I0823219

# BELONGING TO THE AIR

# BELONGING TO THE AIR

A NOVEL

AVERY IRONS

Screen Door Press gratefully acknowledges the contributions of editorial assistants Akhira Umar and Julian Long.

Publication of this volume was made possible in part by generous support from the Thomas D. Clark Foundation.



Published by Screen Door Press, an imprint of The University Press of Kentucky

Scholarly publisher for the Commonwealth, serving Bellarmine University, Berea College, Centre College of Kentucky, Eastern Kentucky University, The Filson Historical Society, Georgetown College, Kentucky Historical Society, Kentucky State University, Morehead State University, Murray State University, Northern Kentucky University, Simmons College, Spalding University, Transylvania University, University of Kentucky, University of Louisville, University of Pikeville, and Western Kentucky University.


*Editorial and Sales Offices:* The University Press of Kentucky
663 South Limestone, Lexington, Kentucky 40508-4008
www.kentuckypress.com



Cataloging-in-Publication data is available from the Library of Congress.

ISBN 978-1-967165-00-1 (hardcover)
ISBN 978-1-967165-01-8 (epub)
ISBN 978-1-967165-02-5 (pdf)

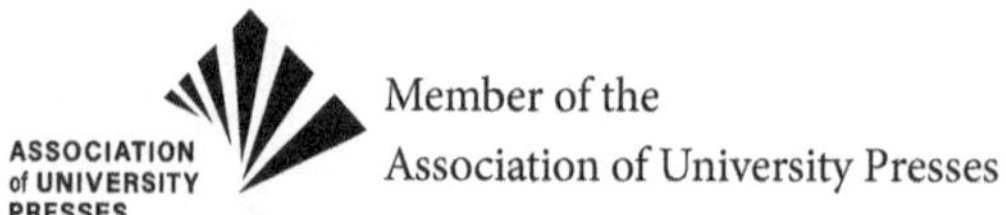

*For Sandra, my mother and friend*

*In Loving Memory of Gregory Duane Rodgers,*
*Choctaw Writer and Storyteller*

# PART I

# August 1912

The youngest member of the Bennett family, named Honest and called "Bird," stared across the kitchen table at her grandmother and then down at the half-nibbled biscuit on the plate between them. The mid-morning sun shone on the oak table and blanketed the old woman. "Granny?" Bird whispered, and eased back her chair.

"Don't sound so apprehensive. You've done what I've asked of you," said her grandmother Odelia, who slipped her fingers around her cup of chamomile tea as she turned to present herself for Bird's inspection. "I always enjoy Mrs. Charles's visits. I trust this one will be especially productive."

"Yes, ma'am." Bird rounded the table, only half-hearing the words. She paid no mind to the last word's half-note rise but would later remember it and recognize the hint of impending mischief. She focused on her task—preparing the woman before her for the world, as represented in this instance by the town's schoolteachers. Bird smoothed errant wisps in Odelia's black and silver plaits, brushed crumbs from the front pleats of her gray dress, and fluffed the poofs of her bishop sleeves. After a quick glance at her own blue pinafore, she deemed everything in order and carried the cup of chamomile in her left hand while guiding Odelia with her right.

Bird hadn't heard the teachers' wagon, but experience had taught her about their incessant punctuality, a cause of biannual agitation. Mrs. Charles's silhouette waited on the porch swing; Mr. Charles had likely stopped up the lane at Uncle Vernon's little house as was becoming his habit. Bird opened the curtains to brighten the room, and Mrs. Charles kept her seat, earning high marks with Bird. Many visitors, colored and white alike, paced the porch, sneaking glances into the living room. When she finally let them in, Bird took advantage of her grandmother's blindness and shamed them with a child's knowing glare.

In contrast, when Bird waved Helena Charles forward, the woman showed no signs of curiosity or unease. She stepped firmly across the threshold, Bird noted, without the demanding heaviness of the white women who came for her mother's services. On this day, Mrs. Charles offered a regal nod—a gesture in which Bird found an instruction: This is how you enter a house, *any* house. The teacher wore a calf-length tan skirt and suit jacket ensemble that seemed a bit much for the August heat. A thin strip of early gray rippled from her widow's peak and fell with the thick crest of hair on her shoulders. To match the teacher's formality, Bird stood with a straight back and extended a stiff arm toward the settee. Only after their guest had settled herself did Bird disappear into the armchair by the fireplace.

"Would you like tea?" asked Odelia. Bird didn't stand. Mrs. Charles had never accepted a drop of tea or water in the four years Bird had been allowed to serve as her grandmother's secretary at these meetings.

With the gesture of hospitality offered and refused, Odelia Bennett began her questioning. "How fare the children?" she asked with a warm soprano, matter-of-factness.

"Very well indeed. This year we will have our largest student population ever and plan to extend the fall session as late into the year as the weather will allow."

"And the reading rates?"

Mrs. Charles rattled off numbers as she fished her notepad out of her satchel with a rush that betrayed surprise. Glancing at her grandmother-suddenly-turned-interrogator, Bird flipped quickly through her own secretarial pad for an empty sheet. Where were the usual questions about updates in the field of colored education, books for the Bennett purse to procure for the school library, or her granny's own melodious musings on the proper balance between practical and philosophical learning for Bennettsville's children? Finding her place, Bird fought to record the teacher's recounting of the number of children reading at each level, those progressing, and those struggling.

"It sounds as if the younger children are having difficulties," said Odelia with such an abrupt directness that Bird almost reached out to steady the teacher who seemed to wobble in her seat.

Mrs. Charles hemmed, "Well . . . it is difficult since so few of the parents can read. However, Mr. Charles and I believe that as the children's skills improve, literacy will diffuse itself among both the younger and older family members."

"I do not doubt your methods, Mrs. Charles. I am simply wondering about your capacity. Perhaps you could use more assistance?" Odelia's tone slowed Bird's pen; the Bennett family's warning lilt had been handed down through the generations to use sparingly and theatrically, right before the possessor pounced.

"Are you suggesting another teacher?" asked Mrs. Charles. Bird didn't know her grandmother's meaning, but she pitied the woman's bait-widened eyes.

Odelia sighed and tilted her head back wistfully. "I do wish I could fund such a luxury. However, I was thinking more practically." She lifted a hand toward Bird. "I do believe Bird could do well under the advanced tutelage of you and your husband. She would also be available to support the younger students. She's quite mature for her age and well trained. I would, of course, compensate you for your work with her."

Despite the referenced training, Bird's mouth opened as Odelia's words twisted around her stomach like bedsheets in a nightmare. Oh, Granny, what are you doing? she thought. Mama won't like this at all.

"We would never turn her away. Every colored child in our catchment area is welcome to attend. I thought Miss Maddy preferred that she be educated here at home."

"Maddy has left all tutelage decisions to me." Odelia's tone suggested that any conversation or disagreement about the subject—from anyone—was only a dance. "I would like for you to work with her on the Romance languages, geography, mathematics, and bookkeeping, in case she decides to carry on her mother's dressmaking."

"Yes, ma'am. That's all possible. But if I may, perhaps it is best to hire a private tutor."

"May I speak frankly, Mrs. Charles?"

"If I may do so as well."

Odelia smiled. "I would expect nothing less. . . . I am also interested in Honest's, shall we call it, her socialization."

Bird gripped the sides of her chair to maintain her seat. What was the old woman talking about?

"Ma'am?" Mrs. Charles grimaced and closed her notebook.

"I want to prepare her for the world, but I also want to find her place in Bennettsville. The child has no friends her own age. Formal schooling seems a good remedy for this."

"Granny!" Bird cried. Heat flushed through her cheeks and underarms.

Odelia raised a hand to quiet her. "It's no fault of her own. She is a sweet and amiable child . . . with too many responsibilities here in the house," she added—an inadequate gesture to assuage what Bird considered an outrageous betrayal.

"I'm not sure what you think I can do, Miss Bennett. There's history in this town that me and mine have no stake in." Bird followed Mrs. Charles's glance up to the portrait hanging over the fireplace, which pictured Bird's unsmiling but not unkindly looking great-grandfather, Ezra John Bennett. He stood broad and tawny skinned in a black suit. Born a slave, he was reputed to have died, cheated the devil with the help of an herb woman, and come back to life with enough cash to build a town for the two lines of his descendants—those from his slave marriage, the line of Abel, and those from his free marriage, the line of Marian. Bird had always doubted most of the story, but Odelia herself told parts of it, and here they were, living in a town that bore his name.

"Nothing that you aren't already doing, Mrs. Charles."

"Perhaps we should speak alone?" The teacher glanced at Bird, who sat tense and motionless except for her eyes, which flitted between the two women.

"Bird should be part of conversations that affect her future," said Odelia.

Bird noted the intake of breath that the woman carefully kept from her grandmother's ears, so similar to her mother's in moments of frustration. When Mrs. Charles broke the moment of contemplative silence and her long study of Bird, the girl recognized the teacher's halting speech as a struggle with care over each word. "There are schools for colored girls of means. It seems that one of those would be most appropriate for Honest. She would not have as much . . . history, shall we say."

Odelia Bennett shook and lowered her head and placed one blue-veined hand into the other—a rare sign of meekness, and her first in this conversation. Bird wondered how genuine or carefully constructed the display was. "Having my child near me saved my life and gave me the will to walk a hard and lonely road. I would not send my daughter's strength away from her."

Bird leaned forward to catch the teacher's eye with a silent warning that the conversation edged toward a dangerous path. There had been a line she'd sensed her entire life—a line of negation, of what wasn't said. Bird could not explain with certainty the forces that had drawn this line, or what lay on its other side, but she felt its presence nonetheless and recognized any mention of her mother's strength or her grandmother's road as cautionary signs. With a burst of defiance Bird mouthed, "No."

Mrs. Charles's neck twisted. "Not even to spare the child?"

Odelia raised her head to the ceiling. She had no temper that Bird had ever seen, but she could close herself like a door, with such a clarity of meaning and finality that Bird could hear the clicks of turning locks. "You seem to know my story, Mrs. Charles, or at least you think you do," she said. "Could you have?"

"No, ma'am." Mrs. Charles conceded.

"You are a woman of intelligence and grace. You've married well and work for the uplift of our people. Bird needs a door—or even a window—and I'm trying to find it. I don't ask for any special treatment for her. She's capable enough not to need it."

"How old are you, Honest?" Mrs. Charles asked.

"Twelve," said Bird.

"The same age as my daughter, Bessie." Mrs. Charles sagged back with the deflated air that accompanies defeat. "Would you like to help with the younger children?"

Bird frowned. "My mother won't like it."

"Why not?"

Bird dared not repeat the words her mother used. Words that combined into phrases with seemingly incongruent parts—*sanctimonious crows* and *happy-gettin' hussies*. And Bird certainly couldn't mention the Minister, who seemed to be at the root of most of her mother's dislikes.

"Would you like to go to school?" Mrs. Charles pressed on the *you.*

Bird stopped. Did she want to go to school? Odelia's head tilted toward her. Bird always did the lacework and pattern-cutting that her mother hated. And there'd be no one to navigate her grandmother through her day, prepare her lunch, read to her, help her down and up from her nap, and keep her company. She didn't want the trouble her granny was courting, but she hadn't ever actually thought about the school in Bennettsville beyond these meetings with Mrs. Charles. Fisk was discussed as an inevitability for her. She dreamed of what it promised: friends to talk to, and to read and sew with. There'd be a roommate, maybe even two. And autumn walks and weekend dances. But these things were all years away. As her mother always said, everything in its own time. Her heart jumped at the possibility of having it now, in Bennettsville.

During rides to the fields with Uncle Vernon or to town with her mother, the adults had sternly warned her against begrudging Bennettsville's poorer children for their dusty legs and worn clothing, but no one in the Bennett house or in the cropper's cabins on Bennett land had encouraged friendship. Still, thought Bird, there are other colored children in Bennettsville whose families weren't tied to the land. The Charleses' two daughters and their son. The Johnsons who owned the grocery store had children. Bird considered all of this and the life-altering proposition for the few seconds allotted to her.

"Yes, ma'am. I'd be nervous though."

"Your first lesson: Our nerves make us sharp. We should listen to them but not be controlled by them. Mr. Charles and I would be happy to have you start with us when the term begins next month."

Odelia Bennett exhaled. "Thank you, Mrs. Charles. Your kindness is always well remembered."

"Yes, ma'am," said the teacher, sliding her notebook back into her satchel and standing to take a bewildered departure.

"That's settled," Miss Bennett said to Bird as they stood side by side on the porch. "We'll convince your mother at dinner." Mrs. Charles walked down the lane to where her husband, Everett, and Uncle Vernon chatted. Bird stopped herself from imagining how Mrs. Charles would describe the meeting and their arrangement.

“She won’t like it,” Bird said aloud what her grandmother should have already known.

“She dislikes so many things. What’s one more?”

Odelia’s plan for a successful argument centered on chicken and dumplings. As Bird hopped down the lane to Uncle Vernon’s little house to request a chicken, she suspected that peace would cost more than her mother’s favorite meal.

By sunset, the soup simmered, and Bird had scooped but not dropped the dumplings. While Odelia dozed in the wingback, Bird read on the settee until lanterns bobbed in the night, and then she darted to the kitchen—slowing just enough to squeeze her grandmother’s shoulder on the way. A few minutes later, the aroma of chicken and boiling dough met her mother at the door. The ride to town, and whatever visiting she’d done, had bronzed Maddy’s skin, lessening the pallidness that always worried Bird. Maddy’s hazel eyes matched Odelia’s, but the former retained their ability to focus and needle Bird until she had to look away. “Good evening, Mama,” Bird said to the words in her book.

“Good evening, love,” added Odelia.

Maddy sniffed the air as she hung her jacket and scarf on the coat hooks. “We’ll see about that.” She regarded their repose a moment longer before marching past them toward the back of the house and the old servants’ quarters that had been converted into her bedroom.

“Let me do the talking,” Odelia said in her daughter’s wake.

Bird almost snorted. She hadn’t planned on saying a word. “Yes, ma’am,” she managed.

Imagining herself the proud matron of a fancy New York City restaurant, Bird placed the dumplings on the table and bowed to her imaginary customers. She admired the silverware’s gleam and regretted that her mother hadn’t returned earlier. They could have hashed out the whole problem before dinner. Such a meal was meant for reconciliation, not argument. But what was done was done. Bird sighed and called to her mother and grandmother. Odelia took her place at the table’s head. Maddy sat on Odelia’s right and Bird on her left.

Odelia tested the dumplings with a peck. "Very good, Bird." Maddy followed suit and agreed with an impressed wink.

Bird blushed into her own bowl. She had done well. The dumplings, fluffy and moist, floated among tender chicken shreds in soup salted just right. They ate in silence for a few minutes, almost unnerving Bird. Thrilled when her mother asked about her lessons for the day, and eager to put off the argument for as long as possible, maybe even to the next day, Bird recounted everything she'd learned about the Panama Canal and her plans to see it when she was old enough, including her preferred season and mode of travel. When Bird could find nothing else to say about the canal or the subject of Central America in general, Odelia laid down her spoon.

"How was town?" asked Odelia.

"Same as always. The delivery from St. Louis never arrived and may not come until Wednesday, which throws off all the work I had planned for the week. Mr. Johnson sends his regards. And Lorna will drop off the pickled onions and your salve next week. How were things here?" She rested her own spoon.

Bird's bite of dumpling turned to stone.

"Mrs. Charles came by for my semiannual report."

"So sorry I missed that." Maddy rolled her eyes.

"Bird is going to help the younger children at the school. There is some struggle, and they could use some additional assistance."

In deep study of the folds and bends of her napkin, Bird forced herself to chew and swallow the stone.

"Helena Charles suggested this?" asked Maddy, her voice an octave higher than her usual alto.

"Not exactly," Odelia admitted, scrunching her face as if struggling to remember just who had said what.

Maddy sipped her water without taking her eyes off her mother. "Who told you that you could make such an arrangement for my child?"

"She's my only grandchild, and she needs more socialization." Odelia Bennett straightened as she defended herself.

"And we decided on Fisk when she's seventeen. She's not doing it." Maddy tossed her napkin over her dumplings and stood.

"Why not, Madeline?" Odelia slid her chair back to block at least one exit from the situation.

"You know damn well why not."

Odelia gasped, and Bird shuddered. This was all going too far, too fast.

"I am still your mother. And this is still my house. You will reconsider your language. If this is about her father . . ."

"It's not about him. It's about how people around here think. I am readying her for the world, not this town." Maddy's chest heaved, and her skin glowed red as coals.

"Maddy, that's like giving a child swimming lessons in the ocean instead of the pond out back."

"I am trying to protect her." Maddy turned to Bird as she said this, and the hurt in her mother's eyes pressed Bird back against her seat. She regretted the afternoon's flight of fancy that had misled her into saying yes to Mrs. Charles. She didn't know what scared her mother so much about her going to school, but it had to be real—the unshakable Maddy Bennett was shaking.

"You can't protect her from your mistakes," said Odelia, nodding at her own wisdom.

"I haven't made any mistakes, Mama, not a single one," said an indignant Maddy, moving to the night-darkened window. "You don't know half as much as you think you do—about me or her."

Odelia scoffed. "I've known both of you since your first breaths. I know you better than you know you."

Maddy spun on her mother. Fearing Maddy's gathering venom, Bird jumped up with a force that knocked her chair down with a loud bang. "Granny," she pleaded. "It's okay. I don't want to go. I just didn't want to offend Mrs. Charles."

Odelia waved down her granddaughter's denial with a snicker. "In this house, a girl can tell her mother what she wants."

"And what about a woman?" asked Maddy.

Odelia paused and then sighed. "Maddy, women . . . we have our own wounds . . . and blindness. I admit to my own in every sense of the word. This house was my refuge, and it's your shelter." Her voice was softer now, calmer. "If we don't do something, it will be Bird's prison. She's got to find her place in the world."

"Any world but this one," whispered Maddy.

"These people, *our* people, are good people, Madeline." Bird winced at the pleading in her grandmother's voice. "Yes, there is history, and not all of it's pretty. But that's true of every place and family. She should learn these things now instead of when she's grown."

Maddy opened her mouth to reply, but Bird could take no more. They would go back and forth, dying down and ramping up, for half the night. She suffered through it when it was about unavoidable things like money or issues with the white people in Tuckersville. Now that she sat at the center of it all, Bird's world shuddered like it might fall to pieces all around her. "Please stop," she said, "I just want this to stop, please."

The older women let her words settle between them. They stepped back from the brink of some place they'd edged near before but never battled toward with such deliberation.

Maddy pressed her hands against her skirt. "We're done. You're excused to your room. I will clear the table," she said to Bird.

Neither woman spoke as Bird left the room and mounted the stairs. She imagined their wills locked together like two rams' horns. Not bothering with her lamp, Bird collapsed onto her bed. Branches of the great oak outside her window swayed in the moonlight. She imagined the seams holding the women downstairs together, as tested as the leaves clinging to the branches even as the changing season and gravity pulled at them. The strain between them had been a near-constant of her life, but now it was clear that there was no point of permanent binding between them. Each woman had her own vision for Bird's life; any momentary overlaps like Fisk would only lead to other forks. She tossed and turned between her options—school or no school, Granny or Mama—until she fell asleep.

In the night's middle, Odelia's slow plod upstairs woke Bird. Guilty and wondering if her grandmother had sat downstairs all this time expecting her return, she rushed to the door.

"Do you want help, Granny?"

"I'm fine child," Odelia answered. "And tend to your dress, Birdy."

"Yes, ma'am," she mumbled, "How did you know I still had it on?"

"All girls have cause to cry in bed at some point. Old age doesn't spare you those memories. Are you okay?"

"Yes, ma'am."

"I'm sorry. I miscalculated. I anticipated her anger. I didn't expect the hurt."

"What's she afraid of, Granny?"

"The thing she's feared since you were born—your reproach."

The next morning Bird leaned against the doorframe of her mother's sewing room. Maddy had skipped her usual biscuit and fried egg and gone straight to work.

"Come in, we got lots to do." Maddy called her forward without looking up from her pinning.

Bird took her place beside their dressing form for full-figured women.

"Mrs. Shaw wants a tulip skirt. I tell her they're going out of fashion, but she won't listen."

Maddy pinned, straightened, and repinned one side while Bird mimicked her work on the other side. "Give her a little extra space for moving," said Maddy, and Bird rearranged her pins until her mother nodded to signal her approval.

After threading the machine, she took her spot at her mother's elbow to observe the sleight of hand that joined two pieces of fabric into fine clothing.

Before pressing the motor forward, Maddy paused. "If you wanted to go to school sooner, you could have just told me."

"I didn't know till they asked me."

Maddy sighed. "I apologize for not asking. I thought you liked being here with me and Granny."

"I do . . ." Bird felt herself coming undone again.

"Don't cry. It's okay to like the sound of both. Life's trick is that we always have to choose." Bird followed her mother's hands as they fed and turned the fabric flowing under the rising and falling needle. Bird didn't feel like she had a choice. She wanted her family, and she wanted the world. But one pushed at her, and the other pulled. She could only go along.

The Minister's baritone notes always woke Bird, no matter how late his visits. Given her mother's mood these past few days, she suspected that there would be no tap on her door and quick aid into her housecoat for a short conversation with her father. Bird tiptoed from her bedroom to the top of the stairs. Her parents' voices drifted up to her.

"Just tell her no, if you're so upset about it," he said, with a tone that was both unconcerned and bored.

"I can't now that Bird's got it in her mind." Her mother's voice was tired and exasperated.

"What could really happen that's so bad?"

"Let's talk about something else. You're not helping."

The Minister chuckled. "I come all this way, and you're in a huff, sitting over there all by yourself. I try to get to the heart of the matter, and you tell me I'm not being helpful."

Bird slid down to the fourth step. The mirror at the stairs' bottom revealed her mother sitting in the wingback, massaging her forehead as she did when she was annoyed. Leaning forward, Bird could see the Minister resting on the settee, his feet up on the coffee table and his pressed white shirt unbuttoned. Bird always wondered how he looked in the house he shared with his other family since he always looked so at home in theirs. He was a tall, thin man. Dark brown with eyes to match. To Bird, he was neither handsome nor ugly. But even in the middle of the night, in his stocking feet, he had presence. Her grandmother always said that presence was a good thing, although she'd never say a good thing about the Minister.

"You know the heart of the matter. The people here got nothing better to do than wag their tongues about me. Who knows what their children will say to Bird?"

Sensing the closing window of her mother's tolerance for any interruption, Bird eased down one more step and wiggled her toes.

"As far as anybody knows, we broke it off years ago," said the Minister. "Who sees me coming here but Vernon? And he hasn't said anything after all these years. You ought—" He paused and cleared his throat. "Bird, come down here," he said.

Bird regretted her impatience; she wanted to hear more.

"I see your toes in the mirror," he said.

She yawned and rubbed her eyes as she descended. "I'm thirsty," she said, "but didn't want to interrupt."

The Minister patted the empty seat beside him. "How's my girl?"

"I'm fine, sir."

"You know it's not polite to listen in on grown folks' talk."

"I was just coming for water." Maddy lifted a glass of water from the coffee table and held onto it for a second, forcing Bird to look up and note the displeasure in her flattened lips.

"Your mama says you're starting formal schooling in a few weeks."

"Yes, sir."

"That's good. A girl as smart as you should keep her head in plenty of books."

"Yes, sir."

"Both your mother and I were good students. We expect the same from you. And there were less opportunities for colored folks back then. I'll check on your marks next time I'm here."

"I'll be teaching too," she couldn't help but say it and hoped he wouldn't reprimand her for pridefulness.

He smiled at this. "I heard that too. I'll ask about your students' marks too. That's the true sign of a good teacher."

Bird sipped without rush. Sometimes, he needed a moment to remember a small trinket he brought her after a long absence. Once the glass was half-gone, her mother shooed her back to bed. Bird lingered on the third step from the top this time.

"You'll have to remind her about her family's privacy, of course," said the Minister.

"You just had your chance to remind her yourself."

"That's a conversation best had between women."

"How convenient." Bird didn't need to glance back at the mirror—she knew well the scowl her mother gave that dared people to say something else.

Bird ignored the sunrise and dallied in bed. Her sleep had been anxious and restless. The mornings after the Minister's visits were never good. She hid in her bedroom as long as she could; the silence on the second floor suggested that her grandmother shared her plan. When hunger finally drove her out of bed and into the hallway's brightness, she eased her grandmother's door open and found the woman gone and her bed made. Still in her dressing gown, Bird tiptoed downstairs before stopping short.

Her grandmother's voice floated from the kitchen. Having long forgotten about the Minister's caution against listening to adult conversations, she pressed her ear to the kitchen door.

"What should I do, Vernon? This has all gone on far too long," said Odelia.

"He just won't loose her," Uncle Vernon answered. Bird pictured her uncle in his overalls in her seat across the table from her grandmother, having taken a polite sip of his tea and eaten just one cookie. He was the most generous person she knew but could hardly stand any comfort for himself. "I'm the closest thing she has to a father. I can go tell him what a man of God ought to know without being told."

"She'll never forgive me. That's the Tucker in her. Holding onto anger runs strong in that line. No good has ever come of it."

"Well, at least Baby Bird didn't get it."

"No," said Odelia. "She takes after me and my mother. We let anger go quickly, but hurts stay with us a long time."

Bird considered this information about herself and her great-grandmother as she sneaked past the kitchen door and to her mother's room. Maddy lay in bed with the curtains still drawn. Her arm covered her eyes. Her chest rose and fell. This was all Bird needed to know. She backed away, careful not to wake the woman. She'd tripped over the night basin once and her mother had turned to her and, with shimmering eyes, said, "Tell me what you mean when you say you love me?" Bird, then ten years old, froze in confusion. "Then how can you say it?" her mother had shouted and sent her running away.

At noon, after Bird had completed her mathematics and sketching, Maddy called her for company on a trip to town to pick up the late fabric shipment. Her mother was pale, slow-moving, and irritable. Taking the reins from Uncle Vernon with a muttered *thank-you*, Maddy stared ahead as he helped Bird onto the buckboard and gave her a supportive arm squeeze.

As they rode, Bird scooted inch-by-inch across the board to her mother's side. When she sat so close that they almost touched, Maddy reached an arm around her. Bird craved the touch, as an acknowledgement of her forgiveness, and for the ability to brace herself against her mother's body.

Of all the things members of the Bennettsville community called Madeline Bennett, no one ever called her a timid wagon driver. She pushed the wagon along the ruts in the roads with no fear or mercy for its axles. Bird curled into her mother and watched the countryside intermittently full with corn, grain, and tobacco. The day smelled of warm earth and lush greenery. They waved to the cabins dotting their route. The harvest had all but the oldest and youngest members of each family in the fields. Those left behind worked in their family gardens, washed clothes, or rested in the shade to wave at passersby.

Bird drank up the town that shared her last name. It was little more than a small grid of houses and a main street that held Johnson's Grocery and an ironworks. It wasn't Paris or New York, but it was much more than her grandmother's garden or her mother's sewing room.

Main Street cleared as her mother drove down the thoroughfare. A few men and women ventured a "good day" as Maddy and Bird deboarded the wagon. Maddy returned the greetings and never offered or seemed to expect anything more.

The grocer, Ernest Johnson, was the friendliest person Bird knew in town. He was a round man in his late fifties, although he was only gray at his temples. He boomed his greeting as the bell clanged to announce their entry.

"Good day, Miss Bennett and Little Miss Bennett." He handed Bird a warm butterscotch candy from his pocket before leading Maddy to the boxes of fabric stored for her.

Two women walked from the other side of the store to the counter. They wore long gray high-waisted skirts and blouses that were just a bit worn but well pressed and neat. As they watched Maddy and Mr. Johnson, one of them spoke under her breath, "As if my money don't spend same as hers."

Fearing the women would say something to her, or look at her crossly, Bird hung by the door and watched the street. She stepped back as three girls about her age walked in, counting their coins. To Bird, they didn't favor enough to be sisters. She wondered if they were friends who walked to town and whether all the kids in Bennettsville did so. She frowned at her own naivete. Here I'm planning on Paris, she thought, and can't even go to Main Street without Mama or Uncle Vernon.

The older girls reached the candy bins and looked for Mr. Johnson, who never let children draw their own candy.

"Patience, girls, the Bennetts are here," said one woman, and the other sniggered.

The girls' questioning eyes found Mr. Johnson and Maddy taking inventory of the fabric bolts. The girls nodded at the older women but glanced awkwardly among themselves. Bird shared their uncertainty about any situation in which adults in public didn't at least cloak their rudeness.

Mr. Johnson glared at the women. "There's no need for any of that, Mrs. Simmons and Mrs. Cook," he said.

"Good day, Diane. Jocelyn." Maddy's direct address forced the women's eyes to hers. "I apologize for any inconvenience, but this shipment is three days late." The women finished their wait in silence. Bird wanted to soak in her mother's boldness, but she stood at the door, terrified, the collar of her dress tightening around her throat. Maddy's gaze locked on her for several breaths and seemed to register a new understanding. Her lips tightened as she turned back to complete her business.

On their return trip, Maddy drove the wagon with a pensive slowness. Her body was rigid, and her attention chained to the road ahead of her. Bird kept to her side of the buckboard. She had erred somehow. The scene in the store had displeased her mother and soured her already difficult mood. When the town disappeared behind a curve and a copse of trees, Maddy pulled up on the reins and stopped the horse. She took Bird's chin in hand and studied her. "You look like your father. You've got his nose and the sharp angle of his jaw. You even have his ears. But you've none of his spunk or steel. I must have marked you by calling you Bird." She exhaled and released Bird's chin. "Lots of folks in this town don't like me, including Jocelyn and Diane. They'd probably say it's on account of my relationship with your father. But I'm not the first woman to ever have a baby outside of marriage. The truth is they never liked me. Not even when we were all girls your age. Maybe it's my color. Or the house I live in. Or that I've never had to work like they have. I tried to make them like me. Odelia still throws money all around this town so folks will like me, and now she's doing the same for you. I've tried to protect you from this, but now I see that I was wrong and Granny's right. I had to learn when I was your age that it's okay for people to dislike you. That I shouldn't be afraid of their scowls, teeth sucking, their words, and occasionally even their hits. That lesson freed me. Not from everything. But from them. From worrying about what they think. From trying to find the magic smile or words that would make people change their mind. I haven't done everything right in my life. But I've lived on my own terms the best a colored woman can in this world. I have regrets. But they are regrets about the decisions I've made—not about what others have imposed on me." She looked at her daughter. "Do you understand what I'm trying to say?"

Tears rose in Bird's eyes. "That the other children aren't going to like me."

"Maybe they will. Maybe they won't. I'm saying that you just can't let it affect you either way. You've got to be your own person and live your own life."

"I'm scared now," said Bird.

Maddy pulled her close and kissed the part in her hair.

"The worst that could happen is it doesn't work out and Granny takes back over. Or, you might make friends and find a different way in the world than I did. You won't know until you get there."

Sitting at her vanity, Odelia hummed a lullaby as Bird brushed her hair.

"What should we dream about tonight, Birdy?" Odelia asked and leaned back against her granddaughter.

"An ocean voyage," said Bird, brushing at the nape, which always made Odelia relax and sigh.

"To where?"

"You choose."

"Then I choose everywhere. We'll be exhausted when we wake."

Bird giggled as her mother knocked on the door. Her hand stopped mid-brush; Odelia's song held true. "Come in dear, we're planning the night's grand voyage."

Maddy joined them at the mirror, pulled Bird in for a kiss on the forehead, and held out her hand for the brush. "I thought old ladies and young girls needed good rest each night."

"That is the world's oldest lie," said Odelia.

“There are many older and juicier lies than that,” said Maddy and threw her head back with a laugh that calmed a nagging worry in the undercurrent of Bird’s thoughts. Her mother would be okay. They all would. Odelia found her daughter’s hand. “I am sorry, Madeline. Old age makes one anxiety-prone and sometimes inconsiderate.”

Maddy squeezed her mother’s hand. “Or maybe, it just makes you see the necessities more clearly.”

Bird relaxed back on her Granny’s pillows, and the two women continued the song.

# September 1912

Maddy swore as the mare brayed and jerked.

"I'ma get Uncle Vernon," said Bird, dropping her satchel onto the porch steps.

"Bird, this is no time to ignore the King's English," said Odelia from the porch swing. Bird ignored the admonishment.

"I've got it," grumbled Maddy. "This is silly. All of this so a child can get a worse education."

"There's more learning in school than happens in books," said Odelia.

"We're going to be late," Bird pouted.

"Honest Bennett," snapped Maddy.

Bird quieted and sank onto the steps. Everything about the morning had promised tardiness. Maddy had been hard to rouse, slow to rise, and then had glared at the oldest Miss Bennett, as Odelia listed for Bird all the ways she should help the Charleses—clearing the blackboard, sweeping the porch, and reshelving any books. Bird had willed them both to keep putting food in their mouths. And now, her mother and the horse each tried to out-mule the other.

Grabbing the horse's muzzle, Maddy stared it in the eye. "Move one more time," she said. The horse accepted its bridle, saddle, and then its mistress. "Well, come on then." She lowered an arm to Bird. "We've got to ride halfway across the county when I got sewing to do." Bird grabbed her mother's outstretched arm and all but flew into the saddle's front.

The freshly harvested fields smelled of dirt and dew. Bird rode tense, trying to give the horse discreet squeezes with her feet to nudge it faster. The rest of the morning crystallized before her. She'd arrive to a schoolroom in full session, and Cecile starting the new students on the alphabet—her job. Maybe the Charleses would tell her if she could not come on time to not come at all.

As they drew closer to the school, small groups of children walking from the cropper cabins made way for them. Only after they passed three or four groups could Bird relax. Late or not, she would be on time. She settled into Maddy's softness, and the woman, in turn, held the reins in one hand and relaxed the other around Bird.

The boys they passed wore ankle-high britches and patched shirts, and the girls wore plain dresses and faded ribbons tied in neat bows. She didn't recognize any of them. She hadn't run through the fields with them—or worked in the fields with them either. She had everything, and they had nothing. They'd all come from slaves, only her grandfather somehow had money, and theirs didn't. She hated to think that life was as simple and as random as that. She'd always wondered what power Ezra Bennett had used to entice a smattering of freed blacks to join his little town. At least weekly, Uncle Vernon complained that the croppers' plots were too small. "It don't make sense that cotton makes a man fat and not corn and beans," he'd tell her grandmother.

"Good day, children," said Maddy leading the horse past a small group.

"Mornin', Miss Bennett," they replied.

"I should've walked," Bird said, once they'd gotten a few strides ahead of the third group.

"You don't know anything about walking like these children do. And you walking wouldn't change the fact that you have a horse that could bring you. Don't flaunt what you have, but also don't act like you don't got it. That's worse; that makes you a liar."

"What if they don't like me?" Bird asked again.

"Then they don't like you. Kids can be mean, and kids can be nice. The coin's been flipped; you'll know soon enough how it's landed."

The little schoolhouse sat squat in the middle of endless miles of now bare fields. Patches of grass and dirt circled the white A-frame wooden building. Arriving children pumped the well's spigot to wash the dust off their legs. Several small children cried and tried to pull their older siblings back toward home. As it dawned on her that she'd given up the daily freedom and the coziness of her home for this stress, Bird wanted to cry along with them.

"Be good," Maddy said as she helped Bird down and then remounted. Bird almost asked to call off the whole misadventure. But I brought it on myself, she thought—with Granny's help. She walked past the playing children and toward the schoolhouse. At the bottom of the porch, she brushed the dust from her dress and straightened her bag with her school and embroidery supplies.

Mrs. Charles smiled and pointed her to the blackboard at the back of the room near where Mr. Charles wrote at his desk.

"Welcome, Miss Bennett," he said.

"Are you ready, Bird?" asked Mrs. Charles, clapping chalk dust off her hands.

"Yes, ma'am." Bird tried to sound confident, but her voice squeaked.

The teacher laughed. "Every day is work, but the nerves lessen."

After Mr. Charles dismissed the students from morning prayer, eight pairs of curious eyes watched as Bird had them sit cross-legged in the schoolroom's back corner. One of the littlest ones, Bird guessed she was four or five, still cried to go home.

Bird held her hands against her stomach to calm it and then began. She asked each child their name and wrote them on the board. "This is, more or less, the *ABC*'s, or the alphabet as we call it in school. Who has studied their letters at home?" Half the children raised their hands. "Tomorrow, you will all raise your hand. Today, we'll work on the first few letters, starting with . . ." she stretched the word out. No one answered. They stared at each other and then at her. Bird thought she might faint. Finally, one brave soul raised his hand.

"Miss, is you a kid or a grown-up?"

"I'm twelve." This admission started most of the children giggling.

"And you a teacher?" a pigtailed girl asked, her face twisted in childish disbelief.

"I'm assisting Mr. and Mrs. Charles."

"You gon tell on us if we don't mind you."

"I hope it won't come to that."

Another girl sucked her teeth and spoke up. "If you gon be teachin' us, you gon have to be meaner."

Bird considered this advice for a moment and the surprise of it. "I'll work on that, and you'll work on your letters and minding. Then we'll be just fine," she said. This seemed fair enough to them, and they watched her write the letter *A* in upper and lower case on her tiny chalk tablet.

"*A*," one of the children shouted.

"Yes!" said Bird. "It's one of my favorite letters and is the first letter in one of my favorite fruits, apples."

"Do we get apples?" The child who'd been crying all along pulled herself together long enough to get the question out.

Bird hadn't expected this. "It can be arranged. I think."

The crying child nodded with approval.

The older children peeked over at her every once in a while. None of the peeks offered any signal of friendliness, so she forced herself not to look up when she felt their eyes on her. She remembered Maddy's complaint to the Minister and wondered what they were thinking about her and her family. She deemed her ignorance to her advantage.

The children bolted into the sunshine for the late morning recess. Thankful to have a moment to herself, Bird found a shaded corner of the porch to embroider as the other children chased each other, jumped rope, and shouted to the skies, grateful for the break. Her solitude was short lived. Apparently, among the Charles family members, responsibility for her during recess fell to the youngest, Bessie. Bessie was short for her twelve years, mahogany in color, and, as Bird would learn, had an attitude that often exasperated her mother and earned her the respect of her taller peers.

Bird didn't notice when the children in the yard stopped playing; she only noticed the silence. Bessie approached her with a theatrical reluctance, her arms hanging at her side and a forced half-smile across her lips. Bird didn't know whether to feel worse for Bessie or herself.

"We're about to jump rope." Bessie pointed to a group of girls standing with a limp rope between them. "Want to join us?"

Bird eyed the fidgeting girls. "Thank you very much, but no." She saw Mrs. Charles watching and assessing. "If you like, you can stitch with me. I have an extra hoop."

Bessie's eyes did a little hop when she saw the hummingbird floating in Bird's hoop and peeked at her mother for instruction. Mrs. Charles gave a slight nod of approval, and Bessie plopped down. Bird handed her a small hoop and fabric, and Bessie clumsily stretched the fabric.

“I don’t know how to embroider,” she admitted after a few seconds of embarrassed trying.

Bird separated the hoops, laid the fabric across the smaller one, fitted the larger one around it, and stretched the fabric as she tightened the larger hoop. “Do you know how to stitch?”

“Of course.” Bessie regained a bit of her pluck.

The other children watched them until Mr. Charles emerged from the school. “We can begin the afternoon lessons if you don’t want to play,” he said, his voice deep, half-serious, and half-playful. Within a single breath, ropes turned, balls sailed through the air, and merriment resumed.

“But how did you learn to sew them?” Bessie asked.

“My mother taught me to stitch, and I just see the birds and butterflies in the hoop already.” She smiled shyly and then laughed at herself.

“Do you have butterflies all over your bedroom.”

Bird shook her head. “I give them to my grandmother.”

If this surprised or confused Bessie, the girl said nothing. Bird began to appreciate the profound un-nosiness of the Charles women. She would tell her mother. Feeling brave and concerned that this would be her one chance to make a friend, Bird opened her mouth and hoped that something interesting or clever would find its way out.

“Are you going to be a teacher when you grow up?” She wasn’t particularly impressed with herself but acknowledged that it could have been worse.

Bessie laughed at this idea. “I’m going to New York or Chicago to be a secretary for a rich man who’s going to marry me.”

“I want to go to New York or to London!” Bird almost shouted, excited by this commonality.

“Are colored people allowed in London . . . I mean that aren’t part white?”

“My granny has been there, and she said there are colored people from Africa there.”

“I’ll go with you then.”

Uncle Vernon picked Bird up at the day’s end. She might have run to him if all the other children hadn’t beat her to it. They crowded around the wagon as he handed out candies like gold coins.

"I'm so glad it's you," she said as she bounced onto the buckboard after the crowd cleared. "We need to take as many students as we can, and we need to get some apples."

"Apples?" he asked, rubbing the gray stubble on his chin.

"For my lesson tomorrow. *A* is for Apple."

"Just so long as you ain't doin' *B* for Bacon, 'cause I'm not slaughterin' no hog tonight."

"I hadn't thought about *B* yet."

"Ya might want to plan ahead," he winked at her as he waved for the children to climb into the back. "You got twenty-five more letters."

The early weeks of her formal education sped by like a roaring train. Tending to her students was the easiest part. They were eager to learn and appreciated having their "own teacher," as she often heard them describe her. It also helped that Uncle Vernon assumed Maddy's school transport duties, and he and Bird piled children into the wagon all along the way. None of the kids, and especially not her students, dared get kicked off "Miss Bird's wagon." She didn't know why they assumed she would kick them off to walk alone; she was serious in manner, but never terribly stern. Either way, it worked for all of them.

The time for sewing and play breaks was short-lived for her and Bessie as the Charleses didn't shirk their part of the deal. Accustomed to her grandmother's wandering lectures and lessons punctuated with garden strolls and tea times, at first, Bird found the new workload daunting and then invigorating. All the new learning required organization and discipline, but the rewards, mainly the impressed nods of her instructors, were worth the effort. Bessie seemed none too happy that her parents increased her own workload to match Bird's. At first, Bird worried that this would ruin their hesitant friendship, but after the school day was done and Uncle Vernon carried home the children who lived east of the schoolhouse before doubling back for the rest and Bird, the two girls worked side by side. On particularly nice days, Mr. Charles sent them out into the play yard to stretch their legs, and everything they discussed seemed vitally important but would later be completely lost to memory.

Ten weeks later, Bird hesitated outside the cracked door to her mother's sewing room and fiddled with the semi-official-looking progress report addressed to Madeline Bennett. Certain of her marks, Bird instead worried about the enclosed proposal that Bird continue her studies at the Charleses' home during the winter break—an honor that made Bird want to dance. The buzzing stopped, and Bird tapped the door open. Maddy muttered over a knot in the machine's foot. An uncut pattern lay in the middle of the floor. Skirts, blouses, and dresses in various states of creation and repair hung over stools, dressing forms, and crates of fabric bolts. Bird had meant to help her mother during the break. She'd tried to do what she could on weekends, but tired eyes and a distracted mind resulted in mistakes that had cost her mother time and money.

"Mama," said Bird, "Mrs. Charles sent my progress report for you."

With a couple more picks at the knot, Maddy turned to her. "I'm sure this is just a formality," she said as she took the envelope.

"Do you want me to try the knot?"

"You never have to ask."

With a few gentle picks and coaxing tugs, Bird freed the foot and spared the work.

Her mother handed her the report back. "I'd hoped to have you back in here with me. I miss my assistant."

"I think the load will be lighter since it's a break," Honest Bennett lied.

"We'll see how it goes," Maddy opened her arms and Bird stepped in. "I'm very proud of you, Birdy."

Next, Bird found her grandmother in the kitchen breading pork chops. The stove was lit and the grease starting to sizzle. Odelia Bennett had proved her ability to still make chicken, hot water cornbread, spaghetti, and plenty of other meals Bird would have not thought possible. Bird offered her help.

"You can set the table," said Odelia. "It'll be four. The promise of my special pork chops has gotten your uncle to agree to eat with us like a proper family this evening."

Bird hadn't known that her grandmother made "special" pork chops. She was learning to accept these new lessons about the people in her life and her life itself. The house had its ways, and the world had its own.

For twelve years, she'd lived only in the first. She now straddled the line between the two, and already the people and the ways of the house were re-forming themselves around the void she would one day leave.

# November 1912

By late November, Bennettsville's dirt roads crackled with each step. Uncle Vernon's wagon had eased enough children's travel burdens that the school teased a few more weeks out of its session. But winter won in the end. The plentitude of threadbare coats and too-short pant legs forced the school into winter recess.

To end the winter session, the Charleses assigned Bird to deliver reports to all her students. Uncle Vernon carried her around to their little houses and cabins, and she'd never felt so young as she stood before her students' parents. Most sat on their porches or at their kitchen tables and humored her, calling her "Miss Bird" and asking about any misbehavior that needed addressing. Despite her nerves, her voice only shook as Pap Giles, a man as old as her grandmother and Uncle Vernon, made his grandchildren stand beside him for her visit. A thumb-sized switch lay across his lap. Bird's students, a five-year-old boy and a six-year-old girl, stared at their feet as she praised their reading and math skills. When she ended her report, Pap Giles gave her a speckled smile, and the children grinned. "Good work, chillun," he said. "We don't have much, but your learning will get you yo due."

As they rode back home, Bird sidled next to Uncle Vernon. He gave her one rein and kept the other. "Would he really have whipped them in front of me?" she asked.

"Yes, he would."

"But they're so little."

"Didn't matter how old you was where we come from. You got whipped, and everyone was made to watch as a lesson."

"You mean back before . . ." she hated to even say the words.

"That's what I mean."

"Was Pap Giles a— . . . too?"

"When he was a boy."

"You're Granny's brother, but he's not?" Bird had never understood how she was related to most of the town, or how they were all related when most folks looked nothing alike.

"We's all cousins little one. With or without blood. And that's all that matters."

The Charleses allowed themselves a two-week vacation between the session's end and Bird's studies at their home. Bird reclaimed what she could of her former routines and tasks. In the sewing room, she tackled a pile of trousers pinned for hemming and a half-dozen monogramming orders. Bird and Maddy again alternated responsibilities for dinner preparations, while Odelia refused to cede her daily lunch making.

"Bird, you spoiled me so much. One doesn't need sight to cook most things. The nose knows first when something is near burning. And only the tongue can taste the salt. And it's the sizzle of the oil that announces the readiness of your pan," Odelia said, stirring a pot of stew, "but sight is nice for reading—one's own or borrowed from someone." So, while her grandmother prepared their lunches, and in the moments she could escape from Maddy's sewing room, Bird read aloud from a knee-high stack of newspapers from New York City and St. Louis. Odelia had a standing request for anything about W. E. B. Du Bois and his national association. Bird rounded out their reading with excerpts from articles about the strange arguments between the suffragettes and the antisuffragists.

"If only men can vote," she asked her Granny, "who votes in our house? And why in the world would anyone not want to have a say?"

Odelia sipped her tea and said nothing for a long moment. "Uncle Vernon votes in our house dear, and those women out east aren't talking about us colored women."

Bird tried to understand a world in which the quiet and retiring Uncle Vernon voted and her opinionated and obstinate grandmother didn't. She studied the picture above the article. Indeed, she couldn't find a brown face in the crowd of banner-carrying women.

After her weeks off, on Tuesdays and Thursdays, Uncle Vernon carried Bird to the Charleses' home for instruction. Their narrow two-story house stood dark gray against the bright blue winter sky. Plain in exterior, with a stoop instead of a porch and faded shutters, to Bird, the inside was a fairy tale cottage come to life. She arrived each morning to a stove-warmed kitchen and a fire burning in the sitting room hearth. For the next several hours, she shuttled happily back and forth between these rooms with her hosts.

Everett Charles led their learning at school but transformed into an absent-minded introvert at home. Reading incessantly, even as Mrs. Charles had him hanging or holding something, he sometimes stopped to share random passages that he deemed necessary for or worthy of them. Those gifted with the information would reply "yes, sir," or "yes, dear." Their words carried the thinnest edge of teasing.

Mrs. Charles curated Bird and Bessie's days. Their lessons turned from the primary schoolhouse topics of literature, languages, history, and mathematics to more artistic concerns like calligraphy, painting, baking, and home decor. Bird had not guessed the woman's artistic talent. She had filled the house with her own paintings of the schoolhouse, the Charleses' home, the town's main thoroughfare, and southern Illinois landscapes. By the end of that first week, Bird was certain that Mrs. Charles had mastered everything worthy of mastery.

Each day of her studies found her happy to arrive and sad to depart. Only guilt held in check her admiration for the family. Her longing for this fullness, this banter and comfort, and this warmth, even in winter, all felt like a betrayal to her mother and grandmother. Hadn't they each wanted this, she once thought as Mrs. Charles taught them the art of upside-down cakes. Granny almost had it. And Mama hoped for it, but the Minister had given it to someone else. Bird did have a half-sister a few months younger than herself. And maybe there was a little brother too. Of this, she was uncertain. Her mother and the Minister had argued once when she was six or seven. Maddy had screamed like a madwoman in the night and thrown everything in reach at the Minister. Before Uncle Vernon whisked her away to her great uncle Louis's house, Bird pieced together that a boy child had been born in a faraway place and this birth almost broke her mother. Over the years, she'd figured out that her mother had tried to leave her, all of them, after that night. Her recovery had taken weeks, and Maddy was never again as strong or happy as Bird remembered from her early years.

On a chilly Friday morning, Maddy opened her bedroom door and said, "I've a different kind of learning for you today." Bird startled and shut her book. "I'll pick your dress. We're taking a gown order from Mrs. Kirby in Tuckersville this afternoon."

Maddy flicked through the dresses in Bird's closet and pulled out a plain gray dress that could only claim a modest neck frill as an embellishment. A few moments later, Bird stood before her mirror feeling like winter drabness brought to life. She met Maddy in the hallway and envied the smart black skirt and sky-blue blouse. "Fabulous," said Maddy aloud, although Bird read in her eyes—"you're neat and clean and don't look like much. Perfect."

As the wagon bounced down the road to Tuckersville, Bird imagined she and her mother riding a canoe on an ocean current carrying them farther and farther from shore. A sea of frozen earth and a cinder-gray sky stretched around them. The land had served as buffer between the towns for as long as any living resident of either could remember. Two words summed up most of what Bird knew about Tuckersville: white folks.

A handful of Bennettsville women cleaned and cooked for families in Tuckersville. The school children threatened each other with this fate considered worse than sweating in fields. Bird didn't know what to make of her mother's own dealings in Tuckersville. Maddy did not cross the buffer as service help, but still, she went. Bird gawked as they passed the first weather worn gray shacks on the outskirts of town. The almighty Tuckersville had shacks? "Mama, who lives in those shacks?"

"There are plenty of poor white folks too," Maddy said under her breath and pressed the horse forward as a white woman in a coarse house dress stepped into the doorway of the nearest shack and stared at them. A small child in threadbare pants and an oversized shirt clung to her legs.

As they neared the formal heart of Tuckersville, the houses grew into well cared for two-story homes with clean, sharp fences. They rode to the Kirby's home, a brick colonial at the far end of a street. "Don't speak unless spoken too," said Maddy as she pulled the wagon round to the house's back, "and even then, keep it short and don't make eye contact." Bird had only vague memories of accompanying her mother to the visits she occasionally made to customers. She'd been five or six on the last such visit and felt mainly like a doll on display for a flowery-smelling white woman.

Maddy tended the horse and then led them to the Kirby's back door. Bird expected her mother to knock, but Maddy let herself into the kitchen with a sharp inhale and began peeling off her coat and hat and motioned for Bird to do the same. Lula Harper, mother to two of Bird's students, stirred a bubbling pot that smelled like beef stew.

"She's in a mood," whispered Lula as she glanced up at Maddy and extended her head back for an expected peck on the cheek, which Maddy gave with the casualness of habit.

"Tell me something new," answered Maddy. "And the little angel?" said Maddy with a sweet voice and sour face.

"He's somewhere around here." Lula noticed Bird. "Hello, little shadow," she said.

"Good afternoon, ma'am," said Bird, embarrassed by her own shyness.

"How did Camille and Brenda do at the end of the term?"

"Very well, ma'am. I can tell they've been practicing their reading at home plenty."

Lula chuckled and beamed. "They getting too good at it. One day my Daddy said he couldn't find his matchbook, and here come little Brenda talking about some, 'when can we read Big Daddy's matchbook?'"

Bird noticed the pride in her own mother's eyes and felt her own heart swell a bit.

"I guess you better announce us," said Maddy.

Lula sighed and wiped her hands before heading toward a white door at the other end of the kitchen. "Good luck."

Lula peeked back through the kitchen door and nodded. A shrill laughter soared in from the other side. Maddy stretched her neck and pushed through the kitchen door. Bird stepped quick to keep up with her.

"Ah Maddy," said a thin brunette woman with too big a smile as she turned around. Her eyes lingered on Maddy for a moment and then slid over Bird with little more than a half-second pause and the barest acknowledgement. “Is today the day? Yes, it must be, the gala is fast approaching.”

Three other white women stood in the foyer wrapping scarves and buttoning their jackets. Their eyes darted from their host to Maddy. “I wanted to get the dress made in St. Louis,” said Mrs. Kirby, “but Wilton wouldn’t hear of it with what we’re spending on the travel, and hotel, and sightseeing. I had to compromise somewhere.” She laughed at a joke she hadn’t told yet, “Who of those snobs in St. Louis will ever know?” The other women nodded agreeably. Maddy stood impassive with a face unreadable even to Bird.

“Off you go, ladies. I’ve got to get these measurements taken before our lunch lands on these hips.”

“Wilton,” she called up the stairs, “Come down here so you can see the dress I’m planning and make sure Maddy doesn’t cost us and arm and a leg.”

A man’s deep and snappish voice called back almost instantly, “I’ve put what I’m willing to pay on the mantle.”

Bird had never been to a play, but she suddenly had the understanding that she was watching a show. The visiting women exited the stage rolling their eyes and laughing.

“Oh, Maddy, I’ve found some amazing ideas in the magazines,” said Mrs. Kirby as she led them into the sitting room. She rummaged through cut out images and pointed at various tops she wanted combined with various bottoms. Of course, cost would be an issue. She’d rather cut costs on the labor than the fabric, so Maddy should keep it simple.

“Is there a theme to the gala?” Maddy asked with the same enthusiasm with which Mr. Johnson took orders for the cheapest cuts of meat.

“It’s loose, not too big of a ta-da. Black tie for the men, something shimmery for the ladies. I don’t want to stand out mind you, just the right amount of blending in.”

This answer was spectacularly unhelpful to Bird, but her mother “mmmhmmm’d” as Mrs. Kirby continued what seemed like random pointing. After a few more moments of this, Mrs. Kirby left Maddy to the magazines and seated herself on the settee. “I also wanted to ask about a maid for the Jensens.” She crossed her ankles and smoothed her skirt.

Maddy stopped turning pages but didn't turn around immediately. "You probably couldn't tell with the coat and all, but Tally is expecting again. Really any girl would do."

Maddy stood straight and turned to face Mrs. Kirby. Bird read the calculations in her mother's eyes. She had cards to play and was planning carefully. "That has always been the problem at the Jensen's, Mrs. Kirby," she said with a matter-of-fact flatness.

The two women matched gazes, and Bird wanted to cry out to her mother. Hadn't this woman just told her, for the thousandth time, not to look white folks in the eyes. After several seconds through which Bird held her breath, Mrs. Kirby finally dropped back further into her seat. "I know, but you have to give her someone Maddy. She's over here crying every day about the fatigue and morning sickness. How about someone to just do the cooking? I'll ask Lula to go and do the rough work once a week until after the baby."

Maddy thought for a moment. "You remember my cousin Sue who worked for the Stacks family before they moved?"

Mrs. Kirby tilted her eyes up to the light as she scanned her memories. "I don't remember her being a particularly friendly woman, but Mrs. Stacks never complained."

Bird sat cataloguing a million questions when a wooden arrow whacked her in the arm. The uncontrollable howl that escaped spun her mother around and a snarling voice cackled from the hallway.

Mrs. Kirby stomped her foot. "Jonas Kirby get in here this moment." The cackling ended, and the hallway was silent for a long moment. "You will come here right now, or I will go get your father," Mrs. Kirby shouted. Bird was somewhat relieved that the woman had it in her to get so red in the face. Maddy caught her eye and gave a subtle nod; Bird nodded back. Blood trickled inside her sleeve, but she didn't need immediate tending.

Jonas Kirby, a dirty blonde and gangly boy of maybe fourteen, slunk into the sitting room. He wore a shiny sheriff's pin on his chest.

"You will give me that right now," said Mrs. Kirby holding out a hand for the bow. Maddy watched Mrs. Kirby without blinking. "If I've told you once, I've told you a thousand times about that damn thing."

"Hell, no," said Jonas, looking from his mother, to Maddy, and then Bird. "When the sheriff really does make me a deputy, it'll be a pistol."

Maddy stepped back, and Bird turned her head to protect against the hands that were about to surely fly. But nothing happened for another long moment.

"Just go to your room, Jonas," said his mother, not bothering to hide the defeat in her voice.

The boy slumped, frowned, and marched back out.

"Just make the dress a bit drapey," said Mrs. Kirby turning back to Maddy. "And you'll make arrangements with Sue?"

Maddy nodded without looking at the woman.

Bird followed Maddy back to the kitchen. Maddy immediately pulled up her daughter's sleeve and frowned at the cut in her skin. Mrs. Harper hustled to the cooler for ice and then over to Bird. "No good's gon come from that boy."

"You be careful over here, Lula." Maddy said holding Mrs. Harper's eyes.

"I can hold my own, and everybody know it," said Lula.

"You okay, Birdy?" Maddy asked as both women turned to her.

"Yes, ma'am. Don't worry about me," said Bird. "She didn't make him say sorry, and she didn't say it either."

"No, she didn't," said Maddy, acknowledging the toe her daughter was dipping into the deep ocean of injustice through which she would one day swim.

"Then, we'd know for sure these is the last and evil days," Lula said as she handed Bird a cookie from a plate cooling on the counter.

Maddy rode stiff beside her. "I'm sure you have thoughts little one."

Bird's mind spun with thoughts and questions. Her mother had looked that white woman in the eye—multiple times. What was wrong with the Jensens? Mrs. Kirby hadn't even tried to make the boy apologize. But one question festered under all of the others. "Wasn't Granny's grandfather from Tuckersville? Does that make some of them kin to us?"

Maddy's quick, sharp glance flashed both appreciation and fear. Bird had found the crux of the matter but had missed something too important for a girl her age to miss. "The history between the towns is deep. The only Tucker blood in Bennettsville runs through you, me, and Granny.

But that doesn't make us any safer. So don't expect it and certainly don't ever count on it. I don't hold much with anybody's religion, but I have to think it was Miss Ada's herbs or protection that kept Ezra and Marian safe after they bought the land from Silas Tucker. It didn't have anything to do with shared blood or love from the Tuckers. May it be a long time before that protection runs out."

# March 1913

On the third Tuesday, Bird woke to tree buds brushing against her bedroom window—the first sign of winter's concession. She threw on her least wrinkled dress and ate her biscuits on the front porch. She marveled at the seasonal tipping point and how much could change from one day to the next. Winter hadn't beaten them and neither had Tuckersville. The schoolhouse would reopen soon, her students would hop into Uncle Vernon's wagon, and they'd all laugh and savor the promise of easier days, at least for a while.

"I'm out here," she yelled when Odelia descended the stairs.

"Tell me what it's like Birdy," said Odelia, easing onto the porch swing beside her. "I smelled the green when it arrived in the wee hours. You know it's the scent of a rider on horseback dragging spring all the way up from the equator."

Bird giggled at her grandmother's annual fancy. "The buds are like tiny green rosebuds showing just the tips of their white petals. It's just a few trees right now, Granny, but there are even bits of fresh grass pushed up."

Odelia clasped her hands. "This old girl has lived to see another spring."

Jarred, Bird turned to her grandmother. She'd never seriously considered that her grandmother would not see a spring. She pushed this new knowledge and worry to her mind's edges.

"Come, Granny," she said, standing, "if you dress quickly, we can check if anything's come up in the garden before I leave for the Charleses' house."

That afternoon Bessie drew flowers in her notepad as Bird searched for pluperfect conjugations out the window. Mrs. Charles eventually gave up and sent them outside to sketch with special attention to the ways the new season changed the light. They walked the perimeter of the yard sketching trees and planning their warm weather adventures.

"Uncle Vernon will take us to town if we like," promised Bird. "I've been saving for candy."

"I want to go swimming as soon as we won't freeze."

"Then you have to come to my pond. It'll be warm enough to wade in by May and to swim in by June."

"Yes!" exclaimed Bessie, "Then, we don't have to worry about my big-headed brother and sister bothering us, or lessons from my mother."

"We have a hammock we can read in, and all kinds of Mama's fabric scraps we can play with. And you can meet my Granny. She's always asking after you, wanting to know when she'll get to meet you."

"Do I have to dress up like Mama does when she goes for her reports?"

Bird laughed. "No, what we always wear is fine."

"What's it like," Bessie asked under her breath, "having a white grandmother?"

"She's not white, just fair-skinned."

"Does she cook the Sunday dinner?"

Bird shook her head.

"Does she quilt you blankets? Or call for the switch when you don't mind."

Bird's head continued to shake.

"You sure she's not white?"

"Maybe she'd do those things if she could see."

"Maybe."

Neither girl could have imagined how the adults in their lives could complicate a simple visit. Although her mother frowned at having people over in her business, it was not lost on Bird that Mrs. Charles added the most complications and demurrals. "Surely," she'd said, "two boisterous girls would strain Miss Bennett's health and Miss Maddy's business." Bird confirmed her family's belief in learning hosting skills from a young age. Questions about travel and meals were similarly dealt with. With all lanes closed but the one leading to Bird's house, Mrs. Charles acquiesced with the condition that the mothers meet to "make arrangements."

On a Thursday afternoon, the Charleses carried Bird home after her lessons. Odelia greeted them from the porch swing. "Good day, Mr. and Mrs. Charles. It's a pleasure to have you for a social visit." Helena Charles stood straight as a yard stick, and her husband removed his hat as they all made polite small talk about the early spring before Mr. Charles turned the wagon back up the lane to Uncle Vernon's place. Bird pecked her grandmother on the cheek and held the screen door open for the guests.

Maddy met them in the living room in a simple skirt and collared blouse. Bird appreciated the conservative tone of her mother's selection.

"It's so nice of you to come by." Miss Maddy offered her hand. With the effort of this simple welcome, Bird understood the reason behind her mother's detached directness: sugariness did not become her.

Mrs. Charles shook her hand. "Thank you for having me. Mr. Charles and I figured that since our daughters have become such good friends, we mothers should be better acquainted." Mrs. Charles glanced at the settee.

Maddy chuckled. "Oh no, let's go back to the kitchen where it's more comfortable. Odelia entertains here, but the only people I have sit here are the white folk who come for their clothes. They are always so curious about how we live, so I just leave them in the room that's exactly like theirs."

The white kitchen walls and countertops glowed yellow in the bright afternoon sunlight. "Would you like tea or coffee, Mrs. Charles?" Maddy asked as the mothers took their seats. "Birdy, why don't you and Bessie go keep your grandmother company?"

"Tea, please. You keep such a clean house."

"It's easy with just the three of us," said Maddy as she poured the tea. Bird watched to see if Mrs. Charles would actually take a sip. With a second, more stern dismissal, Bird and Bessie sulked out of the kitchen and to the porch. Bird opened the screen door and let it bang closed.

"Don't tell on us, Granny." She whispered through the screen door.

"Ok, darling. Just remember the price of my silence."

"Yes, ma'am." The girls tiptoed back across the living room until they could hear their mothers' voices once again.

"Bird is an excellent student," Mrs. Charles offered. "I wish she'd raise her hand more, but when called on, she always knows the answer, and her penmanship is impeccable."

"Thank you. She is a good girl."

Bird flushed, uncomfortable with the praise.

"I appreciate how Bessie is helping her come out of her shell. I didn't know if it would ever happen." Miss Maddy took her turn.

The mothers sat in silence for a moment. Bird imagined each woman sipping and grappling for something to say.

"And this is such a lovely house," offered Mrs. Charles. "Do you have many visitors out this way?"

"Mostly just my customers coming to have something made or altered, and sometimes family."

"You know, naturally, Mr. Charles and I are concerned about the type of company to which the children are exposed. They're so impressionable."

"Yes, I feel just the same way about Bird."

"Well, yes, I'm sure you do. I guess I'll just be blunt; we're both grown women. It isn't such a delicate matter. You being an unmarried woman and all, I'm just concerned about the type of people who Bessie will meet here."

"You mean my mother and Uncle Vernon? She can be as mischievous as a schoolgirl, but I assure you she's quite harmless. And Uncle Vernon is gruff, but that's only to hide all the softness."

"Please don't be coy, Miss Maddy. I'm sure that you have gentlemen friends."

Bird's back snapped straight like Mrs. Charles had just smacked her spine with the schoolhouse paddle. Bessie's mouth dropped. Bird felt the throbbing sting and everything else beneath her mother's pause: a swallowed gasp, the clicking and slow grind of her teeth, and the forced smile that gave lie to the true depth of the cut.

"Gentlemen friends? No, Mrs. Charles. I don't have gentlemen friends." Maddy emphasized the "s." "Bird's father comes by to visit her now and again, usually during the week. Don't you think that it's good for a girl to know her father?"

"Why yes, of course. But don't you think it's appropriate for children to be exposed to a more traditional arrangement?"

"That's a luxury not many of us have. I'm not the only one."

"Why, I know—" Mrs. Charles didn't get to finish her sentence.

"I assure you Mrs. Charles, that I am just as concerned about the upbringing of your child as I am about my own. Whatever Bennettsville's gossips say about me, this is no den of iniquity. This is my home and place of business. These girls mean a lot to each other. I'd hate to see that ruined because of low-minded gossip."

"Well said, Miss Maddy. I didn't mean to imply otherwise. Perhaps it's best if we proceed with that understanding."

Bird and Bessie sprinted back through the house and screen door and landed on either side of Miss Bennett. Their mothers returned to the porch to find them muddling through embarrassed discomfort between them.

Mrs. Charles fitted her hat. "It was a pleasure seeing you Miss Bennett and Miss Maddy."

She extended her hand to Maddy but hesitated and tipped her hat to Miss Bennett. "Bessie, Miss Maddy says that you are welcome to visit on weekends. You be a good girl when you are over here."

Bessie offered her polite goodbyes to the adult women and frowned an apology to Bird.

As the Charles women walk back down the lane, Bird slipped her hand into her mother's. The girl wished she knew words to heal her mother's wound. A high price had been paid for this friendship. All this time, Bird thought, I've been worried what the schoolchildren think of me, and I should have been worried about the schoolteachers. And for this, she forgave her mother's initial anger, current reluctance, and all the days of melancholy in between.

It had all seemed so easy in Bird's imagination. Mr. Charles would bring Bessie over on a Saturday morning, and they would play, maybe read a bit, and eat lunch. Later, she and Uncle Vernon would take her back home again. And then one Saturday afternoon, Bessie stood expectantly in front of the Bennett house. As Bird and her mother stepped onto the porch, Mr. Charles bid them good day and turned the wagon back up the lane. Maddy gave the frozen Bird a nudge before returning to her work. The near silence of her world embarrassed Bird. Who visits a friend's home to read and play with fabric? She wondered at her own stupidity.

"I have some fabrics in the backyard," she mumbled as she stepped off the porch. "I thought maybe we could pretend to be in a play." Bird swallowed and led her friend to the house's back and mound of cloth scraps she'd begged from her mother. They stood before the pile. Bessie glanced around the yard. "Or, anything you'd like to do is fine," said Bird wishing her mother was more like Mrs. Charles who always had activities planned for them, even though most of them were educational. What she wouldn't give for her mother to call out some tasks for them.

An upstairs window opened. "Bird," Odelia's melodious soprano floated out into the blue sky. "Won't you bring your friend here to meet me formally this time."

A relieved Bird feigned duty as she led Bessie through the house's shadows and upstairs to her grandmother's bedroom.

The room was bright and simply furnished with only a four-poster bed, dresser, and sitting table with two chairs. Pictures and framed embroidery nearly filled the walls, leaving just a few inches of faded baby blue paint showing here and there. Odelia sat facing the window in a canary dressing gown and robe.

"Bird, bring your friend here by me."

Bessie trailed slowly behind.

"Odelia Bennett, pleased to meet you," she said holding out her hand.

Bessie giggled and shook Odelia's hand. Bird tried to see her grandmother through Bessie's eyes. She was a tall woman, skinny but with strong shoulders despite her sixty-two years. The wisps of salt and pepper hair that had escaped her bun framed her pale face. Blue veins showed through her eggshell skin. Was the old woman she loved frightening to her friend?

"Do you mind if I touch you? It's how we blind folks see," asked Odelia.

Bird wanted to reach out, to intervene, but Bessie spoke before she could.

"No ma'am . . . I don't mind."

Odelia hands ran down the length of Bessie's arms. Bird glanced around as Bessie took in the bedroom. The pictures revealed a young and beautiful Odelia Bennett who'd been stylish and vivacious in youth and then more solemn as she aged. The pictures' timeline stopped abruptly in her early 30s as if a day hadn't passed since then. Only the old woman sitting before them belied this.

Examining the girl's fingers, Miss Bennett asked, "Your siblings do most of the housework?"

"I do some." Bessie squirmed. "How can you tell?"

"Your fingers are soft like there are older children who do most of the rough work. I tell Maddy she's working Honest too hard. She's a little thing, but her hands are almost as strong as a woman's." Odelia's hand slid to Bessie's waist. "Oh, you're going to be a curvy one. Your husband will like that."

Bessie relaxed and giggled again.

"Do you mind if I touch your face?"

"I think it's fine."

Odelia's fingers found her cheeks and slid along her nose and cheek bones and up to her eyes. "You're quite a pretty child. You're going to be a looker when you grow up. I hope you won't break too many hearts."

"My father says either school or early marriage."

"Those are often the options depending upon the young lady." Odelia smiled.

"Honest, would you and Bessie mind taking me down for tea in the sitting room?"

Bird and Bessie made much ado of making tea and a platter of cookies. Odelia entertained them with stories of grand stores in New York City and ocean liners to and from London. Later this day, when Bird and Bessie retired to the hammock to read, Bessie would ask about the old woman napping in the house. "Why didn't your granny ever get married?"

Bessie stared at Odelia's bedroom window with a concern and sorrow that surprised Bird and set her at ease. Satiating the curiosity would do better than silence's fan, decided Bird. "She did. She traveled lots with a white lady she worked for. She met my grandfather on a trip to England. But some white men killed him in Mississippi for teaching. When her sight got too bad, she and my mother came back here."

"Then why does everybody call her Miss Bennett?" Bessie asked.

Bird could only shrug.

"I thought white people were always happy."

"She isn't white. And no, I don't think so."

# June 1913

The summer would teach Bird that life is a mountain-filled walk. Sometimes the peaks are the rewards after hard journeys, and sometimes they only herald low times ahead. The summer promised two highlights to Bennettsville's children—a wedding and a revival. Bird only concerned herself with the first since Maddy didn't hold much with church and Cecile Charles was the bride-to-be. For months, Bird and Bessie had watched Cecile and Helena Charles fret and argue over countless details—bridesmaids, dress colors, flowers to plant for the bouquet, and how to keep Bessie from theatrics during her march down the aisle as the junior bride. When school was in session, the children talked only of the wedding in their spare moments. The wedding cake centered most of these discussions. They argued about how fantastic the cake would be and how many slices each would have. Rumor had it that Mr. Johnson had gone to the white baker in Tuckersville, an almost scandalous idea.

As Bessie and Bird waded in the still too cold pond on a Saturday afternoon, Bessie debated (mostly with herself) whether she should twirl up and down the aisle or offer her sister and brother-in-law a song as her sister arrived at the altar. Bird guessed that Bessie was mostly joking, but her friend's commitment to the debate and listing of oddly inappropriate songs—"Silent Night, Holy Night," "Nearer my God to Thee," and "Jesus, Lover of My Soul"—gave her pause.

"Why those songs?" Bird asked, straining to keep her voice even.

"My Grandma Charles has us sing them; I know 'em best."

Any singing talent on Bessie's part was news to Bird. "Can I hear you?" she asked excitedly. Only Odelia had the gift of song in her family.

Bessie stood, clasped her hands, faced the water, and began to sway. Bird waited patiently as Bessie seemed to focus her thoughts, and then gave her friend the benefit of the doubt when her first hummed note was flat for any song. She tried not to grimace as Bessie wailed and moaned through the opening lines of "Jesus, Lover of My Soul." By the time Bessie got to the "I love you/I need you/Though my world may fall" and provided her own chorus, Bird had raised her hand to stop her friend. Bessie paused for the response and scowled at Bird's wide-eyed silence. "I know I can sing. This cold water is just—."

Bird stepped closer to put her hand on Bessie's shoulder, the way adults did when delivering hard news. Bessie put one indignant hand on her hip and grabbed Bird's approaching hand with the other. They each knew the next part of this game. Bessie would toss Bird's hand down, and they'd both laugh. Instead, they stood there holding their breaths, their fingers intertwined. Neither girl pulling her hand away or knowing what to say.

They both jumped about two feet when Bird's cousins Ned and Luther roared like bears and dashed out of the wood line toward them. The girls screamed and fell back deeper into the water. The boys' own laughter dropped them at the pond's edge.

The sight of her cousins rolling at the expense of her and her friend took the shock out of the cold water, and Bird stomped onto the dry ground. Bessie screeched and splashed for a moment longer.

"I'm telling Cousin Jeannetta!" Bird yelled at them.

They didn't stop laughing. Ned, the oldest, only waved a dismissive hand at her.

Bessie dragged herself out of the water and stood beside her friend. "That was rude and rotten," she said.

"So was that singing," Ned said. As he managed to stand, he offered a hand to his little brother.

Bird wanted to smash his nose but could only stand there.

"What on God's green earth!" All the children jerked toward the tree line, as Uncle Vernon shouted and barreled toward them.

Bird raised a protective arm, pushing Bessie back a few steps into the water.

Ned and Luther stood smirking until Uncle Vernon burst through the bushes with a small axe, half raised. Then, the boys scrambled back in terror. Uncle Vernon's eyes found Bird and Bessie first. "Who's messing with you?" His intent to hurt someone was clear.

Bird's heart jumped into her mouth, and she could hardly talk around it. "It's just Ned and Luther, sir. They was just playing." Her eyes darted to the boys.

Ned, nearing sixteen, had mostly regained himself and his full six feet, although the girls could see the fray of his nerves in his deep breaths. Luther, small for his thirteen years, stood behind him.

Glaring at the boys, Uncle Vernon lowered his axe. "What ya got to say for yourselves?"

"We were just playing, Uncle, like she said." Ned said, though Bird disliked the impudence in his tone, and the tilt of his chin suggested haughtiness.

Uncle Vernon must have read all of this too. He returned the axe to his pant loop and stepped to within arm's reach of the boys. His frame, tall and broad and built of taut muscles, countered their young and scrawny arms. He lowered his voice. "You don't play like that with girls eva again. Not on this land or in this town. If I hear of it, I'll treat you like the man you think you is. You understand?"

Ned's chin wavered for a moment and then lowered. "Yes, sir," he answered, the chastening's effect genuine in his voice, "I didn't mean no harm. We just came to get fitted for our pants for the wedding."

"Then head on to the house and leave these gals alone."

The boys hurried back into the tree line. Uncle Vernon watched them go before turning to the girls. "Anybody come at you, playing or not, you scream just like you did."

The girls nodded, sobered by the whole episode. After her uncle left, Bird gathered their things. She and Bessie stared at each other for a moment. Bird's face burned. "We've got to go back to the house," she explained, "my Mama's not feeling well today. I need to do their measurements."

Bessie sat in an armchair staring at the window, as the boys submitted in silence to their measurements and left with only a thank you. The mood of the afternoon was dampened, and the girls flipped half-heartedly through books under the towering oak beside the house. Finally, Bessie lay her book down and asked, "Would Uncle Vernon really have axed them?"

"Them or anybody from Bennettsville, probably not, 'less it was bad enough," said Bird, only half sure of her answer.

There was nothing more to say after this, and the girls sank back down into her books, though Bird couldn't even pretend to read anymore. When the Charleses' wagon rattled down the road a short while later, both girls sighed with relief. This was a day that needed ending.

So, both girls gawked when Mrs. Charles and Cecile alighted from the wagon and said they were all staying for a spell. Maddy Bennett matched their shock as Bird explained that the schoolteacher, Bessie, and Cecile were in the sitting room.

"We need your help." Mrs. Charles gestured to her oldest daughter as Maddy came out still in her house robe. "Sewing help."

Still, Maddy said nothing, though Bird tugged on her sleeve to prompt even a "hello."

"Sister Higgins made Cecile's dress." Mrs. Charles began making exaggerated waves to the front door and the wagon that had carried them. "She did a fine job. A fine job. You see, she's always done our sewing. It's just that the dress needs . . . a little letting out now. Unexpectedly."

Maddy raised an eyebrow at Cecile, who managed an impressive blush and half-smile that said she was more embarrassed about her mother than her situation. This, at last, loosened Maddy's tongue and a low laugh escaped. "And how long til the wedding?"

Bird almost choked; she'd been talking about the date and all of Cecile's preparations for months. And they had received their customary invitations, though they only ever sent small cash gifts and best wishes.

"Two weeks," said Cecile.

Maddy turned to Bird. "Put on some coffee and warm up the chicken. It's gonna be a long night."

Bird and Bessie skipped all the way to the kitchen now that their day had reset itself in the most exciting of ways.

Maddy set up her tools and measuring box in the kitchen. The first moments of the gathering pained everyone. Helena had basic sewing skills but nothing sophisticated enough to speak competently with Maddy about her strategy. And Maddy didn't offer any information or small talk. Thank goodness for the yardbird, Bird thought.

Bird placed the fried chicken and cornbread slices on the table without utensils. Helena wrinkled her forehead at the plate in front of her, glanced at Bird, and accepted her instructions. She removed her sweater and picked up a chicken thigh like she would have at home.

"Miss Maddy, did you fry this chicken?"

"Yes," she said, through lips still pinching pins. "Call me Maddy."

"It's so nice to eat good food I haven't had to cook myself." The teacher made short work of the thigh as Bird and Bessie nibbled on their respective wing and drumstick.

"I made the cornbread," Bird offered.

"Well, that is very good too," said the teacher.

Bird drank up the praise she almost never sought so forthrightly in the schoolhouse.

"I keep telling Cecile she needs to cook more. A woman has to know how to cook and keep a house."

"Mama," whined Cecile.

"Don't talk," Maddy ordered, and Cecile quieted.

Helena laughed. "Then I need to say my whole piece."

"You got three minutes," Maddy said as she gathered, pinched, and planned magic for the flowing chiffon dress, edged with lace.

"Why, thank you, Maddy."

And for a few moments, Cecile stood lovely and pouting as she bore the brunt of teasing reserved for soon-to-be-married girls who prefer sleeping in to making breakfast and don't mind the occasional wrinkles on dresses—especially if a cardigan will cover them. The laughter must have been irresistible, for a few minutes later, Bird heard Odelia on the stairs and ran to help her. A hush fell in the kitchen when Bird led her in.

"Please don't stop the fête now," said Odelia as she sat.

"It's more a mission of mercy, Miss Bennett, for my Cecile," Mrs. Charles said with a note of chagrin.

Odelia frowned at the indecipherable silence.

"We're letting out a wedding dress, just a touch," explained Maddy with a professional diplomacy.

Odelia brightened. "Then I was right, it is a party. We celebrate babies in this house. All God's gifts are good."

"Amen," said a relieved Mrs. Charles.

"To Cecile and her motherhood," Maddy raised her glass, and the others followed suit. "Now, Helena, help me get this dress off her before she and this baby bust out of it." Bird studied her mother's smile. It wasn't exactly an act, but there was no light in it. Maddy's eyes lingered a moment longer on the pregnant bride, and Bird looked away to give her this moment with the path not taken.

Cecile Charles married Liston Johnson on the last Saturday in June. This marriage between the schoolteachers' daughter and the grocers' son had won Bennettsville's approval. To mark this approval and hope that the couple's double roots in town would keep them from running off to St. Louis or Chicago, almost the whole town turned out for the event, including Maddy, Bird, and Vernon Bennett—rare attendees to anything.

Bird and Maddy rode beside Uncle Vernon with a staid and dignified air as the heat and humidity pressed on their chests. Inside, Bird could hardly contain herself, craning her neck for a first glimpse of the church. This wedding was the most exciting event she'd been to. Maddy had sewn them matching dresses for the occasion—baby blue crepe de chine that hugged the waist and floated at the ankle. Even Uncle Vernon had accepted a new shirt and tie.

They arrived at a churchyard overflowing with people in their Sunday finery repurposed for the wedding. The women wore sleeveless dresses and sequined hats that had to be painfully hot. The men wore trousers, ties, and shined shoes. Bird and Maddy's arrival earned more than a few second glances. As they settled into their own clump among the other clumps, Bird glanced from her mother to her uncle. Both had a well-practiced comfort with silence. The weather and the couple's plans for the future occupied most of the conversation around them. To their right, Sarah Giles, who'd opted for a full sleeve and ankle-length ensemble, complained to two other women who didn't seem to be paying her much mind. "Don't they know it's too hot to have folks sweatin' out here like this? Ain't nobody ever said a bride have a right to keep a whole town out in the heat."

To their left, the Simmons family plotted Cecile and Liston's future. "Of course, they gon' stay. What they got to leave for? They practically the only kids around here got ready-made jobs. The boy gon' get the store, and his wife can teach the school."

His wife countered, "That don't mean they want to stay. Robert coulda had the iron works, and he left."

"What would a young man want to shoe horses for if there's automobiles out here?" Mr. Simmons waved away her argument.

Bird turned back to her own family. Maddy watched the door of the church. Uncle Vernon raised a hand to folks in the different clumps. Glad she'd come with a plan, Bird scanned the multitudes for her tiny students and found them split between their usual pastimes—clinging to the legs of some older family member or running completely wild through the shielding crowd. She'd promised each little one a piece of candy if they found her and spelled a word or recited the alphabet. This way, she'd have at least some opportunity to encourage conversation between their mother and hers. What could be more natural than complimenting children's smarts and the bride's beauty?

Trying to catch the eye of Josiah Robbins, she caught Mr. Johnson instead, who cut off his conversation mid-sentence and made a beeline for them, dragging his wife Mildred along by the elbow. He boomed as usual and made a big show of hugging Maddy, subtly forcing Mildred to awkwardly follow suit lest rumors blossom. Bird surmised that he took their presence as some honor to himself. Maddy did not dissuade him from this. "Odelia sends her regrets," she explained, "the old and heat are not friends. She hopes the couple will stop by for proper well-wishes soon."

"Of course," Mr. Johnson nearly shouted as he pounded Uncle Vernon's back. Uncle Vernon gave the man an indulgent smile. "I've heard them talking over such a visit as soon as they are back from Saint Louis. Isn't that right, Mildred?" His wife stood with a deferential silence and seemed relieved when a woman used the lull in conversation to insert herself.

"Miss Maddy, so good to see you." A small hawklike woman in lavender satin rushed forward with an extended arm and grabbed Maddy's hand. "And what lovely dresses. I hope you aren't here to advertise your services." Mildred Johnson pulled her husband away.

Maddy laughed with a feigned politeness and reclaimed her hand. "It's good to see you as well Mrs. Higgins. I wouldn't think of doing such a thing. There's more than enough work between both the 'villes to keep us both busy."

"Don't I know it. Although I do hope that those white ladies in Tuckersville aren't as cheap with you as I've heard from other girls who work for them."

"I've never had a reason to complain."

As the women relished their not-so-veiled dislike for one another, Bird waved over Elijah Tompkins. The boy was sweet and obedient in class and would often find a reason to sit in her lap while she read stories. As much as he hung on her in class, candy was not enough to win him away from his mother's legs. Bird searched for a more rambunctious child, but the crowd had started its slow procession into the white A-frame church.

"Wait until you see Cecile's dress," said Mrs. Higgins. "It's simple elegance, but you know the devil is in the details when going for such a style."

"I've heard it's quite lovely," said Maddy.

"Oh my, word of it has spread all the way to your end of the road? We should do tea soon."

"Yes, let's." Maddy had turned away from the woman before she'd finished the words.

The common divisions between the bride's and groom's families meant nothing at this particular wedding, as the guests vied for seats near the open windows. Preferring to avoid the fray, Bird, Maddy, and Vernon took seats off the church's center aisle. They had not brought ladies' fans, a mistake that Bird—a first-time church and wedding attendee, regretted with sincere sorrow. She envied those on the pews' outer edges. The windows didn't do much, but when the whisper of a breeze passed through, those in its path stilled and quieted lest they scare off the skittish air.

Mr. Johnson and Mr. Charles stood at the back of the church in a heated but quiet exchange. Bird wondered if they argued about the delay, when Mr. Johnson broke away and walked straight toward them.

"Didn't Helena tell you? You have seats up front."

Bird had grown used to the fact that she and her mother didn't favor much, at least in features—in that moment, their looks of shock were indistinguishable.

"Oh no, that won't be necessary, Mr. Johnson. We're fine right here."

"I insist. I would certainly seat your mother there. Y'all come out to see my only boy get married and sitting in the back of the church. Uncle Vernon, your seat is by Mister Fred, and Miss Maddy and Miss Bird, you have seats right next to Miss Jeannetta and her girls."

For the first time, the grocer's oversized personality grated against Bird's nerves. Both Bird and Maddy swiveled around for any kind of rescue and found all eyes on them. Mr. Charles bowed his head in apology or prayer. Mr. Johnson grinned and pointed to the front pews. Bird wanted to kick him in the shins.

"Just go, Mama," she whispered, afraid they might linger in this horribleness forever.

If Helena Charles taught Bird how to enter a home, that afternoon her mother taught her to hold her head up in any and every situation. To swallow the bitterness of others like peach marmalade. And to use the hardness in their eyes to ground your step. There were sympathetic eyes, those well aware that Maddy Bennett did not covet such an honor or the associated attention. Bird noted those folks and appreciated them. And she saw the others, those that were haughty and spiteful, indignant that the place of honor, even if unwanted, had been bestowed. Maddy sat beside Jeannetta Bennett who immediately put her hand on her mother's to still the trembling.

A few minutes later when they stood for the wedding party's entrance, Bird slipped her mother's arm around her and felt the burden of the weight that needed sharing. Bessie, possessed by restraint or nerves, marched with a dignified calm down the aisle and offered her sister a humble curtsy to the approval of all, as Cecile and her groom wed before a church full of sweating brows and glistening eyes.

The church emptied into a cooler, cloud-covered afternoon as a wagon, driven by two of the oldest women Bird had ever seen, pulled up with the meal. The women's auxiliary members made quick work of unloading salads, hams, chicken, pies, and biscuits, more food than Bird had ever seen in one place. Mr. Johnson stepped forward to carry the arms-length white sheet cake himself. Bird and all the children held their breath and hoped that anticipation could not knock a man down. Bird, Maddy, and Uncle Vernon had just sat a table when a firm hand grasped Bird's shoulder. Mrs. Charles hovered above her.

"Bird, darling, the children's table is over there." She pointed to a gaggle of girls crowded around Bessie, who glowed under all the attention.

"I should stay here, Ma'am." Bird tried.

Mrs. Charles dismissed her protest, and her mother pointed her glumly toward the girls. As she departed, Mrs. Charles slid into the seat on Maddy's other side. "I thought we were going to have to grease her up to get her in that dress. She's got about one more hour before she and my grandbaby pop out of it." Both she and Maddy hollered with laughter. The two women carried on for a good half-hour, oblivious to the curious glances around them. Helena abandoned her place at the table of honor, eventually calling over other women to join them and make merry at the expense of young brides and hot weather. For everything that would happen between Bird and Helena Charles in a few short years, Bird would tend the sting with her remembrance and appreciation on this day.

# July 1913

With the wedding passed and the school still on break for the summer field work, Bird and Odelia resurrected their old patterns of late mornings, garden strolls, and relaxed reading. The first steep valley of the summer came during the biscuits and gravy they shared on a Tuesday morning. Odelia started her day chatty enough by her granddaughter's measure but then gradually silenced and stilled. Accustomed to these reflective moments, Bird thought little about it until she glanced over from her own musings. The left side of Odelia's body slumped, and the left side of her face had flattened. Bird didn't know what had happened, only that it was wrong.

Her mother's machine hissed from the sewing room, but Bird's body had locked itself in place. She forced out two shouts. "Mama! Granny!" Later she could not fathom how those two words had been complete sentences full of explanation—or maybe it was the shout itself, or the clear terror in it. Seconds later, Maddy stood in the kitchen doorway, and then she kneeled at her mother's side, Odelia's veined hand in her own.

"Get Vernon," she said, her voice a distressing calm.

This simple order, executed so many times, unlocked Bird who flew out of the house and down the lane.

Together, Maddy and Vernon carried Odelia to her bed with Bird trailing in tears behind them. Maddy massaged her mother's temples and cheeks and then bent her arms and legs before covering her with a blanket. "We're here. Rest. Everything's gonna be fine." A tear slipped down Odelia's cheek.

"Go for Doctor Mitchell," Maddy said to Vernon. He was gone the next second.

"Birdy, sit down," she motioned for Bird to sit beside her on the window seat. "It's called a stroke. Something goes wrong in the brain. They can be minor things. Old Ezra had plenty of them."

Bird heard the words not added. Odelia had spoken of her father's strokes plenty of times. News would come down the road that one of the town's elders had "had a spell," and Odelia would grimace and say something to the effect of, "Just like Ezra—wore him down slowly and made short work of him in the end." Bird had had no emotions about these announcements or her grandmother's comparisons. Ezra Bennett had died generations ago, and she didn't know most of the old folks in town. Now, these words hovered over her grandmother. There was no warning. No sign. Was this a slow wearing down, or the short work at the end? Maddy opened her arms for a hug, but Bird pushed her away. Hugs were for happiness or catastrophe—this was . . . she didn't know what this was.

"She will get better," demanded Bird through gritted teeth and hot tears.

"Yes, she will," said Maddy. "She'll need time, rest, care and to know that we're strong."

In bed that night, Bird tossed and turned through memories of the day. The slack of Odelia's face. The undisguised fear in both her mother and uncle. It could have been worse, the white doctor said with little empathy for the frayed nerves around him. This was a small stroke, a warning of what may come, but Odelia would recover. As sleep found her, Bird roamed an empty and shadowed house in her dreams. She called out for her granny, her mother, and uncle, and then anyone who would come. No matter how hard she cried, no one came.

For the first time in her young life, Bird understood what it meant when her mother said she woke feeling like hell. Her head pounded, and her muscles ached, like she had actually roamed the house all night. The sun was high when she threw on a house dress and admonished herself for tardiness to her caretaking duties. Maddy sat at Odelia's bedside and held open arms, and this time, Bird slipped into them.

"Give your grandmother a good morning kiss," she said.

Bird approached with measured steps. Odelia's eyes were closed, but she wasn't sure that the woman was asleep. Bird kissed her damp forehead. "Good morning, Granny," she said.

Maddy stood and waved for her to follow her out. In the hallway, her mother took her chin in hand. "Rough night, little one?"

Bird nodded. "Did you sleep, Mama?"

"Enough."

"I can take over now, and you can rest."

"Uncle Vernon has the next shift. And then Jeannetta is going to help. You, my dear, are going to the Charleses' house for a few days."

"Granny needs me; I'm the one who takes care of her," Bird argued.

"Yes, Birdy. I appreciate that, but you are a girl, and there will be plenty of time in your life for caretaking. Uncle Vernon has the wagon ready. You need to pack enough clothes to get you through the weekend."

Bird pouted, but Maddy held up a silencing hand. "Please, baby. This is how Odelia and I need you to be strong. She'll be fine, and you'll be back at the end of the weekend." A night of crying had puffed Maddy's face, and gray circles ringed her swollen eyes. If Bird felt like hell, she acknowledged that her mother's heart and body must hurt more. She agreed to go. Maddy kissed the part in her hair and said she would rebraid her two plaits before she left.

Mr. and Mrs. Charles greeted them as the wagon stopped. Bird waved shyly at Bessie and her brother Alexander pressed against the window. Uncle Vernon lifted her down, and Bird felt like a small girl again.

"How is she?" asked Mrs. Charles, her hands pressed tight.

"The doctor says she'll be fine. It'll just take a little time."

The teachers exhaled with relief and shifted to Bird. "We have lots going on this weekend to keep you from worrying too much," offered Mr. Charles.

"She'll need plenty of help for that," said Uncle Vernon, and Bird gave him a quick glance of displeasure. He squeezed her into a half hug.

"We'll be seeing my sister and her family at the last day of the revival."

Uncle Vernon had reached to hand Bird her bag. Both of their hands stopped mid-air. "I didn't think y'all went," he said.

"We use most of the week as a break but often go on the last day. It's a good halfway point from my people in Decatur." Mrs. Charles brightened.

For the second time in two days, Bird was stricken. Uncle Vernon gave her a fuller hug and whispered. "It'll be okay, these things is huge and been goin' all week. No harm gon' come from it."

With a sense of wary foreboding, she followed her hosts into their home.

"I'm not sure about this revival," Bird said to Bessie as they settled her in her room. The side of the bed that had belonged to Cecile was now Bird's for the week. "My mama doesn't hold much with church."

"Oh, Bird, it's outside, and there are plenty of other kids," Bessie lowered her voice, "and it's easy to get away from the adults and have fun. And the last day is a show! Now, we've got lots to do. Cecile and Liston are coming, and Mama will be cooking all day. And the boys will load up the wagon with stuff for my aunt and cousins."

Members of the Charles family moved like worker bees, each with his or her own unspoken mission. The girls cooked, washed, dried, and ironed. The boys tended the horse, replaced a wagon wheel, and plotted ways to situate the entire family, plus Bird, in with a hand-me-down dresser.

Bird followed Bessie's lead and took up a washtub. All through the scrubbing, she considered her own mission—to stay behind. She couldn't go to any revival. The Minister could be there. She'd only ever seen him in her house. And he was part of the reason she and her mother didn't go to church, any church—that and Maddy didn't seem to hold with God nearly as much her granny and the other colored folks around them.

On Thursday, she made a direct plea to Mrs. Charles when she caught the woman returning from the outhouse.

"May I have a word, Mrs. Charles? In private."

Mrs. Charles glanced toward the kitchen but acquiesced. "Just don't make me burn my pie, little one."

"Yes, ma'am. I can't explain much anyway. It's just that I can't go to the revival. Mama and I don't go to church. I'm happy to stay behind and read the Bible. Did you know I can name and spell all sixty-six books?"

Helena Charles looked at her quizzically, "Your mama has never taken you to church, even for baptism?"

"No, ma'am. They probably did that in the pond. Basically, the same as with John the Baptist."

Mrs. Charles either laughed or choked; Bird was never certain. "Bird, we're charged with your care and safety. I'm certain your mother would rather us carry you to the Lord's meeting than leave you here alone. One day at a revival, that's mostly hustle and bustle anyway, shouldn't bother Maddy too much. I will explain things to her myself if necessary. And you may find that you like church. A young lady's soul is her own."

Bird sighed as Mrs. Charles left her standing on the back porch. She had tried.

Their arrival at the revival was like riding up to a big city. The wagons leaving had children piled on top of mattresses and about any other household item you could imagine. Like all the wagon drivers, Mr. Charles stopped and stared when an automobile beeped and bounced past. He issued a low whistle and waved to the goggled driver.

"Wagons have been fine since Moses was a boy." Mrs. Charles sucked her teeth with disapproval.

The revival camp was orderly chaos with people moving in indecipherable patterns like flocks of birds. Mr. Charles deposited them near the campground entrance before diverting to store the horse and wagon. Mrs. Charles led their small party toward the hubbub, and Bird almost felt giddy as they merged into the camp's web.

Bessie explained everything as they went. The tent at the center served as the main pavilion for the preaching. Women in white dresses and men in black suits swept between the benches. It would be packed and hopping except for mealtimes. The preachers' tent stood a short walk from the pavilion as did the tents for the women's auxiliary, nurses, and ushers. In the distance, along the camp's eastern and western sides, families traveling from far away towns and cities had raised large tents for their lodging.

Women said quick hellos to Mrs. Charles, and men tipped their hat, but no one stopped to talk. Everyone had some place to be in this temporary town, and Bird matched the Charleses' sense of purpose as Mrs. Charles led them along the rows of family tents.

"Children, keep your eyes open for our people."

Bessie quieted and scanned the distance along with her sister and brother for any faces she might recognize from the crowded wedding earlier in the summer. As they neared the camp's edge, Alexander yelled, "There's Jeannie." He began shouting the teenage girl's name until his mother took his arm and ordered him not to make a spectacle of their arrival. Ultimately, that was her job as she let out an involuntary shout of joy and ran the last few strides as her sister stepped out of their tent.

Bird could hardly track all the bodies whirling around hugging and laughing.

"Who you?" They kept asking of Bird as they grinned and hugged her and then turned to hug somebody else before she could answer.

When everyone calmed down and remembered that introductions were needed for Bird, Liston, and a baby born since the last visit, Bird stepped forward to Mrs. Charles's sister, Laura, and offered her best smile. She had not seen this woman at the wedding—she would have remembered. The woman was even more striking than her sister. She was younger and taller and with an angularity Bird attributed to physical work, but she beamed more freely than her sister.

"Good morning, ma'am," said Bird.

Mrs. Charles placed a hand on Bird's shoulder. "Our star pupil Honest, called Bird, and Bessie's best friend. It's her first revival."

"And y'all brought her for the last day?" Laura shook her head. "Well, you are in for a show baby Bird."

And with that, Bird was family and received her share of random love, chores, snacks, and a few cents to spend as she saw fit. The morning passed in a blink. Instead of going to the children's camp, Bessie and Bird were allowed to attend the young ladies' camp for teenage girls. This perceived honor thrilled Bessie and mostly entertained Bird. Years of reading to her grandmother gave Bird a strong advantage at the Bible games, but the new popular hymns were completely lost on her. And she had no idea what to make of the "young lady lessons" about a young woman's duty to God, her family, and her future husband.

At lunch, Mrs. Charles suggested that Bessie and Bird join the adults for the afternoon preaching. Bessie was thrilled, and even Bird approved this new turn in the day's adventure. She had relaxed; Uncle Vernon was right. The revival was huge, and she was lost in it. In the main pavilion, Bird and her newly adopted family squeezed into a middle bench and took up the general task of fanning to keep the air moving. The white-clad ushers moved up and down the center aisle and edges forcing late arrivers into tiny spaces and shooing away trespassing children. Bird glanced around with amazement at the crowd of beautifully brown people. Everyone was hot but happy. The smell of sweat, perfume, and the evergreens mixed around them. Her astonishment pleased both Mrs. Charles and Bessie. "It gets better," said Mrs. Charles.

Bird made mental notes to relay all she saw to her grandmother. How the preachers ascended the wooden stage one by one, each with his own gravity and energy. Some were big men, and some small in frame. Some were old, and plenty were young. Most wore heavy gray or black robes and poured sweat for it. There was an art to the mopping of brows among them—the patient unfolding of a white handkerchief and the deliberate dabbing of the forehead, or the rushed "wipe and forget" until the sweat slipped into their eyes again. They came from churches with names that invoked mounts, missionaries, streets, and cities. They announced their cities—Chicago, Nashville, Indianapolis, Des Moines—and the greater distances earned more applause and hallelujahs from the crowd. The men led prayers, promised them salvation, warned them of damnation, reminded them of commandments and covenants, and pleaded with them to avoid being left behind. Along the way, a few women mounted the podium to sing or read announcements.

To Bird, this was as much theater as it was preaching, and she was surprised to find herself enjoying it all. Each preacher's performance was better than the last, and as the afternoon deepened, the tent overflowed, and people crowded onto the surrounding grass.

Bird leaned to Mrs. Charles. "Will there be any women preachers?"

"Earlier in the week, little one," the teacher answered.

The man who introduced the preacher who would close the revival spoke so fast, that Bird almost missed her father's name. The Reverend Johnathan Edward Turner, the man had said, and Bird's body was again rigid and locked. He mounted the stage with a Bible in one hand and a handkerchief in the other. His black robe highlighted his dark skin and graying hair. He leaned against the podium like it was the counter at Johnson's Grocery and spoke to the revival attendees like they were old friends.

"I am invisible," Bird muttered to herself. Uncle Vernon's words still stood. Hers was one face among hundreds.

Bessie squeezed her arm. "You okay?"

"I'll need to use the bathroom soon."

"Me too." Bessie whispered back.

The Minister, as Bird thought of him, spoke with a deliberate slowness and gave glories to God. "I don't have to speak fast tonight, or long," he said. "My message is short and to the point."

"Hallelujah," someone shouted, and Jonathan Turner laughed humbly along with the others. Still, Bird felt the audience waiting, like this was the preamble to some previously agreed upon process. The Minister's eyes roved over the crowd as if searching each one of them. Bird pretended to cough and covered her face with her fan.

"I have come to tell y'all that we do our young folks a disservice when we tell them Satan is a liar." He stopped for effect.

"But ain't he though," a woman shouted from the back benches, causing Bird to jump.

"I'm talking to whoever said that," the Minister continued, "and the front of this here tent—to you mothers and fathers of the church. Wise and venerable you are. But we're wrong on this one." The mothers and fathers watched the preacher for their lesson.

"Sometimes, Satan tells the truth. Like when he tells a young man a drink won't kill him. That's the truth. It won't. Or, when he tells that same young man how nice that young lady looks, and that she probably feels even nicer."

"It's all the truth, brothers and sisters. The young folk know it, and us telling them it's a lie makes us seem like we got the problem. If it wasn't true, wouldn't none of us be here. We have to tell them that sometimes the devil tells the truth. And onto all this truth, he adds one little word. And this little word has cost God only knows how many souls a mansion in my father's house."

A chorus of low moans echoed through the benches pushed along by waving fans and arms. The piano player began pounding chords in rhythm with the message.

"What's the word, preacher? You gotta tell it," said an old bald man from the front row.

"I'ma tell it, though we've all heard it, and hopefully, you done all saw through it before it was too late. Satan tells them . . ." He leaned forward until Bird thought the podium would tumble off the stage, "to wait."

"My God, my God," a woman called out.

Another woman stood near the front and swayed. The Minister held his hand out toward her. "Ladies and gentlemen, my helpmeet. The woman who wrested me from the word 'wait.'"

Several folks shouted "Hallelujah's" and "Praise Him."

The Minister's wife was tall and sandy brown, with smooth, glimmering skin. She wore a fine white shirt and simple high waisted skirt. Her black hair was pinned under a cartwheel hat despite the heat.

The Minister continued, "'You can listen to the old folks one day,' Satan says. 'When you're old like them. Just wait a little longer til you got a little mayhem out ya system. Taste the fruit now and clean up the mess later.' But he don't tell them that the longer they wait, the more time it seem like they got. The more under control things seem. Like they have the time and ability to fix it all. And this is the devil's trap."

"God's people, we got to counteract this message. Show them the truth and the lie. Anybody can wait, but tomorrow ain't promised to none of us. To wait is to live in soul danger, and don't nothing on earth feel as good as hell feels bad. And don't no human pleasure feel as good as the presence of my God. Will you tell them?" he pounded on the podium. Mrs. Turner still stood and seemed to have come back to herself. She now looked imploringly at the crowd.

A chorus rose up of "Yes, Lords," and "I tell it every day," and "Give us strengths."

"Tell them," ordered the Minister. "It's your duty. What are you waiting for!"

Bird never knew whether the Minister intended for people to start calling out names at the end of his sermon. When the first child—Leonard Jones—was called out, the men on either side of the boy pressed him to stand up. The Minister held out a hand in his direction. "Don't wait, son." The boy studied his feet. Other names followed, and the young people were prompted to stand. "Ruby Thompson," "Martha

Patrick," "Damond Taylor." With his head bowed and hands trembling in the air, the Minister repeated the names. Most of the growing cadre of young people stood with awkward shyness, although a few stood proud, as if to say, "I'm not waiting." Bessie and Bird looked piteously at their peers, as if the scene unfolding around them couldn't possibly involve them. While Aunt Laura had loosed maybe three "Amens" all afternoon, her sister had sat as motionless and studious as the most obedient children in her log cabin school. So, both girls were aghast when Mrs. Charles's voice rang out, "Beatrice Charles and Honest Bennett."

The Minister made it all the way through Bessie's given name and half-way through Bird's before he must have comprehended the name on his lips. He choked like an unexpected fish bone had caught in his throat. Mrs. Turner spun around in the direction from which the name had come, her hand raised to her chest, and then back to her husband, who was doubled over and gagging. "Help him, Lord," Mrs. Turner begged as she shoved her way past the other women in her row.

Several others took up her pleading, "Help him, Lord," they prayed as the Minister dropped to one knee, and the other ministers swarmed him and pounded on his back.

"Even Satan can't resist a good revival," said a man from somewhere.

Bird wondered if he meant her as the tent's heat closed in around her. A burning sensation tore through her chest and to her extremities. She held out a hand, which Bessie caught as she yelled to steal her mother's attention away from the stage. Bird heard Mrs. Charles's "Lord, Jesus," and then fell into darkness.

She awoke in the dappled shade of the camp's wood line. The white clad nurses fanned her and poured water over her lips. They had loosened her blouse, and she wanted to cover herself, but her arms were leaden. The Charleses and Aunt Laura tarried a few feet to her left with faces drawn like they feared she might die. One nurse placed a wet towel on her forehead, and it felt divine. She managed a "thank you." The other woman dabbed another cool cloth around her neck. "You gon' be alright. I always tell them the tent is too hot and tight for young ones."

"I'm thirteen," Bird whispered.

"Like she said, young ones," the other woman said, looking toward camp's center. "Oh, Lord, as if we ain't seen enough ugly today."

Mrs. Sheila Turner stomped from the tent city toward them. Two people followed her—an old woman and a girl around Bird's age. Her own resemblance to both the old woman and girl was so striking that the world spun again. In her whole life, she'd only ever looked like the Minister. The old woman wore a twisted scowl that clarified that she had no tenderness for or curiosity about this laid out grandchild. The girl, maybe a year Bird's junior, walked with wide-eyed confusion. She glanced from her mother to her grandmother and occasionally over to Bird who tried to sit up. If she was to meet the Turners, she would do it standing with her head held high. One of the nurses held her down.

The Minister's wife stopped in front of Helena Charles and Laura, who'd stepped forward to intercept them. The Minister's wife raised her hand as if to strike one or both of the sisters. "Jezebel, have you no shame?"

"What in the world?" Mrs. Charles edged her sister out and grabbed Mrs. Turner's forearm. Mrs. Charles looked around for an explanation of this sudden violence, but everyone stood with gaping mouths. "You must be confused," she said to Sheila Turner, who yanked her arm away.

"I am not. This is no place for the godless."

Another woman from the crowd of approaching auxiliary members and nurses rushed to speak. "Missionary Turner, this is Mrs. Charles. The schoolteacher from Bennettsville. A very good woman."

The Minister's wife stared at Mrs. Charles. "And who is this child?" She pointed to Bird.

"My pupil," she said.

"Have you no consideration, Mrs. . . ." someone reminded her of Mrs. Charles's name. "This is a big moment for my husband and our congregation. This child's presence is only an embarrassment to him and myself."

"I have no idea who your husband is."

The Minister's wife lurched back and clutched her neck with shock and offense.

"The Reverend Jonathan Turner."

"Well, it seems to me like I have done nothing wrong inviting a child to God's meeting, and she's done no wrong accepting the invitation. From one married woman to another, the rest is between you and your husband."

Mrs. Turner grunted and stomped off, with all but two nurses and three perplexed auxiliary members trailing in her wake.

"Who was that, Mama?" asked Cecile.

"A poor ambassador of God's grace," said Mrs. Charles.

Bird tried to sit up again; she needed to leave this place. Whoever this revival was for, it wasn't for her. "Where is the Min—Reverend Turner?" she asked. The nurses glanced at each other and to Mrs. Charles.

"Well, answer her," said the teacher.

"He is resting in the preacher's tent. Women aren't allowed in there."

"I'm sure a message can find its way to him—Honest suggests that he stops waiting," said Bird. This show of headstrongness further alarmed the auxiliary women, who whispered among themselves. Her message would find its destination. Uncertain of her strength to walk, she forced herself up anyway. Laura caught one of her arms, and Bessie took the other.

She held her head high, though she walked without seeing as they guided her. Her tears fell thick and quick. Laura sat Bird on the grass beside the tent and Bessie assumed caretaking responsibilities while Mr. Charles went for the wagon. Someone handed her a plate of food and instructed her to eat. She obeyed, barely tasting the food until acrid bile threatened to force its way up. As the wagon approached, the families exchanged sullen and short goodbyes.

"I'm sorry," Bird squeaked to Laura as the woman hugged her goodbye. "I didn't mean to ruin your visit or your service."

"Child, you ain't got nothing to be sorry about," she wiped Bird's cheeks. "I'm sorry adults is just plain dumb sometimes. You come on up with them next time. We'll show y'all how to have a good time."

Mr. Charles hoisted her into the wagon where Bessie waited. "I'd like to go home, please." He looked at his wife, who dipped her head slightly.

"You alright?" Bessie asked, as they started moving.

"Yes," said Bird, and then proceeded to cry freely, not caring if Bessie and the others saw her. They kindly looked away and talked quietly among themselves.

The lantern was still on in Uncle Vernon's little house when they arrived well after nightfall. He came out pulling on his shirt and stopped them. Bird's heart sank—Odelia and Maddy had gone to St. Louis. Bird climbed out of the wagon as Mr. Charles stumbled through his explanation for their early return.

"There was an incident with a Reverend Turner, and Bird wanted to come home," he looked off into the night as spoke. "Helena and I are mighty sorry; we hadn't meant to cause anybody trouble."

"Everett. Ma'am. Y'all ain't the one that done caused the problem. I'll explain it to Maddy," he said as Bird ran into his arms.

"That's probably for the best," said Mrs. Charles with a weary voice.

Uncle Vernon's house was little more than a front room with a stove and two back rooms. He sat Bird in the chair beside the little table where he took his meals and lit another lantern. A partially whittled horse sat on the table.

"I thought Granny was getting better?" Bird asked.

"She is. But they got doctors in big cities that know more about these spells than country doctors. They be back later in the week."

Bird wanted them back right now, but anything that could counteract the "wearing down and quick work" was fine by her.

"What we gon' tell your mama?" he asked.

She thought for a moment. Of course, they couldn't tell Mama, no matter what he'd said to the teachers. "That I'd never been away for so long and wanted to come back."

"That's called homesick. You okay?"

"Yes, sir," she paused. "I just don't understand."

"Don't understand what?"

"His wife seemed mean, and his mother too. I couldn't make much of the girl." Bird's tongue wouldn't say "sister," and with a pang, Bird realized that she didn't even know her name. "Why do they get him instead of us?" She'd imagine the Minister's wife as a beautiful and saintly woman—she must have had something special to outrank the admittedly difficult Maddy.

Uncle Vernon began sweeping up his wood shavings. "Sometimes we get what we want, and sometimes we don't."

"But it isn't fair."

"Fairness is stingy. You see much of it around us?"

Bird considered Mama's lovelessness, Granny's blindness, the threadbare clothes of her classmates, and her own full closet. The way folks in

Tuckersville treated folks from Bennettsville. "Why don't folks . . . do better?"

"Folks who is strong enough do what they can."

"What are you doing?"

"So many questions." He shook his head, then cocked it to the side like Odelia did when thinking. "I'm being your uncle."

She shrugged, as if unimpressed.

He laughed aloud. "Not much to that?" he asked.

"I didn't mean any offense. You're a very good uncle."

"Thank you," he said. "Maddy gon find out eventually, and it's better she hears it from us than some gossip."

Bird hadn't considered the rumor mill. "Let's just wait a little while—for Granny to get better."

Uncle Vernon rubbed the gray stubble on his chin. "Just a little while, long enough so it's not too much on her at once. And a good uncle gets little girls to sleep at a decent hour." He sent her to the spare back room to change into her nightgown. It was only after he'd mussed her hair as a tuck-in and busied himself in the front room that she thought to ask him how he was her uncle. Everybody in Bennettsville called him Uncle, but he didn't look much like the line of Abel or the line of Marian. And why did he labor when the other Bennetts did not?

Monday morning brought word that Odelia needed several more days in St. Louis, that Uncle Vernon was to carry Bird to Maddy's customers to explain the delay in their work, and she was to stay with the Charles family. The pair made their own plans. She completed and delivered the easy alterations. She offered to measure for a few others, and most took her up on it. They thought it funny to watch her work but fell into line as she assumed her mother's direct manner.

In the late afternoons and evenings, she followed Uncle Vernon around for his chores. The first two days, he made her stay back so she wouldn't mess her dresses. On the third day, he turned to her as she crept up behind him again. "Ain't you got no clothin' for real work?" She ran to the house for the pants her mother let her wear for fishing. With an appropriate uniform, he taught her to hammer, to repair a door hinge, and to weed in her Granny's garden. He was as much a stickler for a job done right as Maddy, and she liked standing beside him and nodding with satisfaction when they finished a project. Bird enjoyed these days and her pants so much that she vowed to wear them whenever possible. In the evenings, they split the cooking as he didn't care for the sweetness of Bird's cornbread and preferred his ratio of collard and mustard greens—and wanted them cooked to death.

It wasn't until the fourth day, as they sat on the porch in their work clothes watching the sunset, that Bird remembered to ask him how he was her uncle.

He exhaled his pipe smoke. "Oh, the usual way."

She considered this for the moment, making sure this answer really didn't make any sense. "What's the usual way?"

"Ain't nobody ever told you not to ask too many questions?"

"No, sir. Never." She grinned at him.

"Well, I'm glad to be the first. Some questions better left unanswered."

"Then why don't everybody just call you Mr. Vernon, or Mr. Bennett? That's respectful."

"Because you can't go to a mister's house without an appointment and your hat in your hand. Folks need Uncle Vernon," he poked his chest with pride. "They come anytime and know I won't be put out. In fact, I be offended if they didn't come when they needed me."

"So, you really ain't gonna tell me?"

"Mind your language, missy. I may not talk like I got schoolin', but I been listenin' to people that do all my life."

Three days later, Maddy and Odelia returned by automobile. Uncle Vernon and Bird waited for them on the porch. Bird still wore her work uniform but smoothed her hair the best she could. Odelia Bennett smiled big as the driver helped her out, and Bird squealed with pleasure. Some of Odelia's color had returned, and she took sure steps to Vernon's waiting hand. Maddy slid out of the car, took one look at her daughter, raised her eyes to the sky and sighed, but said nothing as she kissed Bird's forehead and slid her arm around her.

"Is Granny all right?" asked Bird.

"As well as can be expected. She's gonna need lots of rest, and absolutely no stress for the next few months." She rubbed the rough fabric of Bird's shirt. "I'll inquire about the mischief tomorrow."

"Yes, ma'am. There's ham and beans on the stove."

"That's the best thing I've heard all day."

Bird expected to find a switch waiting for her at breakfast. Instead, she found her mother making eggs and bacon. Bird swallowed a prideful bragging that she'd helped scald the hog on her mother's plate but gulped as Maddy began the promised inquiry into her mischief. "You didn't stay with the Charleses? You didn't go to school? You didn't carry word to my customers? You didn't do anything that I instructed in my telegram?" Bird answered with increasingly weak "no's."

Maddy placed her fork on her plate. "You did all the sewing and measuring? They didn't complain? You took their payments?"

Bird gained confidence with each "yes."

"What did you tell the ladies?"

"That there was a family emergency. I'd do the measuring, and you'd do the sewing."

Maddy laughed and clapped her hands. "I checked your work. You did good. Uncle Vernon said you minded him well." Maddy locked her eyes on Bird's. "And he told me about the revival."

Bird's stomach and confidence shriveled.

"He said you two wanted to give me time, but the thing for you to know about Uncle Vernon is that he can keep his own counsel, but he can't lie to save his life. And I needle for a living." Maddy carried their plates to the sink. "It wasn't your fault. It was bound to happen. Thank goodness I wasn't there. I would have smacked that Sheila Turner clear through to Tuesday. Your father had a choice to make and chose her. That should have ended it, but . . ." She trailed off as she turned and walked toward her sewing room. Bird would spend many years wondering what words would have finished that sentence. She didn't know if love, or need, or hope would have made her feel better or worse.

Two weeks, later the Minister still hadn't returned. Maddy was agitated and distracted but spoke only through her actions. She rose late, retired early, and mostly sewed in between unless Odelia demanded her presence at a meal or a conversation. The anger Bird had expected to draw after the revival erupted at random times. Maddy seemed to try to keep her aim away from her mother, but Odelia countenanced and suffered her share of blows. As much as she could, Bird assumed care of her grandmother. Her absence from school went from temporary to long-term, and she hardly noticed as the fall holidays approached. In the moments her grandmother and mother thought she was out of earshot, the old woman talked to her daughter of death and burial. She wished to be buried with just a simple headstone, nothing to stand out from those she joined.

Bird wept in her bed over these conversations and the strain between the two women raising her. Even she knew they shouldn't be wasting this time. She thought her mother would come to comfort her, but Maddy stayed on the first floor with her bedroom door shut. Dear God, Bird queried though she wasn't sure anyone listened, what will we do when Granny's gone?

# September 1913

"It's going to get better; it has to," said Odelia. Her index finger traced the top of her teacup. Her skin was pale, and for the first time, Bird thought it sagged. It had been two rough months since the revival. Maddy was a constantly changing season, swinging between hot anger and cold frost. The Minister had not returned or sent word. Bird had done her best after returning to school, but she was distracted and troubled. The Charleses lightened her study and teaching load. This adjustment had embarrassed her, and she'd protested until Mrs. Charles had said, "You are just a girl learning some of life's hardest lessons—those that books can't teach. We'll still be here when the storms pass." The only bright spot was Odelia's improvement. Bird helped her daily through funny muscle exercises and tongue twisters and made sure that she drank the herb mixes Lorna made for her.

On this Saturday, the sewing machine buzzed and then stopped suddenly as Maddy began to cough, a deep chesty cough that raged enough to stop Bird and Odelia's teatime commiserating. Fearing that her mother had choked on any of the multitude of tools she held in her mouth while she worked, Bird ran to the sewing room. Maddy was on her knees, her forehead and hands pressed flat against the hardwood with a blood-streaked puddle beside her. Her grandmother felt her way into the room and found Bird's arm.

"Did you swallow something, Mama?"

Maddy could only whisper, "No child."

Odelia Bennett ordered doctors by the half-dozen. With promises of extra payment, donations, bequeathments, and anything else that could "encourage" doctors to travel to Bennettsville. Most weren't helpful. They asked Odelia about her girl's nocturnal habit, company kept, and drinking before even seeing the patient. One suggested she just hire a new maid and that the pickaninny who answered the door was surely old enough to assume many of the other's responsibilities. Of the two that did actually examine Maddy, both suspected cancer of the liver. "By the time it's clear there's a problem, the point of hope has long passed," they said.

None of the Bennett women believed this until Maddy began dropping pounds by the week as her stomach refused anything but soup and her eyes turned Easter yellow. Finally, one night, as they sat on the porch, Maddy and Odelia in the swing, and Bird on a pallet of blankets on the porch floor, "I'm going to die, Mama," Maddy said.

"No," Odelia spat the word out. "The Lord has taken everything else from me. He cannot take my only child."

"Yes, he can. Are you more worthy than God himself?"

"Are you saying you believe now?"

"No. I'm just saying you wouldn't be the first or the last."

"You can't give up, Maddy."

"I'm not giving up. I'm conserving my energy for what matters most." Her gaze fell on Bird who watched her without blinking.

Bird felt the pangs of mother-love barbing all three of them. She turned toward the yard to cry.

Bird perused the jars in Lorna's pantry like she was in Johnson's Grocery. The shelves rose from floor to ceiling. Each jar bore a faded label and contents of varying hues of brown and green. The words on each jar meant nothing to her.

"Can I help you, miss?" asked Lorna. "Feeling better I see."

"Yes, ma'am." Bird blushed. She'd invited herself into the woman's house under the pretext of a chill and thirst while out for a walk. After guzzling a cup of mint tea in the warm kitchen, she'd ventured into the pantry as Lorna reheated the kettle. "I need some of whatever Miss Ada gave to Ezra to bring him back."

Lorna nodded like she'd been expecting this visit. Bird minded her manners enough to direct her scowl at the floor; she hated the feeling of just playing a part in some fated series of events. Of course, everybody in town visited Lorna to back down death as it came for them or their kin. Lorna's great-grandmother was the free black woman who found Ezra dead on a South Carolina road, revived him, and sent him west to build a freedmen's town. Bird had asked Odelia a thousand times to tell the truth or lie of this story. Odelia only ever said, "He was left for dead, and here we all are. There must be some kind of miracle in that." Bird had maintained her skepticism, but now she needed to believe that there was some power passed down from Ada to Lorna.

"You know, her name was actually pronounced Adé," said Lorna stressing and savoring both syllables. "My mothers gave up generations ago on getting y'all to say it right. My mother believed it was Obatala who spared him. Adé just healed death's damage to his body."

"That'll work too. What did Miss Adé give him?" Bird was undeterred and would say the herb woman's name however Lorna wanted it said.

Running her finger along the shelves, Lorna began handing jars to Bird. "Mullein for his lungs. Licorice and turmeric for his liver. Fennel and hawthorn for his heart. Among other things," she finished. "I've given most of these to your mother since—" she stopped herself, "for years."

Bird deflated. "And they haven't worked."

"They have worked." Lorna pulled Bird into a firm embrace that Bird didn't fight. "Your mother has been gifted much time. I'm sorry. Death came again for Ezra and my mothers could not stop it. I wish I could stop it from coming for your mother, but I couldn't stop it coming for my own mother."

"How do I pray to this Obatala?"

Lorna smiled. "I would think your mother more a child of Osun, but you can ask help of any of the Orishas. Always begin with thanks and remember it's often more than our body that needs healing."

Bird penned letters to her father—a bland request for anointing for a sick and shut-in woman, drafted with the aid of Mrs. Charles. She calculated the days the letter would take to arrive and then maintained a vigilant ear for the Minister's vehicle. The days passed, and he did not arrive or respond. The revival hung heavy over her head. Surely his silence was related to that debacle, and maybe even her admonishment that he stop waiting. A fine time to get right, she thought. With her mother now confined to bed, Bird sensed the urgency and power of the woman's need. If she could just bring the Minister, then maybe somehow something would change for the better. She wrote more letters, each shorter and more desperate than the last. Finally, at her grandmother's childhood writing desk she scribbled, "You never really loved her," and shoved it into an envelope. She had not heard her grandmother behind her as she began to cry.

"If he won't come, then he won't come," said Odelia.

Bird was certain that Maddy had never told her grandmother about the revival. She had respected this desire to avoid further stoking the old woman's anger at the man. Unable to hold the secret any longer, Bird explained the revival and its likely connection to the Minister's disappearance.

"I see," said Odelia as she sunk into the wingback. "I understand why you all didn't want to say anything. But you aren't too young to learn that secrets are like stones that bind and trap us. Now please go get your Uncle Vernon."

An hour later, Vernon rode hard from the Bennett property on the mare. In the intervening hour, Bird had witnessed the first disagreement she'd ever seen between her uncle and her grandmother. Their voices had remained even, but the tension was clear, and Uncle Vernon's eyes stayed glued to kitchen floor despite the woman's blindness.

"I understand, Dilly," he said, "But I think it best that we leave the man where he is. He bound her in life. This is her chance to free herself in death."

"Please do as I ask, Vernon," Odelia had said. Uncle Vernon did not move. His sister spoke again. "She is already free of him, Vernon. The imminence of death has ways of clarifying situations. She doesn't need to be unbound in the way that you think. She needs to make her peace with all of us, about what we've given her and what we've taken from her. This includes Jonathan Turner."

Late that night, the Minister's automobile roared down the lane. Maddy Bennett lay on her death bed. The Minister's Oxfords pounded as he mounted the stairs. A woman's shoes echoed behind his. Bird panicked—he better not have brought his wife, she thought and stood ready with clenched fists. Uncle Vernon made a small gesture of moving his feet out of the man's way, but barely moved them, and then scrambled to stand when a small, dark woman, clearly a Turner by her features, walked in.

"I come to Maddy," the Minister said to the assembled. "Maddy I'm here, and I brought Vera."

Odelia clasped her hands in front of her face and then held them out, Vera brushed past the Minister and into her arms.

"Bird, this is your Aunt Vera," the Minister said without looking at either of them.

Vera turned and took in Bird with the same slow, sweeping glance her mother used on new clients. "You don't know me, but I knew you when you were a baby." Her voice was heavier than most women's. This surprised Bird given the woman's short height. Still, she possessed an attention-catching presence that reminded her of the Minister.

"Yes, ma'am," was the only thing Bird could think to say.

"Mr. Vernon, Miss Odelia. I hate to have been so long absent, and I'm sorry to come under such circumstances."

Vera moved to Maddy's side, a move the Minister had not yet made, and peered down at the woman, feverish with death. "Maddy, we've come."

"She doesn't have much longer," said Odelia.

"We wrote to you," Bird said to the Minister's profile.

The man grimaced. "After the revival, Mrs. Turner ordered the deaconesses to open all my mail. They didn't pass anything on. I didn't know anything until Vernon came to me. I'm so sorry. So, so sorry. Maddy, do you hear? I'm sorry." Maddy opened her eyes a bit and glimpsed him. Tears slid from the corners of her eyes.

"She's been asking for you," said Bird, an uncontrollable urge to hurt this man drove her tongue. Vera watched her, and Odelia reached out for her. Bird ignored them both.

The Minister knelt beside the bed. "I'll pray, Maddy."

Maddy held up a finger and groaned, "No."

"Don't risk your soul to spite me, Maddy. There's still time. Don't wait any longer."

Bird flinched at his words. Her father was a hypocrite, but maybe he knew first-hand about what he'd said at that podium.

"No," moaned Maddy.

No one in Bird's life had died before. Maddy lay still in the bed, her breathing shallow and with a growing rattle. Would her mother cry out in pain or even cry at all? Odelia had tried to hold her daughter's hand, but Maddy pulled hers back. The Minister sat by the dresser and read his Bible under the weak lamplight. Vera and Uncle Vernon sat by the bedroom door like patient guardians of them all.

The night wore on, and Bird grew tired. But no one sent her to bed. If her mother could hold on, so could they, she figured. It was nine minutes after three when the rattle ceased. Bird and Odelia snapped their heads to Maddy. Bird knelt beside her mother as her grandmother called to the Minister who still traced the lines of text with his finger. Vera and Uncle Vernon completed their circle. Maddy's chest rose and fell once and then rose again, more slowly. Bird wanted to call out—to stop her from going wherever she was headed, but she did not. This happening was final, and any appeal would be one more burden for her mother. Maddy's chest rose once more and then fell. It did not rise again.

Shock crested the wave of pain that knocked the air and sound out of Bird. Odelia cried out first. A plaintive, "My child."

Bird reached slowly for her mother's hand, afraid of the rebuke her grandmother received. But there was no movement, no resistance. The fingers, hot to the touch, yielded. She placed her mother's palm to her face. The heat she felt had to be life. She moved her mother's hand to her neck and pressed harder to share her own heat, a last effort to keep her mother from slipping away.

"You may pray now," Odelia said to the Minister.

"Yes, ma'am," he said staring bewildered at Maddy. "Lord, we command this woman to your keep. You know her heart and her burdens. Be ye merciful. In your son Jesus' name. Amen."

They remained together in silence for several minutes. Bird stayed at her mother's bedside, resting her head on her mother's palm. Odelia caressed her daughter's face and closed her eyes; no one said anything when the eyes re-opened. Bird sensed that it was the gesture that mattered. Uncle Vernon stood with his head bowed, and his tears dropped at the foot of Maddy's bed. Bird had to turn away from the man's hurt. Perhaps they would just stay like this, in this room forever. What life was there after this? Sunrise didn't matter, if her mother wouldn't see it. Even as she thought this, she knew it would end. The Minister would leave, and this aunt would go with him. And someone would put her mother in the ground, forever away from Bird.

It was Vera who began the push back into the world and time. Later, this would make sense to Bird, and maybe that was why the Minister had brought her. The Bennetts lacked the strength, and the Minister had no right.

"Johnathan, please help Miss Odelia downstairs and make her some tea," said Vera. "Mr. Vernon, we need things for the preparation. Bird, you stay here with me." Bird had no intention of leaving her mother. She thought Odelia would reject the Minister's taking of her hand, but she allowed him to lead her.

Far too quickly, Uncle Vernon returned with a full wash basin, towels, and blankets. They had been kept waiting nearby, and something about this angered Bird. They had all accepted Maddy's death with such complacency. She tightened her hold on her mother's now cooling hand. When all had left, Vera arranged towels on either side of the bed and looked over to Bird. "I am sorry, love. To lose one's mother so early in life is a tragedy. But some have never even known their mother's love. I encourage you to remember and carry on all she's given you. Are you able to help me prepare her?"

"Yes, but I don't know what to do."

"When we die our body releases everything—spirit, solid, and liquid. It's good for a woman to have a daughter and a friend to preserve her final dignity."

Well-versed in the art of following the leader, Bird mimicked the older woman's movements, removing her mother's dressing gown, pinning back her hair, bathing the limbs, and cleaning that which her mother had released. Each moment both cut and cleared the torment in the little girl's chest. The body before her was a shell. Her mother had gone.

When Maddy was cleaned, Vera asked for the dress her mother had selected for burial. Bird retrieved the red chiffon dress her mother had sewn the week after her diagnosis. Vera raised an eyebrow and then chuckled. It was after sunrise when they called for the Minister. Bird had forgotten about him and struggled to imagine him and her grandmother sitting silent over tea and a Bible all this time. He lifted Maddy with a care that softened Bird's heart toward him just a bit. They were a short procession behind Maddy as he moved her to the casket beside the wagon that would carry her to Bennettsville's cemetery.

Bird followed her grandmother through the day. Neither of them slept or ate even as others pleaded with them to take nourishment. They walked the garden and sat on the porch. The Minister spent the day in Uncle Vernon's house, in prayer and study, as he described it. Jeannetta selected their dresses for the burial and pulled her grandmother's hair into a bun. Bird considered her own two braids serviceable for the occasion, but on her arrival, Mrs. Charles intervened and sent the silent girl for her comb and brush. Bird had imagined just herself, her grandmother, and Uncle Vernon at her mother's burial. But unexpected attendees arrived throughout the afternoon, led by the Charles family, including Cecile and Liston. Fred and Jeanetta helped Uncle Louis into the house and sat him beside Odelia. The old man put his arm around her and whispered something into her ear. Odelia nodded and then glanced at Bird.

Ned and Luther came over and gave Bird awkward hugs. Ned stood with her a moment longer and Bird pressed the lapel of the suit that Maddy had made for him just months before. "I'm supposed to say something to you," his voice cracked, "but I don't know what to say. I know 'I'm sorry' isn't enough."

"It's okay," Bird managed. "I don't think there's anything that can be said."

Men, old and young, hovered around Vernon, who shook hands and accepted hugs. Women, mostly the mothers of Bird's students, arrived with dishes and their children in tow. Bird tried to speak to them as they offered their condolences. She wanted to say thank you and that their care was a balm, but her voice broke each time. Her silent nods were received by knowing arms, even from the littlest children.

Fred and Jeannetta helped Odelia and Louis into a black carriage. Bird insisted on walking with Uncle Vernon behind her mother's casket. The families living in the sharecropper cabins along the way leaned against their fences. The young joined the procession, and the old called out their prayers. Bird gripped Uncle Vernon's hand and wished she was still small enough to be carried. The Minister waited in the cemetery with Vera,

Bennettsville's Reverend Davis, and the hired men. A bench sat beside the grave. Someone sat Odelia on one end and Bird in the middle. Vernon refused the bench's other end. Bird almost begged him when Bessie slid beside her and took her hand.

Reverend Davis read Odelia's favorite psalms and stepped aside for the Minister. Bird willed the fire of her hurt and anger to burn through her eyes. The Minister spoke in a plain baritone without the ease or comfort she'd seen at the revival.

"Some may believe that I've no right to be here, or that the words shouldn't be said. Let he or she who can stand blameless before God step forward." The words had his desired effect. The crowd stood still and silent.

Odelia shook with tears to Bird's right, making Bird thankful for Bessie's solidness on her left. Uncle Vernon stood straight as a soldier and cried as Fred lifted a comforting hand to his shoulder. The Minister spoke of the good in hearts, purity in intention, and the mercy of the Lord. He struggled and stumbled. Maddy deserved much better than this, Bird thought. She silently begged her mother. Please get up, Mama. Please get up. Not for him. He'll leave and never return. But for me. I'll do anything. I promise. Don't leave me. Please, please, please don't leave me. She looked from her grandmother to Uncle Vernon. Their individual frailty was now combined and multiplied, and this terrified her. When they were gone, there would be no one left to take care of her.

The Minister closed his Bible and Reverend Davis motioned to Lue-Ellen Giles who sang "Amazing Grace." Odelia rocked with the melody, and if not for this, Bird would have shouted for the Giles woman to stop. Maddy was no one's wretch. She had lived without fear. And if there were any toils in her life, this town and this Minister had set them in her path. Maybe she wasn't blameless or perfect, but she was a good woman and a good mother. These people could keep their prayers for themselves.

Perhaps sensing something rising in her friend, Bessie began to rub her back. Bird lowered her head and let her friend ease out some of the pain and anger. She hardly noticed when the song was done, and the mourners began to step away in twos and threes. The core group remained standing until Odelia Bennett reached out a hand for Jeannetta to help her up. Mrs. Charles called for Bessie who caressed her for another moment before standing. "I'll be by tomorrow," she said and kissed the crown of Bird's head. Bird didn't move and didn't care about the adults' eyes on her. She would not leave her mother.

"She will come when she's ready," said Odelia.

"We'll sit with her," said the Minister, and Vera nodded beside him.

The group deemed this proper and moved toward the carriage and wagons. Bird and her father sat as the sun arced through the sky. Cut from the same cloth, neither felt forced to comfort the other.

"I spoke to your grandmother regarding your care," he said after a long while. "You know as well as anyone that Sheila is not the type of woman who could give you warmth or likely even kindness. Should something happen to your grandmother, Fred and Jeanetta will assume charge of you. I will compensate your grandmother and Fred, of course."

Bird wondered how many times in life people had been offered "compensation" in direct relation to her. The goodbye laced through his words. She could never go to him, and he would not come back to her. She considered asking the "why" of this, but another question pressed on her more.

"Why didn't you choose her?" She held her eyes steady on the casket before them.

He said nothing for several seconds. "It was a complicated matter between adults," he finally offered. Bird rejected this coward's answer.

"It's not that complicated. I am older than your other daughter."

"Honest . . ."

She cut him off. "I want to know."

"Fine then," he said with a pained sigh. "It is a lesson a father owes his daughter. A man of God can't be yoked with an unbelieving woman." Bird sat with this for several moments. She thought about asking if his actions were those of "a believer," or those of his wife, but she left it alone. It was done. It was over.

"She believed in you," she said as she stood. "I'll see myself home."

Vera met her at her mother's casket. The woman touched her cheek. "You look like us, but there is so much Maddy in you. She'll always be with you, inside you." Vera held her hand to her own heart. "I left my address on your dresser. I'd like for us to get to know each other, and you can come visit me whenever you like."

Eager to feel this gentle woman's arms around her, Bird stepped forward before they were fully extended. "I know, child," said Vera and held her up and let her sob until she couldn't anymore.

With a deep breath and a jagged exhale, Bird turned to her mother. "I love you. I need you." And she walked herself home.

# PART II

# October 1916

Bird hummed with the sewing machine. It was the little motor that would take her places. One like it had taken her mother to East St. Louis and then back because she'd gotten mixed up with the Minister. They'd both fared the worst for it. Well, Bird had to give them the fact of her birth, and he had dutifully mailed semi-monthly funds for her care since her mother's passing. But she'd not seen him or received more than short well wishes since the cemetery. She gunned the motor and shook off the sadness that always tried to edge in on her when she let her mind wander too far. She had Granny and Uncle Vernon, and Bessie, and the Charleses. The school and its students. And all the parts of the town she loved—and those she didn't.

Three staccato taps on the sewing room door made her smile. Bessie bounced in bringing the high noon sunshine and the smell of fall. She stopped behind Bird, pecked her on the cheek, and studied the work under the foot.

"Is that for me?"

"Only if you're a white lady in Tuckersville who likes pink satin."

"I've never much cared for pink," said Bessie, pointing her nose in the air. She pulled a magazine from off a stack of fabrics and plunged into the chair kept clear for the many Saturday afternoons she whiled away before insisting Bird end her work for the day.

Twenty-seven minutes, Bird noted as she glanced at her wristwatch after Bessie cleared her throat and said, "If I had to choose between spending a bunch of time on a shirt for a crabby lady who'll barely thank me and finding fun and trouble with my best friend, I know what I'd choose."

Bird finished her seam before turning around to find Bessie poised like a mischief-minded Egyptian queen. Bird smiled at her friend's pluck. Bessie was a few inches shorter than most of the girls in town, and a full head shorter than Bird, but it still felt like they all had to look up to meet her gaze. When any of the girls poked fun at her height, she'd raise her chin, press a hand to her ample chest in feigned indignation and say she more than made do with what she had. Her curves had come in, as Odelia predicted, and she'd had Bird secretly take in the waists on more than a few of her dresses. "Where do you want to go?" asked Bird.

"Anywhere but this sewing room."

"I do have to check on things at Lorna's and pick up some teas."

"Perfect, let's go," Bessie said with a wink.

"What if she comes back early?"

"She won't."

"But what if she does?"

"She said she'd be back tomorrow. That's when she'll be back," said Bessie, reaching out a hand.

Bird did at least remember to bring a basket for the mason jars of herbs. They huddled together against the fall wind as they walked.

"This time next year, we'll be walking in Tennessee," mused Bird, trying to picture them rushing between red brick university halls. "How's your application going?"

"It's going a little here, and a little there." Bessie chuckled.

"I'm trying to finish by next week."

Bessie's arm stiffened. "How's Miss Odelia? We didn't tell her we were going out."

Bird let her change the subject as had become her habit the past few weeks. "No point in disturbing her nap. I'd told her I was going at some point today. Uncle Vernon and Sue should be back from town soon." They walked the rest of the way in silence. Bessie seemingly lost in the wind-blown clouds, and Bird with her head down wondering what to do about her friend's faltering nerves.

They dropped jackets and scarves in the living room of Lorna's cottage. "Can we have a fire?" asked Bessie.

"How would I explain that?"

"Just tell her we decided to spend the afternoon here. She wouldn't care."

"She'll know," said Bird, moving a few pieces of wood into the fireplace. "She probably already does. She knows everything about everybody."

"Mama says it's best not to talk about her."

"Just because people don't talk about her, doesn't mean they've never come here for help." Bird worked at the kindling while Bessie gathered pillows and blankets for a pallet.

"And what do you come here for?" Bessie asked.

Bird pointed to the mason jars on the credenza. "Teas that help me sleep. And salves for Granny's joints."

She and Bessie lay down facing each other.

"You're too young for problems sleeping."

"There's this whole town to keep going. And less and less help to do it." Other than Lorna and Vernon, Bessie was the only one she talked to about Odelia's lengthening naps. And the moments of confusion that sometimes punctuated the usually hawkish woman's day.

"What about Ned?"

"He's spoiled." She left it at that, not wanting to waste their time talking about her cousin. She brushed her fingers against Bessie's cheek and then along her neck. Bessie scooted closer and they wrapped their arms around each other.

# April 1917

Fourteen Bennettsville men, boys really, enlisted after the country's entry into the Great War. They haunted the schoolhouse for lessons and giddy discussions about venturing out into the world. The possibilities bloomed like tiger lilies in their eyes, and Bird was ashamed they could not see such possibilities in Bennettsville. For years, she'd sought atonement through the schoolhouse. Neither she nor Odelia had regretted the delay in her application to Fisk. So, she used the power that flowed to her as her grandmother aged to squeeze every day of instruction out of the fall and spring sessions and to corral as many families as possible into regular attendance. The Charleses mostly yielded but went to Odelia for an intercession when Bird became too strident in her efforts and requests.

As she and the teachers cleaned the schoolhouse after an evening lesson, Mr. Charles had been especially agitated. Opposed on principle to the boys' enlistments, he refused to deliver the lessons, leaving the task to the female cadre. Another boy had joined the lesson that evening and was eager to see the pride in his teachers' eyes. Mr. Charles had shaken the boy's hand and done the best he could to oblige him before disappearing outside at the lesson's start.

"What do you think education can do for these children?" he asked Bird later when she offered an idea for the next lesson.

"Everett," warned Helena Charles. Bessie traced the words on her notepad.

"The same thing you think, sir." Bird forced deference into her voice.

His face reddened as he watched her. "Shape their minds, yes. But if you want to really give them a chance in the world, review your economics, Miss Bennett." He sulked back out into the night.

Bird abandoned the board and gathered her satchel. She wanted to yell to him that the economics kept her up at night. The little money they collected from the farms barely covered the taxes. The line of Marian lived—and gave—off what they earned from their own land and the remnants of a dwindling inheritance. Bird still sewed for some of the white ladies in Tuckersville, but without Maddy's dressmaking income, the ends hadn't met in years. They only held sacred the money for Bird's education; without eventually using it, Bird had no idea how the school would survive another five years. She'd talked her grandmother into delaying her application to Fisk to maintain their coffers—that and she didn't want to go without Bessie.

"I'll walk home." She headed to the door.

"You will not," said Mrs. Charles. "This is all just hard on him. Give him time."

Bird acquiesced but raised her chin to make it clear that she did not fear walking in the night. She often took brief strolls after her grandmother and Uncle Vernon turned in. The realities of her home and aging caretakers troubled her sleep and worried her more than the shadows.

"Can you visit tomorrow?" Bird asked Bessie as they walked to the wagon.

"My parents have been invited to have a drink with Fred and Jeanetta for the umpteenth time."

"Sounds grand," said Bird, exaggerating her sarcasm. Louis Bennett had died two years after Maddy. His oldest son Fred had reluctantly, and stiffly, stepped into the role begat him.

Bessie laughed half-heartedly. "I'll visit Sunday, if I can."

Riding home, Bird tried to balance Everett Charles's anger and her own helplessness. Yes, maybe if the young men had more land, they would stay. Or, if Bennettsville held anything for them at all. The rest of the world held their opportunities, though hidden and stingy. She'd once thought it held a bounty for her too; now she wasn't so sure. She couldn't leave if Bessie wanted to stay. Her Granny was still alive. The schoolchildren needed her. Maybe this was the most the world could offer her.

Bessie blew into the kitchen like a squall on Sunday. Sue, Uncle Vernon's daughter who'd moved in to help after Maddy's death, had just served

Bird and Odelia their tea. Bird would always remember smiling at the pleasant surprise before reading the panic in Bessie's eyes.

"What's wrong?" asked Bird.

"We have to talk," said Bessie and turned to the staircase.

"Bird! Bessie!" Odelia shouted after them.

Bird gawked first at her shouting grandmother and then at Bessie as she ignored Odelia and blew back out the kitchen.

Bessie shut Bird's bedroom door and directed her to the bed.

"Ned wants to enlist."

"Cousin Fred won't let him," said Bird, hardly thinking this news was worth all the bustle. Her cousin guarded the life of this oldest and favored son with a ferocity that would impress the King of England.

"He isn't. Ned is insisting. They've made an arrangement."

Bird braced her hands against her bed as a subtle energy in her world began to shift.

"My parents want me to marry him." The words spilled out of Bessie.

"How is that an arrangement between Ned and Uncle Fred?"

"He has to marry before he can go. He proposed last night."

Bird stood, and the room wobbled. "And what did you say?"

"I said . . . I needed time to think. Honestly, I did."

"How could they expect you to just up and marry someone?"

Bessie inspected her hands and spoke softly. "He's been visiting. Staying for dinner sometimes. Talking to Daddy."

The picture painted itself for Bird. Bessie and Ned talking on the back porch or walking along an edge of the land allotted to the schoolteachers. Mrs. Charles dishing Ned extra potatoes and pork chops. "For how long?" she asked.

"Since last year. I thought it wouldn't amount to much. I told my parents I wasn't ready for marriage. That I want to travel and go to school. My mother said I could travel with my husband, and that I hadn't shown real interest in further schooling."

"Is the decision up to them?" asked Bird, feeling a sudden Maddy-like coolness on her tongue.

"What are we going to do, Bird?"

"We have to leave now."

"With what money?"

"With mine. We can find work when we get to the city." She had what little she cobbled together for a rainy day and would make Odelia give her the Fisk money. It would be enough for a start.

"Two colored girls alone in New York City?"

A thousand needles pricked Bird's heart. "I see."

"You see what?"

"Whatever you decide about Ned, you've already made one decision."

Bessie started to protest but then held her silence for a moment. "I want things to stay just like they are. Our Saturdays. Mama and Daddy in the schoolhouse. Cecile and her kids down the road. No matter how it changes. It can't be better than this right now."

Bird waited every day for change. "Things have to change, Bess. We can't be girls forever."

"Wasn't it always going to come to this, even if my heart is yours?" Bessie kissed Bird's lips as the hurt settled deep in Bird's stomach and pushed tears out in its wake. "This isn't about him."

"What is it about?" Bird asked.

"I guess it's about growing up."

Bird shook her head. "It's about giving up."

She lay in her bed after Bessie left. With slow, deep breaths she tried to calm her mind as her grandmother had taught her. Relax the toes, and then the balls of her feet, the soles, ankles, calves, and so forth. For the last few months, when pressed for the reasons for her worried sighs, diminished appetite, and nocturnal walks, she'd told her grandmother that she worried over her students, her application to Fisk, and traveling to a new city. She did not detail her fears that one night, the old woman's chest would fall and not rise. Or that Uncle Vernon wouldn't emerge from his house one morning. That the house of her childhood would collapse under the weight of their collective sadness. The fear that this would be her life forever and the terror that it would not. Her mind couldn't call forth a picture of some better, joyous tomorrow as the town died and Bessie became a chipmunk skittering from limb to limb of the tree of their lives. What happened to the girl who could sass anyone and treated their little town as a stage? The girl who had, on a warm Saturday afternoon the year before, placed her hand on Bird's neck and kissed her lips as they lay tangled in the hammock.

Bird and Bessie had thought Odelia was the easiest person to keep their secret from. The old woman could not see that they sat close whenever they could and gave silent pecks when meeting and departing. And yet, one evening after one of Bessie's visits, Odelia Bennett had made the unusual request for a glass of Lorna's cherry wine and sipped it as she spoke. "You know Bird, I am old, blind, and prone to forgetfulness, but I'm not deaf."

Bird's mind had raced and then her heart thudded. There had been giggling and maybe one dramatic moan that afternoon. "I'm sorry, Granny . . ."

Speaking with the air of a diplomat, Odelia advised her. "My mother always said that there is nothing new under the sun. These situations arise. It isn't all that surprising that you would develop feelings for your closest friend." Odelia frowned. "I once tried to get you out into the world, but after Maddy . . . I lost my way. Time will sort it all out and send you a handsome young man. I just encourage your restraint until then."

It had been too soon, Bird knew, to explain she would marry Bessie somehow. Everyone thought they would go to Tennessee, but they would move to New York City. They would be fine. It had to be so. Why else would the God her Granny prayed to every night have given them to each other?

As the morning light shifted around the room, Bird stood in the mirror and reminded herself that she was basically grown and already living the life of an adult. She marched to Odelia's room. The old woman sat in the chair by her window.

"I need my money, Granny."

"I don't think that will solve anything."

"If I can show her that we'll be okay, she won't be scared. She doesn't want to marry him."

"She does, Bird," said Odelia.

The flatness of Odelia's tone cut quick at Bird's heart.

"I don't say those words to hurt you. I've discussed the situation with Mrs. Charles. We agree it's the best course of action."

Bird grappled for her balance, and Sue stepped into the edge of her vision. "Why are you speaking to people about my life, and without me?"

"Bird be calm. Sit down, please."

She remained standing though her legs weakened.

"We understand that you girls mean very much to each other. But there comes a time when we must put childish things aside. Your hearts will heal, and love will come. It's already come for her."

"She doesn't love him."

"Did you ask her that?"

"She loves me."

"Even if that's so, there's no future in it. I see far along the path you want to take. It doesn't lead where you think it does." She pushed an envelope across her little table. "It's a letter from your father's sister, Vera, inviting you to spend some time with her in East St. Louis. You can stay there while everything gets sorted out between Ned and Bessie."

Bird screamed with hurt and rage and a moment later, Sue's strong, hot arms held her up and led her back to her bedroom. She wanted to fight and flail, but her body would not respond. She felt her bed beneath her, and a blanket covered her. Warm hands stroked her hair. Sue made a shhhing sound. Bird sobbed. The betrayal unwrapped itself around her. Bessie. Mr. and Mrs. Charles. Granny. Sue. She'd only wanted love.

Idling in bed for the rest of the day, Bird refused Sue's food and her grandmother's reconciliation attempts. As the evening sun dipped, the old woman sat at the edge of her bed. "It's fine if you hate me. I'd hate myself if I didn't correct you."

Bird couldn't look at her. There was no absolution to offer. She said, "One day you and Uncle Vernon will die. And then, who will be left for me? Bessie was my first and only friend. She held my hand at my mother's graveside. She is my only real warmth in this town. The darkness you see is the darkness I live in. I have asked for little and tried to give much. How can you all take us from each other? It's one thing if we had tried and failed. It's another to have never been allowed to try."

Odelia remained silent for a moment, and then her voice shook as she spoke. "I understand more than you know, Bird. Do you think that my heart hasn't hurt through no fault of my own? Everything I do, I do because I love you. I would have left this world long ago but for my love for you. Go to your aunt. You will find assurance there." She left Bird to tend to the burning wound in her chest. She thought of going to Bessie. She had never doubted before. She could cook, clean, sew, and teach. But she could not fight, at least not the whole world.

Bird resolved to spend the whole next day out of her grandmother's house. If the old woman worried, it was no problem of hers. However, she found no place to go. She couldn't go to the school, the Charleses' house, Main Street, or Fred's house. She followed her childhood paths through the woods, stopping at times to ruminate or cry under one tree or another. Unsurprised when she arrived at Lorna's fence, Bird had the fleeting sensation of stepping into her mother's footsteps. She passed the gate and knocked dutifully on the door.

A moment later, Lorna opened the door with a smile. "I hoped I would see you today. To the kitchen, fresh bread is almost ready." Lorna placed a mug beside her own on the kitchen table and dipped a spoon into the two jars on the table to make her tea.

"What's this?" asked Bird.

"A favorite mix. Chamomile and lavender for my nerves."

"You need tea for your nerves?"

Lorna laughed. "Darling, what woman doesn't? Sit." She pointed Bird to a chair.

Bird dropped into it without complaint. "Granny is sending me away," she said, indignant. She didn't feel like a woman today and would rather her role as child.

"Sometimes, a change of scenery is good."

"And sometimes, it's good for everyone else."

Lorna nodded. "Sometimes, yes."

Bird wondered how much Lorna knew and then realized that her grandmother certainly would have consulted with Lorna. Everyone consulted with Lorna.

"You told her to send me." Bird pushed her tea away.

Lorna stared at her for a long moment. "I told her to act with deep thoughtfulness."

"Is she?"

"She's doing the best she can. She's from Marian's line. She can't help her training."

Lorna dangled the bait, and Bird wanted to resist. But her great-grandmother's name was so rarely spoken, even by Odelia.

"And what did my great-grandmother train her to do?"

"To offer the gifts that bring peace and protect the lines of Ezra."

"Doesn't that include me?" she asked.

Lorna pushed Bird's tea back to her. "You, like your mother before you, have your own path. Hers was a hard one," Lorna sighed at this. "Yours will be hard too. But no path worth walking will take you exactly where you want to go and exactly how you want to get there. It's the reaching and twisting that keeps us growing."

As Bird picked at her breakfast the next morning, Odelia ate with undisturbed calm.

"How long do I have to go for?" asked Bird, when she could control the flaring anger in her voice.

"Why don't you pick some books," said Odelia. "I don't remember Vera being much of a reader."

An hour later, they stood side by side on the porch as an automobile waited for Bird. "In case I'm not here when you return," said Odelia Bennett as she pressed the palm of her hand to the girl's forehead. "You are loved, and you are blessed. By God and by me."

Vera Turner lived in a white, two-story country house nestled among fields that lay east of East St. Louis. Bird searched the landscape for any signs of a city and found only country roads traveled by wagonloads of other colored folks. On their arrival, the driver, a small, quiet man helped her out of the coach, and she stood in front of the house. He cleared his throat as she stared at the brick walkway leading to the front porch. She'd imagined Vera waiting for her, but they were over an hour late.

Bird braved the path, knocked on the door, and waited. Nothing happened.

The driver placed her bags at her feet. "Shall I wait, Miss?"

His eyes looked tired, and Bird imagined a family and a bed waiting for him somewhere.

"I'm sorry to inconvenience you. Just a few more minutes, please. I'll need to find other accommodations if my aunt isn't here. She should be. But maybe there was an emergency of some sort." She fumbled in her purse for the letter to prove that she was to be at this place, at this time.

He gave her an easy smile. "Don't worry miss. I wouldn't leave you here alone. I know some respectable church folks a few miles down the road who can take you in for the night, if need be."

"Thank you, sir." Bird almost hugged him for his kindness.

She knocked again, louder, and still nothing happened. She reread the arrival details of her letter and assured herself of the date, time, address, and description of the house. With nothing left to do, she walked to the house's side, searching for any signs of life or death. A cracked kitchen window revealed a pot on the flame. Bird made her way to the back of the house and followed a sewing machine's buzz. She rapped on the humming window, and a second later, a hand snatched the curtain back. A rueful scowl appeared and immediately brightened into a grin.

"Birdy!" Vera shouted. "Go to the door." Before Bird could turn and take three steps, the back door flew open, and Vera stood before her, mostly unchanged from Bird's dim memories. She was a Turner through and through. "Let me look at you, child." The woman was all hands and hugs. Bird could only laugh. "You look just like your mother." Bird's eyes narrowed; no one had ever said that to her before.

"I thought I looked like the Minister," she said.

Vera laughed at the seeming ridiculousness of this statement. "In coloring and maybe some of his features. But you're long and lean like your mother and grandmother. And you have your mother's eyes. It was really the shape that made her eyes so beautiful; the color was just a distraction. Come in. Where your bags?"

"Up front. I've been knocking. I have to let the driver go."

"So sorry, dear child. I started working and . . . oh Lord, let me check my pot before we're suffering through burnt beans for dinner."

The two women sat across the kitchen table from each other. "Well, how are you?" said Vera, as if this were a weekly ritual, or they knew each other in the slightest.

"To be honest, a little uninformed. I know you're the Minister's sister and somehow my mother's friend."

Vera laughed. The features Bird remembered as stern and serious on the brother, revealed joy and openness on the sister. "I've been his sister my whole life. I'm the baby of the bunch. I guess that means that you don't know there's six of us all together, including a middle brother who died years ago. And then, you also don't know that you've got almost two dozen cousins."

"No, ma'am," Bird whispered, taken aback by the sudden explosion of her concept of family.

"Yes, child," she said, "if there's anything the world won't run out of anytime soon is East St. Louis Turners. Do you want to meet the family?"

"Do they want to meet me?"

"Bird, out-of-sight has never been out of our minds or hearts." The gentleness of her aunt's reassuring comforted her.

"I know I have a sister."

With this, Vera sighed and leaned back in her seat, as if to create distance between her and the words. "Yes, you two favor. A lot."

"I know. I saw her once."

"The revival." Vera frowned. "You have a brother too, six years younger than you. They are both . . ." she hesitated. "Very much like their mother—who isn't a bad woman. There just isn't a lot of space in her world for what she doesn't like."

"What's her name, my sister?" Bird asked, embarrassed by her ignorance of this most basic fact of her life.

Vera stared at her before answering. Bird held her gaze. The question clarified much more about Bird's sense of being a Turner than any thousand answers could ever give her.

"Her name is Deborah," said Vera letting the lament soak through each word.

"I think I'd like to take it slow, with everybody."

"Then let's start just you and me. Please just tell me you like northern beans."

"I love them."

"Then we'll get on just fine."

While Vera finished preparing their meal, Bird studied the gold-framed family members on the end tables and shelves in the living room, only recognizing her grandmother and father in the many pictures. Grandmother Turner, as Bird tried to think of her, stood beside an ornate chair in a ball gown. She did not smile. A few of her aunts and uncles posed with the Minister in what seemed like a recent picture. He could have swept his arms wide to envelop them all.

Vera's dressmaking ruled the house. Maddy had carefully segregated her work from the rest of the house, but in Vera's home, fabric swatches, half-clothed dress forms, and sketches lived everywhere. The woman had a flare for fantastic designs: sweeping dresses, indiscreet necklines, and jewel-tone sequins. Everything Bird had ever sewn seemed so commonplace in comparison.

"Who do you sew for?" asked Bird at dinner.

"People who can afford me. Odelia mentioned you might be interested in a short apprenticeship?"

Bird shook her head—education was always her granny's hook. "I don't think I could do what you do."

"Maybe not yet. I see that you make your own patterns and have a good sense for shape and drape. The fabric in the back room is left over. Make a dress."

"Just make a dress?"

"Yes."

Bird had made countless dresses, and before this moment, would have thought nothing of the suggestion. But looking at Vera's work, it was like the woman had told her to build a ship. That particular stress, she decided, would have to wait for another day. Vera's ability to keep others on their toes and guessing was becoming very clear, but she had some explaining to do herself. "You never told me how you knew my mother. Was it through my father?" She hoped the question would stop the woman mid-bite or at least earn a sigh. Vera kept on chewing.

She matched Bird's stare when she spoke. "Maddy was once one of my best friends. We struggled together under the tutelage of an old barracuda of a dressmaker. I was terrified, and Maddy was unfazed. She was too young to have mastered the ability to ignore people's quirks and jealousies." Vera smiled to herself. "This would be the foundation and downfall of our friendship. I introduced her to your father and was none too pleased when he swooped in with that way of his, especially if he wasn't going to do right by her. But he chose Sheila, and Maddy went back to Bennettsville. I visited a few times; you always smiled for me, you know?" She winked at Bird and cut each of them another slice of cornbread before continuing. "I asked her to bring you to visit us sometime. Maybe if she and Jonathan had really broken it off, it could have happened. You weren't the first outside child born. But Jonathan wanted his robe, his church, his wife . . . and your mother too. It all became too painful to watch. Maddy chose her road, and I couldn't walk it with her. I'd hoped your father had the decency to at least tell you about this side of your family."

"That would have been nice." Bird felt the weight of her loneliness. With every moment in this house and every word Vera spoke, she better understood its contours and all that had been kept from her. "I don't want to see him."

"He and I aren't close. Your grandmother wrote directly to me. If you ever wish to see him, I can give you his address."

After a week, Bird and Vera had fallen into a pleasant routine of design lessons and cooking and eating meals together. Bird took walks along the berry bushes and cornfields and fretted over the dress she'd taken from sketch to pattern, still afraid to cut into the bolt. She thought frequently of Bessie. Maybe she would call off the wedding and send word for Bird to come home, or that she was on her way with bags in tow. Bird waited for any kind of letter, and on the tenth day, one arrived—from Odelia in Sue's hand. It contained just a short note about minding her manners and held more money for spending. The letter made no mention of her return home or the duration of her visit. Bird realized, at long last, that she'd been temporarily banished. She sulked for more than a couple of days after this. It was enough to lose Bessie. It was altogether too much to be sent away from her own home.

"Would you like to talk about anything?" Vera asked over dinner a few evenings after the letter arrived.

Bird only shook her head. Anything she said would surely have her sent away from this place too. And there was nowhere else.

In the days of silence that followed, Bird watched her aunt for the lesson promised by her grandmother. What assurance was she supposed to find—that it was quite possible to lead a busy and financially comfortable life in spinsterhood or that being married to a man had to be better than this fate?

Near the end of the third week of Bird's visit, Vera put her feet up on the ottoman and sighed. Bird suspected, at last, a confrontation about her mood. Instead, Vera announced a trip.

"I need to go to East St. Louis for a couple of days for supplies. I thought you could come, and we'd also take a trip across the river. My friend Mrs. Banneker would host us."

Despite herself, Bird grinned and ignored her aunt's pitying smile.

East St. Louis was closer than Bird had imagined. Houses along the country roads increased in frequency until the city rose before them. Bird had never seen so many brick buildings. The thought of 75,000 people in one place seemed impossible, but here they all were. The city had built itself around a small downtown area of shops and a theater. Men and women walked in everything from fine suits and dresses to overalls. Farmers sold their bounty in wagons on the sides of Main Street. Vera pulled her along when she giggled at establishments with suggestive names like "Uncle John's Pleasure Palace" and "The Monkey Cage." As they navigated the bustling sidewalks, Bird was invisible and exhilarated.

Bennettsville was an all-black world, with this blackness only punctuated by the occasional white body entering and moving with an undeserved entitlement. East St. Louis was something else entirely. There were plenty of colored folks and whites, all moving around each other. Each going about their business. And there were the soldiers. Hundreds of young men with rifles hanging from shoulder straps clumped at the street corners with no purpose that Bird could see.

"The National Guard," Vera explained, "Aluminum Ore workers been striking for over a month now. It's never good for us when white men aren't getting what they think is their due. So, we'll keep our shopping quick." After this, Bird watched the white folks more closely. On every block, gangs of white men stood broad chested and red-faced. They seemed to have made a hobby of glaring and spitting at the feet of the colored men passing by. The colored men grimaced but kept on walking; still, Bird could sense the heat in them. The whole town was a pot on the edge of boiling over.

True to her word about the speed of their mission, Vera kept them moving, only stopping at a notions store to place an order and pick up newly arrived threads. She stopped to speak to other colored women occasionally. "This is my niece called Bird," she said, and no one gave her more than a friendly glance or polite nod. The luggage of her life was less heavy in this place. No one had time to think about this country girl who just happened to be some minister's outside child.

Mrs. Eileen Banneker lived in Olivette Hill. The neighborhood's brick houses sat like squat little castles. Mrs. Banneker's house was smaller than many of the others but was as well adorned and manicured. She opened the door for them as they walked up the stone path.

"This is my darling, Bird," said Vera. "Bird, I'm pleased to introduce you to my dear friend, Mrs. Banneker." This introduction felt oddly formal as they stood on the steps, but Mrs. Banneker beamed and hugged Bird before ushering them in.

"You're so tall, dear, and pretty in such a serious way for a young girl." Mrs. Banneker looked her up and down.

"She is one of those children fortunate enough to take the best of each of her lines," said Vera as she handled their jackets.

Mrs. Banneker's home was cloister-like. The heavy curtains gave the sitting room a somber, dense energy. Family pictures covered the mantle, and books filled the built-ins. A Victrola caught Bird's eye from a corner hutch. Mrs. Banneker pulled a record from a shelf. "A little music with dinner will help us celebrate your arrival." Orchestral music filled the room, as they settled down to soup and fish.

Their conversation followed Mrs. Banneker's wandering train of thought. She wanted to know all about Bennettsville, the school, and Odelia Bennett's health. She'd never had the honor of meeting Miss Bennett, the Elder, she explained, but Vera spoke often of the niece she missed, and the grandmother left to raise her. The woman made recommendations for stores and sights in St. Louis and warned Vera against leading a sight-seeing tour of fabric shops. Vera rolled her eyes.

In between the waves of the conversation, Bird tried to make sense of the woman across the table. She was a tall woman, thin and brown, and wore high collars and her lightly graying hair back in a bun. She was not as reserved as Odelia, but there was a weight to this woman. Bird sensed that all while she talked in smiling loops and circles, Eileen Banneker was summing her up and would eventually evince her approval or disapproval.

Bird responded with her hands folded and asked and answered questions as appropriate. Occasionally, she glanced over to find a bemused Aunt Vera relaxing with her glass of wine, saying little and only clarifying that she and Bird shared many shopping and sight-seeing interests.

They took their after-dinner drinks in the sitting room. Mrs. Banneker had poured Bird a glass of wine in the middle of a story about an argument with a neighbor over the fir tree that would blanket the block in "snow" in a few weeks. Mrs. Banneker had told him that the tree had never bothered her, and he was welcome to cut it down at his own expense. Proud of this response, she raised her glass to herself and looked expectantly at her guests. "Go ahead, but not too much," said Vera as Bird tasted her first ever sip of red wine and deemed it even more bitter and distasteful than coffee.

Bird perused the bookshelves while the women lounged on the couch and caught each other up on their comings and goings. Bird selected a book of poetry and nestled into a wingback, reading and sipping the wine since she had the opportunity. After Vera nudged her and sent her off to bed, she awoke only once to the sound of laughter from downstairs.

The next morning, Vera hustled them out after just toast and jam. There would be plenty to eat on the other side of the river. There had been a brief discussion about whether Mrs. Banneker would join them. Vera insisted. Mrs. Banneker demurred. It was her greatest wish to prepare a meal worthy of Bird's visit. There remained, Bird sensed, a small strain of tension as they departed. Vera dismissed Bird's concerned look back at the house.

"Mrs. Banneker, aside from her many committees, spends too much time alone in her home. Live life, Birdy, in the world and not behind walls, no matter how expensive or well decorated they may be." She said this last bit with a grimace and then shook as if to shrug it all off. "We'll spend most of the day in Mill Creek Valley with our people, but I'll have the driver show us a few sights."

"The Mighty Mississippi," said Vera with proprietary pride as the car carried them across the river.

Bird didn't have the heart to say that she thought it would be bigger. She wondered what she'd think of the Nile or the Amazon. She was beginning to understand the ways in which her imagination was both overexcited and inadequate. As much as she had given too much credit to the Mississippi River, she had under credited St. Louis itself. The city was like an ocean of buildings. As far as she could see, there was St. Louis.

"Does it ever end?" she whispered.

Vera laughed. "Somewhere out there, where the sun sets."

The city was bricks and shops, wide boulevards, cars beeping, and people in finery and work clothes rushing around one another. They rode past Union Station, and Bird hoped with all her heart to one day board a train in that grand place. Forest Park made her think of Monet. If she squinted hard enough at the strolling white ladies, she could blend and smudge them just like the Impressionists. She wondered what Bessie would say if she could see it. Maybe she'd see how easily they could blend into the painting.

Once they reached black-owned shops in Mill Creek Valley, Vera opened her arms at the corner of Jefferson and Market Streets. "Black wealth darling, everything you see around you. You won't find it in too many places, and it must be jealously guarded."

"Granny says the love of money is the root of all evil."

"You misunderstand me. White people love money. They stole this land, and many of the people living in it, for the love of money. And they'd rip any value out of these blocks if they could. Black wealth is a place where we walk safe, proud, and secure. Where we don't bend or beg. Where we can be whatever we want in this world. Where God's birthright to us is uncorrupted."

Bird tried to memorize the buildings that Vera pointed out to her. The Pine Street YMCA where black intellectuals and celebrities gathered. The Dickson home where a prominent abolitionist family had lived and secreted away escaped slaves on the Underground Railroad. The People's

Hospital, the only hospital for colored folks in St. Louis. In between lessons, they moved in and out of shops. Bird bought scarves for her grandmother and Sue, she said, though she really picked the second one for Bessie. They ate and walked and talked, and Bird felt herself gaining a new kind of education. On their way out of town, they rode through The Ville, the other colored neighborhood in the city and past Sumner High School, the city's only high school for colored students. Bird gasped. The three-story high school was as big as a museum. There had to be plenty taught in that building that she and her students never learned in their one-room schoolhouse or at the Charleses' kitchen table. She'd always felt average sized or big in Bennettsville. Hell, the town bore her name. In the car on the way back across the river, she felt about the size of a mouse, and wondered if, for seventeen years, she had only managed to stumble through some basement closet of the world.

They returned spent and hungry, and Mrs. Banneker presided over a magnificent steak dinner. Bird noted their host's relief that Vera had returned in more agreeable spirits. Bird reacted less strongly to the white wine served, and Bird and Vera shared the eclairs they'd purchased for dessert. As they retired to the living room, Vera and Mrs. Banneker were quieter this night.

"Bird, you aren't going to fall asleep in your chair again?" Vera winked and pointed her upstairs. She was happy to oblige; she was tired, and the wine had left her a bit dizzy. She awoke in the middle of the night with a dull pain in the center of her head and a queasy stomach. The white wine had crossed her palette easier, but this made no difference to the rest of her. Embarrassed at the shallow tolerance of her youth, she tiptoed downstairs to refill her water glass. Only the uncertainty of an unfamiliar staircase delayed her long enough in her return that she heard a woman's moan, low and long. Confused, she froze. Did Mrs. Banneker have another guest? A moment later, she almost smacked herself with surprise. Vera loved a woman.

She tiptoed back to her room. It was a lover's quarrel that had Vera cross and Mrs. Banneker stubborn that morning. The past few days began to make sense. The odd formality on their arrival. Her early dismissal to bed—they'd wanted time alone. She gasped and her heart skipped a beat—Odelia must have known. And this was the whole point of the trip, but what was Granny's endgame?

The sun rose on her questioning. The women slept in, and Bird could wait in bed no longer. She slipped on her robe and descended the stairs. Everything in the house now posed a question, including where the hell was Mr. Banneker? Mrs. Banneker came down first, in a simple flower dress and slippers, humming a cheery tune. "Sorry, Bird, the wine."

"It's okay, ma'am. I woke in the night with the Sahara in my mouth and a headache. I don't think it's for me."

"That's what we all say in the beginning. I'll have something for your stomach in just a few minutes. I heard your aunt. I'm guessing she'll be down directly."

Bird only smiled.

Vera and Mrs. Banneker conducted a well-practiced coffee ceremony between them. Cups filled and handed. Milk poured. "Would you like sugar?" asked Mrs. Banneker. Vera frowned at the question but extended her cup. Mrs. Banneker winked at their inside joke. Bird wanted to laugh like a mad woman, but she sat with her fingers interlaced.

"You are quiet this morning, Birdy," said Vera.

Mrs. Banneker handed Bird a cup of coffee. "Her first hangover, I believe. I know you don't like the taste, but coffee and alcohol are famous friends."

Vera and Bird stared at each other for a long, quiet moment. Bird willed her eyes to say, "I know."

Vera held her eyes, as if double verifying the message. "I thought I heard you up in the night," said Vera. "We can talk later."

Mrs. Banneker sat back with a resigned unease.

Bird excused herself to get dressed, and when she returned, Mrs. Banneker had left for errands.

"Do you mind if we stay another day?" Vera looked up from her lacework.

"Of course not."

"Thank you," she said and then groaned. "I've always hated lace."

"It's my specialty."

Vera's eyebrows lifted.

Bird took the work from her aunt's hand and studied the pattern.

"It's for a bodice."

Bird "mmhmm'd" at this obvious information, took a seat, and began to work. "I didn't mean to cause problems with Mrs. Banneker."

Vera stretched her legs on the couch. "You didn't cause any problems, Bird. She is . . . a very private person. She likes you very much, but the stress sometimes gets to her."

"I'd been wondering why Granny sent me to you. She told you?"

"She said that you had a problem, the nature of which I might understand and help you avoid roads best not taken. There's only one reason Odelia Bennett would write for my expertise after all these years."

Vera curled her legs under her and motioned for Bird to sit at couch's other end. "You can work on that later. You have questions?"

"Only a million."

"Then, I'll start where it seems most relevant. Eileen married young—her family's doing." Bird noted the hint of a warning in this, but it was a truth she'd already learned. "Cancer took him probably fifteen years ago. I knew her before then through some of her committee work around town and my dressmaking. And even after that, it took us some years to find our way to each other. We're comfortable. What we have is enough for each of us. Most nights, it's enough to know she loves me."

Bird's heart hurt as she listened. Was this how it always went?

"Your turn," said Vera.

"The same, just different names and places. Bessie. My cousin Ned. I don't know that she loves him, but she's willing to marry him. Granny sent me here. I don't understand any of it. I love her; and it's impossible to love her."

Vera flashed a wry smile. "You aren't the first girl to love another girl, and you won't be the last. I can't tell you why. Maybe love does as it pleases. But we are humans and have told ourselves that we cannot do the same. And for women who love women, or men who love men, doubly so."

It had never occurred to Bird that a man could love a man.

Vera chortled as this realization dawned across her face. "How many trees are in the world, Bird?"

"Who could know?"

"The same applies to people. Some are tall, some are short. Some bear fruit and some give shade. We're all worthy and have a purpose."

Bird thought of her aunt and her father. There must be something in the Turner line that made them section off the love in their lives. But that felt too harsh. Bird had seen her aunt's ease with Mrs. Banneker. Had seen the ache in her eyes when they parted. This world was bigger than they ever would be. They'd just figured a way to love around it. "What do I do?" asked Bird.

At this Vera sighed. "You can only keep living your life. It has already taken you through pain and heartbreak and will likely take you to both again. But there will also be times of love and joy, during which the sun shines so bright that we are sustained through everything else."

Mrs. Banneker returned with an armful of bags and distributed packages and instructions. Flowers on the table. Chicken in the cooler. Vegetables on the counter. With the perishables handled, she handed a small package to Bird and led them all to the sitting room. Bird sat in her favorite wingback and opened a small box containing a pair of pearl stud earrings that glimmered like moonlight on her pond back home.

"Oh, Mrs. Banneker. They're beautiful, but I cannot accept these."

"Please, call me Aunt Eileen and know that a lady never turns down jewelry. This can be a difficult time in a girl's life—when she needs love and support the most. I hope that you two will stay another day. I'd hate to see you go." She turned to Vera. "And we've got to get those earrings in her ears somehow."

With nothing else to do, Bird threw herself into her sewing, turning out dresses at a pace that amused her aunt. When Vera insisted that she go off into the world, she went to East St. Louis and walked the shopping areas. Most people were indifferent to her, and this was fine. She only wanted to see the dresses and had no intention of purchasing anything of great expense. She wrote to her grandmother and inquired about her return. Odelia's response suggested that she spend a little more time.

Bored one day, she boarded the trolley to her father's neighborhood. His church was simple and white with a steeple. It was a little larger than the church in Bennettsville, but not by much. A sign outside proclaimed the church Mount Hope Baptist with Rev. Jonathan E. Turner as its pastor. Bird wanted to go in, just to see it, but knew it looked like every church of the sort, not that she'd been in many. But she was easily marked as a Turner and did not wish to see her father or sister, or heaven forbid, his wife. She walked away wondering about her father's choice. This little corner had been worth more to him than both she and her mother.

She thought often of Vera and Eileen and all the miles between them. Eileen somehow managed to fill her life, just as Vera did. Vera listed all the committees, auxiliaries, and boards on which Mrs. Banneker sat. There were church functions and distant relations who visited. In a few weeks though, she would come to the country and stay with Vera for a week or so. Distance gave them space and safety. Bird tried to imagine this life for herself. Bennettsville was too small. And there seemed to be a lovelorn curse on the women in her family.

"I think I'm going to be alone my whole life," she confided in Vera one night.

Vera disagreed. "The world is a strange, funny, cruel, and sometimes kind place, Bird. You could move here if you like. I have plenty of room. And we haven't had time to introduce you to the Turners yet."

"How would my father feel about that?"

"I don't worry about such things."

"Maybe one day. I have to take care of Granny. If she ever lets me come home."

"She will send for you. If you lose faith in everything else in this world, trust your grandmother's love for you."

# May 1917

After several nervous trips, Bird had gained enough confidence to navigate much of the east side of the river. She wished her students could see the towering confections—sugar castles and cupcake mountains—forever on display on the town's main thoroughfares, the shiny automobiles, and endless rows of houses and apartment buildings. She wanted to ask Mrs. Banneker if any of her committees would help with funding such a trip but still felt shy about requests. She also didn't know how many children or for how long, and Helena Charles was the last person she could write to for guidance.

Only the growing tensions radiating out from the city's main district slowed her down. On her first trips with Vera, people moved with a "city" walk as she liked to think of it. As spring deepened, people moved with quick steps and worried glances. Brief storefront chats gave way to warning nods. On her last trip, she gathered extra sewing notions and dry goods.

"I don't think it's good to go back to the city for a while," she said to Vera, spreading the spoils of her trip on the kitchen table.

Vera began sorting the thread by color. "The same word came down the road after you left this morning. I wasn't sure how I'd rein you in."

"We have angry white folks in the country too."

"Show me a place that doesn't have them."

As a child, she'd thought Bennettsville was such a place. She'd initially thought the white folks in Tuckersville were only rude and putting on airs with their colored neighbors. Her third year in the schoolhouse taught her the danger of their anger.

Micah Childress. She wanted to say his name and tell her aunt his story, but even here sitting safely at the table of one of the bravest colored women she knew, she couldn't risk the boy like that. Micah's aunt, called Solemn, had arranged for him to rake the leaves of a few houses in Tuckersville. And as he raked, he noticed an old woman watching him from the window of a neighboring house. He figured he'd be nice and rake hers too. A day later, she accused him of stealing fifty dollars cash.

The Bennetts and Childresses gathered at Fred's house, and Micah wept like a small child, certain he'd be dead by sunrise. He'd been a classmate in the little school. He was quiet and obedient, and always eager to help Mr. Charles with some schoolhouse repair. Fred gave them the cash he had in the house, and someone carried them to Chicago that afternoon.

Odelia tried to head off the trouble and offered to make restitution to the woman, but the sheriff wouldn't have it. He ordered all working-age boys to the schoolhouse. The other deputies rode through checking the shacks to ensure there were no boys left. It never occurred to them that the folks in Bennettsville had moved as many boys as possible to the woods. A couple dozen boys went to the schoolhouse—those who didn't look a thing like Micah. Bird was surprised when Ned walked in with his father Fred behind him. He was a head taller than the boys beside him and carried himself like a young man well aware of his duty in the situation. When Odelia arrived by wagon, with her rocking chair in tow, Bird led her grandmother to her place beside the boys and whispered in her grandmother's ear, "Ned is with the other boys."

Odelia's head jerked up sharply, but she composed herself. "So be it," she said.

Bennettsville was a well-disciplined military when the white folks from Tuckersville entered the schoolhouse. No one moved or spoke; all eyes shifted between Odelia and the sheriff—a tall, sweaty man. One of his big pawlike hands removed his hat and handed it to the young man who walked at his heels. It took Bird a long moment to recognize the eager, blonde hat-holder. Jonas Kirby must have edged toward eighteen years of age. His chest and arms had filled out, although he was still skinny compared to the sheriff and deputies around him.

Bird's fists clenched as the sheriff let that white woman poke and prod every boy. She even peered up at Mr. Charles for several seconds.

Some of the boys were defiant and stone faced, and others fidgeted with fear. Worry tightened Bird's throat. She could barely breathe. Kirby and the deputies were thirsting to grab someone. And if they did, there would be a fight. None of these boys was a sacrificial lamb. As the old white woman stopped in front of him, Ned stared straight ahead. Behind him, his father inhaled along with every colored person in the room. Fred wouldn't have walked into this room without a pistol on him. And Bird was sure that several of Fred's men waited outside. The old woman lingered in front of Ned. Bird glanced desperately at her grandmother. Odelia was a statue as she listened. She'd said, "So be it." Bird now understood her meaning—if blood was spilled, all the lines of Ezra stood in peril together.

When it seemed like the schoolhouse might combust from the tension, Odelia cleared her throat. The old white woman whirled toward her and huffed at Odelia's audacity to rush her. "They've hidden him away," the sour woman complained to the sheriff.

The sheriff opened his mouth to bark some command, but Odelia cut in.

"Perhaps now, you are willing to discuss the matter privately."

"The boy has run off with my money; there's nothing to say other'n that," said the white woman.

"There's always room for discussion," Odelia countered. "Mr. Charles, please lead our families out."

"Bring the boy back," the sheriff said when the room was cleared.

"Not hardly," Odelia said, and Bird blinked. She didn't know her grandmother had it in her. "There's been peace between the towns for over fifty years. If it costs fifty dollars to protect that, I'll pay it."

"And you're gonna pay every time somebody steals something?" the sheriff asked. Jonas Kirby's eyes rested on Odelia. His lips curved into a wolfish snarl. Bird stepped closer to her grandmother.

Odelia said nothing for a moment, and the white woman shifted from discomfort. "We'll cross each bridge as it comes. Bird, the money."

Not taking her eyes off Jonas Kirby, who shifted his stare to her and the money in her hand, Bird handed the crisp bill to the sheriff, and he handed it to the sour woman. They turned and left without a word.

Odelia sank back in her chair. "Bring the families back in," she said.

Bird thought everyone would have dispersed, but there they stood watching the white folks load into their automobiles and putter off.

"A Psalm, please, Brother Giles," said Odelia, when everyone was reassembled.

As natural as anything, Mr. Giles recited the twenty-third Psalm. As he neared the valley of the shadow of death, the rest of the room began reciting with him, and by the end, there was a sense of triumph among them.

"The lesson of the day, Mr. Charles?" Odelia asked.

He looked up from his desk, a little away from the group. "Children, don't pity or give charity to white folks. They need to believe they have more than us and are better than us, and that we always know this. If not, they'll try to make a believer out of us every time." Bessie took the place of her mother who had gone with the other boys and pressed her hand against his back. Bird watched this gesture again from Vera's kitchen. I should have known then, she thought. My mother is gone, but I've stayed for Granny and Uncle Vernon. Whatever the appeal of the world, Bessie would stay with her family. Vera placed her hand on Bird's, perhaps sensing some shift.

"I'll write to your grandmother," she said. "Perhaps, it's time for you to go home."

Bird raised her hand, "No, please. I know now why she sent me away. I need a little more time." Bird finished her tea. "I misled myself."

"No, young one," said Vera, "The heart doesn't lie. Its truths are many and complicated and often contradictory. To follow one truth sometimes means that we can't follow another. The choices are always hard and hurt-filled."

# June 1917

Bird would get little of the requested time. Near the end of May, word of the first sparks of violence in East St. Louis worked its way from the city's center to the outlying country roads. Men in vehicles or wagons stopped as they passed by, and with these snatches, they pieced together the story. Someone said, the truth of it unknown, that a colored man had robbed a white man. White mobs were beating colored folks on the streets and pulling folks off trolley cars to beat them. For the next two days and nights, Vera kept her shotgun within arm's reach. On the third day, Bird found herself loaded into a car, with a sorrowful hug and kiss, and sent unceremoniously back to Bennettsville.

The little white house off Miller's Road seemed so small on Bird's return. It was a grand house in Bennettsville and wouldn't turn a head fifty miles to the west. Her grandmother and mother had traveled. Odelia had even crossed an ocean and still had come back to this. The car stopped, and her grandmother lifted herself off the porch swing. Vernon and Sue came out of the house. Each face held nervous expectation. Bird shook as she stepped onto the soil of her birth. What could they possibly expect from her except for anger and hurt? She stood a few steps from the porch as the driver carried her suitcases to the bottom steps. The young man glanced between the girl and her family, tipped his hat, and whistled at the brewing storm.

As Bird mounted the porch's top step and faced her grandmother, Odelia threw her arms around her. In her fantasies of her return and this embrace, Bird had promised to stand still. But in this moment, she'd crumbled and wept in the arms of the one who'd hurt her most.

The first days of her return passed without event, in the house or outside of it. She'd not come back with much of a plan. She'd brought books, newspapers, and bolts of fabric to make dresses, for whom she didn't know. She spent as much time as possible in her own room or the sewing room. When she did join her grandmother for meals, she told short tales of her travels and gave the gifts purchased along the river. Her grandmother's welcome was enthusiastic, too much so for Bird. Sue prepared all of her favorite foods—fried okra, black-eyed peas, and hot water cornbread. Odelia chatted incessantly as Bird escorted her through the garden. The old woman had inquired about the next application cycle for Fisk. All was well in the town. The updates about the school pained Bird. Yes, it was nice that Cecile was back helping her parents now that Bessie had moved on to this next phase of her life. There was almost an obsequiousness that shocked Bird. The woman wanted forgiveness but wouldn't acknowledge the harm done.

Bird ventured to town the week following her return. She handled the wagon with more care than her mother, but she received the same reception. Perhaps a few more short hellos and smiles. She wondered if she imagined it all. How long had she actually been gone? She sat in the wagon, the reins still in hand. It had been just a couple of months. On her way to Johnson's Grocery, one of her little ones ran up to her and threw her arms about her legs. Something in Bird's chest cracked a little. Bird asked after the little girl's studies, to which she received promises to count to one hundred. This forced her mother, a woman for whom Bird had sewn pants for each of her young sons, to finally walk over and discourage the girl from infringing on Miss Bird's time.

Mr. Johnson greeted her with genuine warmth and still handed her a butterscotch candy. If he'd opened his arms, she would have dashed into them. She passed on the card of a fabric wholesaler that she hoped he'd consider doing business with on her behalf.

They stepped onto the porch together, and he put his arm around her in a fatherly way. "I'm glad you are coming into your own. The Bennett women are the backbone of this town."

Bird doubted this, unless the backbone is that part of the body thought of least. She returned home to find that her grandmother had held lunch for her.

"How was town?" Odelia asked.

"It seems that in a few short months, I have become a stranger."

Odelia Bennett said nothing.

"What was said of my departure?"

"We were discreet, Bird. Only that it seemed appropriate for you to meet your father's people, given my age and health."

"Only Mr. Johnson spoke to me. I taught their children, Granny. Plenty of them are my kin."

"It will pass, Bird, in time." The words rolled like water off her grandmother's tongue.

"You've said that before. To whom? My mother?" Bird threw her hands up though the gesture was lost on Odelia. "It seems you have found my place in Bennettsville."

Bird left her untouched meal on the table and marched into the kitchen—and bumped into Sue who listened at the door.

"Your granny worried over you and has done her best to protect you from yourself. And all you give her is disrespect and sass," Sue hissed with a pointed finger.

Bird stared at her. At least a dozen cruel responses came to mind. She channeled her mother's coldest tone, which could cut closer than any choice words. "What is between my grandmother and me, is just that."

She walked through the garden, to the tree line, and then down to the pond. Through the thinning trees, she could see Ned's house in the distance. She'd gathered that Bessie was married and pregnant, and Ned was off to his duty station. Bird wondered at any logic that had her thanking Odelia for orchestrating her first heartbreak and ostracization. Her grandmother had once described them as two of the same kind: women that don't take to anger, but for whom hurts run deep and linger long. Odelia Bennett knew what she had done and must have sensed the ocean that now lay between herself and Bird. Maybe one day, she and Bird could share a shore, but Bird wasn't rowing this time.

# July 1917

The gulf between the Bennett women hadn't ebbed by the time East St. Louis exploded again just over a month after Bird's return. The full-on war scene descriptions gave Bird nights of terror-filled dreams. Neighborhoods scorched. Men and women running for their lives. All was devastation where the mobs had rampaged. There were hundreds, maybe thousands, without homes, clothing, and food. But no one bringing news knew the names of the dead or could say how far out of the city the mobs had wreaked their havoc. Bird had no way of knowing if Vera and Eileen were okay.

"Thank God, Vera sent you back," said Odelia after Mr. Johnson departed from delivering another round of updates himself.

"Amen to that," said Vernon from the porch steps.

"I need to go back," said Bird.

"Pardon," said Odelia.

Uncle Vernon's head dropped. He'd done his best to stay neutral and out of trouble with both Odelia and Bird.

"I need to know if Aunt Vera's okay. And if she is, she'll need my help sewing and cooking for folks."

"Bird, the last thing she needs is a child to look after, and just because the National Guard is finally keeping the peace, doesn't mean it'll hold."

"I'm not a child," said Bird and hated the unavoidable petulance in the phrase. "I will secure my own passage."

"You can yell at me Auntie, but you should have known I was coming," said Bird as she found Vera in her sewing room two days later. Odelia had demanded and cried, but Bird still left. She'd tried to explain. Odelia had put Vera back in her life. And the two had taken to each other. Bird had to see with her own eyes that she was okay.

"Birdy, I'm too tired to yell," said Vera. Her words were sluggish and dark rings circled her eyes.

"Where's Aunt Eileen?"

"She's here, recovering. She made it out the first night . . . It's been difficult for her. I'll take you to her later and explain when I can."

The quiet repose of Vera's country home had transformed into a life triage station for almost twenty folks during the first days of riots. Now, aside from Eileen Banneker, five people remained—a husband, wife, and their two-year-old daughter, and two young men just arrived from Mississippi who'd spent their last dollars on a boarding room that had been torched. The family had taken over Bird's room. The young men slept on pallets in the living room that they tucked away during the day. That first day, Bird wondered where she would sleep. It turned out that there was so much work to be done, she and Vera would sleep in shifts. Vera in the bed beside Eileen and Bird on a pallet on their bedroom floor.

There were meals to prepare for those in the house, and bread, soup, and whatever meat could be spared was sent to the city each day to the churches feeding people. Vera sewed skirts and blouses, and when she could sew no more, Bird sewed drawstring pants for the men and boys. Every day, they sent a stack of clothes into the city. At sunset, someone dropped off more donated fabric, and the sewing began again.

It had taken Eileen Banneker several minutes to recognize the girl nursing her. "It's me Auntie Eileen. I've come back to help," Bird tried to explain.

"They've taken it all. Vera won't let me go see it. Tell her I need to see it."

"Yes, ma'am. I'll tell her. Please just rest." She wouldn't tell her aunt. The woman's dire condition was plain to see. Bird could imagine the horrors seen that made this pillar of a woman shrink into herself. Eileen slept with her arms wrapped around herself, and they could hardly be pried open. When awake, her eyes darted all around as she cried. Before she lay down on her pallet each night, Bird sat beside the ailing woman, hummed softly, and stroked the edges of her hair.

As the young family waited for word from relatives in Chicago and walked the roads looking for work, Bird grew accustomed to having their daughter cooing on her hip and curled up on blankets beside the sewing machine. When they departed after their family had scraped together enough for train fare, Bird was surprised at how much she missed glancing over at the sleeping child. One of the Mississippi gentlemen, as they called themselves, took a liking to Bird and was always ready to help should she need to lift more than a spoon to her mouth or a piece of fabric to the machine.

Vera watched with bemused caution. Bird could sense her curiosity. "It's okay if you like him, Bird. He's a nice boy," Vera told her.

Bird considered this. She did like him, but not in that way. "I'd just like to be his friend."

Vera shook her head. "Then, take care. It's easy for boys his age to mistake a young lady's intentions. A giggle may mean friendship to you, but it may mean more to him. Hell, some grown men struggle with it."

So, Bird kept her lines straight and clear, and the boy eventually took note, and the Mississippi gentlemen too went on their way, west to Kansas City. The quiet in Vera's home was restored, leaving Bird to wonder about her aunt. Everyone knew her, and plenty stopped to inquire after her and exchange updates, but no friends visited. Her otherness seemed settled and accepted by all, and most so, by Vera herself.

Eileen Banneker had friends. As word spread that she was recovering her strength, ladies representing various auxiliaries and committees visited. Vera welcomed them and, in soft tones, requested few questions and not too many details on the aftermath. The women gave solemn agreement. Eileen received them in the sitting room, wearing the only clothes she had in the world, simple dresses with touches of elegance that Vera fought through the wee hours of the night to sew for her. Bird served tea and sat off to the side lest the guests stay too long, or Eileen fade. The ladies discussed the dispersal of the newcomers. The wariness of those who still arrived each day and all the churches were doing to help. Eileen promised to resume her duties as soon as she was well enough. The women assured her that she had done plenty, and there was no shame in being cared for. There were already plans for the restoration of her house and where she could stay when she was ready to return. Each group of visitors exited the sitting room more somber than they had entered it. Vera saw them out and then helped Eileen up the stairs and back to bed, where she cried and Vera comforted her.

Bird's mission to the city was two-pronged—to procure what living and sewing supplies she could find and lay eyes on Eileen's house. Bird rode in the automobile's front with her newly introduced Uncle Jarvis Turner. The day before, she'd argued Vera into letting her make the trip. Eileen wouldn't notice her absence as much, and it would be good for them to have the house to themselves for the first time since everything had gone wrong. Vera had agreed with due reluctance.

Still, as the distance closed between her and city, Bird began to doubt herself. What if the prices were outrageous, she had no skills in haggling and no benefits expected from long years of patronage. And there was always the chance that something, or nothing, could set the white folks' anger boiling over again. Her Uncle Jarvis was short like his sister, but bulky, and he walked and talked like he could use this bulk if the need arose. But that would only get them so far.

"You gonna fall out?" Jarvis asked her.

"I'm trying not to," she admitted and relaxed the grip on her purse handle.

"We'll be fine. All the red in the street been costing these stores the green. They think they got us back in place, so they're happy to take our money again."

"Yes, sir, I'll be fine," she told him and herself.

The smell of burning wood and rubber and metal haunted the air long before they reached the city. Both Bird and Jarvis held their breaths as they entered the city proper. Whole sections were scorched black. On some blocks, every single structure had succumbed. Bird placed her hand on her uncle's. He squeezed back. Her eyes burned, and she could not swallow. White people were powerful surely, but how could even they have done this? The fires must have pressed against the sky itself. It was a wonder that any of the city remained. The adults of Bennettsville had trained Bird and all the children to give Tuckersville its distance and due fear. Bird would never doubt this lesson again.

By the time Jarvis parked a block from the city's center, Bird was too numb to feel much fear. She let the practicing she'd done with Vera lead her. She earned odd looks as Jarvis held the door for her at the dry goods and fabric stores. She stood off to the side of the counters after she'd selected her goods, notions, and fabrics, most of the time waiting for the men behind the counter to decide when she'd waited long enough. She waited for the totals before reaching into her purse and was glad that she had folded bills into various compartments of her pocketbook lest she been seen with too much money for a colored girl.

After the last shop, as Jarvis eased the car back into the street traffic, she sighed with some relief and wished she could close her eyes against the burnt city. Jarvis knew the way to Eileen's neighborhood, but the fire-scarred streets threw him. He paused often to decide whether some skeleton of a building or pile of bricks had been a landmark at which he needed to turn. When they were certain they were on the right block, he rolled slowly, and Bird counted the houses, or what was left of them, from the corner.

Bird stopped him in front of Eileen's house, now little more than a dark cave with a sunken roof where the second story had once been. The room she'd slept in—and come to think of as hers when anticipating visits with Vera—was gone. The house that had been one of the few safe places for her aunts in this whole world was gone. Only a few red bricks that girded the front porch remained untarnished. This amazed Bird since even the grass in front of it was blackened.

"I need to get something," she said.

Jarvis's head shook. "Structure ain't sound, and I don't know that anything could have survived this."

"Do you have anything to dig with?"

"You are a funny one," he said with a kindly smile. "Jus' these hands."

Bird looked at her own hands and shrugged as Vera would. "They'll have to do." She pointed them to the sugar maple sapling that had replaced the fir tree. It looked worse for wear with a few bare and snapped branches. It wouldn't survive whatever demolition was coming to these blocks. It had just as much a chance in her aunt's yard.

"Are you going to clean the dirt out of my back seat?"

"Yes, Uncle, I will."

"Alright, then we best get to digging, so we can be out of here by dark."

As the weeks passed, Eileen recovered her strength and took to the porch. The July days were hot, but she seemed unbothered by this. Her exercise consisted of a daily vigil to the newly planted tree fighting for survival about ten feet in front of the house. On a quiet Tuesday afternoon, Bird balanced a glass of ice water for the ailing woman and a pitcher of water for the tree. Eileen reached for her hand, causing her to spill the ice water; thinking the woman close to fainting, Bird dropped both and grabbed for her. Eileen pointed to the large black car approaching the lane. Her voice was barely more than a whisper when she called out for Vera. Bird, still plenty confused, assisted Eileen's abrupt retreat to the porch.

A moment later, Bird understood as the car stopped dangerously close to the sapling, and she recognized the height of the man who stepped out of it. The details were all wrong, but the man could only be the Minister. His hair was completely white, and he now wore spectacles. He'd gained weight in his face and around his waist. He saw Eileen Banneker and bowed his head with a solemn grimace. He recognized Bird and stopped mid-step. "Where's Vera?" he asked, not taking his eyes off Bird.

"Auntie Vera," Bird called back toward the door as a knot tied itself in her stomach.

This time Vera heard. She stepped onto the porch and walked to the edge standing between Bird and her father.

"I knew of Mrs. Banneker's presence here. But not of Honest's."

"She came to help," Vera said, like Bird had just walked from one of the houses down the road.

"I wasn't aware that you two were in touch." The Minister's voice deepened with displeasure.

"Her grandmother reacquainted us. A girl should know her family."

He directed his gaze back to Bird. "You look well, Honest."

"Thank you."

"Well, if I haven't heard of your arrival, then you two have been discreet. At least in that area." And with that, he turned to Eileen, and Bird saw herself disappear from his mind. "Good day, Mrs. Banneker," he said.

"The good folks of East Saint are keen to get you back into town where you'll have more access to doctors and help."

"I appreciate their concern," Eileen Banneker said dryly.

"The doctor's been here twice," Vera said. "Shock and nerves seem to be at issue. It would be unwise for her to return until she is strong enough to handle what she'll see."

"But how much damage will have been done to her reputation by then?" the Minister snapped at his sister.

"My reputation?" Eileen asked in a suddenly firm growl. Everyone else on the porch paused. Bird hid a satisfied smirk. "Is devastation a threat to a woman's reputation? You can assure them I am too old to be out here hiding a pregnancy," said Eileen.

"No one would dare suggest such a thing," the Minister answered too quickly, and it was clear who outranked who among them. "But your friendship with my sister has been tolerated for more than enough years, and the associations we keep can . . ." He searched for words.

Vera Turner winced and inhaled. She looked into the distance as each of his words seemed to slice through her. The woman was weary and had carried too much, while he worried only of reputations.

Bird thought she saw her aunt near faltering and held up her hand to punctuate her command. "Stop."

Everyone turned to look at her.

"Have you had no training since your mother's death?" asked the Minister. The coldness in his eyes and tone shook Bird. "A child is to be silent unless spoken too. Honor thy mother and father that thy days may be long upon this earth."

"Unless the child has more sense than her father." Eileen Banneker lifted herself out of her rocking chair, and Vera put an arm around her waist to steady her. "Reverend Turner, do you know all the things I've done in my life so that my days may be long upon it? How many folks I've honored and submitted to? How afraid I've been of just two things: the white face of death and the black face of hatred? I feared that both would do God knows what to me. Shun me. Beat me. Kill me. I did what many of the fearful do, chained myself to the Bible. Prayed on my knees every night. Married the man selected for me. Did everything I should. And then, still, the white face of death came for me. With torches, ropes, knives, and pistols. They came for everything I had. If I had not been a dark-skinned woman, in a black dress and able to tuck into the shadows, I'd be dead. They laughed and danced in the flames of my home. And when they left to seek other destruction, I ran with the others just as scared as I was. We looked for shelter that no God provided. I ran although my feet bled, and my body shook with fear. I ran until I collapsed on the steps of this house. I cannot stop the white man's blood lust. And I cannot stop the hatred of those who hate the love in my heart. But I can make my stand here. I will not leave this place. It is my home. It took flames to make me see it, but the angel did say it would be fire next time."

The Minister's jaws pulsed, and his nostrils flared. "You are corrupting my daughter."

Bird's own anger flashed. She wanted to throw bricks through his little glass chapel and to say that she had corrupted herself and was happy to be so, but this would do her aunts no good. "I have not seen your daughter here," she said.

The Minister opened his mouth, but then closed it again. Without a word, or another look, he returned to his car and drove away.

Vera helped Eileen into the house, pausing to rest a trembling hand on her niece's cheek. Bird nodded and returned a soft smile. "I'll be okay," said Bird.

"You don't have to be," said Vera.

"Yes, I do."

"What are you going to do next, Birdy?" Vera asked as they sipped a sweet white wine in the living room that evening.

"Stretch out. Read a bit."

Vera rolled her eyes. "You know what I mean."

"What choices do I have? Stay here with you. Go back to Granny's house. Or perhaps, I could show up at the Minister's house with my suitcase and a pitiful look. I'm sure they'd be happy to take me in."

"I think you need to go back to Odelia. You two need to sort this out."

"Sort what out?" Bird asked appreciating the few drops of her mother's sarcasm that found their way into the words. "You think she'll give me Bessie back?"

"Do you really want that sailed ship dragged back to port?"

Bird wanted a million contradictory things. To let it all go and be unbothered. To have her mother back. Relief from the weight of expectation and obligation. To be ignored. To be loved. To be held. To be believed in. She whispered the only words that seemed adequate: "No, but I want to belong."

Perhaps, she sensed, if she had said any other words, her aunt would have pounced. Or misunderstood. But these two words gave Vera pause. They even stopped Bird. She'd never thought of such an apt description of the predicament of her young life. She didn't belong anywhere. Her grandmother had sensed this about Bennettsville and done her best to orchestrate around it. There was no place for her in East St. Louis. She'd dreamed of a life that took her down far roads and across oceans, but the omnipotence of her childhood had waned. She'd never been afraid before, but she knew the world better now.

And then, there was Odelia. Bird now saw the roots of the tense relationship and stifled love that Maddy and Odelia had made do with. Deep down, she admitted that Odelia deserved more than a grudging forgiveness. The woman had been ready to rest so many years ago and had resurrected herself so that Bird wouldn't be alone and without love in the world. Maddy's hurts had caused her to keep the world at a distance, even this friend who'd only wanted to love her and her daughter.

"You and my mother," said Bird.

"What about us?" Vera pressed hard on the last word.

Bird let them rest a moment in the before of this conversation. Surely, Bird thought, she knew I'd ask one day. There was a part of her mother's story that was her birthright. And there was only one person left on earth who could tell it to her. "She knew you loved her?" said Bird.

Vera sighed. "After a while, I didn't try to hide it."

"Did you two ever . . . ? She let the silence convey her meaning.

"That's quite a question for a young lady to ask."

"I would ask her, but she can't answer."

Vera sat up. "Did your mother ever tell you why she called you Bird?"

"Because I was born little; she was afraid I might fly away." Bird couldn't remember where she'd actually heard this story, maybe from her grandmother. But Maddy had never told her otherwise.

Vera shook her head and laughed at the ridiculousness of this. "If Odelia hadn't objected, your given name would be Bird. Maddy and I lay in the grass many a day. Me admiring her and her admiring the sparrows, blue jays, and hummingbirds—their free and simple lives. She called you Bird with the hope that you'd belong to the air and be free like them."

"Maybe I'm too free now. Would she still love me?"

"Of course, she would. You were the hand she fanned herself with." Vera hummed in thought and then was silent for several minutes. Bird sensed she was peeling back years and wading through memories and pain. When she spoke again, her voice was soft and halting. "Although I was always careful, I think your mother sensed the difference in me. There was a difference about her too. A gravity beyond her years. Whatever she sensed in me, she seemed confident that she could deal with me. She thought she could handle most things. I kept my counsel until she was pregnant. Sheila's father offered your jackass father a bigger pulpit than Bennettsville could. He wasn't man enough to tell your mother and started avoiding her, hoping she'd take the hint. One did not avoid Maddy Bennett. She confronted him at my parent's house. My mother begged her not to call him out publicly. They offered her money and to send her to a woman that could solve the problem for her."

At this, Vera turned to Bird. Bird nodded for her to continue. None of this was surprising. She would allow herself the hurt of it all later.

"I think it was that night that Maddy realized the lions' den that was my family. It was almost like she floated above them. They were statues under her gaze. Your father sat in the sitting room corner hiding in his Bible.

"'Ain't none of y'all worth this,' Maddy said and turned and walked out.

"Your father didn't move, so I ran after her. She had moved fast, and I caught her some ways down the road.

"'My brother,' I said, mustering my courage, 'isn't man enough to listen to his heart. He has always taken that which offers ease to him. I was neither blessed nor cursed in this way. I hear my heart and want so much to obey, whatever it costs or how hard the road. The child could be our child.'

"She let me kiss her. It was a simple kiss. Her lips were soft and salty sweet like maple sugar and tears. Her tongue curious and unafraid. That kiss answered every question for both of us. I loved her and would love women for the rest of my life. She loved me enough to accept my kiss, but not as a lover. When she pulled back, this was all clear between us.

"'What will you do?' I asked her, stuffing my disappointment into a deep corner of my heart.

"'I'll do what every woman in my situation does, go back to my mother and bear my shame among my people,' she said.

"'And the child?' I asked.

"'You can tell your people that the child is mine and of no concern to them.' She held up her hand as she spoke in that way you do.

"'I want to know . . . ' I said.

"'Please,' she said. 'Give me time.' And then she walked off into the night.

"Two years later, she sent me a ten-page letter describing everything about you. We remained friends, and I visited often until, somehow, she and your father struck back up a couple of years later. I didn't see her again until the night she died."

Bird was still, her breath shallow and slow. Vera placed an arm around her.

"So yes," she said, "your mother would love you no matter what. You were hers, and she was yours. She would want you to be happy."

"How did you survive it all? Her leaving at first, and then going back with the Minister?"

Vera walked to the window seat and leaned against it. She didn't look back at Bird as she spoke. "I wanted to die, for a long while. Begged for it. I held on long enough that the world must have pitied me enough to offer a little mercy."

"Is there happiness?" asked Bird.

"I wish I could promise it to you, but I like to think you'll find happiness. You didn't get your Daddy's fear or Maddy's coolness; well, you got a touch of the latter. And you've got a bit of money coming to you one day. Nothing chains a woman worse than poverty. You won't be foolish enough to let a man spend it for you. Don't be foolish enough to let a woman do it either. There's probably gonna be more hurting than loving in your life. Savor the loving while you can. You might love some women for years and some just for a night. All are gifts from a stingy world."

Bird stood and stepped sobbing into her aunt-mother's arms. Vera held and rocked her. "And you can get off the road whenever you like. There's no shame in that either. We are meant to survive."

No one waited for Bird on her return to Bennettsville. She had left when it felt urgent and returned in the same fashion. She found Sue in the kitchen basting a chicken and her grandmother in a chair on the edge of her garden.

"I'm back, Granny."

"God is good," said Odelia. "How is your aunt?"

"Spent. We sewed and cooked until we couldn't do it anymore."

"I've held you both in my prayers."

Bird was surprised that her grandmother didn't have any questions about East St. Louis or the people, but she didn't really want to describe what she'd seen anyway. And she knew this tension well, had lived with it for most of her life—this dance between Odelia and Maddy. The adagio and then the crescendo.

"I've brought back the latest edition of *The Crisis.*"

"I'd enjoy hearing a passage, but we should talk first." She motioned for Bird to take the other seat. "I know you're angry with me, Bird."

"No, I'm not angry."

"Then what are you?"

"You know me so well. Must you really ask?"

"Mind your tone, young lady."

Bird stood to walk away.

"Sit down," her grandmother ordered.

"If I cannot speak freely, then I have nothing to say."

Odelia Bennett paused as if considering how many indignities she would suffer this child. "Fine, say your part."

Bird laughed. "My part? You sent me away with the barest of consultation, explanation, or option. You say your part, grandmother."

"I wanted to save you from yourself. Clearly, if this is how you returned, I have erred. I thought your aunt could provide you warning and caution."

"Against what?"

"Things the world doesn't understand and will strike out against."

“What do you understand about me, Granny?”

“That you developed a crush on your childhood friend.”

“I loved her. And she loved me. For years, I’ve read her face as easily as I read yours. I know her dreams and her fears. And I promised I would be strong enough to bear them both. And maybe for a few moments, she believed me. But I was made a liar. It would have been one thing if I had tried and failed her—” Bird’s voice thundered through her own tears.

“And how would you have lived in the world? You’d have been ostracized at best and killed at worst. There have been enough killings in this bloodline,” argued Odelia.

“I’ve already been ostracized. Who stopped to visit me when I came back? I don’t know how we would have lived. I can admit that. And maybe we couldn’t have. Or, it would have been too hard or too dangerous. But you never took my love or my pain seriously enough to even ask that question before you arranged for my departure, behind my back, and sold Bessie to the highest bidder.”

“You don’t know the world. What fear and hatred can do. She chose to marry. That he had been courting her was her own omission.”

“I know enough. I have seen the burned-out houses and blood stains on the streets. And I saw what happens when a woman gives her life over to the white face of death and the black mask of hatred only to have the former come for her anyway and destroy everything she had.”

“Vera, is she okay?” Her grandmother clutched at her chest.

“Her lover, Granny! Fell at her feet after running half the night for her life. All the years they suffered apart, for what? They are together now. I don’t know what will become of them. They don’t either. But at least they are together for it.”

“Vera is a woman. You are a girl—a girl, left in my charge.”

“And when would I become a woman, Granny, in your eyes? In the eyes of this town? When I married a man? Had a baby? I am a woman who prepared her mother’s body. A pain she never lived to know. I am a woman who came back to this town that has never found a place for me except out of respect for you. You ask me what I am. I’m hurt. More deeply than I ever thought you possible of hurting me. I have asked for so little, maybe even just this one thing. This love. And you took it from me. Not the white men or the black men or the church ladies. It was you who ripped it from me."

Odelia Bennett leaned back in pensive silence. Her hands shook her cane. Her voice cracked when she spoke. "I was . . . I am afraid for you. When I first realized what you two were to each other." Odelia lowered her head, "The world took that kind of love away from me. In the worst way. I thought I could keep you from feeling the hurt I felt. But even then, I knew that was folly. Life spreads its cruelty with little discernment or mercy."

"You sent me away and kept her. Do you understand how that makes me look, Granny? If she's Mrs. Bennett, then who am I to this town?" Bird's head spun as she spoke. She had peeled the wound to its deepest layer and found and studied the blade's tip. Her granny cried as the tip must have cut her too.

"Only one of you could have stayed. The burdens have always been ours. To whom much is given, much is asked."

"We could have both left."

"I have secured safe and comfortable futures for both of you."

Bird knelt before her grandmother. "Don't you know that this house and the life you have chosen for me is hell? Didn't you want to rescue me from it once?"

Bird laid her head in her grandmother's lap. The old woman's tears landed on Bird's cheeks and mixed with her own.

# October 1919

Bird lingered in the chair at Odelia's bedside as the old woman settled under her covers and smiled sleepily. They'd taken to eating their breakfast at the little table in Odelia's room. Bird called it their queenly luxury. Neither woman commented that it was too much effort to move Odelia up and down the stairs for a nibbled biscuit and sips of tea. Fall winds pressed against the windows, and Bird closed her eyes and inhaled deeply. She wished Maddy were with her. They'd once shared this bedside and held each other up. But now, Bird was alone. Everything's okay, right now, she told herself. Odelia's fine. Vernon's fine. I'm fine. And that's all that matters today. She wiped a tear and rose quietly to clear the dishes.

"Come on in. I'm just about done," Bird stopped the sewing machine long enough to call out to whoever knocked. It was likely Lorna coming for the very window treatments under the foot. Bird zipped along the last hem and leaned back to check her work before remembering a guest's arrival. "You've got timing," she said, pushing her chair back. The last syllable barely passed her lips as she turned to find Bessie standing in the doorway. Neither woman spoke. Bird was more than willing to cede the first word to the woman who hadn't crossed the threshold of her house in what seemed like years.

"I don't know why I'm here, or what to say. It just came to me this morning," Bessie said, her hands kneading each other. "I want to know how you been, and how you're doing? I have a son now, named Sed."

"I know, congratulations," Bird said, and wondered if Bessie had expected her to send a gift. "I been alright—just sewing and keeping Granny and Uncle Vernon out of trouble." Bird glanced at her watch. "I was thinking about tea."

"That sounds good."

"I'm not sure where to start," said Bessie as they settled in at the kitchen table. "There's a lot we never got to say."

"Not for lack of opportunity," said Bird. If you've come for a path made easy, she thought, you have chosen the wrong day, and maybe even the wrong lifetime.

"I regret that, and I'm sorry for it. I didn't know how to say what needed saying. Any way I said it would have hurt you. I was making grown woman decisions without seeing the grown woman hurts they would cause." She inhaled and glanced up at Bird who hadn't moved. "But I made the right decision for me. So, I think that means it was the right decision for us. Maybe it's too much for you to consider friendship, but I wanted to at least clear the air."

Bird's mouth was bone-dry, but she didn't dare lift her cup lest a shaking hand give away the trembling anger in her heart. "I know why you made the decision you made. But I deserved better from you and Odelia . . . and your mother. It felt like we both had feelings but somehow, I was the most wrong. I guessed you told them it was all just me." Bird stood and walked to the sink. It had been a fall afternoon like this one when Odelia and Helena Charles had made the uneasy arrangements for her schooling. "Whatever was said, the price I've paid has been more than I owed. I'm still not ashamed, and I'm fine to keep to myself. Anybody wanting friendship with me can't be wanting my shame too."

Bessie leaned forward and placed her hands flat on the table. "I told my mother the truth. She still gives me the evil eye sometimes. She knows what I was coming to do here today and so does my husband. I don't care much what anyone else in this town thinks. I've had enough of caring about that. Everybody has their idea of who Mrs. Bennett should be and talk amongst themselves about it while smiling at me. I need a friend who will tell me about myself, to my face, and be mad at me for years, if necessary." She smacked the table at the end of this, and Bird could only imagine who had done what to raise her ire.

The first laugh escaped Bird. She tried to hold it in, but it was all ridiculous. This town full of kinfolk and the history that bound them. This whole world and all its contradictions. Bessie Charles Bennett and Honest Bird Bennett still needing each other as friends. Bessie straightened her back with feigned indignance. "You want to laugh," she demanded. "Wait till I tell you the stink Sister Higgins started for me wanting to order red velvet for the church pews. Or, how I almost got cast out for salting the watermelon on Township Day."

The salted watermelon broke the dam of Bird's composure. "Bessie, I been telling you for years, don't nobody want salt on their watermelon."

"That's how my people do it," Bessie protested.

Bird had learned this the hard way during a visit with the Charleses to see Helena's family. Bird had minded her manners so well as the dazzling tray of sliced watermelon was carried out of the house. She'd waited patiently in line and not begrudged the old folks and then the children who'd gotten their small rectangles of divinity first. And then, she'd bit into hers and damn near choked on the salt. Bessie had clapped her on the back. "Someone spilled salt on this piece," Bird croaked, and Bessie looked confused. "It's all got salt on it." Bird looked around at everyone enjoying their slices and kept the rest of her thoughts on the matter to herself as her Granny would have demanded. And she was very polite when she declined a second helping.

"Well, you've married into the Bennetts. And folks here won't stand for you desecrating a watermelon like that."

"Backwards town," said Bessie, cutting her eyes as she lifted her teacup.

Bird chuckled and allowed herself to nestle just a bit back into the familiarity of this friendship long considered lost.

"That was Bessie?" Odelia asked, after Bird had settled her in the living room after her nap.

"Yes," Bird measured the hesitance in her grandmother's question. "Did you have anything to do with this visit?"

"For once, I haven't been meddling in your life. How'd it go?"

"Well enough. I'm surprised you didn't join us."

Odelia scoffed. "It may have taken me several decades, but I have finally learned that the way to stay out of trouble is to give it wide berth and still step carefully. I do hope reconciliation is possible. Division in the family is no good for the town. I tell you this from experience. Your Uncle Louis and I had our share of disagreements over the years, and I can't tell you how many times I've wanted to throttle Fred."

Taking some issue with comparison of the duplicitous crushing of her heart to a mere disagreement, Bird let it go.

# June 1920

Bennettsville's common knowledge held that Odelia Bennett did not die. Neither did she succumb or pass away. She simply took her leave. Bird would explain to inquirers that her grandmother had sat beside her in the garden as she read to her, and then the next moment, she was gone. The presence or absence of a body was debated—a debate intensified by the private ceremony attended only by Bird, Vernon, and Fred Bennett's family, per Odelia's long-standing request. In the end, the truth made no difference to either camp. They both agreed that after seventy years, the body of a woman forced to raise a town of kin was as tired as the shawls she wrapped it in, and as easily shed.

Odelia, they said as they retold Bird's story—even when she was in earshot—had rested her eyes and opened them and found that she could see a world she hadn't seen in over forty years. She started walking, and Bird—known for the intensity of her concentration—had failed to notice that the last true Bennett daughter had sauntered away. Of course, the old woman should have said goodbye. But how much do the old owe the young? Odelia had done her part for her granddaughter, the rest of them, and then some.

Bird agreed that her grandmother hadn't died, but silently protested that she knew the second the woman had left her. If the others had felt or could even fathom that stillness. That terrifying moment when every blade of grass and tree leaf waited for Bird's reaction. Would the girl stand, or would she fall? Bird kept reading, because it was her voice that was the only movement left in the world. She read until it broke, and the stillness had mercy on her and dissipated. Only then did she close her grandmother's Bible and weep at her feet, for there was indeed a body.

Even as she cried, Bird knew that this body had never actually been her grandmother; it had only held her spirit and light.

If time passed after Odelia's death, Bird couldn't tell. The arriving newspapers marked time for the rest of the world, as did Vera's letters, and the stories of those driving through. But Bird, inside herself, could feel no difference between one day and the next. Summer gave way to fall. One of the Giles boys married a Higgins girl. Bird received her invitation and sent the customary gift. In October, Bessie birthed another baby boy, this one named Theodore. Sometimes, she accepted Bessie and Ned's Sunday dinner invitations, and sometimes, she could not bear the thought of being squished among everyone else at the table and the brushed over awkwardness of it all.

Her life had screeched to a stop, like a train stuck on a suddenly ended track. Odelia had planned and plotted so much. Did you foresee this nothingness, Bird often asked the night. She walked the hallways to avoid sleep. She only had two dreams, one of a maze-like empty house, and the second of unknown women who brushed their lips against her nipples and moaned as their bodies pressed against hers until Bird's body exploded. She woke from one dream wanting to scream, and from the other afraid that she had.

"What you doing, Birdy?" asked Uncle Vernon easing into a chair beside her as she watched a mid-December snowstorm from the dining room table.

"Just tending the snow, Uncle. Somebody has got to," she winked at him.

"I mean what you doing with your life?" he said.

Bird shrugged. She hated feeling sorry for herself in front of him, but she was sorry and didn't see a way to fix it.

"I hope you not waiting me out?" he said.

Bird couldn't face him. "I won't leave you, Uncle Vernon."

"And if I tell you I want you to?"

"Wouldn't matter. It's me being selfish. You're all I have left."

"Nonsense," he shook his head. "You got your cousins and this whole town."

She took his hand. "Please don't say that. You know what I mean. It's the same reason you spent a lifetime with Odelia living in that little house down the lane. We aren't that different, you and me. Sometimes I wish I could have stayed that little girl following you all around the house in work pants while Maddy sewed, and Odelia napped in the wingback."

He squeezed her hand. "If I could stay for ya, little one, I would. I'll stay as long as I can, but when I go, you got to get out into the world. Odelia wanted to make you for this town, but deep down, she knew you were made for this world, Birdy. And it's waiting for you."

# August 1921

The Chicago woman drove into Bennettsville just after sunset on a Tuesday and parked in front of Johnson's Grocery. As those who passed on the story told it, she'd gone into the store and let out a "Hallelujah" to rival the angels and said she'd never been so glad to see colored folks in her life.

"Folks in Brownsville told me to make it across the state line and find a 'ville, and someone would put me up for the night. Nobody told me that every town here has a 'ville in it—Edwardsville, Belleville, Collinsville, Tuckersville, and Bennettsville. I drove through one town and, I tell ya, I'd be hanging from a tree by now if I drove any slower. Where's y'all boarding house? A woman is tired."

No one really knew what to make of the woman, and Lorna's place was full with someone else's visiting family, so they pointed her down the road to Miss Bird Bennett's house. A few minutes later, the Chicago woman stood on Bird's porch with her hand on her hip. Bird had stood behind Sue, who'd opened the door, and felt the cool, fresh air blow in with the woman.

"Mrs. Jedda Hollis," she'd said after they'd ushered her in. She was a striking brownish-red woman with high cheekbones, a mischievous curl to her smile, and curves everywhere else. She talked to Bird all through her reheated supper about coming back from a funeral in Tennessee and meeting her family in Chicago who had ventured west for another funeral.

"You're welcome to stay," said Bird working hard to hold her own in this tornado of energy.

"You don't mind if I wait a day or two for a telegram? If they need to stay out west longer, then I'll need to head there instead."

"Take as long as you need, though there isn't much to do."

"I'm happy to just sleep," said Jedda. "There won't be much of it soon enough, when my little ones get a hold of me."

Bird enjoyed the pleasant confusion and amusement that surrounded Jedda. Sue, on the other hand, sucked her teeth at every chance. "That woman don't make no sense. She need to go on home and prepare for her family's return. Something ain't right. Keep your valuables hidden in your closet." Sue's suspicions only deepened as the Chicago woman's visit lengthened into a week and then another.

"You sure you don't need to be moving on," said Sue as she laid out dinner one evening.

Bird scowled, and Jedda laced her fingers. "I hope I'm not putting you out too much. I'm not from the city and hate to be there when my husband isn't there. I'll take country life any day."

"You are welcome to stay," said Bird and ignored Sue as she huffed and puffed out of the room like an overburdened locomotive. Bird had grown to like the company in the evenings as she read or did the lacework that Vera sent. The tornado that had arrived, she suspected, had just been the bravado the woman needed to enter the town and find a place to stay. Jedda Hollis tended toward sleeping in, long walks, reflective musings at night on the newspaper, and daily checks for telegrams with Mr. Johnson. She admired the dresses Bird sketched and the ones she made, asked about the style and construction, and even described some newer styles she'd seen in other cities.

Some days when Bird could steal time, Jedda drove them around without destination until they puttered into a meadow and lay out in the sun. During their first of such ventures, Jedda offered Bird a puff from the joint she rolled. Bird thought of Sue smelling reefer on her dress, giggled, and took a dainty puff.

"Did you get this here?"

Jedda twisted her face at her like she was crazy. "I got it from Lorna like everyone else."

"Of course," said Bird and shook her head. "I thought she might have been a bit more discreet with folks visiting from out of town."

"I have a way of making people feel comfortable," said Jedda as she released two steady streams of smoke from her nostrils.

"Something tells me this town won't be same after you leave."

"You know, you are not the first person to tell me that," Jedda said with a wink and playful blown kiss. "You're welcome."

She offered Bird another puff. Bird declined; she was already starting to feel nauseous and light-headed. "Everything in moderation," she explained.

"Some things in excess," said Jedda before a deep pull and subsequent rolling laughter.

"I suggest you mind your attentions," said Sue one day, after Jedda had looked over Bird's sketches and requested a blouse.

"Excuse me," said Bird, jolted out of her amusement by the brusque tone.

"Just what I said," and she walked away. Sue's hawk eyes continued, but Bird refused to give her the satisfaction of changing her patterns. For her part, Jedda went out of her way to make chit chat and compliment Sue's everything, which only annoyed the woman further. Bird was guiltily relieved when Uncle Vernon and Sue received word of a relation in Ohio not faring well and the need for them to visit. Bird shook her head as Sue launched one last offensive on the morning of her departure.

"I believe it's best if we move you over to Miss Lorna's house. With all her sewing, Bird can't possibly do all that requires of hosting."

Jedda glanced from Sue to Bird. Uncle Vernon sighed and took up his hat.

"We'll be just fine. I've learned from the best," said Bird.

Jedda smiled, and Sue pursed her lips.

When Bessie arrived the afternoon of Sue and Vernon's departure, Bird understood that Sue had called in reinforcements.

"Just checking in," said Bessie whose theatrical skills hadn't developed much beyond what she had when they were twelve. "Haven't seen you in a while."

"Not much has been going on. Just enjoying the warming weather."

"And keeping up with your company? She's out?"

"Upstairs napping, I believe. It is nice to have fresh blood in town. We get so closed off out here, especially in the winter."

"I heard she's thinking about moving on soon," Bessie took the carafe of tea from the cooler and poured them each a glass.

"Funny, I hadn't heard that. Folks clearly don't have enough to talk about if they are making stuff up."

"She's going to have to go to her family at some point."

"Of course."

"Do you know what you're doing?"

"I believe I am well-versed in being friendly, maybe some folks around here need to study up."

"These folks around here are looking out for you. Things have been going well. No point in courting trouble."

"Excuse me, what things and what trouble?"

Bessie wiped the ring of sweat on the table from the carafe. "Things!" She looked Bird in the eye.

Bird sat back. "Ahhh, I understand. Well, you can tell folks they need to mind their own damned business."

"Some things people can't help but talk. We both know that."

"And you're talking with them now?"

"I'm carrying a message. Things been going well, settled down. It's been so hard since Odelia left us, finding the balance. Why upset it?"

"Things are going well, as long as there is a lonely and frigid Bennett woman in this house."

"Bird!" Bessie clapped her hands in shock.

Bird threw her napkin on the table. "Seems like this visit is over."

"I'm just trying to be a friend."

"Then I don't need enemies."

"Now I see why they have Sue out here supervising you," said Jedda that night as Bird stood at the stove frying their dinner.

"You're saying you don't want chicken."

"I'm saying I want wine too."

"You know where the glasses are. Wine is in the pantry."

Jedda poured their glasses and took a long sip. "Mmm, you made this?" she asked.

"My cousins down the road. Washington, DC, can't keep Bennetts from their wine."

"It seems like everybody in this town is a cousin."

"Just about. Don't worry—we import spouses."

Jedda raised her glass in the direction of the road. "Who was the woman here earlier today? A cousin too?"

"Bessie Charles Bennett."

"She's married to the headman, right? I've not had the honor. You two seem about as good a mix as hot grease and cold water."

"Then I guess you heard all that?"

"Open windows. I couldn't get mine to shut." She winked.

"We were close once. In the years after my mother died."

"What happened?"

"Same thing that always happens—life."

Jedda sipped her wine and shook her head. "That's happened to me a few times too. Your mother died when you were . . . ?" Jedda let the questions ending hang.

"Thirteen."

"I'm sorry," her tone was sincere and sobered. She stood silent for a moment and then seemed shaken as she realized Bird was watching her. "I was thinking of my children. Our babies think us all powerful when we feel so powerless. I fear they won't ever understand."

Hearing these words as if from a deep well of pain, Bird tried to speak to it, to say what she could to any of Maddy's pain that lingered in the house. "They understand," she said. "And they will be okay. I had my grandmother and others to help soothe hurt."

"The famous Miss Odelia," said Jedda.

Bird sipped again. It was strange how all the titles shifted after her Granny's death. Granny had become Miss Odelia, and Bird became Miss Bird. Bessie was Mrs. Bennett. There was no need for a "Miss Bennett," or no desire for one. "She did well by me." Bird stood too quickly in an attempt to use clearing the table as a way to step away from the conversation's turn. She lost her footing and nearly sent the dish sliding off the table.

Jedda secured the dish with one hand and Bird's wrist with the other.

"Wine and fine dishes don't complement each other. I'll clear the table."

The pressure on her wrist was firm. Bird could feel the softness of Jedda's fingers and the woman's strength. Jedda smelled of rose water. Had they never stood so close?

"You are my guest," Bird said through her clouded thoughts.

Jedda sucked her teeth. "That's enough of that for tonight."

"Then you'll pardon me if I take some air?"

"That sounds like an excellent idea."

Bird sank onto the back steps and tried to cry as quietly as possible as the dishes clinked in the kitchen and Jedda hummed. I'm just a silly girl, she chastised herself and pushed the ache of desire as far down as possible.

The full moon rose as Bird gathered her dignity. She came to herself as Jedda sat beside her and nudged her to take a glass of water.

"You alright?"

"I will be. How about you?"

"In this moment, yes?"

"And the next?"

"That's the question, isn't it?" Jedda stretched her arms into the night and pulled herself up. "We should sleep this off."

Bird reached for her arm. "Can we sit for a few more minutes? It's been nice having someone to sit and enjoy the evening with."

"Then you are a romantic," Jedda said.

Bird's head snapped up, but Jedda stepped further into the night. Bird blushed at the constancy of her silliness but stood too and walked a few paces behind her.

"I've never understood this garden," Jedda said.

Bird chuckled. "It's a garden designed for smelling more than seeing. My grandmother was blind. She preferred to smell the lavender first, then hyacinth, gardenia, and freesia, and finally the roses."

"All these weeks and no one ever mentioned that." She turned back, and Bird wanted to memorize her silhouette in the moonlight.

"I guess it doesn't matter much now. She saw plenty of things—things that most people miss."

Bird had not felt the tear on her cheek until Jedda reached up and wiped it. Not thinking, and not completely sure why she did it—need, desire, familiarity, pain, loneliness, all of this—Bird nestled into the touch and savored the second that her face rested against this hand. Jedda cleared her throat and slipped her hand back into the apron Bird usually wore.

Bird almost choked on her horror and embarrassment. "I'm so sorry. I didn't mean anything," she stammered.

Jedda was pensive and stiff. "We should turn in." She turned and left Bird in the night.

Bird paced her room trying to think of anything she could say to fix this mess. She was a jumble of panic, confusion, and frustration. And there had been the wine. She collapsed on her bed and heard Odelia's instruction to mind her dress, so she hung it up. Odelia couldn't argue too much about sleeping in a slip. But sleep would not come. Fretting over what to say in the morning, Bird tossed and turned between the implausible and the stupid. Eventually, she determined that more wine was the easiest solution to end the long night.

"I'd advise against the habit," Jedda said from the living room shadows.

Bird almost dropped the bottle.

"And I'd advise against lurking in the shadows," said Bird, annoyed as she replaced the cork.

Jedda laughed. "I'm not lurking, just using the moonlight to write by."

Bird slouched into the wingtip. Jedda was a posed statue at the window seat with a hardback book, paper, and pen in her lap.

"But now, the note is unnecessary. My telegram came the other day. I'm heading back north in the morning. I appreciate the hospitality and am sorry to have stayed too long."

"You didn't say anything about it."

"We were having so much fun worrying Sue, and I didn't want to give her the satisfaction. But now, I see I've got the whole town riled up."

Bird's chest and cheeks burned with shame. "I'm sorry, I didn't mean anything. The loneliness is too much sometimes."

Jedda placed her writing tools beside her. "I know. Sometimes the starkness of the relief makes it seem all that much worse when the relief ends." She regarded Bird for a long moment and then said, "Bird, I reached for you first."

Confused, Bird replayed the moment of indiscretion. Jedda's hand had risen slowly and rested with gentleness. Bird had reacted to her own longing and missed the other pertinent details about the touch.

"I didn't mean to mislead you."

"You left so abruptly."

Jedda laughed. "I'm good at exits. It's a skill I recommend. And so tomorrow, I will make a grand one." She headed to the steps, and Bird jumped to intercept her. "You are a girl, Bird, and I . . . I . . ."

"I'm the woman of this house," said Bird.

"Bird, you are twenty-one, and I'm thirty-two with children and a husband, as rocky as that all may be."

"I understand that you have to go back but not tomorrow."

"Then what do you want, Bird?"

"The same as you. A few days of relief." Bird held Jedda's eyes, and her own breath as she stepped in closer. She ignored the remnants of her silliness and insecurity.

A curious smile played on Jedda's lips, and with a swift lean in, Bird kissed it. Her body both thrilled and ached as Jedda's arms slid around her neck and their bodies clung to one another. Jedda tugged at Bird's bottom lip and started to pull her toward her room.

"My room," said Bird, "I'll explain in the morning."

"Are you going to tell me your story now?" said Bird as they lay tangled in bed in the morning light.

"My story?"

"Why you been here for weeks, and where you going back to?"

Jedda turned onto her back. "I've told most of it. I'm going back to Chicago to my husband and son and daughter. They've just been there, never have left. My husband gets mad sometimes, and it's best if I go away."

"Mad about what?" Bird kissed her forehead.

"Stuff I can't control. We married when I was sixteen, and I've done my best to be a good wife. But he wants a woman with passion for him, and some things the body just can't fake. I had a crush on a girl when I was eighteen or nineteen, and he figured it out. Ever since then, he accuses and shouts and sends me away when he thinks my attentions have wandered. Funny thing is, I've told him he can do whatever he wants and bring home any baby he needs to, but that's not enough. So, I go away and wait until he calls me back, and it starts all over again."

"Could you leave?"

"I wouldn't ever see my kids again. They already don't know what to make of me or the situation. What about you, what are you going to do?" asked Jedda, rolling on her side to face Bird.

"I don't know what to do or where to go. I just know that I shouldn't stay here. There has never been anything for me here."

"Bessie Bennett seemed to think you have a future here," Jedda said.

"Bessie Bennett was part of the whole start of this mess," said Bird. "She loved me and married my cousin."

"That old story," said Jedda, giving Bird's ribs a soft tickle.

This did get a laugh out of Bird. "It seems that everyone here is okay if I'm the next Odelia—frigid and lonely, and only speaking when called on."

"Why not go to St. Louis? It sounds like your aunts adore you."

Bird shook her head. "Like this house, that town isn't for me. It's the Minister's and his family. I thought once that maybe I could squeeze in, but it would be just like here."

"Then what are you going to do?"

"You could come visit every summer, and we could scandalize folks."

"Something tells me you won't be here next summer."

Bird considered this and raised her hand into the sunlight. Jedda matched it and curled her fingers around Bird's. "I want to savor this day."

"Then let's do just that."

Bird hung the laundry as the car drove Uncle Vernon and Sue down the lane. She waved and took up her basket to meet them at the porch steps. A Giles boy tipped his hat to her as he hustled the suitcases out of the trunk.

"You are a sight for sore eyes," said Uncle Vernon. Holding on to Bird's waiting hand, he heaved himself out of the car. When stable on his feet, he planted a whiskery kiss on her cheek and then retrieved his hand. "I'm old and tired, but not that old and tired, Birdy."

Sue bustled around them, "Are you old and tired enough to get yourself up those stairs and occupied while I get dinner on."

"There's chicken stew on the stove," Bird said and took up a suitcase.

Sue gave her an appraising look that, in the end, signaled some type of reluctant approval.

"I got to get out this suit, and then I'll be up to the house."

"You can eat just fine in that," Sue said.

"Not no stew."

The Giles boy glanced at Bird and shook his head as if to say he'd had a long car ride of this. He opened the back door. "Come on, Uncle Vernon. I'll ride you back down the lane."

Vernon grinned at them and then climbed back into the car. Sue frowned as the car drove back down the lane. "Don't let that slow rollin' fool you. That Giles boy drive too fast and stop too hard." She looked around the yard and back to the barn. "Miss Jedda has departed us?"

"She left this morning." Bird tried not to flinch under Sue's studious gaze.

"Tis for the best. Nothing about that woman made sense."

"She made sense to me," said Bird as she took up her basket and left Sue standing with whatever questions this assertion raised.

# February 1922

The morning Vernon Bennett died, the ice on Bennettsville's tree branches dazzled like diamonds in the sunlight. The winter had been especially hard, and by November, the women had forced him to move into the big house. Sue had threatened to march through the snow to collect his belongings herself.

"This house weren't meant for me." Vernon had protested.

Bird had reached out and placed her hand on his. "Nothing in this whole wide land was meant for any of us, Uncle. But we've done the best we can." And with that, he had acquiesced. When he had the first stroke in mid-December, he complained that the house was making him soft. His body and mind weakened in the following weeks, but he sat up daily in his dress shirt and suit pants to grant an audience to those who came to visit him. Word had spread through town, and it seemed like no one could bear to let him go without a goodbye. He accepted their kisses with a half-smile, and those who took his hand received the best he could do as a squeeze.

When finally, on the second to last day when he could rise no more, Sue sent word that his transition had begun and those who hadn't been able to visit could offer prayers and thanks to greet him on the other side. Bird, Fred, Lorna, and Sue sat with him the last day and night. He fought to hold on, and Sue was lovingly terse with him. "We'll be fine, you old goat," she said, and he groaned his protest. For once though, he could not see her and the way his suffering and laboring weighed on them.

It was Lorna who had known the words to release him. The woman had knelt beside him and whispered in his ear. "Your Mama and Ezra are here for you. They have as much to say as you do."

Vernon's eyes opened and glanced around the room, landing and lingering on the open bedroom door. He inhaled deeply and exhaled, one last time.

Bennettsville closed down for him. The weather warmed a bit and eased the burden of those who trekked on foot to the church, from the church to the cemetery, and finally back to the Bennett house. The house was so full and everyone so close, they had to throw the doors and windows open.

Bird just wanted to sleep and think about her uncle. The last few years of her life had been a meditation on Odelia and Vernon. She tried to hold onto every bit of them that she could. A foresight she'd been too young to have as her mother had wasted away. She understood that those moments together were like the few last warm breezes of fall before winter descended on her life and never left.

# July 1922

Bird's gaze traced the high arched entrance to the LaSalle Street Station. Like Chicago itself, the station stood as a monument to the fortitude of stone and the human imagination. In this heart of the city, even the blue sky battled for prominence. She'd used the hours between her connections to walk to the river, window shop, and procure a couple of sandwiches for the trip. Bird almost laughed aloud when she thought of the ticket to New York City in her purse. Porters carted the trunks of the white men and women in fine suits and silk dresses and stockings. They'd ride the 20th Century Limited and drink from crystal for their sixteen hours, while she'd ride for two days, but get there just the same.

A lanky porter with coloring and a toothy smile that reminded her of Vernon slipped her suitcase from her hand. He checked his pocket watch, "I've time to assist one more passenger to her train," he said.

"Oh, I'm not on the Limited," she stammered.

"Maybe on your way back."

Bird blushed. His eyes roved as he led her through the crowd, anticipating even the subtlest movements around them.

"Never gone so far?" he asked.

"No," she said. "And I'm not coming back."

"Home for us," he lowered his voice, "is where our people is. You gon' find good people in that city. I can tell just by looking at you. It won't be the first people you meet. Those first folks will smell the country on you and try you. You get yourself some city clothes and hair, you'll look like everybody else except the nice will shine through on you, and then your people will find you."

Bird couldn't help but pat her hair and glance down at her traveling dress. It took everything she had not to sniff her sleeve. Did she smell country?

Chicago's ruler-straight streets gave way to rowhouse neighborhoods and then smatterings of lone homes, until the train chugged through the countryside. Every once in a while, people—sometimes colored and sometimes white, almost always in worn out clothes and with somber mouths—stopped their labor to watch the train pass. It was strange to see these glimpses of other lands that were both so familiar and so foreign. She knew the lethargy of these lives and the pull of something from across the hills and plains. Although, for her, an excising push out of Bennettsville had aided the pull.

The deepened creases in Vera's forehead as they parted in St. Louis had been warning enough about her New York City experiment. Bird had feared that her aunt would call the Minister to issue some threat or confiscate her money. But Vera had stayed her hand and let Bird toddle off into the unknown. If only Maddy had lived, Bird thought as the day outside dimmed, we could have left Bennettsville together, her in this seat right next to me. Maddy would have taken New York City by the neck and refused to release it until it had submitted to them. Bird feared that she'd cry and embarrass herself but found no tears. She'd cried the last of them out at the cemetery as she stood over Maddy, Odelia, and Vernon's graves and explained that Bennettsville was not the whole of her story.

Two days later, with sore legs and a cramped neck, Bird reconsidered the magnitude of any battle to subdue New York City. She rode the last stretch into Manhattan pressed to her window, country-ness be damned. The buildings and people defied counting and even physics. How could any little island hold all of this, and she could only see a sliver? The gray and brown buildings stood with an austere air, as if to say, we'll be here long after you all have passed on. We are the city, not you.

If the LaSalle Street station had impressed her, Grand Central made her want to surrender and marvel. The stone pillars held up the heavens themselves. She ignored the jostling and groans of those swirling around her and laid claim to the awe of this moment. Her moment. She stood in her childhood dreams made real.

Bird took the first exit she found out of Grand Central; the signs may as well have been in a different language. She panicked a bit when she considered that she was on 42nd Street and needed to be on 137th Street. The city and its people buzzed around her. I'm not the first to arrive untethered, she soothed herself. I can count, and I can walk one hundred blocks if I must! With a deep breath and humble tone, she stopped a colored woman whose dress was as modest as her own.

"Harlem?" she asked.

The woman glanced back and forth between Bird and the direction she'd been walking. "You've got to get to the Main Line and head uptown," she said hurriedly. Bird teased out the slight remnants of a southern drawl, but the Main Line meant nothing to her.

"I can't be late for work, or I'd take you." The woman seemed genuinely sorry. "Walk three blocks that way and you'll see the stairs down into the station. Give your money to the man in the booth and make sure you head uptown."

"Thank you, Miss," said Bird.

"Good luck!" said the woman with a wave.

"I can and will do this," said Bird setting out in the direction indicated. "Just walk with me, Mama."

With the assistance of Eileen and her church's Ladies Auxiliary, Bird had secured lodging in an apartment on 137th Street. Her hosts, an elderly retired couple, added acclimating her to the city and finding her a beau to their usual pastimes of cleaning, Bible studying, and stoop chatting. By her third week with the Williamses, Bird was certain that there was a block-long list of eligible bachelors scheduled to join them for dinner a few nights a week.

During the day, she window-shopped for sewing machines and explored the fabric stores in Harlem and downtown. She gawked at the high price and low quality of the fruits and vegetables, and the number of both that she didn't recognize at all. After several days surveying

Harlem's fashions, she purchased two blouses and skirts off the rack, both big so she could visit a couple of seamstresses to check their processes and prices. The first woman owned a hole of a shop on 131st Street and wound in all kinds of advice about city living. This was done so skillfully that Bird didn't know what to think when she quoted a price six times what Vera would have charged and then told Bird not to tell anyone about the discount.

The second woman worked out of her home on 129th Street and matched Bird's suspiciousness.

"I thought all you country gals knowed how to sew."

Bird smiled as sweetly as she could. "I was the baby and marked for teaching."

The woman looked her up and down and was not impressed. "Even a teaching woman should know enough to make her children's clothes."

"So I've heard more than once over the years."

The woman sighed and quoted Bird a price much more in line with her expectations.

After weeks with no success in finding Bird a suitable beau, Mrs. Williams started fretting over the cost of such frequent dinner guests and the difficulties of the Christian duties foisted upon her; Bird sought other accommodations. The room for rent ads in the colored papers were either vague enough to be useless or unabashed about their lies. There were plenty of for rent signs around Harlem; she would rely on her eyes and luck.

With just three stories, the red brick brownstone stood short and squat beside its taller, sandstone neighbors. Bird appreciated the house's character. A black wrought-iron fence protected a garden of lilacs, lilies, and gardenias in terra-cotta planters. The tiny yard garden held spotless white iron chairs and a matching table.

Bird rang the doorbell to the garden-level apartment. After a moment of silence, she knocked on the window, as she'd learned this was not considered rude in New York City.

"Don't rush me," shouted a voice from inside the apartment. A curtain slid aside, and two large brown eyes set in a long brown face looked Bird up and down. The window curtain closed.

"Yes, miss," said the woman who opened the door and stepped from the shadows, her wide smile emerging like the sun from parted clouds.

Bird exhaled. "Good day, ma'am. I'm Bird Bennett, and I've come about the apartment for rent."

The woman's eyes gathered at their corners, her lips knotted, and she studied Bird for another moment. Bird stood expectant and still until the woman motioned for her to back up and exited into the yard area. She had to be sixty years old, Bird figured, and no less than six feet tall. She wore a simple apron over a heather gray house dress. Her thin graying hair rested in two plaits. She walked on legs that seemed stiff as sticks, though this didn't slow her down much.

"I'm Mrs. Louise Hurtis. Where you from? And who yo' people?"

"I'm from Bennettsville, Illinois, and my people are the Bennetts, ma'am."

Louise's eyes gave nothing away.

"And how do you earn yo' livin'?"

"I'm a dressmaker, and I do alterations."

"Good steady work. And what's yo' gentleman caller's name, and what he do?"

"Excuse me?" asked Bird, though she knew this routine.

"Yo' boyfriend?"

"I don't have a boyfriend, ma'am."

Louise narrowed her eyes. "That's what all y'all young gals say these days. Then I hear giggling and sneaking around and footsteps too heavy for a little gal like yourself. We'll see."

"I guess we will."

The apartment was simple with a large front room, open kitchen and dining room, and good-sized bedroom with a French-doored side room. Bird imagined a waiting area for her customers by the living room window and her work and storage space along the adjacent wall.

"I'd need to use the space for sewing and measuring customers. I'd limit the hours of course."

"I got no problem with honest work in this house."

Bird took this as a good omen. "It's perfect then, and I can pay you for the first three months up front."

Louise tsked at her. "I'll take just the first two. I bet you don't got a lick of furniture to your name. Get yo'self set up. This here's a hard city; a woman needs at least a little comfort where she lays her head."

# PART III

# February 1928

The last pick-up of the day left after talking Bird's ear off for ten minutes. Bird finally cut the woman off with the excuse that she needed to flip her sign lest others try to run in. Hearing Louise's slow plod on the stairs, Bird left the door open and scooted to stir the stew on the stove.

"One of your packages," said Louise, tossing the large manila envelope of correspondence collected by Bird's lawyer in East St. Louis on the kitchen table.

"Your check's there," said Bird.

"I thank you," said Louise. "The new girl, Irma, says she's starting her move-in early in the morning."

Bird shrugged; she'd lost count of the girls who'd come and gone in the third-floor apartment. What was one more? "I just hope she don't drag her chairs like that last one."

"I put it in the lease," said Louise, pulling down the bowls from the cabinet. "Rent is due on the first, call the landlord for any problem with the drains, and if you drag yo' chairs, you answer to the second-floor tenant."

"It's about time!" said Bird, ladling the stew into their bowls.

"Plans for the evening?" asked Louise.

Bird looked around her. "Seems to me I've already started my plans."

"How you know I don't got after-dinner plans?"

"You're already in your house dress Louise, and it's not even 6:30."

"Don't want to spill nothing on my finery."

Bird chuckled and shook her head.

Louise shimmied her sharp-edged shoulders. "You don't know me; I might change my mind."

"Don't let me stand in your way." Bird added a pinch of salt to both their bowls.

Louise nodded in appreciation and waved for a bit more. "You know I can't taste things the same. Just don't want you to feel obligated."

"I'm not obligated," said Bird, "If I had a dime for every time I've told you that, I could ship salt directly from the Red Sea."

Louise refused to accept that New York City had done just what Bird had hoped, absorbed her without question or notation. In the first few years, she'd sometimes made the rounds at readings and political meetings and received the occasional soiree invitations. Eventually, she lost interest. She read for enjoyment, not argument. She had no taste for heavy drinking or late nights. She was surprised that a dinner and an evening cup of tea with Louise had become her favorite Friday night activity. The woman had a sharp wit, good commentary on the day, and didn't broker in mean gossip. There was a strong religious streak that Bird navigated, although this wasn't hard since Louise wasn't much for church going herself.

"Just know I'm praying for yo' young man," said Louise, cutting a large piece of beef down to size.

"What young man?"

"The one who clearly ain't got no sense of direction since he ain't found you yet."

"Louise," Bird sighed.

Louise ignored her annoyance. "Open your package. What's happening in Bennettsville?"

Mrs. Charles's twice-yearly reports served as Bird's most consistent source of updates on her hometown and kin. Lorna sent notes three or four times a year, usually recounting some memory she'd had about Maddy or Odelia. The notes tend to start with something like "I was recalling the other day and was sure that Maddy would have wanted me to tell you about the time . . ." Most of the musings were humorous anecdotes that Maddy would not have told herself, like the time as a girl that she'd poked one time too many at the Harper's goose and hollered the whole quarter mile it chased her down the road.

In contrast, Mrs. Charles's notes were brief and politely impersonal, so much to the point that she often just passed them across the table for Louise to read for herself. This letter started like the others and then diverged.

Dear Bird,
I hope this letter finds you well. All is well here in Bennettsville. The winter was hard, but an early spring has more than made up for the hardship. Ned and Bessie finally welcomed a girl in early March, Jean. She's plump, demanding, and if you miss a beat, she lets you know. STEDDY (what Everett calls Sed and Theodore) don't know what to make of her since she's already running them around. Ned and Bessie send their regards, as does Everett.

The planting was a little early, so we plan to eke out a couple of extra weeks of the summer session. Here's to hoping against a late frost. The student body will be thirty-seven for the summer session. We graduated six students from the eighth grade at the end of winter session (a record for us). Mabel Simmons's aunt in St. Louis is going to enroll her in the ninth grade there. We are praying on her focus and success. I've included a separate chart with the usual breakdowns by grade level.

I also write to announce that Mr. Charles and I will be moving up north to be nearer my sister at the end of the summer session. We have loved our years in Bennettsville and have been so thankful to share the love of learning with those who are now kin by blood and law. Now that our children are settled, I'd like to spend this next stage of my life with my sister.

I (and many others) do hope that you will return before too long. Bennettsville can't glitter like New York City, but it was built by your mothers' hands and the will of the Lord. As Matthew 7:25 says, "The rain came down, the streams rose, and the winds blew and beat against that house; yet it did not fall, because it had its foundation on the rock." And that rock is our salvation. Please know that I have always prayed for you as I pray for my own children.
With affection,
Helena

Bird didn't notice that her hand shook until Louise touched it. Louise gently tugged the letter away and lay it face down on Bird's side of the table.

"You okay?"

"I'm just surprised." Bird's mind raced from Bennettsville back to Harlem. Things that were known in the former were unknown in the latter. "The schoolteachers are leaving, moving north." She considered what little truth she could offer. "I didn't leave on the best terms with them. And it seems there's no sorting it out now." Had she believed she and Helena would reconcile one day? She heard the creaking of a lid opening somewhere between her heart and her stomach. A note of pain wafted through her, and she forced the lid shut again.

"The Lord moves in mysterious ways. Trust in him," advised Louise.

Bird glanced up at her, "If life has taught me anything, it's that there's not much to trust."

"Then I was right, the Lord done sent you here for me to tarry with you. Some folks can't tarry alone."

"If that means friendship, Louise, I won't turn it away."

That night Bird lay in bed re-reading and considering the letter, all that it said, and everything it left unsaid. Bessie had three children and a town to lead to show for herself. Was Helena saying that she'd been right all along—that there was some cosmic lesson that Bird still hadn't learned? She was even lapsed as a prodigal child.

Bird wanted to laugh as she considered what they must all imagine of her life in New York City—liquor filled and women crazy. If these walls could talk. There'd been one woman, during Bird's second year in the city. A quiet woman a few years older than Bird. Every couple of months, she brought in a dress for taking in, modest dresses made for office work. On her first three visits, she'd said little and submitted to Bird's measurements with closed eyes. On the fourth visit, she arrived just as Bird prepared to flip her sign and asked to try on the finished dress before taking it home. Bird turned back to her work to give a moment of privacy, and when she turned back around, the woman stood nude on the measuring box with her arms at her side and her lips pursed tight—as if daring Bird to deny the truth they both knew about the other.

Bird reached first for the woman's face and her stomach fluttered at the simple pleasure of touching her cheek. Raised on measuring folks, her clients' parts were merely things to be lessened or accented. She was the illusionist who pressed and tucked their bodies into fabrics and made them into who they wanted to be. She'd touched breasts, lifted buttocks, and made space for penises. She'd never touched one of their faces. The woman kissed the palm of Bird's hand and then her wrist. Before she left in the morning's wee hours, the woman had said she would not be back, and she kept her word.

The new girl did move in early. As she buried her head under a pillow, Bird figured she must have gotten the early bird rate for those who don't care if their new neighbors hate them. When Irma knocked on her door at eight o'clock exactly, Bird gave up any hope for friendly neighbor relations.

"You must be Bird," Irma said as soon as Bird opened the door. She stood a head taller than Bird and wore a jacket and skirt ensemble that screamed Helena Charles.

Bird stepped back from the woman's friendly enough, but sharp eyes. "Yes, I am."

"It's a pleasure. Miss Louise has told me all about you."

"Did she now?"

Irma chuckled as she tracked a mover carrying a lamp. "That's for the bedroom, northeast corner, please," she instructed the man. "I figured since I'm making all this ruckus, I should at least introduce myself."

"You're just moving to the city?" Bird did her best with the paltry small talk skills inherited from Maddy.

"Moving back," explained Irma. "I'm getting settled, and my fiancée Rupert will be joining me when he's done in the service. We'll be here just long enough to save for own place."

"Congratulations. Let me know if you need anything."

"Thank you. Well, I should let you get back to . . ."

"Yes, thank you," said Bird barely pausing before she shut the door.

"Maddy Bennett, I am certainly your child," Bird said aloud as she sat at her kitchen table already regretting her brusqueness and thinking about baking something to round the edges of this rocky start. Just don't let the woman be a schoolteacher, she thought.

# April 1928

The thing about New York City, that Bird would realize much later in life, is that you never notice changes as they happen. One old store closes and a new one opens and becomes part of the landscape. Like one building coming down and another going up. Folks moving on to the block and folks moving away. The changes get integrated as easily as air in the lungs. Most people don't notice the little changes that add up to big changes. Or the small pivot points that later are recognized as forks in the road or dead ends.

Irma turned out to be a pleasant enough hospital record keeper. A year later, she brought home Rupert who was six feet and five inches tall. Bird immediately feared for Irma's ability to feed this man and safely birth his babies. For his part, Rupert calmed his fiancée, and Bird came to appreciate the echo of his laugh throughout the building. She also appreciated that he had no qualms about asking if she ever offered a "wedding dress discount for an upstairs neighbor." He'd nearly doubled over with laughter when she answered that she did, but most folks never forgave her afterward.

Bird would have been happy for her New York City living to continue in this way and couldn't have imagined anything that would have upset too much since Louise hardly raised the rents. And then came the woman needing trousers. Bird knew little about most of her clientele, just their measurements, preferences for cuts, and that they could pay. They streamed through her apartment just as white people had moved through her mother's house—the less said, the better. This earned her a more specialized clientele willing to pay more for her services and tip well for her discretion—people who coveted designer imitations, scandalous unmentionables, or gifts that didn't match the proportions of their husbands or wives. Bird took the orders and asked only the necessary questions. When one of the men she regularly made shirts for asked about the trouser-needing woman, Bird handed him her card.

Leah arrived in gabardine trousers several sizes too big and an ill-fitting button-down shirt. Bird took it all in and frowned.

Leah stepped back, "Charlie told me it was all right."

It took a moment for Bird to decipher the woman's suddenly wide and frightened eyes.

She brushed away Leah's concern. "I'll sew you whatever you want. It just looks like we're gonna have to start your wardrobe over from the beginning." She pointed at the button that wouldn't close because Leah's cup-runneth-over hips wouldn't fit into the unforgiving men's shirt, and where the shirt badly needed darts to create room for her breasts. "Come in and undress down to your underclothes, so I can get your true measurements."

"I'm not used to women being so forward." Leah grinned, moving with an impressive smoothness for her five feet ten inches.

"Seamstresses and doctors, we're not shy—and we're not cheap."

Bird worked methodically and talked Leah through her colors and fabrics—heather blues to compliment her ochre coloring and breathing fabrics like cotton and linen. She pointed out styles like single-breasted suit jackets and lower-waisted pants that gave the sense of masculinity while working with her height and curves.

"Where you from?" Leah asked.

"Illinois."

"Everybody open there, like you?"

"No. That's why I left."

"What did you want them to be open about?" Leah gave her a sly smile.

"Button-down collars," said Bird.

Leah came to Bird's once a month to pick up one order and place the next. After the second visit, she stopped trying to make small talk. Although she would sneak in the occasional question that Bird made short work of.

"You go to church?"

"No," said Bird. The following questions about any family in New York, friends, and hobbies all elicited the same response.

Bird felt Leah trying to piece together the puzzle she presented, and in her quiet moments after Leah's appointments, she found herself amused. As she sewed, she added little flourishes that she might have charged extra for but didn't.

Leah arrived late for her appointment in September. Bird pointed her to a chair while she finished up a seam on her machine. "Your watch broke?" she asked Leah when she finished up.

"No, sorry. I was delayed at work."

How would this woman describe her line of employment? Bird was curious but held fast to her rule.

"You're a wizard at that machine. I only ever saw my mother sew with that kind of speed."

"She didn't teach you anything?"

"Big girls like me end up in the fields. More money in picking cotton than sewing the family's rags together." She raised her hands, large and calloused even from city work. "You give lessons?"

"Here and there, mostly teaching daughters on the block how to mend and repair, if their mothers never learned."

"Can you teach me?"

Bird laughed. "You trying to put me out of business?"

"Never that. Just curious."

Bird retrieved a leftover cutting. "Sit down, let's see if you got it. It's all about knowing how to get the machine and your hands to work together."

"I know how to work with my hands," Leah raised an eyebrow.

Bird ignored her and placed the fabric under the foot.

"You got the pedal? Now just press it and guide the fabric straight. Don't force it, just guide it."

Forgetting herself, Bird placed her fingers on Leah's to guide them and then jerked them back. Leah seemed not to notice as she twisted and turned the fabric while figuring out how to control the speed.

"Do I have it?" Leah asked once the machine purred and stitched a straight seam.

"With a little work. But I doubt you have the time."

"That's true. At least, it's good to know that I could've."

Bird moved aside so Leah could find the door.

"My clothes?" Leah pointed at the shirt and slacks hanging on the rack.

"Sorry," Bird laughed at herself.

"Some of the others I work with, like mine and Charlie's clothes. Maybe you could come down this Saturday, and I can introduce you around. Get you some more business."

"I've got about all the business I can handle. If someone is really interested, and you think they're all right, you can bring them with you next time."

Leah opened her mouth as if to try a new angle.

"Please, don't." Bird looked away.

"Am I wrong?"

Bird met her eye, "No, you're not wrong. I've lived here long enough to see the road you walk and where it leads." Bird didn't agree with the temperance laws and didn't think much of the folks behind them. But the underground scene seemed like one bad turn following another.

"I come to your place every month. I've seen your road; you ain't never seen mine. Let me take you out, just as a friend. I promise. New York City is no place for folks who want to be left alone."

"But it is."

Bird's memory tried to soften her half of the conversation when Leah missed her appointment the next month and the month after that, but the truth was what it was.

# October 1928

Bird buttoned and then unbuttoned her overcoat twice as she walked the long boulevard to the back entrance of Leah's club. Leah had only ever seen her in plain house dresses and aprons. As Bird planned her outfit, she knew if there was ever a time for effort, this was it. She'd bought the calf-length, brown linen coat hoping the wide herringbone collar said classy but casual—like she wore it every day. But letting the coat hang open showed off the auburn crepe de chine blouse that highlighted her eyes—another procurement just for the trip.

After a groan of frustration with herself, she left the coat unbuttoned and pulled open the rear entrance door. "I have a package I'd like delivered." She said to the skinny, gray-haired man sitting beside a beat-up host stand just inside the door.

"Ms. Bentley don't accept gifts."

"It's for Leah. It's a shirt I owe her. I'm her seamstress."

He gave her a brighter, appraising look. "You wanna make a shirt for me?"

"No. Will you give it to her?"

"I'm not a delivery boy. Somebody get Big Lee. She's got a delivery." He shouted down the dim corridor behind him, and a boy of no more than ten poked his head out of a doorway. "You heard me," the doorman shouted, and the boy took off running.

Bird stepped back against the wall and waited. She hadn't expected the club to be so dingy. Young women skittered through the back hall in pitiful excuses for costumes that were much more glitter than actual fabric. Big men moved in and out of doors, shouting profanities. The doorman looked at Bird and shrugged. "Rehearsal for a new show," he explained.

As he spoke, a woman in a golden leotard and train that shimmered like the sun when it caught the light strode toward them with a strut bold enough to impress Cleopatra. Her lips curled like a haughty cat. "Lee says she isn't expecting any packages and doesn't need any." She stopped to savor Bird's reaction, a shocked silence, before whipping the train around and heading back down the hall.

"Hell, nah," said the doorman. "That gal is evil. And evil got enough advantages. Give me the shirt, lady. I'll get it to Lee. I wish somebody could've have saved me from just half the evil women I got mixed up with. If it works out, my name is Samson, and I look good in baby blue."

Bird spent a few days listening for the door as she sewed. She minimized her trips out and shortened her baths before giving up. Maybe Leah had sent the golden ostrich with that message. She resigned herself to once again attending readings and speeches. On a Friday night, she dressed in a modest but flattering suit to attend a debate. She stopped on the second step. Leah stood at the bottom of her stoop.

"I owe you for the shirt," said Leah, reaching into her pocket.

"It was a gift."

"Where you going? Can I walk you?"

"To a debate. If that's the way you going."

"Ahh, to the respectable negroes."

"Aren't I respectable?"

"Are you?"

Bird blushed. "I'm not sure what I did to give you the impression that I was anything but."

Leah stopped. "My apologies. I won't bother you no more."

Bird's head spun. How had everything gone so wrong so fast? She grabbed Leah's arm.

"What's happening here?"

Leah turned, the hurt in her eyes made Bird catch her breath. "I thought since you sewed for me, and then sent me the shirt, that you could be interested in me."

"I am interested."

"But you're going off to those respectable fools."

"Aren't you respectable?"

Leah howled. "Everybody knows everything there is to know about me."

"Wait, what does respectable mean to you?"

"What does it mean to you?"

"It means I'm discerning and selective about the company I keep."

"But do you tell people? Did they know where you're from?"

Bird glanced at Louise's apartment and sighed as she proved Leah's point. "Walk with me," she said moving them out of earshot. "No one here knows. It hasn't really come up. There was no hiding it in a little country town."

"Here, most folks hide it. They'll hug and kiss up on you in some back room and act like they don't know you in the light of day. Me walking you to that debate will end your respectability."

"Is it just as simple as hiding it? People have to look out for their livelihoods. I'd like to spend time with you. But I also need to keep my living situation and clientele. Where do the unrespectables go?"

"Buffet flats, whist parties, and dinner clubs at people's apartments and houses. You don't know that? How long you been here?"

"Six years. I went to some readings when I first got here, but never seemed to click in. I figured I was just too country. And I didn't really think I'd find anyone here anyway. Until . . ." They stopped at the corner, and Leah pulled them back against the shadowed wall of the corner market.

"Until . . . ?" Leah grinned and stepped a little closer.

"Until you stopped coming by." Bird scowled at her for making her say it aloud and tried not to obviously look out for neighbors among the endless stream of people entering and exiting the store.

"Why don't you come with me to work tonight."

"I don't like that scene."

"You ever been to my club?"

"The back door."

"Well, you done seen the respectable scene. At least come look at the other side. Then, you can decide what you want to do."

"I already know what I want to do."

Leah raised both eyebrows, and Bird blushed again. "I want to get to know you better," she clarified.

"You might as well see the parts you're worried about. If you can't take those, no point waiting around a few months and falling for everything else." Bird didn't resist when Leah pressed her hand against her back to guide her as they retraced their steps back to her apartment.

Bird cut her eyes at the over-sized ego in front her. "Can I go dressed like this?"

"You look like a secretary."

"I don't have much else."

"You at least gotta lose the blazer."

Bird cringed. The blazer made her look smart. She remembered the ostrich woman and figured that looking smart wasn't the point. She excused herself to return the blazer to her place and check her make-up. In reality, she barreled into her apartment, stripped off the jacket and blouse and tore through her closet before slamming the door in frustration. She ripped a red satin blouse sewn for a customer off her pick-up rack. Please don't let me run into Lily Burns tonight, she thought. Somehow, with just two hands, she re-applied her lipstick, added a bit of rouge, and traded her French braid for a French roll.

She caught her breath before opening the front door and hoped that Leah would interpret her use of the stoop's handrail as elegant—as opposed to a needed crutch since she could hardly feel her legs.

Leah whistled. "If you clean up like that in just five minutes, next time, I'll give you ten."

"Make it fifteen, please, so I can use the restroom," said Bird.

"Hey, it's the seamstress." Samson took Bird's hand and kissed it.

"My friend, baby blue."

"Remember, baby girl, I got these long arms."

"Size 20 neck?"

"Hey, you good," he said with an approving nod to Leah.

Leah tried to sit her at a table, but Bird insisted on a far corner of the bar. "I'd be sitting there by myself. Looking like somebody's lost country cousin."

"Nah, people would just think you're a VIP." Leah motioned to the bartender and then pointed to Bird and then herself. "Sebastian, meet Bird. Please keep her glass filled." Bird was skeptical—Sebastian looked barely old enough to know how to open a bottle of wine, let alone be bartending.

"I don't drink," said Bird.

"Lord, Jesus. Just get one drink," Leah paused, "Seabass, a French 75. You'll like it." The boy gave an exaggerated bow.

"Should I do anything else?" Bird asked.

"Enjoy the show. I'll come out and check on you when I can. If things get rowdy just keep to the sidelines. If they get a lotta rowdy—like you see badges—someone will bail you out in the morning."

Bird started to protest.

Leah placed a hand on Bird's hip and leaned into her ear. Bird was surprised to find herself silenced. Leah's voice was low and soft, her hand reassuring and suggestive. "Everything's gonna be fine. Have a good time."

Who am I, and what am I doing, Bird thought as Leah flowed smooth as silk through the crowd. The club vibrated, and Harlem's night owls shone in their tailored suits and flouncy dresses the color of rubies and sapphires. The beautiful and proud sons and daughters of Harlem hooted and shouted and hung on each other. It seemed like they all knew each other—like they'd stepped out of their daytime lives and resumed this never-ending party. Bird wondered if her crystal-stemmed drink would give her any of the devil-may-care attitude floating around.

The shouts dropped to whispers when a low bass note thrummed through the club. The lights shifted the room from dusk to dark except for a spotlight at center stage. If anyone had asked Bird, she could only describe the performances as syncopations of fluttering arms, luscious thighs, and winking smiles riding high on trumpet shouts and string bass plucks. The dancers and musicians moved, and Harlem and Bird Bennett moved with them.

After the show, Leah acted as if it was completely natural that they'd then go somewhere else. They were well into the wee hours of the morning, and Bird worked to stifle a tired protest. She had agreed to see it all. Leah knocked twice at the dinner club door and whispered some phrase Bird didn't catch. The door opened, and a young man peaked through the chain. "Glad you here," he said as slid the door open, "I was worried I was my own tonight."

Leah shook his hand. "Not yet. Holler if there are problems. Esau, this here is Bird. I'll teach her the passphrase. She's good people."

"Pleased to meet you," said Esau, flattening his tie and attempting suaveness. Leah playfully pushed him aside.

They walked a short corridor that opened into a joined kitchen and small dining space. A heavy-set, brown-skinned woman was posted at the kitchen stove. She wore a house dress, paisley headscarf, and apron and stirred a pot big enough to feed the block. Leah kissed her on the cheek.

"Mama Mazie, this is Bird."

Mazie looked Bird up and down. "You changing your crowd, Lee? Looks like I need to get some meat on those bones for you."

"Nice to meet you as well," Bird said as Leah led her to the table closest to the corridor. She glared at Leah.

"What?" Leah asked with feigned innocence.

"Why did you bring me here?" she whispered.

"Ahh, she don't mean no harm. She likes you."

"She doesn't like me."

"She will like you."

"No, she won't."

"She's one of my closest friends. We go back to my first days in Harlem. She got me through. That's why I want you to meet her. I don't got family other than her. And if I tell her to like you, she'll like you."

Bird didn't believe this for a second.

"I promise," said Leah, and Bird rolled her eyes.

"What you got cooking?" Leah asked when Mazie came to their table with a hand on her hip.

"Grits with sausage and shrimp."

"Two bowls."

They ate and talked the best they could between all the folks greeting Leah and requiring introductions as new patrons arrived. The people were all colored folks, and Bird loved that they were fine and loud, having clearly started their parties elsewhere. Most paused to read the night's menu by the kitchen entrance before passing through an archway leading to a living room and bedroom converted into a dining room and lounge with two- and four-seater tables. A few eyes darted toward Mazie, but no one spoke to her.

"What'd you think of the show?" asked Leah.

"I enjoyed it. I hadn't been to one before. I just don't think of going out at night as my thing."

"There's daytime New York and nighttime New York. You miss out on one, and you don't really understand the other. You don't really know anything about a person until you know who they are at night too."

"What do you appreciate about daytime New York City?"

"Beautiful country seamstresses hiding in their apartments." Leah pressed her foot against Bird's.

Bird gave a mock scowl and was about to defend herself when voices rose from the front corridor. Leah excused herself, stood, and squared her shoulders.

"These gentlemen are insisting," said Esau as Leah reached the door. Everything in the kitchen stopped. Mazie looked over to Bird who understood that she was supposed to give some kind of signal if things took a bad turn.

Leah moved Esau to the side and became a brick wall.

"We said the passphrase," said one of the men. "You know me," said another.

"The law says no white folks and colored folks mixing, even in private parties such as this."

"Come on, Big Lee," said a voice.

"Have a nice night, gentlemen." Her voice lowered, and the door slammed. Voices rose for a minute and then faded away.

Bird relaxed and moved her hand sideways through the air to say, "It's done." Mazie nodded and removed her right hand from her apron pocket. She met Leah and Esau in the hallway. "It was that Lewis guy. Don't let him back in, and none of them other fools. You got their faces?" Leah asked Esau, who nodded that he did.

Leah sat back down and dived back into her bowl like nothing had happened.

"What was that?" demanded Bird, more excited than scared.

"Probably some undercover detectives."

Bird's eyes bulged.

"Don't worry, they try it every few weeks. Guys like that just want to get in and see what's going on so they can lean on Mazie for cash. Maybe do a raid when they need to produce numbers."

"You act like it is nothing."

"It's the city at night. Can you handle it?"

Leah studied her with a raised eyebrow. Bird looked around at the other folks having a good time. There was something missing in her life. She wasn't sure this was it exactly, but she wanted a few more tastes from the pot.

"I think so," she said.

The streetlights caught the mischief in Leah's eyes and the beauty in her handsomeness. Bird pulled Leah to the side of the stoop for modesty's sake. Taking this as an invitation, Leah bent slightly and pressed her full lips to Bird's whose body ignored her more hesitant mind and pressed in close.

"Can I come up?" Leah asked, not hiding her intentions.

Bird shook her head. "I need a little more time."

"Not a problem. Lesson on Thursday?"

"Same time."

Leah pecked her on the cheek and walked off into the night. Bird wanted to call after her but didn't. Lightheaded, she mounted the stoop. Her apartment was silent and empty, like her life—which just moments before had been bright and boisterous. As she undressed, she glimpsed herself in the mirror. The body of her girlhood had passed. Her breasts hung a little lower and her hips curved suggestively. Somehow, along the way, her body had become that of a woman. Its wants were no longer nervous and frenetic. She slid into slacks and a sweater, grabbed her change purse, and headed back out into Harlem's night.

She strategized ways to avoid looking ridiculous. Apparently, a little more time had been only five minutes. There were plenty of women in Leah's life who were decisively willing. Bird slowed. What if she hadn't gone home, but instead to find one of those women? Bird felt stupid for spending the night kindling the fire and then sending it to another woman's bed.

She studied Leah's graystone. Leah had said she lived on the second floor and hated the street noise. A shadow moved by the window Bird guessed was Leah's apartment. After climbing the stairs, Bird almost turned around at the apartment door. Leah would think she was crazy.

Then, she remembered her empty apartment and the fullness that was just on the other side of the thin sheet of wood.

"Damnit," she said aloud as she knocked.

Leah opened the door in her trousers and a white t-shirt. She held her hand out for Bird to come in. "My apartment is simple." She didn't lie. It was just a studio with a bed, table with a hot plate, and a worn couch.

"I'm sorry for barging in. I . . . I . . ."

Leah smiled at the dither Bird had worked herself into.

"I thought I needed more time, and then you were gone . . . Look, I'm too old to be this silly. I'm usually not. I'm a very serious person."

Leah poured Bird a drink from the whiskey bottle on the table. "What are you trying to say?"

Bird sat the glass back on the table without drinking it and let her lips and pounding heart explain things for her.

"Are you sure?"

She kissed Leah again.

"Enough said."

Later as they lazed in bed, Bird thanked herself for the moment of bravery. Leah lay on her stomach with her head on Bird's arm. Bird's fingers traced the crisscrossed scars on her back. Leah stiffened a bit as Bird explored them. "What happened?" Bird asked.

"Proof that there's no beating the devil out."

Bird kissed the scars and held her until they both slept.

Leah was hers, if not in every way, then in enough of the ways that counted. Bird became scarce on a couple of weeknights and always on Saturday nights. Occasionally, she went to the club with Leah or met her at Mazie's. But they both preferred it when she waited for Leah's return at night. It would be the morning's wee hours. She'd arrive cranky and tired, smelling of booze and smoke. She'd eaten at Mazie's, so Bird would draw her a bath and wash her back. She'd lay next to Bird and complain about how much her feet hurt. Bird would shimmy closer, and the silk of her gown was distraction enough. Their lovemaking was patient, sparing plenty for both the moon and the sunrise.

Bird maintained her Friday nights for Louise, who commented only once on the change in Bird's routines.

"I notice you keeping late nights these days," Louise said over a cup of tea after dinner.

"Some nights," Bird admitted.

"Most times, I done seen late nights lead girls into troubled days."

"Louise, I'm almost thirty years old."

"Just saying what I've seen."

"Thank you, I do hear you."

Louise left it at that. Irma, Bird noticed, seemed a bit more distant, leaving Bird to wonder if her neighbor had seen or heard one of the rare times Bird let Leah in during the night. Preferring to avoid conversations that would force lies or truths, Bird gave the woman her distance.

# September 1929

The summer of 1928 passed into the winter of '28, and then, before Bird knew it, the summer of '29 had arrived. Leah was sometimes hot and steady, and, at other times, cool and distant for weeks. Bird could discern no patterns and resigned herself to peace with it. She wondered about other women or addiction but could find no evidence of either. Leah called them her moody moments. Eventually, Bird came to appreciate them. She would not lose herself in this woman or give her the key to her joy like her mother had given to her father. Leah's distance protected her.

Besides, Bird didn't trust love. That throw-yourself-into-the-street-for-love, or jump-off-the-bridge love, or take-it-to-the-dirt-with-you love. Humans were too fickle for all that. She'd seen enough of the world to know that neither riches nor poverty perfected love. It was about as magical as sewing two pieces of fabric together. No matter how strong the fabric or skilled the maker, the seam eventually gives out.

In their cool periods, and even during some of the hot ones, Bird resumed her walks and returned to the occasional lecture hall. On the nights she was bored, she went to Mazie's on her own, sometimes for a drink and sometimes to fry what the regulars started calling Miss Maddy's Fried Bird. During their cool periods, she and Leah would speak, and then Bird would be off into the crowd or kitchen to do her own thing, coming and going by herself.

Bird counted herself among the world's realists. A Black woman better not be anything else. You worked for your living, and you died on a day you couldn't choose. The astrological alignment that gave her health, a friendly place to live, a business that put food on her table, and the warmth of a woman in her bed was as transitory as the moon. She tried to stave off the many things that could break the spell. When she stayed over, Leah came and went during the height of her clients' pick-up hours. She was ordered to contain her heavy footfalls. And they made love on the mattress pulled to the floor. Whatever Irma heard, she kept to herself. So, Bird was furious when the day of revelation came and had nothing to do with Leah, and everything to do with Bird being a woman alone on a street at night.

As a rule, she carried with her a razor Leah had given her and taught her to wield without fearing the feel of slicing flesh. She stuck to the main thoroughfares, kept her wits about her, and avoided deep shadows. As she left Mazie's on an unseasonably cool September night, she noted the slightly emptier streets and walked fast. She and the man in the Panama hat noticed each other at the same time. Without missing a step, he flicked away a glowing cigarette and changed his direction to match hers. And it was that simple, she would later think. An opportune moment for him and nothing to stop him.

"Shit," she whispered, picking up her pace and turning her head to make it known that she had seen him. The sounds of his steps matched hers, but his stride was longer, and he gained on her. Bird turned onto her block and was ready to run when she spotted the slow-walking, over-sized silhouette that could only belong to Rupert. She called out and hated her voice for faltering in the panic, but he stopped anyway and turned back toward the sound. Spotting her and the man a few steps behind her, he shouted "Hey," in a warning growl.

The footsteps behind her stopped, and she ran to Rupert who placed an arm around her shoulder and raised a fist at whoever lurked behind her. The man in the Panama hat lit another cigarette and continued his way down the street. Only after he passed did she cry.

"You okay, Miss Bird?" Rupert asked setting down his toolbox and gently pulling his arm from around her.

After several breaths, she could speak. "I will be. Everything happened so fast. If you hadn't been here . . ."

He shushed her. "I was here. I'd cursed the train I missed in Brooklyn, but now I'm glad. God is good. I don't want to tell you what to do, but it ain't safe for a woman to keep the hours you do. Let's get home."

Bird no longer felt the night's chill or the thudding in her chest. Her legs moved on their own down the block and up the stoop. Rupert opened the door for them and held it for her. She had nothing left for the shock of Irma standing at the top of the second-floor landing in her bathrobe. Her arms lay on her swollen belly. "Rupert, you jackass, and Bird, you bitch," she said with an emotionless voice.

It was worse, Bird thought, that Irma hadn't shouted. Then, someone could yell back that this wasn't what it looked like. Instead, the accused stood stunned. Rupert whirled around to Bird like she should be talking. What the hell could she say, but she tried.

"I ran into trouble, Irma," she stuttered. "A man on the street. Rupert just saved me," she said, her voice trembling. It was all too much for one night. "I promise you, Irma. That's what happened."

Finally, Irma crackled with fury and loosed the guttural yell of a woman betrayed and shook the banister. There was nothing more for Bird to say; the woman was angry and hurting and saw the obvious instead of the subtle. "Don't ever speak my name again," said Irma. "Rupert, we will discuss this further in the morning. You can sleep in the living room."

"I'm too big for that couch," he complained.

"Then you can sleep on the floor," Irma yelled.

Bird let her dress slip to the floor and fell into her bed. The Harlem night carried on around her. The occasional beep of a horn or a shout from somewhere. A neighbor's Victrola sang to the stars. Bird considered the shouts. How many had she heard in her years in this bed? How many had she ignored, or not heard at all? The city has its price, she thought. And at some point, we all pay our share of the toll. She slept in fits and hated the morning when it arrived. The clock read eight thirty, and she cussed as she rushed to get herself decent enough to get through the workday. Customers came and went and accepted their clothing or handling without remarking on her tired smile. She only did the simple tasks, those she could do with her mind in a million other places. At 6:30 p.m., she flipped her sign and sat at the table waiting for the knock that came at 6:35 p.m.

Louise stood at her door with Irma and Rupert behind her. Louise spoke first as they all took up battle positions in the kitchen. Irma and

Louise sat at the table. Rupert leaned against the wall nearest the front door, and Bird gave what weight she could to the kitchen counter.

"Trouble done come to my house," started Louise, "and I aim to get it sorted out. You two got explaining to do." She looked from Bird to Rupert.

Rupert raised his hands in exasperation. "I done said all there is to say. I was coming home from a job and heard a woman's voice call my name behind me. It was Miss Bird with a man coming up behind her."

"That's the truth," said Bird. "I know what it looks like," she spoke to Irma, "but I did not and would not."

"All this time I've tried to figure you out," Irma gave a rueful laugh. "I knew no good could come from a woman who don't let her dirt show even a little bit. I thought you'd have the decency not to shit where you sleep." She fixed on Rupert. "You want me to believe you about last night, and what about all the other nights? You savin' women all over the damned city? My brother's saying y'all going to the Elks every night. You say they joking, but we don't have extra money to show if you doing all this work."

Bird rubbed her temples. She could only vouch for last night. The rest was up to Rupert, at least she thought so until Louise leaned toward her. "And your other nights," she said, "I done let it go along enough, but this is the house of a God-fearing woman. And what's done in the streets can still bring trouble home."

"I been working in Brooklyn," said Rupert. "I got the job almost done. It won't pay til I'm done."

"Rupert! That don't make no sense!" shouted Irma. The crack in her voice begged for truth.

"Fine," he said, throwing his hands into the air. He slid his hand into his pocket and raised a key. "It's a house. In Brooklyn. For us. Your brother's been helping me, and maybe we tip the bottle. But ain't nobody seen me in no Elks or anybody else's club."

Irma stared at the key and then at the man who held it. Her eyes seemed to trace back each day and imagine the details of this story. After several moments, in which they all held their breaths, she nodded. Bird hoped this revelation would end the conversation, but then they all turned to her. She still held a missing puzzle piece. Bird looked from one to the other. Irma was skeptical, Louise rigid, and Rupert drained. Bird considered her options. If pressed, she'd always thought she would just make some sheepish admission of seeing a man on the outs with his woman. That line wouldn't win her any sympathy or grace this evening, and it wouldn't help Rupert.

"There are things I have preferred to keep private," she straightened as she spoke first to Louise and then Irma. "But Rupert, you saved me, and for that, I owe truth in this conversation. I am with a woman. I stay with her some nights and was coming back from her last night."

Louise lowered her head. "I feared such an affliction."

Irma gasped and raised her hand to her chest. She looked at Rupert; he shrugged as if to say this news certainly had nothing to do with him. There, Bird thought, you all wanted the truth, now what do you have to say? Not a damn thing. Done with the conversation, she nodded to the door. "I have had a hellish day. Can we just leave things here for now?"

Irma hugged Rupert and they walked out with his arm around her swollen waist. Louise paused at the door and started to say something but shook her head and shut the door behind her.

The suit pants needing hemming got rested on the Sabbath day. As did the work dresses and party gowns. Bird spent most of the morning in bed. It was always going to come to this. And it would happen again and again, even if she moved into another brownstone. She thought she and Louise had been friends. We weren't, Bird admitted; true friendship requires truth. She could try a big building but couldn't bring herself to imagine for more than a second if a whole building wanted to turn her out. There was no way she could keep her business.

Louise tapped at noon. Bird poured herself a cup of tea from the just starting to rattle kettle and shouted for her to come in. Apparently, it was plenty Christian-like to evict someone as the city's preachers still bellowed from their pulpits.

"Afternoon, Louise," said Bird.

"Afternoon." Louise frowned. "May I visit for a spell?"

"Of course," Bird ushered her in. "I was just sitting down with tea. Care for a cup?"

Louise looked around, unabashed in her absorbent gaze, as if she hadn't been in this kitchen a hundred times.

"No, thank you. I will take a seat though."

They regarded each other across the table. Louise's eyebrows knitted together with consternation, but they held no anger or malice. "I tend not to mind the business of grown women, especially those who pay their rent on time," said Louise.

"That sounds mutually advantageous."

"But some situations require comment."

"Do they?" Bird asked.

"Yes," Louise said with a surprising firmness.

"Then comment, Louise."

"Your friend isn't here?"

"No, she's not."

"Is there anything you want to say to me?"

Bird almost spit. Louise was about to be disappointed if she wanted an apology or begging. "You've come to my table. You can do the talking." Feeling the edge in her own voice, Bird reined it in. Letting things get out of hand would only mean she'd be packing her stuff and headed to Leah's tonight instead of having a few weeks to find a new place.

"This is my house, and I answer to the Lord. I avert my gaze when girls run around and stay out with they boyfriends. I was young once, and I know how young men are. I doubt the Lord minds all that much if a couple can't quite make it to the altar before indulging. But two women carrying on is too much for me not to see. I've always liked you and appreciated yo' company, but it ain't right to disrespect a God-fearing woman's home."

Bird wanted to slap the righteousness off Louise's face. Breathe, she told herself. This is only a bump against an old bruise. It doesn't hurt like it hurt back then, that lifetime ago. And the pain calmed itself a little more with each breath, and she could truly see the old woman sitting across from her. It had to be a hard life fearing so much. We're raised to be afraid, Bird thought. Of men. White people. Sin. God. Sex. Dying old and alone. Bird read the fear in the straightness of Louise's back and the corners of her eyes. She feared for herself and for Bird. Odelia had worn this fear like a shawl years ago. How could she put them at ease, help them see she didn't need their fear, just their love? Maybe if they could see that, then she could explain that looking into a lover's eyes and seeing your own reflection was sacred too.

Bird folded her hands in front of her. "I'm not ashamed of who I am, Louise. There has been no disrespect intended. I . . ." There were so many things she wanted to say, but it wouldn't matter in the end. It never did. "Then you accept my thirty-day notice?"

"It ain't my intention to toss you out into the street. We all lived peaceably before your friend."

Bird shook her head. "You and Irma have made your feelings clear. Whether I have someone or not. I am who I am. You accept my notice?"

"If that's how you want it," Louise stood. "I'm praying for you and that you are able to humble yourself before the Lord."

"It always strikes me as odd how folks tell me to humble myself as they look down on me."

Bird packed her overnight bag and walked to Leah's place looking out for rental signs along the way. Her world had taken a jaw-breaking hit, but Harlem, as always, kept on. The children playing hopscotch on the sidewalk, the church folks leaving afternoon prayer services, and the market goers struggling with their bags. She thought of the city's toll again. If you're going to make it here, there's no room for self-pity.

At Leah's, she knocked, and after hearing the woman's exhausted "go away" groan, let herself in with her key. Leah pulled the pillow from over her head and watched as Bird exchanged her street clothes for a satin nightgown although it was only three o'clock in the afternoon. Leah ran her hand over the gown cupping Bird's breast as Bird slid into bed.

"I thought you were asleep," said Bird.

"I'm awake now."

"I've come to join your moody spell."

"What happened?" said Leah, kissing her neck. Bird lay back and surrendered to the pleasure.

"I have to move."

"Louise?"

"I'll tell you everything later. She said I was disrespecting a God-fearing woman's house."

Leah pressed her nose to Bird's cheek. "Don't cry," she said. "You can move into my place."

"Thank you, but I can't run my business out of here, and most of my clients come from within walking distance. I don't know if I have it in me to start all over again."

"What you saying?" Leah's back stiffened.

"I'm not saying anything Leah, just telling you what I'm up against." Bird pulled Leah on top of her, kissed her neck, and rocked them both until Leah relaxed and couldn't help herself. Bird fought past the day and Louise, and the man in the Panama hat, and Bennettsville, and deep into the heat and need of the woman she clung to, and the peaking pleasure that was almost too exquisite to bear and, in so many ways, impossible to live without.

The days ticked by. Irma no longer spoke in passing, and Louise regarded her with a somber politeness. Bird dreaded each necessary interaction. In spare moments, she walked the neighborhood spying rent signs and sussing out what she could about the owners. She inquired of her regulars and let Leah spread the word at the club. There was an opening in Mazie's building that she regarded as a last resort. It was too far to bring many of her customers with her. And the sign on her front window had been her best advertisement.

Louise knocked late one evening. "I've heard of an opening in a big building, not too far from here. It might suit your needs better." She held out a piece of paper.

Bird hoped Louise could not discern the red of her eyes in the evening light. She didn't know why she was taking this so hard.

"You okay?" Louise asked. "I've been praying for you."

"It's just the grind, Louise."

"It's Satan who tells us we can't control our sinnin'. But the choice is ours in the end, and that is why we each stand accountable before the Almighty."

Bird popped. "Who among us can choose not to love for a whole lifetime, Louise? If that is the decree of your God, then I wish all you fools luck when you meet him." Louise hopped back as the door slammed in her face.

"Shit," shouted Bird as she threw on a jacket and stomped out to Mazie's for a drink, slamming the front door behind her too.

"I could use a drink, and I thought you could use help tonight," said Bird as Mazie opened the door. Already, the apartment smelled of simmering greens and fried pork chops.

Mazie took her coat and pointed her to the kitchen. "You're just in time to peel potatoes."

"I'll do anything." She slammed the first whiskey and sipped the second.

Mazie watched this without judgment. "Leah told me about it."

Bird nodded, curving the potato skins into the sink. "I've got to figure out how to move and take my clients with me, or I'll be on the train back to Illinois by winter." The admission barely scraped the mountains of her concern. Mazie was Leah's friend, and there was only so much she could say to her. She couldn't, for instance, say that all this drama was over Leah, and she wasn't sure how long they would be together. Leah had made her limitations clear. It didn't pain Bird to think they were only meant for a season. A welcome and needed season, but just a season.

"When I took the place, I thought I'd never meet anyone. That kind of love has never been kind or generous to the women of my family."

"You know Leah don't stay too long in any one place or in anyone's arms."

Bird would always appreciate this woman's candor, even when it cut. "I know, Mazie." She met her eyes to be clear that she was no fool, or at least not in that way. "Either way, I'd like to find a way to love and eat."

"Ain't nobody told you loving and eating ain't for us?" Mazie laughed and threw a towel at her.

"I didn't believe it when they told me." Bird laughed despite her predicament and the gnawing understanding that there was more truth than joke in the words.

# October 1929

Bird finished her Sunday sewing and ventured out into the Harlem bustle. She had exactly seven days to find an apartment. Someone had snapped up the opening in Mazie's building, much to her relief. She strolled down as far as 110th Street admiring the buildings with a park view that she couldn't hope to afford in this lifetime. Golden leaves laced the boulevards. The city was a mystery and a miracle. It was hard, dirty, and stingy with its sustenance. But there was a hum beneath its surface, or some might call it a siren's song. She could so easily pack up her few things and head back to the Mississippi River. But she wanted to stay, maybe to age, weather, and eventually crumble like the brownstones around her. If the city could just hold her upright until then, although it, she admitted, claimed to be no man's God. Maybe their master, but not their benefactor.

Two days later, she awoke and learned the full extent of the city's disavowal of obligation even to the world. The news tore up and down Harlem's streets. "Them white fellas downtown is crying." "They markets done crashed." She sat on the front steps as her neighbors argued up about whether this trouble would end the world. An old man with a carved cane the color of amber and a matching fedora stopped in front of Bird and said, unsolicited, "Mark my words, anything that makes a white man panic is bound to bring us to our knees."

This soothsayer got Bird moving. She flipped on her radio and hung on each word when Louise tapped at the door. The old woman accepted tea, and once again sat across from her.

"I am a woman of convictions, but I'm not cruel. From what I hear, this thing going on downtown is gonna be bad—for everybody. You've already had trouble finding a new place, and it don't look like it's gonna get any easier."

"What are you saying?" Bird kept a straight face but wanted to holler with relief. Apparently, Louise's convictions included keeping a tenant who'd paid on time, every time. Bird was nervous about her own savings, but she had enough cash to hold her for at least six months, and maybe even a year if things stayed stable with Leah.

"I'm saying, you should stay, for now."

"That doesn't give me much certainty."

"For a year then."

"I mind my business, and you mind yours?" Bird sauntered up to the line. "I have heard your counsel. I'll answer for myself, if it comes to that, and I'll be sure to leave your name out of it."

Louise sighed. "Then it seems we have an understanding."

# July 1931

Bird had waited a long time for this letter from Vera. She'd always thought she'd be unmoved, but her hand shook as she read. "You okay?" Louise asked, stopping her spoon mid-stir. Bird wasn't sure. She handed the letter across the table. The Minister died in his sleep on a Sunday night. He'd grown a bit older than his years, which he attributed to the work of laboring for souls. His doctor described it as a weakening heart. He'd intended to leave all his children some money, but the crash had ruined that.

"I'm sorry, Bird. Were you close?" Louise folded the letter and set it on the table between them.

"No. I'd seen him maybe once in the past twenty years. I was his outside child."

"A child is a child," said Louise, sipping her coffee. "At least he wanted to do for you in the end."

Bird accepted this. The Minister had cared about endings, but he hadn't known how to handle the durings.

That night, a familiar knock on Louise's window pulled them from the general lament. Irma had come as promised. Bird hopped to the door, and Louise tucked away the little nip they'd added to their mugs. Despite her formless grief, Bird squealed as little Taylor dashed in giggling as her mother bustled through the door behind her.

"I promise she knew where we were going as soon as we hit the block."

Taylor, a child of Rupert through and through, had no hesitation and was certain she owned everything in Louise's place as she ran directly to the fabrics Bird brought for her play and the caramel chews Louise always set out for her.

"Catch us up on everything," demanded Bird as Irma settled into the highback and rested her feet on the ottoman.

"Chile, ain't nothing different in Brooklyn. We just hoping Rupert gets paid, the heat stays on, and the tenants at least pay some of the rent." Bird and Louise joined this song. Since Irma and Rupert had moved to Brooklyn, Louise had taken in a steady stream of folks moving from here to there every couple of months—with new jobs starting the very next week, they always swore. Bird paid what extra she could to offset those who sneaked out in the night leaving unpaid rent behind.

"You look tired," said Louise.

"Louise!" said Bird. "Ignore her, Irma. You look good. I have a few things I think would look good on you." Bird pointed to the blouses hanging on the rack that she'd designed and begun selling.

No longer concerned with her feet, Irma headed to the rack.

"Rupert ain't taking me no where I can wear these."

"You're going with me to Leah's club tonight," said Bird. "I want to see this new woman, Charmain—or Charming, as she insists on being called." Bird rolled her eyes.

"I thought that you and Leah were being nice about everything," said Irma, pulling a low-cut blue satin blouse from the rack.

"We are. I just want to see. And have a drink that didn't come from Louise's purse, and who knows where else before that."

"Girl, I'm tired. I came here so you could get up with Taylor tonight." Irma frowned but held the blouse to her chest and admired herself in the mirror.

"We won't stay out late. One drink and a peek. I promise."

The end with Leah had been as simple as the pain that accompanied it. Leah hadn't lied. She wasn't the settling down type, even if she had stayed with Bird for almost three years. Sharing the bed. The closet. And the bills. Even if she and Bird had become known as "them two" to everybody on the block. Her "trips out of town" became more frequent. Her hours at Mazie's grew longer. And the other woman's perfume grew stronger. One day, Bird had had enough, looked up from her sewing machine, and told her just to move her stuff over there. Leah had packed as told but had stopped at the door. "I had to leave a few things in the closet."

Bird started to protest. She'd grudgingly let Leah store cash at her place. She didn't need it there without Leah also there to protect it and her.

"It's just till I see . . . if things will stick. Or, I find another place for it."

Folding her arms, Bird pursed her lips.

Realizing her mistake, Leah slumped. "I always knew you'd stick; we'll always stick. Like me and Mazie. Her and Alicia. And Esau. And Samson."

"It's hard to feel that kind of sticking happening when people don't have the decency not to make a fool out of you."

"I'm sorry." Leah lowered her head. "I didn't know how to say it, but I mean it." She tried to smile.

"Two weeks," said Bird, her voice flat and without sympathy.

Leah nodded. "You still coming by the club sometimes, right?" She sounded like an apprehensive child.

Bird didn't know if she should laugh or cry. "Maybe," she said and pointed Leah to the door.

Samson held down his spot at the side door.

"Bird!" he shouted. "Ain't seen you in a hot minute." He glanced at Irma. "Who's your friend?" He adjusted his bowtie and leaned forward.

"Samson, meet Irma. She's married and a woman of deep faith."

"Your fella treat you right?" asked Samson, pulling off complete sincerity.

"Yes, sir, very right," Irma said, tilting her head with enough coquettishness to play along.

"Then, I won't make no trouble," he crossed his heart.

"That's good of you, Samson," said Bird, patting him on his shoulder. "You'll let Leah know I'm in my usual spot."

"I got you."

"Miss Bird!" Seabass grinned at the bar. "We've missed seeing you around."

"We come. We go, Seabass. Don't get attached."

"You're a special one, Miss," he said with a bow. "Two 75s?"

"Yes, please, and I won't be mad if you spill in a little extra champagne."

Seabass winked at her.

"You're in rare form tonight," said Irma, trying to get comfortable on the stool. "Everything all right?"

"The world's gone to shit. I'm here spying on Leah and her new woman. And the Minister's Lord has finally taken him home."

"Ahhh, your father. I'm sorry, Bird. Want to talk about it?"

The orchestra began a slow melody. "Not really. Not much to say."

Bird spotted Charmain as she and a friend arrived in the middle of a dance number. She was just as Mazie had described her—the kind of woman you'd figure Leah would take up with. Bird had considered that an amazingly unhelpful description. Now she understood. Charmain strutted in like everyone had turned out just to see her entrance. She stood with a regal patience while the maître d' held out her chair. Her purple satin and lace dress highlighted her full figure. When Leah appeared through a side door, Charmain stood and kissed her cheek. Leah placed her hand on Charmain's hip and whispered something in her ear that made the woman laugh.

"That's her," said Bird, elbowing Irma.

"Who?"

"Irma, keep up," Bird growled.

Irma caught up. "Ooooh," she said.

"Right," said Bird feeling embarrassed by the little curves she'd been so proud of.

Leah navigated the tables over to them. Charmain turned to watch with a proprietary seriousness. Come on, said Bird to herself, you got eight years of New York City attitude lessons. Act like it.

"Y'all finally found your way out of the house. Good to see you, Irma," said Leah, giving Bird a quick kiss on the cheek. Bird acquiesced only to vex the new woman who still stared at them.

"Just getting lil Mama out for a breath of fresh air," Bird explained.

"Much needed," said Irma, playing her part.

Leah grinned at both of them. "I can't say much for the singing tonight, but it'll still be a good time. I'll cover your drinks."

"Thank you, kindly," said Bird and reached out and pulled Leah in for a hug. Leah stepped in, not hiding her surprise. "You still have stuff at my place," Bird whispered. Leah was a month late in picking up the lockbox full of cash that Bird had futilely pushed even deeper into the closet.

Leah groaned. "Just a little more time. Deposit some of it if you're worried about it."

"I'm not a laundry woman or a bank. But I do know how to spend. Now run along before your little friend gets upset."

"I got everything under control." Leah stepped back. Her smile had dimmed, but Bird couldn't worry about that.

"Famous last words," said Bird as Leah walked away.

"You trying to get her back?" Irma asked.

"No," Bird sighed. "It was just a season for all that. I'm trying to stay friends, though she didn't make it easy with all her playing around when she just had to be up front."

"We'll see," said Irma.

"You can see. I know."

The singer was indeed not much to listen to. Irma and Bird exchanged glances and then giggled behind their glasses. A couple of seats down, a maple brown woman in a twinkling black party dress said, "Lord, Jesus," and stared at the singer in distaste. "I sound better and could wear that dress better."

"No, actually, you couldn't," Bird spoke to her with the firm authority of an expert in her field.

"Bird!" said Irma, grabbing her arm. Bird shooed her hand away. The woman gaped at her.

"No one could, really," Bird continued. "It's a poor imitation of an Anne Lowe. The lines and drape are all wrong. I can practically see the threads hanging from here." Bird took a long sip of her drink. "All that being said, you'd be better in something with long lines and a semi-loose drape. If elegant scandal is what you want, a neckline that dives deep and a little wide, that clings just enough to give the hint of bare breasts without telling it all, if you know what I mean."

"If you don't mind my asking, who the hell are you?" said the woman.

"H. Bennett, Proprietress of H. Bennett Design and Dressmaking. People call me Bird."

"I've never heard of you."

"What's your name?" asked Bird.

"People call me Anna Silver."

"I've never heard of you either."

Irma almost spit out her drink.

Anna Silver frowned into her glass. "That's the problem all around. Pretty dresses are nice, but I prefer to be known for my voice."

"Think about it this way," said Bird. "The dress makes them stop and look, and your voice makes it so they can't look away."

"I like that, Miss Bennett. You have a card?"

Bird slid it across the bar.

A month later, she cajoled Irma into going back with her to see the fruit of her labor. The club lights darkened, and a single spotlight appeared on Anna Silver in a gown that flowed like a river of silver. Anna sang like a dream and added a few subtle twitches of the hips that made Bird and everyone else forget about the dress too.

# February 1932

Even after years of visiting and cooking at Mazie's, Bird had never imagined a day in which Mazie would pull a slow drag at her kitchen table. Bird had opened the door, and Mazie strolled in without asking for an invitation. She'd peeled off her winter layers with the deliberateness of a woman who knows her audience will wait without comment. She wore a church suit with a cloche hat. The suit fit so poorly, and Mazie looked so uncomfortable in it, Bird wondered if she'd come for sewing services until Mazie sat at the table and said, "They was raided. They took 'em all. Leah, Charlie, and Samson. Everybody."

"But that doesn't happen up here," Bird protested.

"Maybe somebody ain't paid the bills," Mazie shrugged. "I'm closing down for a few weeks to be safe."

Bird studied Mazie's suit again. "And you're going to bail out Leah," she said like she was figuring a math problem out loud.

"I just bailed out Charmain."

Bird rolled her eyes and sighed. "And I've got to go get Leah."

"Absolutely not. I've come to tell you to lay low and stay out of it. The fools drinking got tickets. Leah and the others will be up for bootleggin', interstate trafficking, abetting prostitution—you name it. And I heard that she may have sent one of them white boys off with a black eye and cracked ribs. They gonna come for everything she got. You don't want them thinking what you got is hers too. She got anything here?"

"A few things." Bird sat back and took several deep breaths to still the anger and panic that chased it. Leah's cash still sat in her closet. She could never explain having thousands of dollars hidden away.

"Get rid of everything she won't miss."

Bird didn't know if she should be honored or humbled. Mazie did come to personally deliver the information but was clearly concerned she would do something stupid.

"It's the life, darling," Mazie sang in a few low notes. "Don't go see her until after she's sentenced. I'll let you know when I get word, either way. If anybody asks you anything, you just one of the chicks pecking around."

"So, we're just going to let her go to prison?"

"She can plea, cooperate, or keep her mouth shut. We'll know soon enough." For the first time since she'd arrived, Mazie let sadness slip into her eyes and voice. Bird inhaled. This was serious. Leah was in trouble, the kind of trouble that would send her away. She'd told Leah that she didn't want this life. Now she understood that she didn't want it for either of them. Being Big Lee had given her the freedom to be herself in the world, and Bird got some of that freedom by association, but now it would cost Leah a different kind of freedom.

She and Mazie sat together at the table in silence for several minutes. Bird wasn't much for praying but did ask anybody listening to lend a miracle or two. When Mazie lit another cigarette, Bird realized that the woman didn't want to go home. Bird had never seen Mazie's apartment empty and couldn't even imagine it.

"Well, if you're not cooking, you might as well eat here," said Bird. "I can show you how to properly make hot water cornbread."

Mazie snorted, sat back in her chair, and put her feet up on the chair beside her.

# October 1933

The Angel Gabriel came to Bird's door in a threadbare wool coat and tattered boots. At first, Bird thought the tall figure beyond the glass door was confused and homeless. Every few weeks, one old man or another still came searching for Leah. Bird sent them away with an apology and a request that they spread the word: Leah doesn't live here anymore. Most had taken the news with a respectful calm as change was constant in their world. A few had become belligerent, calling her all manner of names, and threatening to break down the door.

"Can I help you?" she asked with a brusqueness learned by necessity, gripping the seam ripper in her apron pocket.

"I'm looking for Leah Reynolds." The voice was deep but simple in its request, nothing gravelly or worn.

Bird relaxed a little. A boy, far too young to have needed Leah's services, stood before her chilled to the point of stiffness.

"She hasn't lived here for a couple of years now."

The young man lifted his eyes to hers, and she almost fainted as she gazed into the spitting image of Leah. His face sagged with exhaustion. "I done asked all over Harlem. Anyone who knew her said this was where she lived. You know where she's moved to?"

"Why do you want her?"

"She's my mama."

Bird inhaled. Her mind raced through the years with Leah and over Leah's body. She hadn't spoken of a child. "You look like her," said Bird, grasping for anything.

"Yes, ma'am. That's all the proof I can offer you."

"Come in." She held the door open.

"I don't want to bother you. If she ain't here, you can just point me on."

"She isn't here, but I know where she is. And it's somewhere you can't get to. Now come on in. Let me get you some food and warmth, and then you can decide what you want to do."

She led him to the kitchen table. He hesitated to take off his coat and then tried to brush off the dirt on his clothing. He sat down once she began pulling down pots and pans and turning on burners.

"You kin to me?" he asked.

"In a manner."

He waited for further explanation.

Bird didn't know what to say. His head shifted back, and his eyes narrowed like Leah's did when she suspected someone wasn't on the up. She put a glass of water in front of him.

He reached for it and then pulling his hand back, the refusal clearly paining him.

"Who are you?" he asked.

She hesitated again and then sighed. "Your mother lived here with me for a few years. My name is Honest, but everyone calls me Bird. What's your name?"

"You got a funny name like me. Call me Gabriel," he chuckled.

Bird blinked, not understanding the boy's humor.

He loosened a bit. "She named me The Angel Gabriel. And she's not here?"

Bird nodded and smiled, and then sighed as she braced herself to give him hard news. "She's away for a while."

"You mean she's still in prison?"

Bird pushed the water toward him again. "How did you know?"

"People said."

Bird wondered what kind of person would tell a lost boy this news and not at least see him to safety. She wanted to fault the city and what it could do to people, but that wasn't fair. No one could take on extra mouth right now, especially that of a teenage boy bigger than plenty of grown men. "She's due back in a year."

If the information shocked him, he didn't let it show. "How can I get there?"

"You can take a bus, if you have money."

He shook his head. "How many miles is it?"

"Too many to walk, especially on this side of winter."

"She never said she had a son?"

The truth rang in Bird's head and shook her heart, and it would destroy this young man. So, she bent it. "She said it hurt too much to talk." Leah did have a hurt she couldn't talk about; they had lived around it.

Relief shone on the boy's face, and he plunged into the bowl of white bean soup she put in front of him. He ate with tidy efficiency and only glanced up when he reached the bowl's bottom. "That was very good." She poured him a second bowl and excused herself to make a phone call.

"You have a phone?" he guffawed.

"Yes, sir."

In the hallway, she dialed Mazie. "Praise the Lord," said the voice on the other line.

"Esau, it's Bird. I need to speak with Mazie."

"Hey, Miss Bird." She heard the young man's grin through the receiver. "You know Mazie hates phone calls at night."

"She can get mad at me."

A moment later, Mazie fussed her way onto the phone. "You dying?" she asked like she wouldn't have minded if Bird answered yes.

"I'm in a delicate situation. There's a young man here, for Leah, probably fifteen or sixteen years old."

"Is it The Angel Gabriel?"

"Yes."

"Did she ever tell you about him?"

"No."

"I'll take a taxi."

"You can call me Auntie Mazie." Mazie rushed into Bird's kitchen with her coat still on. The boy named after an angel hardly had time to stand before she pulled him into her arms.

"Yes, ma'am," he said and again tried to groom himself. "I mean Auntie Mazie, ma'am."

Bird intervened, offering to take Mazie's coat to get the boy some space. "Auntie Mazie was your mother's first friend when she arrived in New York."

Mazie beamed. "I got her through, and I'll gladly do the same for you."

"No thank you, ma'—Auntie, I'm going to keep on 'til I get to Bedford."

"You told him where she is?"

"He already knew. Harlem can't hold water. I'm trying to tell him that he needs to cool his heels until she gets back."

"True enough," said Mazie, taking Bird's seat. "As your Auntie, I insist that you wait here for your mother's return. Bird's got plenty of room."

Bird tried to keep her bulging eyes in check. Mazie spoke with the confidence of an elder ordering her clan about. Leah had Mazie to show her the ropes. Bird had Louise. She would be The Angel Gabriel's bridge. Bird willed her roiling stomach to calm. They needed a new lodger, though she'd have to figure out how to pay his share without touching Leah's stash if she could.

The open bedroom upstairs contained only a bed, dresser, and writing desk. "Tomorrow," she said to Gabriel, "we'll make it homier."

"This is fine. I don't need much," he said.

"I insist," said Bird. She showed him how to run a bath and returned to the living room where Mazie waited with a glass of wine already poured for her.

"I believe his dear Auntie Mazie has an extra bedroom," she said. "And this might all be a bit awkward since his mother didn't return any of the letters I sent her."

"Your business is much more suitable for child rearing than mine. We can split the expenses. His shoes must cost a fortune. And as for Leah not talking to you—she only needs to talk him."

Bird gulped her wine.

She did everything she thought prudent including a doctor's exam, a couple of pairs of new pants and shirts until she could make him more, and a letter sent to Virginia without a return address declaring the boy safe and lodging with family. For his part, The Angel Gabriel shuffled along with the compliance of a displeased but trained child. Bird had passed the vocational school countless times and done little more than admire its size. She never imagined herself mounting the stairs to register her "nephew."

"It'll be fine," she said as they waited on chairs outside the attendance office. "Just let me do the talking."

He blinked at her. She thought reticence had made him lug slowly behind her. She now saw the terror behind the boy's eyes.

"I'd rather just work, ma'am." He paused, "I don't got much book smarts, but I got work smarts."

Bird stretched her neck to calm her growing impatience. They'd been through this every day for two weeks. He could do it all, he swore—save up for a place for him and Leah. Buy his own clothes. Chip in on the groceries. He could do everything but go to school.

Bird froze. She whispered, "Son, can you read?"

As he started to respond, the office door opened. A plump white lady in too much green glanced at them and then the form in her hand, and then around the empty waiting room.

"Gabriel Bennett."

"Yes'm," said Gabe.

Bird cringed. She'd have to tell him they didn't have to do *that* up here.

"Yes, and I'm his aunt." Bird stood.

"I see he doesn't have any documents—no birth certificate or school records."

"Our family had a fire last year. His mother's trying to get what she can from the county. And you know how informal country schools can be."

"I'll process the paperwork now, but you bring it on as soon as you can."

"Yes, of course." Bird savored the lie.

The woman paused as if she was waiting for something else. Gabriel glanced between the two women. Bird said nothing.

"Miss Armstrong will register him for classes." The white woman flapped her hand toward an unseen desk on the other side of the wall.

Bird stepped forward. Gabe kept his seat. Bird furrowed her brow and hissed his name as she entered the office and was embarrassed to realize that she hadn't fixed her face in time.

"I'm so sorry." She swept her dress beneath her and sat as Gabe finally lumbered through the door. Bird turned and was surprised to find beautiful merriment sparkling across the desk. Miss Armstrong was cocoa brown with wide eyes that curled like her full lips as she smiled.

"If I had a dime for every time I'd seen a face that tight, I'd be a wealthy woman," said the attendance secretary.

"I'm so sorry Miss . . . Miss . . ." Why couldn't she remember the last name she'd heard not even a moment ago?

"Sharon. Sharon Armstrong." She held out a dainty hand.

"My nephew is a very polite and bright young man. He's just a bit nervous." And I'm a mess, thought Bird as she appreciated and quickly released the woman's slender hand.

"How many years of school did you attend in . . ." Miss Armstrong glanced at the paperwork in front of her. "Virginia?"

"I was born and raised there, excepting the last few months of course," Gabe answered.

Miss Armstrong handed a sheet of paper across the desk. Gabe read the Bible verses typed on it with ease.

"Are you looking forward to Monday, Mr. Bennett?" asked Sharon as she wrote down his class schedule.

"Are there any classes with work programs, Miss?" Gabe asked, and Bird wanted to elbow him.

"Some of the instructors can try to help you find employment. There isn't a lot to go around these days. It's a good time for a young man to focus on his books."

"Yes, ma'am," said Gabe, not hiding his disappointment or his stubborn disbelief.

"The family prefers he focus on his studies," said Bird, trying to mix firmness and pleasantness.

"That's what we're here for." Miss Armstrong handed Gabe his schedule with a nod to Bird that said *I'll keep an eye on him.*

"Thank you," said Bird as The Angel Gabriel slumped in his seat.

# November 1933

Several weeks later, Miss Armstrong leaned against Bird's kitchen counter holding her satchel in one hand and an attendance report in the other. "It would be most accurate to describe Gabe as a selective sampler of his education," she said. "He attends metal working and carpentry most days. But his math and composition teachers say they couldn't tell him from Adam." She'd arrived at midday as Bird had one customer settling an overdue bill and another waiting for measurements. Bird had hurried her into the kitchen and tried not to seem rushed with her listening.

"He leaves every morning like he's going to school and comes home talking about all the stuff he learned," said Bird, flustered. "I have no idea what to do."

"It happens, a lot," said Miss Armstrong. "Try to refocus him, show him the gain from an education. And if that doesn't work, you can't force him. He's going to follow what he believes is most important right now, and it may not be his education."

"I used to teach, back where I'm from." She did her best to explain her frustration to the woman regarding her with amused concern. "Even in a little country town learning could do a lot for a child."

"I'll remember your qualifications next time we have an opening."

"Oh no," said Bird, remembering the customers in the front room. "I don't mean to be short, but my adventures in aunthood and business ownership have not mixed well. I'll talk to him; can you send a note if he doesn't improve?"

"You know, there must be a stack of my letters home floating around the city's sewer system. I've sent two to you already."

"Ahhh, I see," said Bird, realizing that angels could lie and lie well.

Tired and exasperated, Bird posted her first letter to Leah in almost two years. She suspected the brevity would say as much as what she did include.

> Listen here, Leah.
> You don't have to write me. But you do have to write him. He wants to work instead of going to school because he's worried y'all won't have a way to live when you get back. Say something to him and give a little help, damnit!
> Bird

The Monday morning after Miss Armstrong's visit, Bird walked with Gabe to the train station claiming the necessity of a trip downtown for supplies. She held her peace as he complained about a test and a project that wouldn't work in his carpentry class.

She took a seat at the far end of the downtown platform and only had to wait for two trains to pass before Gabe walked down her side of the platform and leaned against the wall. Bird followed him on his route doing quick jobs at a barbershop, grocery store, and fruit market. As he counted his change after the fruit market, she stepped forward. He jumped back like she was a ghost from a past life.

"How about I buy us lunch?

"You been following me all morning?"

"I have." She led him into a diner. He dropped into the two-seater booth with silent indignance.

"Show me what've you made today," Bird said after a few bites of a turkey sandwich had taken the sting out of her temper. He laid $1.30 on the table between them.

"Hard earned," he said.

Bird took a ten-dollar bill out of her purse. "Hard earned," she said. "I respect that you want to make your way in the world and that you want to do it honorably. You been trying it your way. How about I show you a few different options."

She paid for their sandwiches, and they hopped the train for a long ride downtown. Sitting next to her, he picked at the callouses on his massive hands. Be gentle, she told herself. Folks down south had probably told him his whole life that he was made to labor. As they moved into the wealth of lower Manhattan, Gabe marveled at the marble buildings and clean streets. She stopped them across the street from a preparatory school for boys. The boys, all white, huddled in twos and threes in the brisk air, talking and laughing.

"You want me to go here?" he asked incredulously.

"No. I want to protect you from these boys and a future of breaking your back for their wealth. If you want to get ahead in the world, look for people who will prioritize you and your future, not just what you can do for them right now." White men in long coats rushed around them as they surveyed the buildings and then walked to see the Statue of Liberty. "She doesn't look a thing like us," said Bird to the boy gripping the railing beside her. "Our people came in chains to do the worst work and then die." He nodded and was solemn as he considered this.

They rode in silence back to 135th street and walked to a hardware store. The owner greeted Bird with a loud hello that always made her think of Johnson's Grocery back home.

"Mr. Young, would you mind telling my nephew Gabe how you got to running your own store?"

Mr. Young led them around the store telling Gabe about the first hammer he'd received from his grandfather and learning by watching his uncles fixing their own houses. Then, he took them over to the ledger book. Gabe blinked several times at all the numbers. "Knowing all that other stuff earned my customer's trust. Learning accounting keeps them doors open."

As they walked home past the Amsterdam News, she bought the day's paper. "People make the paper and the ink, write the stories, and print them off. It all takes training and learning of some sort. Your mother and I want you to do what you want with your life. You worried about what's going to happen in a year when she's coming home. She's the mother, and you're the child; you let her worry about that and figure it out. In the meantime, you can make a few cents here and there. Or, we can figure out how to get you skills you can build into something. The white boys you saw have connections and privileges that no one of their ilk would offer to you. I don't have much in comparison, but I'm offering you what I can. The Angel Gabriel, you have paid your dues. Don't make struggle; plenty of that comes for us in life."

"I want to try plumbing," he said after a moment of thought.

"You go to class, and I'll talk Rupert into letting you help with the extra work he does on weekends. Deal?"

"Deal." He held out his giant hand, and Bird felt the tenderness of a boyhood saved in his shake.

When they got home, Louise had left a letter on the kitchen table for them. Gabe turned over the envelope postmarked from Bedford, New York, and then stared at the handwriting on the letter's front. "It's addressed to both of us; you want to open it?" he asked Bird.

Bird shook her head. He eased the envelope flap open with a gentleness that impressed Bird. He separated the several folded sheets that bore his name and handed the rest to her. "Can I take it to my room?" he asked.

"It's your letter, Gabe," Bird chuckled. "You can read it wherever you want, and you don't have to tell me what's in it."

"Thank you." He clung to the letter like it might disappear.

Bird flipped over her own letter and laid it beside her sewing machine. After all this time, she'd expected a quick "Thank you" or an "I'll explain when I get back." But now, several handwritten pages lay before her. Certainly, a story. Any story Leah had to tell her now would be a hard one to read. She would wait until the workday ended, and she could retire for the evening and hold whatever Leah needed her to hold.

> Hello, Bird,
>
> I owe you plenty of explaining. This the best I can do for now. I don't sleep much in here. I'm doing every bit of time I got. But last night, I slept long and hard enough to even finish a dream. I was back down south standing on the old mine road that I once walked from the bottom of Virginia to its top. The dream always starts the same. Me walking to my Grandma's house under the burning sun. I fight making this walk but can never stop myself. I walk in the middle of the road and watch the edges for my cousin, Gabriel's father. In some dreams, he jumps from behind a tree or a clump of bushes. Or, like it

really happened, he waited for me leaning against the shed. I'd seen him waiting on me the whole time.

In my dream last night, I was almost to Grandma's fence when I realized that he hadn't jumped out. And there wasn't no more hiding spaces. I broke out running. I would see the old woman again for the first time in decades. I'd finally beaten them, at least in my own mind. And then I heard them shouting. Ugly shouts. The devil's shouts. I hollered, wanting to run the other way, but my feet wouldn't turn and kept on dragging me toward the crowd of my own kin, aunts, uncles and cousins huddled in front of my Grandma's farm house. Get her. Show her how it is. See she likin' it. They yelled. Only two men stood outside the circle. One cousin holding the other back as he lunged and cried. At least someone tried to stop him, and them, I thought as I watched and remembered. Some drooled. Some laughed. They all hated me. They always hated me. They wouldn't have stopped him if he'd just gone on and killed me when he was done. I didn't understand then. And I don't understand it now. It must have been something in them. It couldn't have anything to do with me sobbing in the dirt.

But this time, I was outside the circle. And I was Big Lee, not little Leah. I pushed through them, knocking them to the ground. And they backed up, shocked at the grown me before them. I expected to see The Angel Gabriel's father, but he wasn't there. It was just little girl me, crouched in the center of the broken circle. She held a baby wrapped in an old quilt. I wrapped my arm around the girl-me's shoulder and stood her up. She cried into her little bundle as I led her past them and north along that old mine road. The girl never looked back, even after she stopped crying.

She asked me why, after we'd gone a ways. Grown me shook my head and told her that I've spent a lifetime wondering that. Wondering what it was about me that could make them hate me so much. I told her to let go; it was them and not her. And that she needed to make her life her own.

> She asked about her baby. I pointed further down the road and told her to keep going north until she reached the city of lights. If she loved hard on her baby while she could, he'd find his way to her there.
>
> I have no right to ask you to share this burden, but I've prayed for my son to find me every day since they took him from me. You know the love a lonely child craves. I'm asking you to protect and love him until I get back.
>
> Yours truly,
> Leah

Bird wept over the letter for half a night. What kind of people rejoiced over the destruction of a child? A child of their own blood. And Leah had somehow survived. Carried it all for so long and so many miles, and still lived and loved. Bird had kissed the scars of her back so many nights. Let there have been at least some healing in those kisses, she said to the night.

Bird pictured Vernon by the pond, axe in hand, towering over two frightened boys. She'd thought him excessive all those years ago; but he'd paid the insurance on her safety and for so many girls.

The next day when Charmain arrived on her doorstep, Bird noted Leah's thoroughness. She had sent truth and help.

"I've brought some clothes for Gabriel and some cake." Charmain patted the shopping bag slung over her arm. Her tone was matter-of-fact, and Bird noticed that she'd assumed her identity was known and no introductions were required.

"Gabe, you have a visitor," Bird yelled up the stairs since they weren't standing on any ceremony.

The woman's veneer cracked as Gabe trotted down the stairs. Charmain extended a nervous hand. "I'm Charmain." She glanced at Bird. "Your mother's friend. I'd like to visit you every now and then."

Gabe glanced at Bird, who didn't dare move a muscle. She'd wanted help, and she'd received it. Of course, it made sense for Leah to send Charmain. At the very least, this confirmed that they were serious.

# January 1934

For her next visit, Sharon Armstrong arrived just before Bird flipped her sign on a Friday evening. The woman carried her satchel and couldn't have looked more like a high school attendance secretary if she tried.

"Good news or bad?" asked Bird as she opened the door and waved the woman in.

Sharon glanced back to the street and then stepped in. "I hope you don't mind a quick visit. These kids have me running around Harlem. They must think I like the cold."

"Then, I'll take it that it's bad news. Tea? Rest your coat?"

"I couldn't impose," Sharon demurred.

"Trust me, it's a social etiquette requirement where I'm from."

"Then let me not offend you."

Sharon wrapped her fingers around the teacup, and Bird forced her attention to the sugar bowl. I am too old for this, and this woman is probably too young. She guessed her to be twenty-six or twenty-seven.

"He's doing better, but doesn't attend every day," explained Miss Armstrong.

"What could he possibly be doing?" asked Bird, perplexed.

"He's made a few friends. Good boys, although they're at the age where their combined intelligence isn't too high. I'm keeping an eye on them."

Miss Armstrong's asserted ownership of this situation loosened the knot in Bird's stomach enough to keep her from all out panic. "He hasn't said anything or brought anyone home."

"Welcome to adolescence."

"Any thoughts on what I should do?" asked Bird and then remembered her supposed role as Gabe's aunt. "You must think I'm a mess. I didn't expect to be raising a teenage boy . . . or anticipate the complications of doing so in this city."

The attendance secretary shook her head and smiled, her eyes soft with amused empathy. "Just keep the boundaries firm the best you can. The worst trouble is found at night. Keeping him home then is half the battle."

"Do they teach you all of this in attendance secretary training?"

Miss Armstrong laughed. "I wish. Just watching the trials and tribulations of the families at church. It's no easy task getting them through these years. You try to raise them one way, and the city is selling them everything else."

"And that is the truth." Bird's mind raced to think of anything to say to keep this woman from standing up and leaving. "Are you from Harlem?" she blurted with a desperate awkwardness.

"Brooklyn. My great-grandparents came up after freedom in the Carolinas. You're from Virginia?" There was a note of a test in Miss Armstrong's voice.

Bird hesitated. How could she avoid digging this hole of a lie any deeper? "It's complicated. Let's just say by way of Illinois. My family comes from all over the South." This was true enough Bird figured.

"Oooh, that makes me think about Mr. Robeson's *Showboat*. Have you seen it yet?"

"Years ago, during its first run."

"I won't miss it this time."

A question flitted across Bird's mind. She could so easily say, "I'd love to see it again too. I could look for tickets. Maybe next weekend?" Instead, she held onto her teacup for dear life. A glance ventured across the table found a shy gaze that made Bird's heart pound. Bird was both disappointed and relieved when Louise knocked on the door and let herself in.

"I got the pig feet for the greens," Louise called ahead of herself and then stopped short at the kitchen.

Bird could only laugh; at least this confirmed her country credentials. "Mrs. Louise Hurtis, please meet Miss Armstrong, the attendance secretary at Gabe's school. Our young man is mostly attending these days."

Miss Armstrong stood, "Which is better than not hardly attending." She looked around like she might find her coat and the front door in the kitchen.

"Thank you for the update. I will heed your advice." Bird led her to the door and wanted to ask Louise why she didn't turn around and put the damned pig feet in the cooler.

Curiosity killed the cat, Bird told herself as she waited outside the theater box office window. A few tickets couldn't cost that much. What was the point of raising a child in the city if he didn't get to see the excellence to which he could aspire? And these so-called friends could use some guidance too. She imagined she and Miss Armstrong wrangling ten boys in their Sunday best to the theater district until the clerk told her the price for twelve tickets.

"There's no group discount?" she asked.

"Sorry, not these days," the clerk said and looked over her shoulder for the next customer.

Bird headed back to the train. There was one more place she could try. She checked her watch. If she hurried, she could finish her business without having to see anyone but Mazie and Alicia.

"I want to take Gabe to see *Showboat*," she blurted to Mazie.

"Then take him." Mazie chopped celery like it had wronged her. "If you want me to go with you, you know I don't go in for the theater."

"I want to take him and some friends he's fallen in with. It'll be good for them, but the tickets are a bit much for my budget."

"How many do you need?"

"Twelve."

Mazie finally looked up.

"You taking eleven boys to the theater by yourself? You trying for sainthood?"

"Not exactly. The attendance secretary may be interested in coming along and helping me." Bird flushed as Mazie grinned.

"Have you asked this secretary lady if she's even willing to put herself through all of this, for the children?"

"I know she wants to see the show."

"Bird, how old are you? And how have you ever gotten a woman before?"

"I'm clearly thirteen," said Bird, indignant. "And you know my resume is short in that area."

Mazie sighed and went back to chopping. "Let me see what I can do."

The next Tuesday, a young man who only asked her name and looked her up and down, as if to verify her identity against some description he'd received, delivered an envelope with seven theater tickets and a note from Mazie. "Give yourself a sporting chance with the secretary and only take five boys. I want an update."

By 3:00 p.m., Bird had hustled out her last appointment and commissioned Louise to handle any customers who dropped by to pick up their clothing.

"Where's your hat?" asked Louise, as Bird turned to the door.

"My hat?" she asked, not hiding her impatience.

"I never stood for a man calling on me without a hat."

"Louise, I am not a man."

"But you are going calling. Wear the taupe tea hat. It frames your face so nicely and flatters your brown. And shows you got a bit of fashion about you."

Bird whirled back to Louise. "What do you think I do for a living old woman?"

Louise was unmoved. "What we do for others, we must also do for ourselves."

"Better?" snapped Bird as she settled the hat into place.

"Much. Good luck."

The asking had been easy enough. Bird had got wind of tickets and remembered their conversation. She hoped that Miss Armstrong hadn't already seen it yet or didn't mind seeing it twice. Miss Armstrong had blushed but accepted her part in the venture without hesitation. The hardest part had been getting Gabe to agree to corral his friends and talk them into dress slacks and shirts.

She ushered this spindly combination of young man arms and legs through Harlem, onto the train, and to the theater where they arrived with five minutes to spare. Miss Armstrong waited for them out front and flashed a nervous smile to the group.

"Hi Miss," the boys offered in a loose chorus.

"I hope you didn't think we'd stood you up," Bird tried to say lightly as she read a new stiffness in the secretary's shoulders and general demeanor.

"Not at all," said Miss Armstrong, struggling to affect some of her usual warmth. "You're actually earlier than I thought you'd be, and who knew you all cleaned up so well." Despite their commitment to sulking, the boys stood a bit straighter and ventured eye contact after the compliment.

"Is this the crew?" said a man's voice behind them.

As Bird turned to the voice, Miss Armstrong answered, "It is, and their benefactress, Miss Bird Bennett."

A tall, light-skinned man had asked the question and beamed an owning look around all of them that made Bird immediately dislike him. At his side stood a woman who looked so much like Sharon Armstrong, Bird blinked with disbelief. The woman scanned Bird up and down before offering a limp hand.

"Miss Bennett, please meet my sister Mrs. Carolyn Burgess and her husband Deacon Ralph Burgess. The Deacon runs a young men's ministry at my father's church."

"And when I heard of this little adventure," the Deacon cut in and clasped Gabe's shoulder, "I knew the good Lord wouldn't want me to leave two young women burdened with what should be a man's responsibility."

Bird felt all eyes on her. Gabe and the boys seemed prepared to respond to whatever signal she sent out. Bird forced Odelia's cheery lilt into her voice. "Then, it will be a little meeting we have here."

Deacon Burgess laughed. "Yes, indeed, a few gathered in His name."

Their seats were high in the balcony, with the Burgesses a few rows away. Bird tried to relax as the house lights dimmed and the curtains opened. The boys had settled in and showed grudging signs of excitement as the concert A sounded and the theater quieted. Miss Armstrong sat statuesque—beautiful and unyielding through the acts and said little at the intermission. By the last act, Mr. Robeson had convinced the boys and even saved a bit of the night for Bird. As she led her crew back uptown after a Deacon Burgess–led prayer circle in the middle of Broadway and stilted goodbyes that Miss Armstrong barely participated in, Bird took comfort in the boy's spirited rehashing of scenes and all the pride with which they carried themselves through the New York City night.

For two weeks, Gabe came and went from school, or so Bird assumed. "What'd you learn today?" she'd ask him over dinner, and he'd rattle off some feat of mechanical skill. She wanted to ask after Miss Armstrong but held her tongue. He'd started mentioning more information about his friends, but nothing about anyone else. Louise listened with mirth to these conversations.

"Perhaps you should drop in and check his attendance?" Louise asked as they cleared the kitchen one night.

"I was being silly," said Bird. "All's well that ends well."

"I done seen attendance secretaries on this block five times in all my years here and four of them was that woman at this house."

"The fifth time?" asked Bird.

"A different lady. She'd misread the street number."

Bird threw a tea towel across the table. "Louise, I got the tickets and wrangled five boys. I could have only added a rose."

"Back in my day, if a suitor got distracted, you sauntered around and did a little reminding."

Bird tried to imagine Louise sauntering. "Thank you, Louise, really," she said, appreciating how far they'd come. "It's best if I leave things where they lay; silence is its own answer sometimes."

Two days later, Louise waited—with mail in hand—for Bird to finish with a customer. She placed the envelope on the sewing machine. "Looks like somebody has something to say." The envelope's corner said only "S. Armstrong."

> Dear Bird, it has taken me this long to recover from the malady of embarrassment. I try to limit my friends' exposure to the righteous quirks of my family. Can I make it up to you with dinner? Friday? 7 p.m.? The Bistro on 148th and Lenox? Sincerely, Sharon

Louise nodded with approval. "Two days isn't enough time to make a sharp enough dress. You'll have to buy one."

Sharon waited for Bird at the appointed corner. Bird sighed with relief at the comfort with which the woman stood while waiting, without anxiety or self-consciousness, and instead a pleasant surveyance of the world passing her by. They greeted each other with a quick hug.

"I've never been here," said Sharon, "but one of the teachers at school raves about the gumbo."

"Mmmm," said Bird, "Apparently one of my great-great grandmothers was from Louisiana. I've always wanted to try it."

They navigated a narrow staircase and into an entryway so dark that only the subtle sounds of music and the smell of spices and frying oil kept Bird from turning around.

"Your eyes will adjust ladies," said a man's smooth voice. "A table for two?"

"Yes, please," said Sharon as she pointed Bird ahead of her. Bird raised an eyebrow; was Sharon sending signals or being polite since she'd picked the restaurant? The question was both arousing and nerve-wracking.

As they followed the maître d' into the restaurant's main dining area, Bird's eyes did adjust to the low lights and candles. The tiny establishment held several large tables in the center, with two-seaters around the edge. Someone had designed the two-seaters for intimacy and discretion.

The maître d' seated Sharon first and then turned to Bird. Bird almost spit as she looked up into the coal dark eyes of Sebastian. He grabbed her and nearly lifted her off her feet.

"It's always so dark in the entryway, I hardly recognize any of the old crowd until we reach a table." He glanced from Bird to Sharon and chuckled. He'd grown up a bit over the past couple of years, filled out in the chest, and switched his hair to a heavily pomaded side swoop.

"It's good to see you, Seabass," said Bird. "Trouble didn't find you?"

"No, ma'am. I was out with the flu—been flying straight ever since. I look good, right?"

She inspected the cut of his suit and the calm behind his eyes.

"You do, Seabass."

"Well, don't let me keep you from your very lovely company," he said with a wink as he held her chair out and Bird slid in. Bird focused for far too long on her napkin, unsure of what she would see or should say when she looked up. Sharon watched her as she filled each of their water glasses from a carafe in the table's middle.

"Bass and I go back a few years," she said.

"Yes, to the old crowd. There's a lot you need to tell me about yourself."

"There is," Bird paused and matched Sharon's gaze. The woman flinched. "A lot. I should . . . I thought we could spend time together, but I don't want to make trouble for you."

Sharon leaned forward, alarmed.

Bird pulled a bill out of her wallet and placed it in the table's center. "I know Bass because he was a bartender at a club the last person I dated worked at. Her name is Leah. She got caught up in a raid not too long after we called it quits and is upstate until next year. She's Gabe's mother. So, if you go around with me—people know about me." She slid the bill across the table. "In case you want to stay and eat, and for carfare home."

Sharon grabbed her hand and squeezed. "Stay, Bird. Please."

As Bird stood to leave, Seabass walked up with a bottle of wine in hand. "You looking for the bathroom? To the back and left."

"Yes, thank you."

Bird caught her breath in the dank room and expected Sharon to be gone on her return. She remained at the table.

"I ordered the gumbo for us," she said. "I've never dabbled much into spirits, but the wine seems good to me."

Bird sat down.

"You mentioned making trouble. I don't know that there's any trouble that I haven't already made for myself. I do want to spend time with you. I didn't know about your openness, but things are hard to hide in Harlem. I'd hoped we could walk and talk after the theater last week, but my sister barged in. She heard me mention you and the show and thought I sounded funny. I was supposed to have been purified of this trouble years ago."

"I'm sorry," said Bird.

"For what?"

"The weight."

Sharon leaned forward and put her hand on Bird's. "Right now, I feel lightness."

"Then let's dine slow."

After dinner, they walked by the river, and Bird fell in love with New York City again, and Harlem, and walking in the cool night air.

"And what happens when Leah comes home?" Sharon asked the question Bird sensed she'd been working up to.

Bird shrugged. "I think she'll go to Charmain's in Jersey. I'm worried that Gabe will give up on school then."

"She won't want to come back to your house?" Sharon's voice was soft as she poked around Bird's life.

Bird stopped so she could say what she had to say and give it the seriousness that was due. "Leah and I shared a season, and there was much good in it, but I don't think either of us was surprised when it ended. If I was mad or hurt about any of it, it was about the how. I knew she wasn't the staying-in-one-place type. And I'd just asked that she be up front with her moving on plans. She said she would, but when it came to it, she wasn't. I deserved better than that." With the last words, she turned to Sharon and held her eyes. She hated saying it, talking about the ending in the joy of the beginning, but she had to look out for herself. "And I ask the same of you."

Sharon gazed down the street ahead. "I understand."

"You're sure Gabe isn't home?" Sharon asked as they climbed Bird's stoop.

Bird pointed to his bedroom window. "He sleeps with his light on. Every night. All night."

"What's he afraid of?"

"He won't say. I can only imagine what he saw or went through on his trip here. And maybe even when he was back with Leah's family."

Bird offered wine and coffee as they removed coats, scarves, and shoes in the foyer. Sharon opted for water and the restroom. After pointing her guest to the back of the apartment, Bird checked her hair in the hallway mirror, then her breath, and then the locks on the doors. The tightness in her stomach was as delicious as it was torturous. She had never been an adept seductress, but she was the leading lady in this scene. If there's a God, she thought, she'll be naked in my bed when I get there.

Sharon was fully clothed, save for her jacket. "This is lovely," she gestured around the bedroom that Bird had decorated in an English countryside style she'd once seen in a magazine. "I pegged you for simpler tastes."

Chuckling, Bird opened the French doors that led to the little side room she used for reading. "I don't have much use for a proper living room, but I do appreciate some comforts."

Sharon hiked her skirt just a bit and tucked her legs under her as she sunk into the couch in the reading room. "That is very good to know," she said. She accepted and sipped the water Bird offered.

Bird leaned in the door frame between the bedroom and reading room. Sharon seemed ready to play her cards slowly, and Bird feared that all the wine and the long day would beat her desire. Why did everything have to be so complicated, especially those things that could be so easy? She'd have to be decisive. She remained in sight as she stepped back into her bedroom. "What are your plans for the rest of the weekend?" she asked as she unbuttoned her blouse and laid it at the foot of her bed. She considered letting her skirt fall as well but decided on more restraint. She turned to find Sharon's eyes intent on her.

"Please make yourself comfortable," Bird suggested.

"I am suddenly self-conscious," said Sharon.

"You remember what I do for a living. There were ten half-naked women here just this morning."

"In your bedroom?"

Bird shook her head. "No, just four in the bedroom. I was barely on time for dinner."

"Then you might find it all boring." Sharon sat down her glass and unbuttoned her shirt. "Really though, do you sleep with your clients?"

"It's not that kind of business. And how many women do you think are out here falling into other women's beds? We are a small tribe, my dear." She noted Sharon's blink and backed off. "If you really want to know, just two in six years."

"Leah and . . . ?"

"You should be a detective."

"Noted."

"There was a woman who came for alternations near the end of my second year in the city. She had an air of sadness around her. I was lonely and likely had an air of sadness around myself too. We comforted each other." Bird wished for another glass of wine as she considered the memory. It had been another two years before Leah had entered her life.

Sharon crossed the room to her. "I hope I didn't make you sad. I'm not the jealous type, I promise. I just feel inexperienced and embarrassed."

"It only marginally matters how much experience anyone has," said Bird. "I've never kissed you before. Or your neck, or the bend of your elbow. I want to learn all the ways to please you." She stepped closer; Sharon held her breath. "Will you show me everything I need to know?" She lifted Sharon's chin and kissed her parted lips, and then her neck. Sharon moaned as Bird's hands slid to her breasts.

"Yes," whispered Sharon, and that was the most beautifully said word Bird had ever heard.

To the best of her ability, Bird let the lessons and constraints of her life guide her—or guard her, she admitted to herself as she waited at the front of the train platform as train after train passed. Gabe kept them mostly honest. The risk of one arriving before the other departed had kept Sharon's nervous visits to the weekends when the boy could be safely confined to Brooklyn with Irma and Rupert or Jersey with Charmain. She'd put off this visit to Mazie's for over a month. There was a commitment of sorts in bringing someone to Mazie's—an announcement without any way to spell out all the caveats and messy details. Though Mazie would read them quickly enough and would probably tell her how long this would last, if Bird had the gumption to ask her. Sharon waited at the window of the first car of the next train as it rolled into the station. Bird bounced up grinning, leaving her ruminations on the bench behind her.

Esau chuckled as they entered. Bird rolled her eyes at him and pulled the near-frozen Sharon by the sleeve. She'd asked for a discreet place to meet during the week. There was only one place in Harlem that Bird knew of that was clean, comfortable, had good food, and kept secrets better than time itself.

"Ma'am," Sharon said to Mazie with a slight nod after their introduction.

Bird waited as the two women appraised each other. She'd expected this bit from Mazie; Sharon's ability to hold her own impressed.

"Nice to meet you, finally," said Mazie with a feigned annoyance.

"Everything in its time," said Bird, leading them out of the kitchen.

"What if we see someone I know?" Sharon whispered.

"Then we buy them the house special—a drink called 'discretion.'"

The combination lounge and dining space was only half full. A few regulars ate at the two- and three-seaters against the far wall. A group of young men slurred through a notably eloquent argument. "What a man writes today, he couldn't have written a month ago," a sallow young man argued to the others. "He is changed, and his understanding of the world is changed with every moment he's lived in the intervening days."

One of the men across from him folded his arms, the other shook his head and took a long drag of his cigarette. The latter raised his drink and sipped heavily before speaking, "Maybe he couldn't, but it is because creation is a spontaneous act. The outcome of innumerable variables and circumstances."

"That's what I just said," said the first man.

Bird and Sharon listened, looked at each other, and laughed. "The writers," explained Bird. "They are very passionate and often entertaining, until Mazie tires of them, or they start yelling at each other and she boots them out."

"I thought it would be smokier and darker, more dangerous," said Sharon, studying the other tables.

"We can try a Saturday night if you prefer something seedier. Thursdays are for the folks who can't get out on a Saturday night."

"This suits me just fine," she whispered as she leaned in, and her lips brushed Bird's ear.

"Drinking or eating?" asked Charmain, somehow suddenly standing above them.

Bird sank back into the couch. "Drinks, please. Two vodka tonics."

Charmain didn't move. Sharon glanced back and forth between them with undisguised curiosity. Bird obliged them both, deciding to make nice and say Charmain's name the way she would have. "Sharon, Charming. Charming, Sharon."

"What a lovely name," offered Sharon.

"Thank you," said Charmain, a little friendlier. "I'll have your drinks in a moment."

"Another friend from the old crowd?" asked Sharon after Charmain had disappeared into the kitchen.

"Not hardly. She's the woman Leah moved on to." It took everything Bird had not to add, "and her name's really Charmain."

Sharon's jaw dropped. "Then, I owe her a debt of gratitude. Is there a drink called that?"

Bird laughed. "She'd prefer one called a big tip."

"A small price to pay." Sharon nestled into Bird's arms.

Bird slid her hand around Sharon's waist and rested it against the curve of Sharon's thigh. You can enjoy this for a little while, she told herself.

# March 1935

If asked to list Gabe's primary interests, Bird would say food, plumbing, sleep, and plotting his way to Bedford. She considered him blind to just about anything else in his life, and hers. She used this to her advantage. It took just a little orchestrating to keep Gabe and Sharon on separate tracks around her. On the night the twain converged, Bird had to admit her folly. She didn't have a God, but she held a healthy respect for the fates. That night, she remembered a poem she'd once heard about the entwined fates of the *Titanic* and the iceberg. In the vastness of the ocean, the ship and the ice had found each other, almost as if there'd been no choice for either. Other twains had met in her life and bloodline. On a country road, white men with a shotgun had crossed the paths of Odelia and her young husband. An unclaimed child who'd never been to church once found herself under a revival tent and her father's shadow. Sharon and Gabe had to meet one day.

The middle of the night knock at her bedroom door panicked Bird. Gabe's hands were blunt devices without subtlety. Louise wouldn't have dared. This gentle, almost apologetic tap didn't belong to anyone welcome to enter her home at odd hours. Someone inclined to breach her space and then knock had to be crazy. She threw the blanket over Sharon, who woke and stiffened. "Someone's here. Don't move and don't make a sound." Bird slid into her house robe and grabbed the switch blade in her nightstand drawer.

"Who is it?" Bird braced her weight against her bedroom door.

"It's Rupert. Gabe's okay, but he got hurt."

Bird ripped the door open and pushed past the hulking, humbled man. She had a vague sense of shared terror behind her but the fear of everything else in the world had dropped away. "Where is he? What happened?"

Rupert pointed to the front room. "We was working on a boiler pipe and the steam escaped," he explained, stumbling after her.

Gabe sat in one of the customer chairs, in a shirt with a ripped-off sleeve. A clean white bandage covered his left arm. He wobbled a bit as if half asleep or mostly dazed. Bird knelt beside him and took his face in her hands. "I'm okay. I got ahead of my training," he mumbled.

"I'm really sorry, Bird. I'd give anything for it to have been me. We went to the hospital and got it looked at. It'll scar, but the muscle was spared. I covered the bill." Rupert cried as he spoke.

"It ain't his fault, Bird. He told me he'd do it, but I wanted to show him I could," Gabe's voice pleaded with her.

Bird dropped back onto the floor and studied the foot long bandaging wrapped around the boy's arm. He was too young for such an injury and might not get lucky next time. In her panic, she wanted to yell at someone. Rupert would have been the easiest, and he would have taken it and maybe thought he'd deserved it. She had extended Leah's trust to him. But the boy was headstrong. And it could have been worse—his face or his life.

"It isn't anybody's fault, Rupert," she said, and the room exhaled around her. "These things happen. I wanted to keep him out of the streets, but maybe he's too young to be working with you."

Gabe bolted up, now crying himself. "I'm not, Bird."

She put a hand on his uninjured arm. "Son, the thing about being young is that we don't know what we're too young for."

"There's little jobs, Bird," said Rupert. "Or, he could just visit. It's good for him and us. Taylor loves him."

Bird nodded, "Keeping visiting is fine. Let's revisit the working when he's sixteen."

Gabe opened his mouth, and Rupert raised his hand. "She's right, son."

The boy started to lower his head and stopped midway; his eyes focused on something in the distance. "Miss Armstrong?" he asked.

Both Bird and Rupert's heads jerked back. Sharon hesitated in the kitchen entryway and Louise leaned halfway across the apartment's threshold.

"Oh," said Rupert.

"I . . . was worried . . . and forgot myself," said Sharon.

"I figured something must be wrong with all the stomping around," said Louise, though her presence was clearly not the reason for the moment's rouging surprise.

"I didn't realize," Rupert trailed off.

Bird willed herself to turn back around and meet Gabe's accusatory stare. "But what about my mother?" he demanded.

"You know?" Bird's eyes popped.

"Of course. You said she lived here, and I only see one bed. And folks back home whispered about," he paused, "things."

"I'm going to get dressed and go," said Sharon.

Bird rubbed her temples. "Sharon, please just go back to the bedroom. Gabe, we'll talk about all this in the morning. Go to bed. Rupert, you can do whatever you want."

"I'ma go home," said Rupert. "I'll be back to check on y'all after work tomorrow."

"Suit yourself. Everybody move," Bird ordered, and to her relief, everyone complied.

The next morning, Sharon slipped out before breakfast and Gabe's groaning pleas for any kind of pain relief. Louise took all this movement as an invitation and joined them at the kitchen table.

"Y'all look like hell," said Louise, dropping butter into her grits.

"You're one to talk," said Bird as she applied chipped ice wrapped in a towel to Gabe's arm. He choked down his aspirin and looked like he was feeling all of his earned misery.

"I'm sorry, son," said Bird. "If I would have known this was possible."

He grimaced. "It'll heal. I should have listened. Feel bad for Rupert. I've never seen a man that big cry. I want to keep going. He's teaching me . . . everything. And I can help in other ways."

Louise and Bird locked eyes. Rupert was teaching him the things she couldn't, maybe even Leah couldn't. Ahh, thought Bird, the boy has found a father. She'd hoped for a friendship or uncle arrangement. Laying claim to a father was much more beautiful and much more complicated. Rupert clearly cared for the boy, but Bird wasn't sure he sensed what was developing on the other end. She sighed and sipped her tea; she would have to talk to him, and hopefully not spook him. "You're welcome to keep visiting, Gabe," she said and stopped the boy's anxious picking at his hand.

It would be a day of difficult conversations. "And do you have questions about me and Miss Armstrong?"

Gabe shook his head. "I have questions about you and my mother."

Louise made a movement to stand. Bird raised a hand to stop her. Everything should be clear among them all.

"Gabe, your mother is with Charmain."

The boy stretched back as he considered this. "I wondered about that, but then, why she got me living here with you unless this is where she wants to come back to?"

The edges of Louise's mouth turned up acknowledging the logic of this.

"There are things you can ask of some people that you can't ask of others. Your mother and I go back years; she and Charmain were still pretty new when she got into trouble. And Charmain has her own boys to fend for. You can have a lot less responsibility here and focus on yourself."

"And when my mother comes back?" Gabe's raised eyes held a mix of guilt and sadness.

"My love, you have come all this way for your mother." She tightened her hand on his forearm. "I know you'll go with her wherever she goes. You are always welcome here too."

Gabe sat back with relief.

"I do have to ask something of you, Gabe," said Bird. "It's not right for an adult to ask a child to keep a secret for her, but I don't see a way around it given the circumstances. Miss Armstrong could lose her job if folks knew that she stayed here sometimes. Please don't tell anyone, not even your friends."

Gabe snorted. "I wouldn't tell them knuckleheads anything. Will she come back?"

"I don't know. I hope so."

# April 1935

Alda Price was never on time. The woman didn't work, had three children in school, and a husband at work, but still couldn't find her way to Bird's house by closing time. And then, she had the nerve to want to gab, keeping Bird or Louise at the door for twenty minutes. Sharon had just laid the chicken on the table, and Gabe was pouring the water when the doorbell rang.

Bird pushed Gabe toward the door. "It's Alda. She owes me a dollar twenty-five. Hers is the blue dress."

Gabe knew the drill. He answered stray customers with polite ma'ams and sirs. His schooling was going well. Yes, he was still growing. No, he didn't know if he'd be as tall as his father. Beyond this, they got nothing else out of him and cut their small talk short. So, when the boy was back in less than a minute, Bird thought little of it until he hovered at the kitchen's edge, which was not his norm once the meat hit the table.

"It's a lady for Miss Armstrong," he said, still going back and forth between the formal and familiar, afraid that he'd slip and say the wrong one at school. "She say she your sister."

Sharon's glass stopped, suspended halfway between her lips and the table. Bird's carving knife missed the joint and jammed against the bone. "Something must be wrong," said Sharon. "Wait here." She stretched out a hand to keep Bird in her seat, as if anything but rope could do that.

Bird ignored the hand and left the knife in the chicken. Carolyn Armstrong Burgess stood in the brownstone's foyer. As she peered from under her dripping church hat, Bird thought she looked like a woman who had battled her way to hell and then was mad to find it actually existed.

It hurt to see eyes so much like Sharon's rove over her like she was the pestilence Carolyn clearly thought she was.

"You are hard to find, sister," said Carolyn, both despairing and angry.

Sharon stopped mid-step. Bird willed her to see the trap laid before her—baited with guilt, shame, or something akin to love, or all three.

"I didn't know I needed to leave an address every time I dined with a friend. You remember Bird Bennett."

Carolyn inhaled. "I've come to get you, before you find yourself in irredeemable peril."

"Peril?" Sharon said, almost laughing. "Let's talk tomorrow. I was planning on staying the night at Mommy and Daddy's anyway." Bird inched forward to offer whatever support proximity could. She imagined asking Carolyn to join them, slipping the wine away, and trying to win her over. If pressed, she could search deep for her grandmother's grace and charm. This was fantasy though. Carolyn reminded her of Helena Charles and the type of people who wouldn't break bread at the table of anyone they considered a sinner. That is until, she thought of Maddy letting out Cecile's wedding dress, a little more of life caught up with them.

"I've given you plenty of time to get all this out of your system." Carolyn grimaced like she stood in a burlesque parlor. "Reverend Coventry has been invited for dinner tomorrow, since you can't make time to see him again."

Sharon straightened. Bird flinched and then hated that she had let anything show in front of this woman.

"I keep my own calendar," said Sharon, "and decide where to spend my time."

As if to call her bluff, Carolyn said, "If you don't come with me now. I'll have Daddy here in an hour."

"Carolyn, I am a grown woman."

"You are weak . . . and misled," said Carolyn. "I should have intervened after the theater. I will have to answer for that."

Sharon crossed her arms. Carolyn balled her fists.

"Do I need to find a telephone?" asked Carolyn.

"I don't answer to you."

"I wish, for your sake, you did, sister."

"Carolyn!" Sharon yelled.

Beneath the anger and hurt loaded into the yell, Bird heard the resolve splintering. In two steps, she had swept Sharon into the sewing room.

"Let go of my sister," said Carolyn, raising a hand in the air.

Bird called on a lesson from both Maddy and Helena Charles—the stone face and chest puffing that will stop another woman in her tracks. Letting her know that whatever she started, you were prepared to finish.

"Bird," this time Sharon let her anger out into Bird's name. "I have to go sort this out, or it'll be a bigger mess."

"You don't have to go."

"It's not that easy, Bird. She's serious. She'll have the whole damn congregation up here carrying on outside of this house. I'll have her calmed down before the train even hits West 4th Street. And I'll be back in a few days."

Bird shook her head and wished Gabe would turn away. "If you go with her, either they won't let you come back, or you'll decide you don't want to."

"I said that whatever happens between us, it wouldn't be like this. And I meant it. I'll be back."

Bird let go of her arm and wanted to sink to the floor but held her stance. She had her pride even if Carolyn could care less if she danced, cried, or died. Bird had crawled up and down this road. She'd thought she'd been smart, drew her line in the sand, and demanded respect for her feelings. But she'd still had lessons to learn. She'd thought that people could see the ways they were about to hurt you. Like a driver realizing that if they didn't stop at the traffic signal, they'd hit the woman crossing the street. Now, she saw in Sharon's assuredness, her lover's complete obliviousness to her own reckless driving.

Louise found Bird sitting at the kitchen table in front of the decimated chicken. Bird had finished carving the dark meat for Gabe, and he'd asked if he should go get Louise.

"I'm fine," she'd said. "No point in letting the chicken go to waste."

He didn't ask anything else. Once he'd finished as much as he could, he excused himself and eased downstairs. He'd simply told Louise that Miss Armstrong's sister had come for her, and it would be best if she checked on Bird.

Louise frowned at the butchered chicken and the woman who sat pale behind it.

"I didn't know what to do last time. I'd hoped it wouldn't come to this. I'll do better this time."

"She said she'll be back."

"Hmph," said Louise. "It's good to know women do just like men." She poured Bird a shot of the hard medicine from deep in the cupboards. "Shoot it back, and I'll help you to bed."

Not knowing how she would possibly get up from the table on her own, Bird downed the nip and accepted the aid. At least then, Gabe wouldn't find her stuck in the same place in the morning.

The days dragged Bird into the next week and then another. She stopped counting and sewed, cooked, and ate and lived as well as anyone could. These things were all easy enough. The rent was due. Gabe preferred eating over not eating. She could fit the pieces of her life together like the steps in a dance. If her feet followed the correct movements, wouldn't the song take over at some point? Louise began coming up after closing hours each night, and they fell back into their pre-Leah rituals of tea and neighborhood talk. Gabe joined them sometimes. Bird felt both his boredom and how this gesture of adolescent sacrifice was meant to show care and concern the best way he could.

On a Saturday night, when Gabe had gone to Irma and Rupert's, Louise dealt them a hand for hearts after dinner.

"You taking this one harder," Louise said.

"How do you figure?" asked Bird.

"With Leah, you got mad. Every word you said had a bit of fire under it."

"She didn't handle her business respectfully. And she was too old not to." Bird paused. "Sharon . . . didn't get in as deep. Leah still has stuff in this house, and hell, a child too. Sharon was barely here. I just didn't realize it. I'd only be spitting fire at myself. I should've known better. A mistake I seem to keep making."

"If folks saw everything for what it was, humans been done died out years ago."

"Everybody except you," said Bird. "You never let anyone get in this house after your husband died."

Louise shook her head and tapped her cards on the table. "I was married fifteen years. Loving was good, and it was hard as hell. After Jimmy died, I just didn't want to do it again. I was old enough that I could read the road ahead. And most folks don't offer too many surprises, and what surprises do come usually ain't the good kind. I been with myself for a long time, and it's been good enough. I'm always on time, have good conversation, and get myself all the right gifts," she laughed. "I'm the best steady I ever had."

"But did you get lonely?" asked Bird.

Louise nodded. "Of course, and still do." She waved her hand toward the yellowed ceiling. "We thought we'd eventually fill this place with children and grandchildren, but it never happened for us. Sometimes, I swear I hear echoes of all the laughter that should've been. But we is always alone," Louise went on, talking more to herself than Bird. "We're in this big old city and alone at the same time. We're sitting here talking to each other, but really, we're alone. You seeing the world one way and me seeing it another. Not fighting that, and learning how to be with ourselves makes the difference. Most folks never get halfway there."

"Maybe it's easier if you choose it," said Bird.

"Really, ain't no choosing what just is."

A reluctant Gabe confirmed the finality of Miss Armstrong's departure. He came home one night smelling of reefer, arriving just as the dinner table was set. He picked at the table as he told Bird, "They hired a new attendance lady and said Miss Armstrong moved back to Brooklyn to tend to her family."

Bird kept passing around the fixings, trying to keep the anger out of her movements. She hated that bad news always came before dinner time. Louise lowered the plate of pork chops to the table, and the loud thump made Bird jump. She fought to keep her tone even. "Why don't y'all start without me," she said, and then excused herself and didn't get up until Louise made her get ready for her appointments the next afternoon.

The next night, she read at Louise's as her host snored on her couch. The night carried the first whisp of the season's real warmth. If Leah were still in the picture, she'd go to Mazie's just to get out into the air. She missed the hum of energy in the room, the sense of togetherness of a boat full of strangers in a tucked away pocket of Harlem. "To hell with this," she said to herself. "I'm a member of that club, and Mazie probably halfway likes me." A bleary-eyed Louise let herself be escorted downstairs. "Where you going this time of night?" she asked.

"I'm going to fry some chicken. Alone or not."

"Bring some back," said Louise.

The few two-seaters edging the living room were full. A group piled on the couch. Men and the working girls negotiated in the corners. Mazie and Alicia sweated in the kitchen.

"I've heard complaints about the quality of the fried chicken since I gave up my apron here," she said in the kitchen doorway.

Mazie put her hands on her hips and stared at Bird for a long second. Bird swallowed and straightened. Mazie then howled with laughter. "You know, I still got fools coming in here asking like they knew yo' Mama. 'Licia, get that bird in some water. We havin' a midnight special." Mazie held out an arm to stop Bird as she headed to the spice cabinet. "Charmain is coming through here at eleven. I don't want no trouble."

"I just want to make some chicken and have a couple of drinks."

"Does that mean you don't want to get paid?"

"Have you ever paid me?"

"Fair enough," Mazie said as she wrote the new midnight special on the board. Mama Maddy's Fried Bird.

When Alicia finished tending the greens and started delivering the orders, Mazie demanded her update. "What happened to your lady friend?"

"Her family came for her. A month ago," Bird forced the words out.

"I'm sorry. I know you liked that one. I was glad you'd found somebody better suited to you."

"Better suited than Leah?"

Mazie shrugged. "Just cuz it works don't mean it's built to last."

Bird dropped a heavy-handed shake of cayenne into the flour. "But it can be good nonetheless."

At this, Mazie smiled. "I can't argue with that."

Bird fried until the chicken ran out. "Folks wanna know if you comin' back next Friday," said Alicia as she hustled in and out with the thighs. Behind her, Charmain stepped into the kitchen.

"Mama Mazie," she said, giving a preening kiss to the proprietress.

"Bird," she said, like the name tasted bad in her mouth.

Good thing I'm done, thought Bird, she would have chilled my grease. "Charmain," Bird returned.

Mazie sighed. "You bout ready to take over for 'Licia? Mattis be by to get her home soon."

"I'm ready," said Charmain. "I didn't know I'd be sharing tips."

"Just felt like making chicken. I don't have my hand in anybody's pocket."

Later on, Bird would remember thinking, "and that's all that needs to be said." But some folks don't know when to stop. It's getting in one last word that has separated many a fool from his teeth.

"Back in the kitchen. Couldn't keep another one, eh?" asked Charmain.

Bird didn't even see it coming. The anger exploded out from her chest, and somebody was about to get burned. Maybe if she'd read it a second sooner, Mazie would have intervened, or maybe not. It was all going to have to get sorted out somehow. Better here in her place than in front of Gabe. In two strides, Bird had crossed the galley kitchen, whipped her right hand across Charmain's cheek. Charmain fell back into the dining area, landing on her rear. All conversations and heavy petting stopped.

Bird had never stood over anyone she'd knocked down before. Charmain glowered and hardly looked defeated. It had been the surprise that got her, but she wasn't making any moves to get up. "Keep my business out your mouth," snarled Bird.

Someone in their audience snickered, and a few "mmmphs" rippled across the room.

Bird was already heading for her coat when Mazie stomped out of the kitchen. "Everybody knows, and you two best of all, ain't no fighting in my place. Go on, get."

Charmain smirked at Bird, and Bird wanted to smack her again.

"You too," Mazie told Charmain. "Just 'cause ya on yo ass, don't mean you ain't in it."

Charmain didn't argue. Mazie had spoken and protesting would only get her a second lump or worse. Bird sauntered toward the door feeling like the Queen of Sheba. Let folks chew on that.

"Well, I'll be seeing you," said Bird as she started down the hall toward the steps.

"Not if I see you first," said Charmain.

The night was brisk, and Bird was fine to let the walk home calm her down. Charmain crossed to the other side of the street. Bird searched for the similarity that drew Leah to both of them. It certainly wasn't temperament, or body. Bird was plain and thin, and Charmain was curvy and well proportioned. They shared no interests, other than, she guessed, a woman who knew her away around a bed.

As they neared the downtown stop that would carry Charmain back to her Jersey connection, Bird slowed. She'd have to cross the street and pass the station, and she had no interest in crossing paths a second time—she might not win twice. Charmain stopped at the station steps and then walked past. Bird crossed the street and watched her walk further downtown into the Harlem night. Bird stopped. New Yorkers walked. Folks could walk from Harlem to midtown, if need be, and maybe if they were mad or hurt enough to the Tenderloin or the Village. But there was no walking to the PATH train from Harlem, no matter how nice the night.

"Shit," Bird said and scuttled across the street. She wanted nothing to do with Charmain. The woman all but spit in her eye any chance she got. But she was looking out for Leah's son, Leah's money, and now apparently, Leah's woman.

By the time Bird reached the midpoint of the next block, Charmain was at its corner. She shouted the woman's name the way her mama had intended it. Bird was sure that everybody in a three-block radius had heard her. Charmain kept walking. Bird walked to the corner and shouted, "I'm not chasing you." If this wasn't the damnedest bull-dyke drama she'd ever been in. Charmain stopped. "You can at least meet me," Bird said. Charmain obliged, and they met on the dark street.

"You missed your stop," said Bird.

Charmain glowered. "I'm walking."

"That's a long walk."

Charmain shrugged.

They stared at each other.

"You need train fare?" Bird said, since it wasn't her pride involved.

"No," said Charmain getting her back up.

"Ok, then, good night. Have a nice walk." Bird swiveled around and started walking away.

"Yes," Charmain said with the defiance of a child caught in a lie. "I'd planned on using the money I made to buy my way back."

Bird wanted to advise her that she shouldn't have been running her damn mouth then. But that would do no good. She inhaled and tried to think it all through. People didn't spend train fare just to make train fare. It was the end of the month. Two good nights at Mazie's could go a long way to making ends meet. Bird had a couple of dollars stuffed into her bra, but that wouldn't do this woman any good.

"I don't carry cash at night," she lied, "I'll get you something from my place."

"I don't need your money."

"Yes," said Bird, "you do. Tell Leah, she can pay me back. You gonna stand there looking mean, or can we get this taken care of?"

Charmain accepted with a grudging grunt, and the two women walked in silence.

Bird hung her coat and slipped off her shoes to her feet's relief. "My purse is in the back," she said. "Rest your coat. There's seats in the kitchen."

"I'll wait here."

"Suit yourself," said Bird. In her room, she pulled Leah's lockbox from the back of her closet. She had no idea how much Charmain earned in tips or what Mazie paid her. Mazie didn't hold a grudge so Charmain could salvage one night. There was also the algebra of what wouldn't hurt the woman's pride. She could hand over train fare, but what good would it really do for a woman with two boys.

She took three twenty-dollar bills and stuffed them into an empty envelope. She'd likely take her turn getting smacked, but at least she'd try. Charmain leaned against the wall as Bird came out. She handed over the envelope and hoped Charmain would leave without opening it. Never one to cooperate, Charmain slid open the envelope. Her face didn't change as she fingered the bills.

"I don't need your charity."

Bird sighed. "It's not charity. When things ended, Leah left money so I wouldn't be in a lurch over the rent. She went up before I could pay her back. So, I'm giving it back to you. You two can settle up."

Charmain stared at her, and Bird willed the woman's stubborn streak to rein itself in. "That true?" Charmain asked.

"I can go wake Louise for her Bible if you need me to swear on it. But I don't see any point in making a God-fearing woman cuss."

"You don't got your own?" Charmain said like Bird had just said she didn't have any panties.

"My grandmother's is somewhere around here."

"Never mind. Didn't peg you for the non-believing type."

Bird shrugged.

Charmain asked for the restroom, taking her turn to emphasize the long ride back to Brooklyn.

Having fried a bunch of chicken and not eaten a piece, Bird submitted to her hunger. With tired bones and a full belly, she would sleep good. The ham sizzled and seared, and Bird dropped an egg in for company. Charmain appeared in the doorway and sniffed at the air in a way that made Bird think of her mother. Bird waved her spatula over the meat and crackling egg. "It's a long way."

"I wouldn't want my growling stomach to scare the other folks."

Bird dropped in another egg.

Charmain hummed over the plate with approval. "I'm sorry about what I said," she said. "I just wanted to get your goat. I do know these things hurt."

"I'm sorry about your cheek. I didn't know I was so close to popping."

"Chile, have you a few kids, and you'll get to know that feeling well. Half the time, you want to pop at them, and the other half, you wanna pop at the world. And sometimes, you do both." She took a petite bite of ham, whistled, and then cut bigger ones. "Girl, if we gone eat and talk like this then, we need something to drink."

"Vodka or gin in your tonic?" asked Bird.

"Me and that ho gin fell out years ago. She's the only other bitch that's had on my ass since I was a girl. How'd you know my drink?" Charmain eyed Bird as she pulled the liquor from its thus far Gabe-proof hiding spot.

"That night, I saw you at the club. Figured it had to be one or the other."

"I thought you'd be sore with me for all that."

"That was between me and Leah. It didn't have anything to do with you. She should have been a woman about her business."

"You still interested in her?" Charmain asked like she was tiptoeing up to a smoking volcano.

Bird handed her the drink and met her eyes. "No," she said. "We were done before you came on the scene but hanging on because we did actually enjoy each other." And Bird thought, don't you see me falling apart over this next one.

"That's what she say in her letters, but I think she just trying to keep me on the line."

"I can't vouch for her intentions," said Bird as she considered Leah's contradictions, not helping with money despite having plenty of it, but wanting Bird to get Gabe and Charmain to be friends. "But she's not one to stay anywhere she don't want to be. And going to prison is second only to death in terms of excuses."

"True that," said Charmain, raising her glass with a belly laugh.

Over two more vodka tonics, they'd sorted out Bird's path from Illinois and Charmain's from Pittsburgh, more than a few of Leah's cohabitating quirks, and the fact that Mazie likely never got attached to any of them. The wall clock struck three in the morning as Bird showed Charmain to the unrented room upstairs and moments later fell into her own bed. The next morning, Bird found a note slid under the door. "10 p.m. at Mazie's. Don't make me have to come find you."

"Ah Lawd," said Esau, when Bird knocked on Mazie's door at 10:15.

Bird gave him a playful scowl.

Mazie and Charmain conferred at the living room's edge.

"Hey, it's the chicken lady," someone said.

"Mo' like the slap-you-silly-lady," said one of the regulars. Charmain glared at him.

Bird walked up to Mazie and Charmain with purpose. Mazie's hand slid into her apron pocket. Bird and Charmain stared at each other for a long moment. Someone cut the music.

Bird broke first and let out a peel of laughter. Having won this round of the standoff, Charmain threw her head back in redemption.

"Y'all stupid," someone said.

"They think they on Broadway," said an exaggerated baritone in the far corner.

"Who want chicken?" asked Charmain, and hands went up around the room. "Then quit fussing at me and my sister."

"That was quick," said Esau, and both Bird and Charmain's set jaws shut him up.

# June 1935

Louise answered the telephone, and for this Bird was grateful. What would she have done without the moment that allowed her to comprehend that Mrs. Bennett of Bennettsville, Illinois, was on the line? Some long-buried pain conjured an image of her grandmother sitting prim in the wingback, waiting for Bird to answer. Bird sat on the phone seat, receiver in hand, and gave herself another moment to compose herself. Surely all this composing is costing a fortune, she thought, and that's why people reach back across years and thousands of miles through the mail. A stamp costs hardly nothing. Jarring the hell out of somebody should cost more. Somebody must be dead. Bird felt crass and uncaring, but this information could have been conveyed through her lawyer. They had standing orders to send flowers whenever such an occasion occurred. Who could it be that Bessie felt the need to break the silence held for most of a decade?

"Hello, Bessie."

"Hello, Bird. How are you?"

"Fair to middlin' as Odelia would say. How are you?"

"I've had better days, but if all was keen, I wouldn't be calling you."

"Then, let's get to it."

"You've taken after Maddy instead of Odelia then."

"Life pushes us in one direction or the other," said Bird.

"There is truth to that. Then I won't waste our money dragging this out. You need to come home."

So surprised by this, Bird snorted and then had to cough.

Bessie let the fit pass before continuing. "Your folks in Tuckersville have been menacing to get us to uproot. They beat one of the Giles boys last week and mean to force us out one way or another. We need to sell."

For a second, Bird savored the fact that Bessie was a cussing woman and then zipped on to the business. Bessie had to know that she hadn't profited from the land in years. She hadn't collected rent since Odelia died. "You don't need me to come back for that. The lawyer can handle it. Ned can set the price—I don't care."

"Bird, if it were that easy, I'd be on the phone with the lawyer. Everybody wants to sell but Ned and Bony and his kin. Everybody's waiting for them to come around, and Fred won't say nothing to him about it. I thought seeing a boy near dead would do it. But they say no white men are going to run them out."

"Then you need to be talking to your husband."

"You haven't married then?"

Bird gave a long pause. "No, not in the traditional sense," she said, and immediately regretted it. She didn't even know what the hell that meant. "I'm . . . unwell right now, Bessie. I don't think a trip back would be good." Bird hoped she wouldn't have to explain more than that; after ten years away, she didn't want word going around that she was struggling to hold her own with the world.

Without missing a beat, Bessie answered, "Then, you really do need to come home and let your people take care of you." Bessie waited. Bird looked around the dim hallway. She wasn't doing anything anyway. Just sewing and waiting and wasting away. She had no desire to go back to Bennettsville, but something was pushing her back toward her unfinished business there.

A week later, Charmain's boxes lined the hallway and back into Bird's kitchen. Her twins had left their baseball mitts at the bottom of the stairs, explaining to Bird that this would keep them from forgetting them as they ran out of the house first thing in the morning. Bird had looked to Charmain who'd smiled sheepishly and promised they wouldn't damage the walls or break any windows.

"I'll get 'em right," Louise said under her breath. "Just gimme five days, four if my rheumatism don't act up."

Bird did her best to unclench her nerves. Everybody had agreed to this impending disaster, or in Gabe's case, had grunted. By the end of the summer, they'd all be blood-tight or legendary enemies.

As Charmain's boxes emptied, Bird's traveling trunk filled. She'd planned to pack light, only summer dresses, walking shoes, and the like. And then she thought the children would appreciate some small trinkets and treats all the way from New York City. She dug out the still faithfully mailed annual reports for the last couple of years. The school served nineteen children, down from her years. But according to Bessie, everything was down in Bennettsville these days. The population, the crops, and the spirits.

Bird only half heard the doorbell as she considered the woes of her hometown. She still had no idea what Bessie expected her to fix. Her kin had chosen Ned, not her. When Charmain stood fretting and fidgeting in the kitchen door a moment later, Bird wondered what the children had broken already.

"You got company," said Charmain, "and girl, do she got timing."

Bird considered the stragglers who'd not come to retrieve their garments (and pay for them) when Charmain almost smacked her with her eyes. Then Bird understood; she took one step forward, and then one step back.

She started toward the door again with no idea what she or Sharon could possibly say when, or if, she opened it. Sharon had left her clothing. Books. A few albums. Her family could have sent someone for those things. She stalled at the first door. Opening it would be like opening the thin seam that was finally starting to put her heart back together. The lock clicked, and the silhouette outside the front doors straightened.

"It's been months," she said to the glass of the front door.

Sharon huddled in close to the opening door. Her arms wrapped around herself. Her blouse was far too thin for the unseasonably cool June night. She trembled despite the clear effort of steeling herself. "You can call me a lot of things, but you can't call me a liar. Can I please come in? At least to warm up for a few minutes."

On principle, Bird hesitated but then swung the door open. They stood in the foyer. Sharon eyed the brownstone like she hadn't seen it in a decade.

"Is Gabe home?"

"No."

"Is Louise going to shoot me?"

"Probably not."

"Reassuring."

"What do you want?" Bird asked, feeling herself tense as Sharon seemed evasive. There was plenty she needed to be saying.

"I'm trying to do what I said I would do. I said I'd come back. That I wouldn't hurt you like I'm sure I did."

"If that's going to be the end of the story, I'd rather you stayed wherever you were."

"I didn't want to hurt you ever. I . . . I thought . . ." She looked back toward the street in exasperation. "I thought I could sort things out, calm them down. But then it came down to choosing. And I had to choose my family. They gave me the best they could. It's hard, Bird. You lost everything . . . everyone so young. My parents are still here."

"You have no idea what I've lost," Bird said and felt Maddy's ice in her veins. "What are you doing here?"

Sharon began to cry. Bird stood in place. Tears would not resolve anything. She had cried herself to sleep every night for two months. Cried into people's clothes, the meals she cooked, and as she walked down Harlem streets.

"I'm trying to come back. I'm trying to tell you what kept me away. I tried to be what they wanted me to be. Just like I always have. I was that person, and they were so happy. And I wanted to throw myself off the Brooklyn Bridge. They didn't care that I was dying. Didn't care at all, so long as I was who I was supposed to be. They didn't care if I spent a whole life miserable if that misery got me into their heaven."

The handle on Bird's anger slipped. She fought to hold on to it. Bird looked at the boxes around her and her trunk. She'd left Bennettsville in silence—her reasons similar enough to the woman standing in front of her. She led Sharon to the kitchen.

Sharon slurped the chicken stew she'd been offered and glanced around. "Are you moving?"

"I have to go back to Illinois to tend to some family business. Charmain is moving in to save a little money and help with Gabe."

"Y'all have made peace then?"

"It took a little bit to find our way, but we did it."

Sharon searched her soup.

"Do you need a place to stay?" Bird asked.

"I have a friend not too far from here. She'll let me stay. Can I clean up a bit first and gather my things? I'd rather not show up looking a mess."

Charmain approached Bird as she was washing Sharon's bowl, touched her arm to stop her, and then backed up a step.

"Your business is not in my mouth, but I do need to say this. Girl, you reacting when you need to be responding. That woman done crawled through her nightmares to get to you, and you talkin' bout she ain't done it quick enough."

Bird sat at the kitchen table wrestling with this medicine and her anger for half an hour. But Charmain was right. When Sharon left that night, there was no clear path back to her. The woman would have to fight her own way through whatever filled her own valley of darkness—a hard battle that few ever won. A nagging voice whispered that it wasn't even fair to ask Sharon to fight after just a few months together. Bird knocked on the bathroom door.

"Come in," said Sharon. She lay in the deep water staring up at the ceiling.

"I'm sorry," said Bird. "Those first few weeks you were gone, I might have fallen at your feet if you came back. As more time passed, I had to . . . to harden my heart against hope and everything I feel for you to keep it beating and keep myself pushing through each day. I have been advised to let it soften. Do you want to talk about what happened?"

Sharon closed her eyes and sank further into the water. "I was found unsatisfactory. He stood, hat in hand in my father's living room and told him while I was a good woman, I was not the helpmeet sent by God for him. My father stared at him, and my mother at me. He and my father went into the study for all of two minutes. I could hardly look at my father when they came back out. All he said was that the devil can have me. My mother gave me a slap that held about ten years of rage. A child given the keys to the kingdom, choosing sin and damnation. She told me to leave and never come back. That I will perish with the unsaved and will not be mourned."

"'I will live, and I will be loved,' I told her," said Sharon. "I'd hoped for open arms when I came back, but I know I broke my promise to you. I've said and done my part. Where we go next is up to you."

Bird slid to the floor and leaned back against the tub's side. She could pull this woman into her arms and her bed. Or, she could make them slow walk through their next steps. Only fools want a guarantee, she thought, finally figuring out they don't exist. But she wanted them to make decisions based on their truths and grounded in their hurts and hopes. They'd skipped that part the first time.

"I've got to go to Illinois tomorrow. You can stay here. Charmain can make it happen. Maybe with a little space and less pressure, what's next will be clearer when I get back."

"I want to go with you."

Bird shook her head. "Sharon, it's a long trip to sort out a mess I left behind years ago and that's only gotten bigger. And it now involves crazy white folks."

"I want to meet your people and see where you come from. It sounds like this might be my only chance." She pulled the plug on her water, and Bird handed over the towel.

"You can't say I didn't warn you."

## Illinois

The livery car eased down the highway, and Sharon rolled down the window and held her out hand to feel the passing air, humid and fresh, smelling of the green fields surrounding them. They'd long since passed out of St. Louis and East St. Louis and into the territory of county lines and towns worth little more than a blink.

"You said there was corn, but I didn't understand that's all there was. What in the world did you do out here?" said Sharon.

"Grew corn, shucked corn, and ate corn."

Bird oscillated between amusement at Sharon's bewilderment and nervousness at what would happen when they reached their destination. She'd lost track of all the turns and landmarks along their way—the old grain mills and sawmills and general stores of other random small towns. She guessed that they still couldn't stop in any of them. Bennettsville was the oasis in the long desert bridging the north and south.

"Bennettsville's just down this road," said the driver, channeling all the excitement that should have been hers.

"Can you stop at the grocery on Main Street before carrying us on to my house?"

"You got it ma'am."

Main Street remained in good repair—the houses with nice paint and now with concrete sidewalks and fences. A few heads turned as they passed by. Bird wished she was the kind of returnee who could roll her window down and shout hellos and promises that she'd soon drop by for a visit. Instead, she let the car continue its solo processional and stop in front of the grocery.

"Good afternoon, we'd like three ham sandwiches and Coca-Cola's from the cooler, please," she said to the lanky young man behind the counter as Sharon browsed the few aisles.

The young man looked between the two of them. "Miss Bird," he said to the correct woman.

"Why yes."

The boy grinned and slapped the counter. "Folks been waiting on you. My Aunt Bessie says I'm to call as soon as you get here."

"Liston Jr.?" she asked, not believing her eyes. "I used to hold you when you were a baby."

"You and this whole town," he said laughing.

"Your grandfather?" asked Bird, now seeing the traces of that side of the family in him too.

"He's home smoking his pipe and talking folks up and down the road. He still comes in a bit, but less when I'm back from school for the summers." He pointed with pride to the Tuskegee banner hanging behind the counter. "If you going straight to Aunt Bessie's, you don't need to get any food, folks been cooking for days."

Bird blushed. She hadn't thought it might be rude not to go straight to Bessie's. But how could she come home without going to her own house first? She had to see it. "I'm going out to set eyes on my house. Can you ask her to pick us up from there?"

Liston Jr. laughed and began making their sandwiches, "Most folks said you'd go there first."

"Not a bad town y'all got here. Nice to see colored folks with such a nice place," said the driver after he'd dropped their luggage on the porch and received his pay in cash and lunch. Bird admired the massive oaks and maples that rivaled any marble masterpiece. She had so completely underappreciated their magnificence.

"My Uncle Vernon's little house was there," said Bird. There was a field of alfalfa growing there now. "And this is my Granny's house." Bird chuckled. "I thought it was so grand as a child."

"It's beautiful, Bird," said Sharon with sincerity. "I used to imagine something like this when my grandparents talked about the house they lost down south."

Bird took her hand and led her up the porch steps and into the house. The unanticipated mixture of nostalgia and regret burned her eyes and tightened her throat. She offered only simple explanations as she guided Sharon through the rooms. Sharon waited at each room's edges as Bird stepped in, seeing at first through the eyes of her childhood and then as the woman she had become. Odelia's house—it would always be that for her—had aged well enough, but it had not been loved. Who could have loved it but the child who loved the women who'd lived in it? It now seemed an awkward size, too small for a large family and too big for a person alone or even a young couple. Plenty in Bennettsville had resided there for a while but never chose it as their home, leaving the house hollow, the wood floor and fixtures thirsty, and the air stale and dusty.

"There was once life here," she said to Sharon in the dining room. "It was quiet, and its colors were cool, but you could feel it." Bird imagined the fire in the fireplace, the aroma of simmering soup, and bright quilts ready for grabbing.

Bird stopped at the door to her mother's bedroom, touched the handle, and then turned away almost bumping into Sharon. Sharon put a hand on the small of Bird's back.

"This was Maddy's room. I can't go in there yet."

Sharon stepped aside without question. Bird was thankful to not have to add that this was also the room she'd cried and died in.

"The sewing room is this way," Bird said leading Sharon to the room that had seemed much bigger when she was a child. Now, it only contained castaway items from who knows how many families. "Her sewing machine was there. And the dressing forms that I thought were giant dolls were lined up against the wall. It was a room of textures and humming, Maddy's and the machines." Bird rested a hand on the stack of boxes that stood in the machine's place. Sharon stood behind her. Bird nestled back into her embrace. "She'd be fifty-four if she'd lived. I was terrified of her in so many ways and loved her fiercely in so many others." Sharon's grip tightened, and Bird let herself be fully held.

At Sharon's suggestion, they returned to the front grass to eat their lunch. At least, the summer sun hasn't changed, thought Bird as she lay back and Sharon laid out their food and grumbled for not thinking to ask the driver if he had a bottle opener.

"I can say this is the countriest place I've ever been," said Sharon. "Who in the world let you move to New York City?"

Bird thought back to the porter in Chicago. He'd been right; she must have reeked of the country when she deboarded in the heart of New York City. "I survived somehow; I must be lucky as hell."

"Did you think you'd come back?"

Bird chewed and thought she'd told the porter she wasn't. "I don't think I was sure one way or the other. I knew I should, but it's been much easier not to. Once I stepped out of the story, I didn't know how to step back in."

"Somebody makes the way for you," said Sharon, nodding to a car turning down the lane.

The car bounced and beeped an ecstatic tune. Bird hooted. "That can only be Bessie. She always did make an entrance—no matter the circumstances."

Bessie hopped out of the car, slammed the door, and checked her sundress before strolling to where they now stood.

"They let you drive that thing?" Bird quipped.

Bessie stopped in her trademark hands-on-her-hips pose. "They say they ain't seen nobody drive like me since Maddy Bennett tore up and down these roads in a wagon no less." Her face had rounded as much as her hips. Still, Bird could see the Bessie she knew in the light in her eyes. Bird didn't mention her surprise that they let her travel this close to

Tuckersville alone, but Bessie likely still didn't ask permission, and she'd always been fearless—well, almost fearless.

"I'm glad her legend continues," said Bird, wading deeper into Bessie's current. There was something immensely good about seeing this woman.

The air between them was easy as was their hug. Bird had forgotten how country women smell—of sweat and earth—and held on a little longer, not to Bessie, but to the smell of her grandmother and mother. When she stood back, Sharon was right beside her with her arm extended.

"And this is my friend, Sharon Armstrong," said Bird.

Sharon cut her eyes at Bird. "Her companion," said Sharon. "Pleased to meet you, Mrs. Bennett."

Bessie looked back and forth between the two, Sharon smiling, Bird's face saying, "There you have it."

Chuckling and nodding at all that was unsaid, Bessie said, "You know you're sleeping at my house tonight, no matter what crazy thoughts you got going on."

"We'd appreciate the hospitality," said Bird, and Sharon sighed with relief. "Maybe we should go get settled," asked Bird, turning to Sharon.

"Sounds good to me," Sharon said.

"So, who exactly will be joining us tonight?" asked Bird as she leaned forward to the front seat between Bessie and Sharon.

Bessie laughed. "I kept it small. Me and mine, Fred and Jeannetta, Lorna, Ernest, and Cecile, and Liston. Liston Jr. is mad that he has to mind the store and can't ask you a million questions about New York City."

Bird relaxed; the list wasn't small, but it was manageable.

"But you should be prepared to see just about everyone else over the next few days. Everybody's got something to say."

"And what does Ned say about my return?"

"He's very happy to see you," said Bessie with a practiced formality that told Bird she was lying.

The completeness of the lie became clear when Ned met her at the top of the porch with a too-big smile and arms opened wide. He was a bit taller and thicker and still had a head full of tight curls. His skin was still beautifully smooth except for laugh lines. Age had done well by him.

"Welcome home, cousin," he said. "I hear you've come to fix this big mess." Bessie glared at him.

"I've come to stand with the family, whatever is decided," Bird said and was glad when the rest of the evening's attendees stepped out onto the porch.

"My, my. She done found her way home," said Lorna with an exaggerated southern accent and threw her arms around Bird. Lorna felt smaller and frailer in Bird's arms, although she still smelled of her homemade potpourri. "I didn't think them trains ran but the one way."

Bird stepped back and forward again into her arms. "I've missed you," she whispered, and Lorna held her tighter.

In a blur of arms, she'd been hugged all around and was pleased to see that they'd folded Sharon right into the mix. Only Bessie and Ned's children stood back looking to their parents for cues. Bessie waved the children forward as Ned beamed. "You remember Sed?" Bird couldn't believe her eyes. The gangly boy in dress pants and a collared shirt looking just like his father had as boy, couldn't have been the baby she'd once known. "And this is Theodore and Jean, our youngest." The baby girl Helena Charles had written about must have been five and curtsied to put blue bloods to shame. This could only be the child of Bessie Charles. Bessie's eyes lingered on Bird and relaxed. Bird's happiness was genuine. It was breathtaking to see the children of her friend, both of their flesh and blood.

Liston Jr. hadn't exaggerated the amount of cooking that had been done. They had remembered her favorites—chicken, ham, black-eyed peas, hot water cornbread, fried okra, and dressing, along with plenty of other dishes. Ned and Bessie sat the table's ends with the adults squeezed between them and the children at a side table. As everyone bowed their heads for Aunt Jeannetta's throaty and lengthy prayer, Bird absorbed the faces around her and their unfamiliar laugh lines or sorrow lines. This is how it would have been if I'd stayed, Bird thought. Eventually, we'd all have found some semblance of peace. But we wouldn't all have paid the same costs? Life had dealt them their hurts as she'd gotten her own fair share. But they hadn't walked through them together, and Bird felt the deep loss of these separated journeys. They'd all been raised on the two lines of Ezra, but that was wrong. They were all one family and had always been—and always would be. Sharon reached over and took her hand in her lap and squeezed, as if to say, "You don't have to pray, but join them." And so, Bird did.

The next day, the old men came first to Bird Bennett's porch. Four squeezed into an automobile driven by someone's grandson. Bird recognized two of them immediately, Midas Simmons and Anthony Giles. It took her longer to place the others.

"Jus' come to say welcome home and pay my respects."

"Thank ye for coming," said Simmons. "Surprised you ain't done forgot about this lil ol' town."

"There's no forgetting home, no matter how far you go," said Bird.

"True dat," said Giles, and Bird sensed he liked to talk. "I still remember my boyhood home down in Tennessee. Could probably still name who lived in what house and on what street."

"There wasn't but one street," one said, and the rest laughed at his chagrin.

Bird smiled with a respectful politeness, resigning herself to enjoy this banter. The New Yorker in her wanted to get down to business, but that wasn't their way. The conversation veered all over the Midwest and South, through the seasons, through Tuckersville and a still-menacing Jonas Kirby and his lot, up and down Bennettsville's Main Street, and then to the matter at hand.

"Ned, his heart in the right place. This supposed to be a town for us—"

"But twasn't never gon' work. Not from the start. Even Ezra knew that. He bought us what time and safety he could wit his own blood."

With this, they all turned to her and waited.

"What do you want me to do?" she asked. She looked out across the half-grown fields of corn across the road. Those stalks came from their labor, as good as money growing out of the ground. They had to be scared or just done, if they were willing to walk away.

The men all looked to the oldest among them, Simmons, who glanced at her and then joined her gaze at the fields. "It's time for us to go, Miss Bird."

Then, the grandmothers and mothers ventured down the lane. As the mothers exited the auto and wagon caravan, Bird felt Sharon shift with discomfort.

"They've brought pies and fruit. It would be rude not to introduce you. Then, you can tend to those things," she said.

Sharon stood ready to make herself welcoming and then busy. Welcoming the women was difficult for so many reasons. Her mother would have been their age had she survived. Maddy had been gone almost twenty years, an absence that only seemed to belong to Bird. Some of these women had shunned her mother and were delighted when she was brought low. Their communal knowledge of this history forced them into extreme politeness and formality. Bird was not a child come home; she was pain and shame remembered for them all. As if to mend some bridges, they complimented and fawned over Sharon who tapped into the grace of a preacher's daughter and then disappeared.

The story was the same. Only Ned and a few didn't see what needed to be done. The time for moving on had come. There was trepidation in this. Four generations had been born since Ezra had bought and then defended the land. So few had left. What did they know about the rest of the world?

Still, they needed to protect their children and find a place that offered them some chance at a future.

Bird gave them the only promise she could. "I'll talk to him. I don't know that it's my place to come in making demands. I gave up that right years ago. But I'll do what I can."

At the day's end, while Sharon gathered the visiting gifts they'd accumulated, Bird slipped into her mother's bedroom with the light steps she'd always used as a child. There was a bed tucked into the corner behind stacks of boxes and stored furniture. Not a trace of her mother remained. "Mama," she whispered. Only silence answered her. Sharon approached from the kitchen.

"Everything about her is gone," said Bird.

"You're here," said Sharon.

After a late dinner with Sharon in the kitchen, Bird found Ned in his study sitting in front of an empty fireplace. She slipped into the wingback across from him. Once upon a time, this was how Odelia and Louis had planned it. And then, it had all gone wrong.

"I'm not surprised to hear Kirby's name in everybody's mouth. Is he the sheriff in Tuckersville now?"

Ned puffed his pipe. "He was for a while, maybe seven or eight years back. They thought he'd just keep his spite and violence for us and didn't like it much when they had to live under it too. But he's still got plenty of folks who'll do what he says."

"I don't know there's anyone I could make headway with over there anymore," said Bird, tasting the guilt of a duty abandoned.

"Sounds like you've been busy enough over here. It's bold to undermine a man and sleep under his roof." He laughed but the edge was clear.

"Our kin requested my return. You know I have to hear them out."

"Have you forgotten our charge, cousin?"

"Our charge?" Bird accented the *our*.

"To keep this town going."

"My charge, cousin, is to protect its people. And they want to go."

"The lines of Ezra are safer together," he said and glanced at the door as Bessie and Sharon stepped into it.

"With white men marauding and beating us—how long before they kill?" Bird felt her heat rising. "Far as I can tell, Lorna hasn't managed to bring anybody back from the dead. That's a gamble no one wants to take."

"You are turning this town against me. We need to work something out. Not run. But you don't know anything about that."

Bird tilted closer to him. Both women tensed behind her.

"I did not run. I left." She struggled to grip the rage rising in her chest and stood. Ned stood to match her. "We will find other accommodations," she said to Sharon.

"You can stay, Miss Armstrong; I've already sorted one out before." Bessie and Sharon gasped. Bird whirled back to him like a twister and punched his nose. He doubled over to catch the gushing blood.

"You will not disrespect my woman, or yours, in my presence or theirs," Bird said through gritted teeth. Bessie was between them a second later, and Bird wished she would stay the hell out of her way. "And you don't know nothing about this town turning its back on you. That's when don't no one have a kind word or a bit of help for you. Don't seem to care if you living or dead. And breathe with relief when you a girl sent off into the world by their noncaring. And your cousin and oldest friend don't come for you or even check on you." Bessie had stopped and the room stilled except for Sharon now with one hand on Bird's arm and the other on her hip, whispering in her ear coaxing her back toward the door.

Sharon pushed her to their room and shut the door. Bird began grabbing clothes out of drawers and shoving them in her travel bag.

"What are you doing?"

"We're going to Lorna's."

"We don't have a car, Bird."

"We can walk."

"And the white men?"

"They're on the main roads. We'll take the woods. I know them better than I know Harlem."

"Bird, this is crazy."

"If they wanted us to stay, they'd be in here apologizing. I was a girl in this town and had to abide all this. Now, I'm a grown woman and don't have to take none of it. You can stay and come to me in the morning. But I'm going."

Bessie waited for them downstairs. "Where you going?" She looked as tired and exasperated as Bird felt.

"To Lorna's."

"You walking? In the night?"

"I'll take the woods and fields. "

"Bird, we trying to pull the town together. This just gone blow everything up."

"Not my problem."

"Then whose is it?"

Bird turned around, even more pissed off now. "Fine, it is my problem. But all y'all made it clear that I wasn't needed. And your husband clearly still feels that way. I didn't ask to come back here, Mrs. Bennett." Bessie read the warning between the words and said nothing as Bird marched out the door leaving Sharon behind.

Five minutes later, Bird felt both childish and obstinate as she stamped around the clearing beside Ned and Bessie's house. She would not sleep under that man's roof. Maybe Bessie could tolerate his disrespect. And Sharon, she didn't even know what to say. Maybe this is what she'd grown up with. Maybe her manners and sense of survival raised her tolerance level. They could do what they wanted, as would she. She slipped into the barn, grabbed a black blanket, and wrapped it around her, mostly to ward off the mosquitoes. She skittered through the moonless night feeling out any clearing or half path that led in the direction of Lorna's house.

She didn't feel nimble. She was used to brisk and heavy-footed Harlem walking. They beat the ground lest it rise up and spring away. She came to Millers Road first and listened for a long while. The world was so silent she almost felt alone in it. When she was as certain as she could be, she moved low across the dirt road. The next field held neat rows of baby corn stalks that would irritate her legs; she counted this a small price for her pride.

Holding fast to her adamant disbelief in any creature called the Devil, Bird couldn't help recalling the stories children exchanged about his nighttime activities. He didn't come with horns but instead in overalls and a smooth smile. The answer she'd decided all those years ago was to keep on walking. To refuse to be lured by overt friendliness or sly riddle.

However, she did believe that the night held evil. And like magnets, good and evil too often found each other on nights like these. As she passed through the center of a field, two headlights, bright as stars appeared over the horizon. Bird almost broke her neck dropping to the ground. They were at least a quarter mile away. Instinct told her to move, but slowly. She'd been cutting diagonally across the field; now she squirmed straight—anything to get away from where she'd been. "Odelia, have mercy on your foolish blood," she whispered. As the slow rolling truck neared her on its perpendicular track, she pressed herself into the narrow trench between the corn rows.

The truck passed without slowing any further. Two white men talked in deep tones. She couldn't make out what they were saying, but she heard the jocularity in it. As if to prove her right, the horn blasted, and a man's yelp whipped into the night. Just passing time having fun, scaring the niggers, she thought.

She raised her head to see the truck's taillights shrink down the road. None of this would end well, she told herself, if she didn't start acting smarter. Letting Ned get to her would doom them all. When the night was quiet and still again, she crept to the road, darted across, and then sprinted as best she could to Lorna's house.

There was no light on in Lorna's house. She knocked softly at first and then remembered she was not a meek child and knocked hard enough to wake a sleeping old woman. After a few minutes, she sank back against the door and peered out into the night. Still a few minutes later, a shuffling behind the door pulled her from her haze of thoughts.

"I'm packing," Lorna's voice shouted behind the door.

"It's me, Bird."

The locks began clicking and as the door swung open, Lorna's eyes flew through sternness and bewilderment to terror. "You been hurt, child." She grabbed at the blanket wrapping Bird and pulled her into the house.

Bird had not considered her appearance—the smudged dirt on her dress. The grass in her hair. Her reddened eyes and legs. "No, no. I'm fine," she repeated as the woman panicked around her. "I'm not hurt, just prideful," she finally admitted.

This stopped Lorna's fussing, and she sighed, slowing down to take full stock of her. "Then, you is your mother's child."

Bird told most of the story to Lorna as the woman prepared a wash bucket for her, and Bird washed the night off herself in the kitchen—an eye roll from Lorna had ended her bashfulness about her nakedness.

"I didn't think much of that arrangement when I heard about it," the old woman mused when Bird was refreshed and in a borrowed night gown. They sat over tea and cold ham and biscuits. "Too much pressure and unresolved history there."

Bird found no fault with this summary of the situation.

"But this ain't the time to let pride cloud your sight," said the woman in gentle reproof.

Bird stared at her mug. It was the same herb mix that Lorna had always served her.

"Y'all need to get this sorted out amongst you. If you two split, the town gonna be split. You two got to lead together."

"I don't see that I have much part in all of this. Everybody's scared to cross Ned. Some folks gonna leave one way or the other. I gave up my stakes a long time ago."

"Did you really?" Lorna raised an eyebrow.

"Enough not to claim any right in this decision."

"That's exactly why I told Bessie to bring you back, daughter of Marian."

Bird heard the challenge in Lorna's words as the night flowed like a river between them. Lorna now regarded her with an oldness behind her eyes that made Bird think of a timeless cabin in the Carolina woods.

"Go ahead, ask your question, girl."

"Does the answer matter?" asked Bird, no longer sure to whom she was speaking, Lorna or Adé.

"Perhaps yes, perhaps no."

"Fine. Why Abel's line over Marian's? Why couldn't the two be equal?"

"Show me two equal things in the world."

Bird was too tired for riddles but going along was the easiest way forward. "The maple and the oak, Lorna. They're both trees. Using the same sun and water and air."

Lorna nodded. "And if one was favored over the other, given more of this sun and water and air? And what if someone took a knife to the one? Not big enough to chop it down, but big enough to peel its bark off a strip at a time. Would they still be equal?"

"Yes, but one is abused," answered Bird, grasping for Lorna's meaning. "Are you suggesting that my great-grandmother's line would have mistreated Abel's line?" asked Bird, getting her back up on behalf of Marian and Odelia.

Waving a hand dismissively, Lorna said, "No. If my grandmother feared that, she would have never helped Marian birth Odelia. You think too small—of the petty weaknesses of humans. Can you fathom the blessings of Gods and how they've guided the generations since before time had a name? Ezra's is the line of millions of Africans traced through generations of pain, like the bark peeled back. A line needing healing. A man, who despite his white father and birth far from Africa's shores, received Obatala's blessing. One day, Ezra's line will be that of healed sons and daughters of an African claimed and blessed in this land of treachery. You need not believe, Bird—we can't help but play the role we've been called to."

"And what is your role, Lorna? You have no daughter either."

"The work of my mother's line is done. As is yours. Since the first woman walked this earth, we have planted and harvested. And now, we carry our mothers to rest. The price has been high, but Obatala has not left us out of his blessings."

"What will you do now?" Bird asked.

"I've always wanted to go back to South Carolina. In my dreams, there's a little cabin undisturbed in the woods. It feels warm, like a home waiting for me. Maybe it's still there."

When Bird awoke the next day, Lorna and Sharon's voices wafted down the hallway. Her suitcase was now by the door. She donned a simple dress and pinned her hair back. She'd hoped to at least get a little coffee and food down before facing the consequences of her actions.

Lorna and Sharon sat at the kitchen table with a half-eaten pound cake and coffee between them. The kitchen was warm. Lorna had been up early cooking.

"You missed breakfast. I got a little sausage left and can make you an egg if you like," Lorna said with a look of pity on her face.

Sharon had stiffened when Bird entered the room. She had yet to look up from her coffee cup.

"This will do me fine, thank you," said Bird.

"Then, I best be getting ready to set out on my errands. It's so nice to have guests."

Bird held out a small envelope to her. "We may be here for a while, please accept something for our boarding."

Lorna hesitated. Perhaps, if it were just a night or two, she would have refused. But this indeed was shaping up to be a longer trip. "Thank you," she said accepting the envelope, no harm done.

Bird's pride was a whole other matter. She swallowed as she took her seat. "I should start with an apology," she said.

"That would be wise," said Sharon.

"I'm sorry. I scared you and made you worry. And I was being prideful. I . . . I just . . . there's history there, Sharon. I could not tolerate his disrespect."

"Let me continue for you," Sharon said. "And you almost put others in danger. Once we figured out you really had gone, Bessie had to block the door to stop Ned and his men from going after you. They argued half the night and terrified the children."

"Then what should I have done?" asked Bird, tapping her fingers with indignation.

Sharon looked at her like she was stupid. "Gone upstairs with me and held your peace til the morning."

Bird shook her head. "You don't understand."

"You think you were the first woman to be disrespected."

"No, but maybe I'm the first to realize she doesn't have to brook it."

Sharon's eyes rolled hard. "Sometimes, family means you accept stuff even though we don't have to. If we all ran off every time somebody angered us, we'd be alone."

Bird felt the intended sharpness in Sharon's words and stared at her. Sharon did not blink.

Finally, Bird said, "I have to tend to business at the house. I can stop at Johnson's and make arrangements for a car back to St. Louis and a train ticket for you."

"Is that what you want?"

"You know what I want."

"And you think I don't want that?"

Bird sighed. "No, I think you want to please everybody and instead of standing up for yourself, you sacrifice yourself and anybody trying to stand with you."

As Sharon smarted and then stared into her coffee cup, Bird gathered her things for the trip to town.

With each second that passed, Bird felt her heart breaking along familiar fault lines. Can't she hear this rending? Bird thought, but Sharon was trapped by two irreconcilable urges.

When she could take no more, Bird whispered, "It's okay," and left the house.

Bird walked and simmered. She'd cuss if she ran into anyone. Let them think she was crazy. They'd thought that all along. That she got it honest, straight down the bloodline. She should've have stayed and rubbed their noses in her crazy. Flaunted it like they flaunted their righteousness. Their togetherness. Accentuating that she was an outside child to both a man and a town.

Aided by the summer heat, her simmer exploded into a rolling boil, and she screamed something that seemed too deep and guttural to be a decipherable word. There was no point to any of this. Ned and his fools had to see the lynch mob coming down the road. If they thought they could beat it, so be it.

Bird turned abruptly just outside of town. She didn't want to see anyone. She would ask Lorna to arrange a car to St. Louis the next day. Too much daylight had already passed to get it all sorted this day. She intended to cut across the patch of trees that separated the Owens' and Simmons' farms. As she approached, her feet hesitated and corrected her course. She had been in town three days and not visited Odelia and Maddy. They would know why and take no offense, but it was time.

With relief, Bird found that the cemetery was well cared for with the grass trimmed and the weeds banished outside the fence. Maddy and Odelia lay side by side in the back corner with just a bit of tree shading them from the high sun.

Bird knelt first in front of Odelia. "I'm back, Granny," she said. "I figure this is your doing somehow. Not the trouble, but the calling." She looked back in the direction of town. "I'm not sure what you want me to do with these people. And I don't know that either my mind or my heart is in a good place for all this mess." She relaxed back against the granite and sighed. She imagined Odelia in the wingback listening to her complaining.

"What do you have to say, Mama?" She always pictured her mother beside her on a wagon's buckboard. Her brown profile against a blue sky. Bird longed to snuggle against the reserved woman's arm. This was the closest she would ever get again. She closed her eyes.

She awoke in her bed in her childhood room.

Maddy sat at the windowsill and frowned at her. "What are we doing back here? I liked Harlem. Should've tried it myself."

"Tuckersville is after the land. Things are getting bad."

Maddy checked her nails. "It was always coming. We can't have nothing. Tell these old stodgy fools that there's a whole world out there and nothing going on here but black blood in the dirt."

Bird sat up and pulled her knees to her chin. "I got more problems, Mama."

"Sharon," said Maddy.

"I don't want to ask too much of her . . ."

Maddy interrupted her.

"Ask her for what you need. If she says no, then that's it. Keep it moving. Trust me."

"You waited for the Minister?"

"How do you think I've earned the right to say what I'm saying? I loved a man who could only love himself. And you love a woman scared to love herself."

"Would you have loved me, Mama?" Bird asked the question that had worried her for almost twenty years.

Maddy walked over and placed her hand on her daughter's cheek. "Never doubt it, Baby Bird. Never doubt it."

The gentle hand on the cheek became a jostle on the shoulder, and Bird opened her eyes to find Sharon kneeling in front of her.

"We've been looking all over for you. You need to stop going off by yourself." Sharon stood and turned back to Bessie's car.

"I am my mother's child," said Bird, letting herself rest against the headstone a moment longer. Maddy's wry laughter floated on the wind.

Sharon slid into the front seat beside Bessie who started driving without a glance back at Bird. "I came to see if you'd come back to our house, but seems like you're good where you're at," she said.

"It's good to spend time with Lorna." Bird watched the fields.

"I'm bringing Ned by later on to apologize."

Bird sighed. "That's not necessary."

"Yes, it is."

"Bessie, I can't deal with Ned and apologies. I have half a mind to tell you just to keep driving us to St. Louis and ship our stuff. There isn't a thing I can do to help this town." She kneaded one side of her neck.

Bessie and Sharon exchanged glances, to Bird's dismay. The last thing she needed was for them to join forces. Bessie pulled to the side of the road. "I'm sorry," she said. "You told me you weren't well, and I insisted. I just thought you didn't want to be bothered. Or maybe that you were afraid to come back. But it does mean something that you're here." She wiped the sweat at her hairline and rolled down her window. As if they'd been given permission to acknowledge the heat and humidity, Bird and

Sharon rolled theirs down, too. "People can tell that you didn't come with spite. And that it's hard being here for you. There's a lot of blame to go around for that. I'll own my share of it. And we gonna get on with that after we get this mess sorted out. You're one of two who can sign papers, and unless you're absolutely rich out there in New York, you still have a horse in this race. A proper sale could go a long way toward helping folks start up somewhere else. If Ned gets us run out of town, we all lose everything."

A proper sell. Bird heard echoes of Mr. Charles in his daughter's reasoning. Their economics lessons continued. White folks had already stolen a lot more land than this from the Indians; she wasn't sure they'd be willing to buy what they were so accustomed to taking. But just maybe there was a chance. "I'm here; I'll do what I can," she said after several breaths. "I need help getting Sharon back to St. Louis."

"I'm staying," said Sharon, without emotion, as she turned back toward the road ahead of them.

"I asked her to stay," said Bessie, "to help me keep you together."

Representatives of the families began arriving soon after dinner. Lorna, Bessie, and Sharon made tea and coffee and cut slices of cake and pie. There was no plotting war without some sweet potato pie going around. Bird willed herself to leave the back porch, but she needed a few more minutes with the stars she so rarely saw in Harlem and the glass of cherry wine she nursed. She imagined Odelia beside her shaking her head. Her job had been clear and obviously couldn't be done from a thousand miles away. Staying in touch was the least I could've done, she thought. I even have a telephone and never used it to do the things that mattered most. But if I stayed, there'd be no Leah, Gabe, Louise, Irma, or Sharon, at least not for me. They knew her and loved her without shame or hesitation, even if it took Louise and Irma a little while to come around. Bird groaned as car doors slammed and Ned's laughter carried through the night.

A few minutes later, he stepped out the back door and took the seat beside her. "I owe you an apology, Honest. I shouldn't have said what I said the other night. I was raised better than that. Uncle Vernon would've knocked me silly too." He chuckled at the thought. "And I should say, it wasn't that we didn't ever think about you or how to get you to come back.

We didn't know what we could say. So much had happened. The more years passed, the worse it got. What did we have to offer you, especially after New York City?"

Bird fought back tears. "I should've come back sooner," she said. "I didn't know how or what to say after the years grew. And I wasn't sure how folks would . . ." she paused. "Not everybody here did right by Maddy."

He nodded. "Kinfolks. We are complicated."

"That is the truth," she smiled and laughed. "Here we sit under all these stars, fretting when we should just be standing in awe."

"I've got to warn you," he said with an impish smile. "It won't be ten years next time. Me and Bessie coming to that city. You think it's ready for us?"

"Not at all," said Bird. "But we Bennetts know how to make things our own."

"That reminds me. We better get in there before Bessie has us relocating to Iowa City or some foolishness. And I brought a watermelon fresh off the vine. Last I heard, she was looking for some salt."

Bird hooted and jumped up. "Ned, you should have started with that. We could've sorted the last ten years out after the melon was safe."

It had been a decade since Bird had rolled down Millers Road into Tuckersville. The run-down shacks on the outskirts of town were now leaning hovels, like they and the people living in them had finally decided to give up the ghost. If she were a believing woman, she'd say that the crash of '29 had swept across the land like something out of the Old Testament.

The last time she'd been this way, she'd been driving her own wagon and likely had a dress or several orders of alterations in the back. She'd never liked the trips and had always been nervous that she'd say the wrong thing or take the wrong tone. She'd pretended to be Maddy or Odelia but could never move between the towns with their self-assurance. Neither had shown her the well from which it came. She wished Bessie would drive a little faster so they could get this trip over with a little sooner, but as much as anxiety moved her, she guessed that it slowed her friend. Their mission, as decided by the families, was twofold: Don't get killed and see if Salina Kirby could finally talk some decency into her son.

"How many times have you had to visit Salina Kirby?" Bird asked.

"I could probably count it on two hands. Not so much of late. More so in the beginning after you left. It was pointless when Jonas was sheriff. Once Lula retired, Mrs. Kirby never asked for anyone else. From what the girls say, she now stays to herself and in the house. Jonas still lives with her; so, we best make it short."

The houses in town were still well-kept but maybe not as pristine as her memory saw them. They parked in the back driveway of the Kirby house and were greeted by a skittish white girl at the servant's entrance. She only nodded and disappeared when they gave their names and requested to see Mrs. Kirby.

Several minutes later, the girl was back. "Mrs. Kirby tires easily but she will see you in the sitting room for a few moments."

Bird paused as the girl opened the door wider. She'd never thought she'd step over this threshold again. As they walked through the house, she braced herself against the cloistered sadness. They found Salina Kirby tucked into a chair by her front window. Bird blinked. The years had not been good to the woman. She was small, pale, and dressed only in a nightgown and housecoat. A plain cotton scarf covered her hair. She stared at them both as they stood awkwardly in the middle of the room.

"Bird Bennett, you look more like Maddy now than you ever did when you were a girl. Y'all have a seat." A bony hand waved them to the settee.

"It's good to see you," said Bird, trying to maintain her composure. She half meant the words. This woman was part of her history—a complicated part, but part of it, nonetheless. And she was one of the few women of her mother's generation who could say Maddy's name without guilt or shame. Bird made a note to find the Harpers and ask what illness or catastrophe had struck her. "I'm sure you know why we've come."

Mrs. Kirby laughed. "You sound like your mother and get straight to the point like her. But you don't know what Maddy knew. There's no fixing this mess that's been brewing for a hundred years. You can thank Silas Tucker for it all.

"I understand, ma'am. But there's got to be some type of peaceable solution."

"There's nothing here for the young men, and the same is true in Bennettsville," said Salina, turning back to the window. "Jonas has promised to get what folks think is their due. And y'all are standing between them and that."

"Ezra and Marian paid for that land. It's ours by deed. We won't be run off," said Bird, forcing her growing anger into the hands clinched in her lap. Laws, contracts, and deeds mattered until white folks decided they didn't. Then, they just took what they wanted. Bessie's knee pressed hers, a warning to calm down and not make things worse.

"There's not much I can say to Jonas these days." Salina glanced at the clock on the mantle. She was ready for them to leave.

"Yes, Mrs. Kirby. I only ask that you give them this information for our attorney," said Bird as Bessie took a piece of paper with the attorney's information from her purse and laid it on the coffee table. "If they'll negotiate, we'll sell to them," Bird continued. "But if not, we'll sell to the highest bidder, which we all know will be other white folks they can't run off the land." She wanted the satisfaction of adding that if more blood was spilled, it would be on both sides but held her tongue. Mrs. Kirby gave her a shrewd smile, like she'd read her mind and really didn't care whose blood was spilled anymore.

She only said "I'll see what I can do."

That night Bird lay in bed unable to sleep. They'd played their first card; she didn't want to know what Tuckersville would play next. A light tapping on the door pulled Bird from worry.

Sharon strode in her robe and made herself comfortable on the bed.

"Well," she said.

"Well," said Bird, not wanting to send her away, but not wanting to deal with the heaviness that remained between them even as the world swirled around them.

"I've come to make peace."

Bird laughed.

"What's funny."

"What is peace?"

"We used to have it."

Bird paused before conceding this point. "Yes, we did."

"We have to decide if we want to get it back or not."

"You make it sound that easy."

"Maybe it's easier than you think."

Bird shook her head.

"I know it seems hard when you insist on staying mad at me," said Sharon, turning on her side to face Bird directly.

"I'm not mad at you; I just don't know what you want."

Sharon exhaled, and the silence swelled between them. "The world doesn't allow what I want."

Bird sucked her teeth. "The world doesn't give one damn about you or me or anybody else. It's the folks who look just like us who say they care about us but don't want us to have what they have for themselves."

"Those are the same people who clothed and fed me—and do love me," said Sharon.

"That's irony for you." Bird shrugged, not caring if she came across as flippant as she felt. She was coming to like this sense of not caring how each and every one of her words struck each and every person.

"Irony is you of all people not caring."

Bird turned to her. "You think I don't care?"

"I think you are too hurt and angry to spend any time thinking about how I'm feeling."

"If I didn't care, I'd have put you in a cab back to Brooklyn. Any woman can learn to lay under a man and moan."

"What do you want from me?" demanded Sharon.

"I thought we wanted the same thing. I just refused their—" Bird jumped up, ran to open the window, and took several quick breaths. The smoke on the air was faint but growing stronger.

She whirled on Sharon who now stood frozen between the bed and the door.

"Get Lorna up. Stay inside until you hear from me," Bird ordered.

Sharon didn't flinch and was out the bedroom door one step behind her. Bird yanked open the credenza and pulled out the pistol that Lorna had promised the night before. She held her breath as she peered out the front window curtains. The night was a black afghan, but the smell of smoke thickened. She darted into the yard that was silent except for Lorna's cussing at the window. She ran to the front and saw the faint yellow glow to the north like the sun was birthing itself from the soil. A coyote howl, dipped in the evil of a man's voice, ripped through the night.

Bird dropped to her knees. A screen door shut behind her. Shaking hands pulled at the pistol as firm and familiar hands wrapped around her waist.

"What's burning?" asked Sharon.

"Her home," answered Lorna.

The devastation was plain long before they reached Odelia's at sunrise. At least three fields had also been burned, the little croppers' houses with them. The town gathered in clusters around the smoldering remains. Ned cursed as he drove Bird, Sharon, and Bessie down the road. Bird sipped the flask that Bessie had handed her as they piled into the car. She wondered if anyone cared enough to count all the colored towns burned out from one coast to the other. What transgression had earned colored people this purgatory? This would go on forever, the insatiable emptiness of white people and their belief that black misery and blood and fire and death could fill it.

With the fields and trees scorched, Bird could see the smoke from her childhood home far down the road. Sharon gripped her hand. A couple dozen men, women, and children had assembled and marked the vehicle's approach with downcast eyes. They'd already knocked down the blackened cross. The house was charred rubble. Bird thought first of the dining room table and then her grandmother's wingback. She remained still beside Sharon as Ned and Bessie stepped out and moved to talk to those who waited. Bird wondered what she had thought would happen. It was a good enough house, with good enough things, but it was the house of her people. No white man would live in it. They would raze the town, erasing every remnant of Ezra's lines. It was worse than nothing to them; it and the town showed all that colored people could do and be. It was a sty in their eye.

Bird motioned to the door, and Sharon let them out. Bird held fast to her hand and Sharon only let go to put her arm around her waist as they walked through the growing crowd and its murmured sorrows. Bird stopped at the edge of the charred remains and knelt. The house had collapsed in on itself. Only a lone wall stood in the middle of it all. Never in her life had she felt the need for penitence more, not for her sins, but the sins of the world. If those who hated could not kneel, then the hated would have to do it and hope that it saved them all.

With closed eyes, she offered her regrets to her mothers. She had left out of necessity, but the guilt weighed on her. The privilege had been hers, and she'd shirked the burden, and now everything might be lost for everyone. Sharon's hand slid to the small of her back, and Bessie's rested on her shoulder. Bird heard and felt those present gather around and join her silent prayer. She felt their need and love, and perhaps their own regret. Mistakes had been made all around. Now, the only way was forward. "Granny, please just tell me what I need to do," she whispered. "Where do we all go from here?"

Her eyes followed a tendril of smoke as it floated and curved above the mound bound for the sky. She closed her eyes and saw their little town—so defiant and so vulnerable. The roads emanated like wheel spokes and connected them to the country roads and highways that led to other towns and cities. Roads enough for any way her blood wanted to go. New York City lay to the east, but only a few would follow that trail. Some would go north. Others west. A few to St. Louis. Some of her blood would see the great Pacific—a sight still unseen by anyone in their line.

As the vision faded, Bird trembled. A woman hummed a soft song behind her. A cascade of reaching arms led all the way back to the last gathered. Something had happened. Sharon would call it God. Bird would concede communion. Bessie smiled; it was her hand that connected Bird to all the rest. This woman never spoke of her own charge. Of course, Odelia had given her one. To be a bridge. Bird lowered her head with the weight of this new understanding. Odelia had seen so much, and so far ahead—the hard roads and chasms—and done the best she could. That, at least, Bird could accept. She'd done the best she could.

As Bird stood, she accepted Bessie's arms around her and then nodded as Bessie stepped back opening the space between Bird and Ned.

Sensing that he needed to speak first, for himself and the people slowly emerging from a shared daze, Bird stood silent and waited.

"What do you think, sister?"

She inhaled and asked Odelia for the words these people needed. She met as many eyes as she could. "We need to step onto the roads that will take us back out into the world."

"Ending our togetherness," he said with a sadness that held no spite.

Bird reached for and held his hand. "Brother, we can be grateful for all these years we've had together. Show me the fruit of any man or woman that has stayed in one place forever. This was our cradle out of bondage. And now we are free. And perhaps, healed enough. This world is Ezra's birthright to us. To each of us. And by his life and death, we will step out into it with the bounty due us. Trust we are still together if we believe that wherever our blood flows, arms are open to each of us."

"Our children will forget," he said.

"We have to tell them. All of it," Bird said. "We bear no shame or grudge. Tell them the two lines are now one. How we made this town. It is nothing without us. And when we go, the white folks will see the blessing has gone with us."

Ned looked to his wife and took her hand with his free hand. "Then if we are leaving," he spoke out to their kin, "if we are all in accord, that's what we will do. We aren't running. If they want it, they will pay us what we are due." A murmur of "amens" settled this last point. Bird wanted it to all just be done. A black man's due would break the whole country, but she tipped her head in assent. This wasn't the end of anything. They were just getting started.

Come sunset, the tribes of Bennettsville were ready. They had plucked their way through the web-like logic being spun in Tuckersville. How dare them niggers not run? How dare they sell the land their ancestor paid for and bequeathed them—and for which they held the deed? They should have just dropped all the necessary papers in the center of town before running. This insolence of landowners selling had to be punished. Right is right. Fair is fair.

Understanding all this as plain as the brown on the back of their hands, the families had loaded anything of value and sentiment and sent it out of town on any available truck, with three women with the smallest babies. By sunset, the families were divided into the three corners of town furthest from Tuckersville. Bird, Sharon, the Burdess family, and Lorna and had assembled at Ned and Bessie's to wait out the long night and maybe days ahead of them. With the curtains on the first floor drawn and a few men perched with shotguns on the second floor, everyone downstairs took turns resting, eating, and distracting the children.

Sharon and Bird ate alone in a kitchen corner. "I can't say you didn't warn me," Sharon joked.

"I am sorry," said Bird. "I thought it might get bad, but I didn't see all this."

"My great-grandfather's people were run out of their town in North Carolina. I've heard those stories all my life, mainly as the reason I should never go back. I wondered how they survived that terror. Now I know they must have been ready to survive or die."

Bird inhaled. "This isn't your fight. If things get bad enough, you put one of the little ones on your hip and run with your back to the sunrise. You'll smell the Mississippi and see more signs of people before you see it. Then, you put the sunrise on your right side and head north. You'll find some colored folks before too long."

"And what will you do?"

"I have to stay. To the end. Maybe I should have stayed all those years ago. I don't know how I could have, but maybe if I'd found a way, I could have headed this off. After I left, there was no one to hold the line." Odelia stayed, she thought. And even Maddy. Had it been so bad that she couldn't have stayed?

Sharon shook her head. "You didn't owe your life to this town, Bird. It's funny. I always thought you didn't understand what you were asking me to do. Now I . . ."

Bird held up her hand.

Sharon pushed it down. "I see. And we are both gonna get the hell up out of this town."

The sweetness of the kiss offered and accepted made Bird's heart and stomach flutter, and then the cracking thunder of a shotgun firing made them both jump.

By the time they reached the living room, pistols and shotguns were in hand, and adults were tucking children into the crawlspace beneath the stairs.

“Where you think it came from?” Bird asked Ned.

“We didn’t hear no hooting, so I’m guessin’ out by the farm.”

They’d come from the north as suspected, but that didn’t mean another contingent wouldn’t come up from the back. The shots had two purposes: to tell Tuckersville that the Bennetts were prepared to fight, and to tell the Bennetts that the enemy was among them.

The next shot was a much louder and closer boom.

“That’s Samson’s place,” said Ned. “They didn’t shoot back. They’re headed this way.”

Three minutes later, lights appeared far down the road. Two trucks and coyote howls taunted the night. One of the men raised a rifle into the night sky to respond. Ned told him to save the bullet, and Bessie moved the bigger children from the corridor back to the kitchen. Bird pointed for Sharon to go with them and holstered the pistol she’d let lay for most of the evening. Maybe the metal made the men feel stronger. Having it beneath her arm only reminded her that death was out and about this night. The truck lights slow-rolled and stopped twenty yards from the house. Bird, Ned, and the Burdess brothers stepped into the porch and squinted against the lights. They wore their weapons clearly or held them at their sides. Anyone in a truck could take a shot, or many, and have them all dirt bound before they could raise a barrel. Bird hoped that the men in the trucks were smart enough to know that there were other, unseen, barrels aimed at them.

After this short eternity, the truck lights cut off and the doors opened in quick succession. As Bird’s eyes adjusted to the restored darkness, the white men materialized. Eight of them and their shotguns and downturned mouths.

“Awfully late for visiting,” said Ned.

“Watch your mouth, nigger,” said Jonas Kirby, stepping toward the house. “Don’t forget who you dealing with.” Bird remembered him as a skinny kid, hungry to show his power. He’d grown more grizzled and mean. He’d become exactly who he’d always wanted to be.

Ned said nothing to this; he’d made his point. They weren’t afraid.

Another white man lit a cigarette. “We heard there’s land for sale. We thought we’d come see it.” The others laughed behind him.

"You can send all offers through our lawyers," said Bird.

The white men laughed again. "Ain't no point in neighbors bothering with big city attorneys."

"Then you've come with cash?" asked Ned.

"We ain't stupid, and y'all don't know how this works. You priced yourself too high. Tells folks right away these here some darkies that don't know what they're doing. We can save y'all a lot of headache and foolishness."

Bird looked Kirby in the eye to see if he could really say this with a straight face.

Ned smiled. "We will note your interest, but we'll see what all comes in."

Kirby put his hand on the pistol at his hip. "Nigger, it's whatever we pay you."

Ned cleared his throat, and the lights on the second floor came on. The white men looked up, shifted their feet, and looked back at the porch. They had recognized the silhouettes of men with rifles trained on them.

"We don't have an issue with you having the land," said Bird, looking at each man. "My great-grandfather paid Silas Tucker a fair price, and we will receive a fair price. If not you, then from someone else. If you care to make a serious offer, you can do so to our attorneys, Blum and Sons of East St. Louis."

"Y'all big talking for folks don't nobody care about," said Jonas.

"Don't matter to us none. All that matters is our name is on the deed," said Bird.

One of the men spit at the ground between them. "Y'all niggers gonna regret this."

Bird and Ned said nothing, just stared at him, the worst insult they could answer with.

Kirby and the other white men grumbled back to the trucks, revved the engines, and swerved out. Someone in the third truck fired a shot into the night and screams came from the house. The bullet had gone through the upstairs window and a voice called out, "It hit the wall" to calm everyone.

"What we do now?" asked Bony Burdess.

"Lay low and take the first real offer we get," said Ned.

Three mornings later, three vehicles from Bennettsville proceeded bumper-to-bumper down Millers Road toward the highway. Bird sat upright and stone still in the passenger seat of the first. The young man driving, Nicholas Wilson, whistled a little tune she didn't recognize. In the back, the town's oldest grandfather and grandmother, James Wilson and Linda May Tuttle, sat in silence.

They expected the white men just where they found them, about a quarter of a mile before the accessway. Six men hung around two trucks with shotguns in hand. Nicholas stopped whistling.

"Just ease up to them," said Bird, putting her hand on the dashboard like it was the brake. "Make them walk a bit. They won't want to talk far from their trucks." As they stopped, the other cars in the caravan did as planned and stopped about thirty feet behind them. "If I don't reach for mine, you don't reach for yours," Bird patted her holstered pistol, worn in plain sight.

The tallest white man and another who looked like a bulldog came over, holding their rifles.

"Y'all alright back there, Pop?" Nicholas asked.

"Jes fine. Mind your tone, ya hear? We focused on the war, not the battle."

"I hear," Nicholas said. Both he and Bird rolled down their windows.

"Seem like a lot of folks to go talk to a lawyer," said the bulldog man. The tall one strolled past the car and looked back at the other cars but didn't get too close.

"The eldest of each family will speak for their kin," Bird said, looking him straight in the eye.

"Ain't that democratic." He sounded out the last words.

"Yes, it is."

The man stared at her for another moment before loosing a big, wolfish smile and said, "We'll be seeing y'all real soon then."

Bird rolled up her window as the Wilson boy eased them around the backing up truck. "No, you won't," she said.

The three cars rode in a tight pack all the way to East St. Louis. Bird's eyes remained on the side mirror even as the elders in the back relaxed and the tension eased out of Nicholas.

"Well, we got the first part done," said Nicholas, grinning.

"We thank ya Lawd," said Granny Tuttle.

"Now for the rest," said Bird. She thought of Sharon who'd stayed behind. One more young body meant one less spot for an elder. The white men hadn't peered closely into the other two cars and had missed the three and four children tucked at the elders' feet. They had found a way out for those too old and too young to run for their lives if necessary.

Bird and her companions would proceed to the attorney's office and begin what semblance of a negotiation they could muster. The last two cars would separate a few miles outside of the city and travel to Vera Turner's home with a note of explanation from Bird, a stack of cash from Ned, and a warning to borrow every tent they could because a whole heap of folks were on the way.

Their processional into the law offices of Blum and Sons was slow and dignified. Pop had straightened his suit coat, and Granny Tuttle donned the hat that had sat protected on her lap all the way from Bennettsville. The office was simply outfitted but comfortable. A young man in a cravat met them as they exited the elevator, and he correctly guessed the appropriate woman to offer the first handshake. He was young with chestnut hair and a greenness that appropriately complemented his earnest attempt at professionalism.

"My father will be with you in a moment," he said as he ushered them into a conference room. Stacks of paper and books covered most of one side of the table. Bird wondered why they hadn't cleared old work for new, when the young man, tracing her glance, explained sheepishly. "This is all about your land, Miss. Some of it dating back before the war," he paused for emphasis, "The war between the states, that is." Bird was impressed.

"It's been a long time, Miss Bennett," said a voice from the doorway. "I wish the circumstances were more pleasant."

"It's good to see you again, Levi," she said, remembering this ruddy man with dark hair and eyes from the one visit she'd paid him before departing for New York. She'd basically just said, "Mail me anything I need to know and don't give anyone my address."

"I thought I'd be passing the files onto my own son when he passes the bar next year. But Tuckersville was bound to get the land one day, for all their trying."

"This generation prefers shotguns to court procedures," said Bird.

The lawyer frowned and nodded. "Not unlike their grandfathers. One has ways of being more convincing and forceful than the other."

"We have agreed to sell, but we want market value." She handed him a sealed envelope, and explained, "my updated codicil leaving my portion of the land to a distant relative in New York should the sale fail, or I am unable to complete it."

"And Ned's portion?"

"He has agreed to sell and will arrive tomorrow to sign the papers if we get that far."

"And should he fail to arrive?" Blum said with a softened voice.

"Then his wife will sign and her kin after her, if necessary."

"If you get fair value for every acre, we're talking around $50,000." They all inhaled. "But," the lawyer added sharply, "I don't know too many country fellas who have that kind of money, especially these days. You all need to take some time to consider your walk away amount."

"Can't they finance?"

"That Miss Bennett, for many reasons, is the question of the day."

Of the white men across the table from them, she only recognized Kirby. He seemed to have dug up and brought the most genteel intimidators among his neighbors. They all stared at her as Blum turned the paper that had been slid across the table. She almost laughed but suspected that would get somebody killed. Her lawyer whispered in her ear.

"How bad do y'all want to be done with this?" Blum asked.

"We will get a fair price," she said aloud. The old folks behind her "mmhm'd" without having seen the paper. Bird couldn't fathom why these people trust her so much now. They hadn't trusted her to run her own life ten years ago, and now they wanted her say on everyone's.

The Tuckersville lawyer spoke up. "This is a cash offer, Ms. Bennett."

"I am aware."

"Are you also aware that securing financing will complicate and slow things down? And no one wants that."

"Then the gentlemen from Tuckersville should have visited their bank before burning down my house. We are in no hurry."

The amen chorus behind her backed her up again.

"You sure those you left behind feel the same?" said Kirby with a sneer.

"I'm sure."

More pieces of paper slid across the table. They adjourned to separate rooms for strategizing several times, until Blum held up a hand. "It seems like we are at an impasse today. Perhaps a good night's sleep will do us all well." The musky and frustrated Tuckersville men glanced back and forth between each other and then across the table at Bird. There was heat and hatred in their eyes. The scorch wouldn't show on her skin, but she felt it, nonetheless. She channeled one of Maddy's inscrutable faces and thanked her mothers for the calm repose with which she sat under their gaze. Weary but not broken, she held the line. She lifted her chin just a bit to show them that she would hold it again tomorrow. Kirby slammed his chair back, and all the men followed his march out of the room.

The white men leaned against their cars and glowered as Nicholas Wilson held the car door open for her and then the elders. She considered having him drive around a bit, but neither of them knew the city well enough to shake off anybody, and they'd be in a worse situation if they got lost in the wrong part of town. It was a five-minute drive to the hotel, and Bird could only shake her head as two white men rested against the wheel wells of an old Ford in front of the hotel Blum had booked for them. "Of course," said Bird.

Granny Tuttle put her hand on Bird's back. "Don't worry after them child. The lines of Ezra are so prayed up the devil himself couldn't touch us."

"Yes, ma'am," said Bird, "We're all counting on that." Still, Bird thought it prudent to tell the front desk clerk that their room numbers were not to be given to anyone, colored or white.

In her hotel room, she surveyed the East St. Louis night's glimmering lights. The city she'd left all those years ago had mostly rebuilt itself. How haunting it must be to walk daily on the made-over streets. She'd never know. There was no going back to Bennettsville, for any of them. Eileen's words echoed in her memories, the white face of death. Odelia, she thought, stay Tuckersville's hands for one more night. That's all we need.

The next morning, both sides of the table looked worse for wear. Bird couldn't hide the bags and worry lines under her eyes. The white men slumped in their seats and spoke to each with sharp tones. The day's first offer slid across the table. Blum turned it over. If they kept squeezing these pennies, Bessie would be a grandmother before this was through. Bird passed it back to the elders. It was still ten thousand dollars below their bottom line, but she wanted them to see how things were looking. As expected, Pop spoke and said, "No, sir, we not there yet."

The white men groaned. Kirby shouted, "That's plenty for a bunch of niggers!" The other men shushed him though they were all red and angry with beads of sweat forming at the edges of their hairlines. As they argued in whispers, she wanted to throw her head back and cackle. That was all the cash they had. They better pray for financing. If it went on the market, someone would snap the land up. Don't get haughty now, she told herself. She wrote her guess to Blum.

"Then they are about to get desperate," he wrote back.

She checked her watch. She needed to hear from Bessie or Ned; they were supposed to have called as soon as they reached Vera's. The Blum boy would have brought in the message. She checked her nerves. She was doing her job, and Bessie and Ned were doing theirs.

"Name your bottom line," snapped the other lawyer.

"Does this mean you have reached your top price?" Blum blocked for her.

"We need a moment," grumbled Kirby, straightening his tie.

After they'd all returned to the table twenty minutes later, Bird heard Ned before she saw him. For once, she appreciated his flair for making an entrance.

"Mr. Ned Bennett," a voice boomed from the hallway just behind a scuffle of feet she imagined as Blum's son hurrying to stay ahead of him.

Ned strolled into the room in a houndstooth suit. Despite her fatigue and shot-to-hell nerves, Bird couldn't help but grin at him as the men from Tuckersville gaped.

"All is well, cousin," he said as he claimed the seat beside her that Blum had just vacated. He nodded to Blum and the elders in the back.

"What do you need me to do?" he whispered.

"Help me send these assholes to the bank."

"Yes, ma'am," he whispered with a wink.

"Mr. Bennett has arrived to confirm that our family is insistent upon fair market value or publication regardless of the impact on the timeline," announced Bird.

"No hurry whatsoever, gentlemen," said Ned, his smile gone.

A red sun hovered inches above the western horizon as the cars carrying the Bennetts' negotiating team reached Vera Turner's land. Bird felt like they'd reached a beautifully overcrowded promised land. The sight of the tent city and all the people milling around was ridiculous. The cars started honking as they rode down the lane, and people came running from all corners. Within seconds, the cars couldn't make it through the sea of folks, so Nicholas Wilson threw the car into park, and Bird was out of the car and on the dirt road before she knew it. Thank goodness Ned loves a crowd, she thought. He was on the roof of the first car drawing the crowd toward him. All had been forgotten and forgiven between him and his people. Everyone was ready for this rejoicing.

"Get Bird up here," he shouted, "Where's Bird?"

Despite the Wilson boy's protective grip on her arm, the crowd wrenched her away and pulled her forward. Before she knew it, she was slipping off her heels and being lifted onto the car to stand beside him.

Ned raised a hand, and the relocated town quieted down. "This little lady done sent them white boys packing without a penny to their name." The town roared at his words. "I swear she ain't blinked once today." Bird couldn't help but laugh. It was all so much; she could barely breathe.

Sharon, Vera, and Eileen waited for her on the front porch, and she focused on them. If she could just get to them without falling down, she'd be okay. When Ned had the town rapt, she held out a hand, and someone helped her from the car's hood. She slipped through the crowd, surrendering to hugs along the way. She couldn't tell if the porch was ten feet or a mile away, until she finally mounted it with tears falling freely down her cheeks. Vera and Eileen held her in a joint embrace before releasing her to Sharon's arms. Later, Bird wouldn't remember climbing the stairs to her aunts' spare bedroom. She only remembered softness beneath her and a familiar scent and warmth nestled beside her. She drifted for several moments along that line between waking and sleep only understanding that she'd crossed over it as she sat up in a stiff, narrow bed in a firelit cabin. A little black woman with a crown of cornrows rocked in a chair by the fire.

"Is it done?" asked Bird, not sure exactly what she was referring to, but the question felt right.

"Fledgling, it's never done—as long as there is a star to shimmer in the night sky and a child of the Gods to see it. But it's better now. Some of the balance restored. It's hard to see that with these fickle eyes, but you can feel it?"

Bird inhaled the fire, smoke, and incense. Something did feel looser and lighter in her arms and back. Like she'd been fighting to hold something up or hold something back for so long that she might float away with all this new lightness. She lay back. "Yes, Mama Adé, I can feel it."

"Good then, rest now child."

She slept through the night and most of the next day and only woke because Sharon shook her.

"They've been calling for you. Say they can't have the night's meeting without you."

Through swollen eyes and an aching back, Bird dressed and descended the stairs behind Sharon.

"I can't believe I slept so long," said Bird, sore from the hours of stillness.

"The wounds you don't see need more healing time than the ones you do see," said Lorna, sliding a cup of broth across the table.

After Bird had sipped what she could, she and Sharon walked hand in hand into the summer night. A bonfire burned in the yard's distance, and her people waited in its glow.

"Here they come," someone shouted, and bodies moved to the left and right to make way for them. She nodded to Ned and Bessie who sat near the fire's center. They nodded back and let her take her seat where she chose in the middle of everyone. Sharon sat first and folded her arms around Bird. The flames jumped toward the sky as they sang hymns and spirituals. Bird joined in when she could, but she preferred to listen to Sharon's alto harmonize with the rest. She expected a prayer or a speech from Ned, but he seemed content with being one of the chorus. They had both laid their burdens down.

They passed two days waiting for word from Blum. Building new lives gave them plenty to do. There were maps to study, messages to send, and supplies to purchase. A small committee had already begun to plan the first family reunion. Bird had chuckled as Vera swallowed with relief when they voted to have the event in East St. Louis proper. On the third day, Blum called with good news about the bank's approval of the sale and a promise of checks in a few more days.

The next day, Vera placed her needle work in her lap and watched a car cresting the horizon. Bird watched her with curiosity. The woman studied the vehicle and then turned to her. "Your sister is coming. I didn't think she would." Vera turned to Bird and Sharon. "But if you live long enough, you've got to be wrong once." She offered a discomfited smile.

Sharon glanced at Bird and mouthed "Sister?"

Bird shrugged and tried to quell her stomach. "We've never met. I don't know that the word applies. We just have the same father."

The car slowed in front of the house and stopped with a slight roll. A tall, brown man in an olive linen suit exited and walked with leisure to the passenger side and opened the door. While the man strolled to the trunk, Deborah Marcus née Turner gave a regal wave to the porch.

Vera stood with a creased forehead and spoke without turning to Bird. "If it comes up, you were born in 1906."

Bird stared at her aunt and then glanced at Sharon who looked on with a wide-eyed discomfort that mirrored Bird's own. As if enough hadn't happened in the past two weeks. She'd been dragged back to Bennettsville, had her house burned down, agreed to sell her stake in the town, and run for her life. She was living in a camp with her roster of living relatives. And now, she was being re-aged as she was forced to accept an unrequested visit from the daughter her father claimed.

Deborah's dress was well-cut and a burgundy that flattered her brown skin. They still favored both in face and form. Deborah was more graceful, Bird could see. She carried herself like a lady of standing. Bird's heart pounded, and her mouth dried. She had packed away her curiosities and girlhood nightmares about this woman more than a decade ago, but everything else she had crammed into that vault had spilled out in the past few weeks. This cleansing of her soul was thorough. This was the chosen of her father, the girl who had been deemed worthy, given his name, and favor, and his birthright. As her chest and throat tightened, she realized that she'd been afraid to stand face-to-face with this woman and see what the world had wanted her to be, her own inadequacies made plain. The fear and pain tugged at her, and she reached for Sharon's hand and was grateful when Sharon held on.

Waiting as her husband pulled a crate piled high with clothing from the trunk, Deborah's eyes roved over what they had all started calling Camp Bennett, to Vera, to Sharon, and finally, they rested on Bird. The sisters held each other's gaze. Bird decided on starting things off with a smile. The woman had come to visit, even if unannounced. Deborah smiled back, not brightly, but neither had Bird's been.

Vera moved to the top of the steps to welcome her other niece. A pang of jealousy shot through Bird when Vera and Deborah hugged and rubbed each other's backs. She dismissed it in the next breath. It was a season for gratitude. Vera's presence had been delayed in her life, but precious and urgently needed when they'd connected on the cusp of Bird's womanhood.

Vera stepped aside to open the space between all the members of this very uncomfortable party.

"Deborah Marcus, your sister Honest Bennett."

Deborah extended her hand. "It's good to finally meet you, Honest. This is my husband, William." William flashed dazzling white teeth. "My pleasure, Ms. Bennett."

"Please call me Bird. It's my family name. And this is my companion, Sharon Armstrong." Bird felt every word in these sentences threaten to choke her. The memory of Deborah and her grandmother at the revival, and the snarl on the latter's face and the neutrality on the other's floated past her as she offered her family name. Until this moment, she had never really understood the way giving someone your name was giving them power, some insight into the depth of you and your story. And Sharon. She should have let Sharon go. If this fraught reunion was hard for her, what did it mean to Sharon? Sharon and the Bennetts had found a rhythm and come to some understanding; she was in the clan. She was Bird's. And now, here stood another potential purveyor of judgment. Of denial.

"Ms. Armstrong," said Deborah with a slightly uneasy nod. Bird blinked despite herself.

To move the visit along, Vera scooted everyone into chairs. "We brought clothes for the Bennetts. Evangelist James will be dropping more by," William offered to the silence.

"Thank you. They are much appreciated," said Bird and then had nothing else to say.

"How is Mrs. Banneker?" asked Deborah.

"She is well," said Vera. "Loving having all the children around. She is practically running a schoolhouse in the backyard. She will be sad when the legal matters conclude."

William and Deborah nodded in unison. "And where will everyone go?" Deborah asked Bird.

"Lots to Chicago, some west, some south to Nashville. I'll go back to New York City."

"How exciting."

"It's home."

"I hear the rents are outrageous."

"Somehow, we all manage to make do," said Bird, not meaning the slight edge in this. Did this woman really mean to come to make small talk?

"We cannot stay long," Deborah said. "I found something I thought you might want to have, Bird." As if on cue, William pulled an envelope from the crate. Deborah removed a photograph and handed both to Bird.

In the picture, her father stood alone, a robed young minister in front of a white A-frame church. He held a dark Bible in one hand and an oversized cross in the other. He stared into the camera with the fierceness of a newly appointed lieutenant in his Lord's Army.

"Daddy was maybe twenty-five then," said Deborah.

"He was quite handsome, in his own way," said Bird, unsure of what else to say as she took the picture. Her mind struggled to apply the word "Daddy" to the man in the frame.

"Thank goodness those strong features lend themselves to femininity," said Deborah, and William chuckled beside her. "I grew up in the church, thought it was more our home than the house we actually lived in," she continued. "I always wanted a sister. I am sorry that circumstances did not permit our . . . I heard Momma and Daddy arguing about you once, and I hoped they'd bring you to live with us. But Simeon was also just a baby and difficult. Momma could not have handled another baby. I just wanted you to know that I thought of you and hoped for you."

Bird strained to hear the last words spoken through her own new understanding. Vera's request about 1906 clicked. No one had ever told Deborah that Bird was the older sister. That their father had abandoned Maddy and his child for her mother. That he sold Bird and Maddy for this church and the life he led and provided to her, her mother, and Simeon. It was startling how life so vehemently protected one daughter while burdening the other. Vera had stopped breathing. Anger flashed in Bird's breast, and the Maddy in her tempted her to even the scales just a bit. The words rose in her throat as Sharon's hand clasped hers, as if she'd sensed the danger Bird edged near. The weakness of a moment that would cause years of regret. Bird accepted the reminder she needed—that she sat next to her love having been delivered with her kin from death's perils. She was alive. She was whole. She was strong. She was loved.

Bird stared at the sister sitting across from her. They'd likely never meet again. Bird wouldn't know the roads she walked. None of it had been either of their doing. She doubted the woman even remembered the revival. Let us meet and part with peace, Bird thought. "I hoped for you too."

Bird found Sharon in their bedroom, lying on the bed with her eyes closed.

"I'm sorry," said Bird, "I realized too late that watching me and Deborah would remind you of Carolyn."

Sharon patted the space beside her on the bed, and Bird lay down beside her.

"Why can't they understand?" asked Sharon.

Bird sighed. "I've been wondering that for more than half my life. Odelia used to say there isn't anything new under the sun, but some things people don't want to accept or understand."

"So, what do we do?"

"Hell, if I know. I've tried it all. Lived here. Lived there. Left—multiple times. It's all landed me right here, right now. Broken in some places and strong in others." Bird took a deep breath. They had to sort things out now or never. "I've finally figured out that I have to belong to myself first, for my own sake. And I want to belong to you for as long as you'll let me." Bird placed a hand on Sharon's stomach.

"And I want to belong to you."

"How do we do this?" asked Bird.

"We love each other. You have to trust me, Bird."

"It won't be any easier than when . . ."

"Than when I left? I left because I thought the price of loving you was too high. My family has been my everything. And I did what I needed to do to keep them. But the thought of a lifetime, my whole lifetime like that, I realized that the price of not loving you was too high. I'd looked for a sign from God for so long and didn't see it was there all along. The miracle of you from this place and me from that place finding each other in a city of millions. I'm not fool enough to turn away from my miracle, but there must be one thing agreed between us."

"Yes?" said Bird.

"We need a proper a living room."

Bird cried with laughter. When she composed herself, she forced herself to name the unspoken. "And your family?" she asked.

Sharon sighed and slid into Bird's arms. "I will believe that they can find that same love the world deems impossible, to love me."

"They love you."

"I know. That will have to be enough for me for now."

Sharon brushed her fingertips across Bird's lips. Bird kissed them and then kissed her wrist, working her way to her lips and neck as they loved each other in contented gratitude.

# December 1935

Irma and Rupert arrived first. Followed by Louise who only plodded up from her apartment when she was sure there were folks to fuss with. Bird rearranged the table's center piece for the hundredth time. Checked the chicken and dressing. Placed the white wine out the back window. Anything she could do to busy herself. Gabe descended the stairs at a quarter to six. Irma howled, "Rupert, watch out, if I was ten years younger!"

"You'd still be too old." Rupert laughed at his own joke as Gabe presented himself to Bird.

She re-tied his tie and ran her fingers over the part in his hair. "You are the dapper one tonight."

He grinned with a mixture of nerves and excitement.

"Now have a seat before you find a way to spill something on yourself."

The incomplete party occupied itself with conversation and stilled itself immediately when Charmain's key rattled the door.

A moment later, Gabe stood in front of Leah. Bird appreciated that their styles and suits complemented each other.

"The Angel Gabriel," said Leah.

He grinned. "Why you give me that funny name anyway?" And everyone laughed at these first words from son to mother.

Leah cried as she lifted her hand to his cheek. "So everyone would know all the goodness you'd bring."

The boy stepped forward and wept in his mother's arms. They hugged, and rocked, and laughed, while the small family they'd accumulated looked on with hands clasped and wet eyes. Bird stood back between the living room and foyer. Sharon slid an arm around her waist and kissed her cheek. Bird marveled at life. She felt the occasional glances her way. Her heart was a jumble of love and happiness. Whatever her face could make of all that, everyone was welcome to share.

# Acknowledgments

My sincerest thanks to:

Crystal Wilkinson for your words, for selecting *Belonging to the Air,* and for guiding the final edits. Sharing Bird's story is a dream come true.

Margaret Kelly and the team at Screen Door Press/University Press of Kentucky.

The Kimbilio community, especially David Haynes and Diana Napier, for creating one of the most amazing and nurturing spaces of my writing life.

Ravi Howard for your time, expertise, and mentorship through the Kimbilio Mentorship Project.

LeAnne Howe, Audrey Petty, and Alex Shakar for the encouragement and guidance as I stretched myself for writing projects from the past, present, and future.

Henrietta Mountz for your thoughtful edits, comments, and constant encouragement.

My mother and father, Sandra Palmer and Kerry Irons, for raising me to be myself, live my life, and be a proud bookworm.

All my mothers, fathers, aunts, uncles, and friends. You know who you are. I have been so blessed and thankful for the love you shared with me.

Sarah, Kai, and Falcor for your love, unwavering encouragement, and standing shoulder to shoulder on this journey with me.